Praise for Carry Me Home

"In *Carry Me Home*, Dorothy Adamek gives a familiar tale a fresh Australian twist. With gripping characters, a playful romance, delightful writing and heart-rending moments, this novel held me tight and wouldn't let me go. Why, this gifted writer even makes mud romantic! A sterling debut!"

–Sarah Sundin
Award-winning author of *Through Waters Deep*

"As irresistible and winsome as a Phillip Island sunset, Dorothy Adamek's *Carry Me Home* is beautifully written and a lyrical portrayal of the power of forgiveness."

–Siri Mitchell
Author of *Like A Flower In Bloom*

"Reading Dorothy's debut novel is a walk with friends from the cliffs to the sea. The first steps take your breath away by the beauty, the next leave you laughing at calamity at hand, and the rest leave your heart full for the good company. Each word is profound – shells lovingly placed by the author to be gathered and kept. When you reach the shore, you do it with tears in your eyes and a realization that you are changed."

–Joanne Bischof
Award-winning author of *This Quiet Sky*

Carry Me Home

DOROTHY ADAMEK

For Lola, Hannah would love for you to read this book —

Happy reading,

Dorothy Adamek

Crabapple House

Carry Me Home
Crabapple House Publishing

National Library of Australia Cataloguing-in-Publication entry:
Author: Adamek, Dorothy, author
Title: Carry Me Home / Dorothy Adamek.
ISBN, print: 978-0-9944-5720-2 (paperback)
Subjects: Historical Fiction. Phillip Island (Vic.)—Fiction. Australia—Fiction
Dewey Number: A823.4
First Edition, 2015
Print Edition

Cover design by Kelli Standish, PulsePoint Design
Cover images by BigStockPhoto
Cover photography by Jason Lau Photography

Crabapple House
www.dorothyadamek.com

Dedication

To my parents, Bill and Sophie Tassios.
Thank you for letting me read past my bedtime.
You knew when to hold me, and when to let me go.

To my darlings, Sophie, Tom and Matt.
Thanks for offering to tattoo Finella and Shadrach onto your arms. That won't be necessary but I so appreciate the way you've cheered your mama's crazy author ride. You three are the very best.

To my Beloved, John.
You knew when you married me that writing was a part of my world. You had no idea how much it would become a part of yours. Thank you for believing in me, sending me away to write, to grow, and become who I am today. None of that would have happened without your strength and generosity. I am blessed to see the world through the endless possibilities you joyfully share with me. Embracing the author dream is but one of these joys. Doing life with you is all the joy.

Acknowledgements

"A friend is someone who knows the song in your heart and can sing it back to you when you have forgotten the words." Benard Meltzer

Rel Mollet, you are this friend. You kept the song alive. You saw the storyteller in me and there's no part of this book you have not added to with your wisdom and instinct. I don't know how God decided two Melbourne Bretho-girls should meet in an Indianapolis hotel bar, but He did, and I am richer for it.

Catherine Hudson, not a day goes by when I don't thrive on your love and wise encouragement. Narelle Atkins, you never let me forget my writing always belonged to me and fought like a mother bear to keep it that way. Alison Tassiou and Christian Daly-Thomson, no one does legal high kicks like you two.

Kerryn Tepe, you listen and make me laugh more than anyone can, and there's no way I could ever measure your place in my world.

Preslaysa Williams, Elaine Fraser, Jalana Franklin, Alexandra Marbach, you critiqued early versions of *Carry Me Home*. Margie Lawson, you taught me to write. And edit. Jason Lau, you captured the setting with your camera. Julie Gwinn and Kelli Standish, you edited and created cover art and clothed my book for the marketplace. Thank you, each one.

Sarah Sundin, Siri Mitchell and Joanne Bischof, you blessed me with your reading time and endorsements. You opened that door for this debut author. And I thank you.

And to the many who've prayed and invested their hearts, to those who've shared in my anticipation, I owe you my most humble thanks.

And now good-morrow to our waking souls,
Which watch not one another out of fear;
For love, all love of other sights controls,
And makes one little room an everywhere.

The Good-Morrow
John Donne

I

July 10, 1875

Aboard the Aurora

Departing Liverpool for Australia

Aunt Sarah says I must mark the days.

She says they are, each one, touchèd by God and I must look for His fingerprint at day's end.

Each afternoon while Father naps in his adjoining cabin, Aunt Sarah says I am to listen for coughing and attend to him, as always. And in the stillness of our ocean crossing, I must write in this journal Aunt Sarah calls my Everlasting.

Wrapped in organza remnants from my wedding ribbons, this journal is nothing of my mother's by which to remember her. Bound with a leather spine, it's a clean book of alternate parchment and tissue sheets. Each turn of the page brings the whispered lift of a translucent veil, the crackle of stiff paper. And perhaps, even permission to confide more than I care to speak aloud.

Charged to fill it with the evidence of God's goodness, Aunt Sarah insists I add pressed petals from my new homeland. Something beautiful. Worthy. At least in her eyes.

Already I dare to disobey.

With England disappearing through my porthole in sea mists of grey and blue, I fear I may never again see God against the backdrop of my birthplace. So I entrust this parting thought to my Everlasting.

I, Finella Mayfield, promise to look for and collect God's fingerprint in a strange land chosen for me by my father. I promise to become wife to a man I've never met, and live the life designed for me since my girlhood. My motherless girlhood, which already stretches six long years since my fourteenth winter.

And I promise to never forget the days I leave behind and the mother stolen from me by a wretched thief.

May God have mercy on the sinner. For I have none.

Phillip Island, Australia
September 21, 1875

Shadrach Jones lugged a small crate of spring potatoes from his wagon to the little church house.

Not that their bachelor preacher, George Gleeson, would know what to do with them. Still, George would be grateful, and there wasn't much Shadrach wouldn't do to repay the debt he owed.

"Brother!" His sister Molly ran ahead, her boots clapping against the verandah boards. "Brother, come quick. Bad things." She beckoned with her rag doll, a flag of waving calico.

Accustomed to her simple-minded ways, Shadrach took his time crossing the yard. The beach twinkled like a tempting emerald through the tea tree gully, and somewhere not too far off, seaweed steamed in the sun.

"We've only just arrived, Molly. What could possibly be wrong?" Dust still swirled in the churchyard from their ride into the village. "We don't say 'bad things.' We say, 'I need some help, please.' Remember?" He juggled the crate and patted her rosy cheek. The cheek of a little girl trapped inside a young woman's body.

"But, it is bad things." Molly pouted. "Something bad happened. In George's house. Look." She pointed to an upturned chair on its side in the kitchen doorway, and a trail of wood chips that snaked across the normally spotless kitchen floor.

Shadrach stepped inside. The starched tablecloth hung askew and dangled like a lopsided grimace, exposing the well-scrubbed tabletop. Molly followed and righted a cup from a tea-stained pool of spilt brown sugar.

Muffled voices echoed from the front of the house and fear needled the hair on Shadrach's neck. What had happened in the little church house?

A fire withered in the grate, and along the brick hearth, kindling lay scattered like an abandoned game of pick up sticks.

Louder voices escaped the front room, followed by a tortured cry, the kind of cry only uttered by the wounded. Shadrach dropped the potato crate. More than spilt sugar threatened the morning and he wanted to rush to the trouble, but Molly whimpered. And Molly always came first. She folded her rag doll under her chin, and a pinch of regret tumbled somewhere in his gut like the vegetables rattling in his box.

He knew better than to spook his sister. He drew her close.

Mrs. Lawson, the plump housekeeper, appeared in the doorway. She fanned her sweat-flushed face with her apron. "It's young Mr. Gleeson. Snakebite."

Molly squeezed Shadrach's hand, and his lungs tightened in reply.

"Snakebite?"

"Probably copperhead, but doc's not sure. You two stay right here. Snake must've been sleeping in the woodpile, but who knows where it is, now? I found him on the floor when I got here, already delirious. Mumbling about a ship in Melbourne." She stabbed the fire with a poker and dragged the chimney crane and cast iron kettle over the wakening flames.

"But he'll be fine. Won't he?" Shadrach spoke the words as if no other answer applied. Not with Molly listening.

"Doctor's in there now. Almost did my heart in. Running all that way to fetch him." Mrs. Lawson wheezed, but nothing slowed her efficient service to their beloved village preacher. She folded the tablecloth and teacup into a tidy bundle.

"Sit here, Molly." She patted a chair. "We don't want a repeat of your last visit, do we? It's beyond me why a girl like you gets dragged all over this island."

This old story? Now, of all days? Shadrach knotted his arms across his chest, but it didn't keep his heart from sinking. He blew out a slow breath. "Molly's perfectly happy with me on my errands. Last time was an accident, you know that. She was meant to stay indoors."

"Meant to and did are two different things, my boy." She laid a hand on his shoulder. "The girl nearly fell in Spencer's well. Word is, you let her stumble from one disaster to another." Her frown mellowed. "May not be the time to say so, but a young farmer like you needs a better plan if you hope to keep your sister out of harm's way."

Shadrach didn't know what Mrs. Lawson had heard about Molly this time, but if his gut could be trusted, today was not the day to try to undo village gossip. He looked beyond the kitchen door. But the room held him in like a fox in a trap.

The housekeeper swept the dust and wood chips into a pile. "Poor Mr. Gleeson. I found him halfway between this life and the next, right here." She tapped the spot by her feet with the broom bristles.

Molly pumped his hand. Mouth open, she hung on every frightening word. Shadrach squeezed back.

Why was it that whenever he needed to get cracking with urgent farm work or make a simple trip to the village of Cowes, he also needed one eye fixed on his sister?

You know why.

One guilt-filled glance told him exactly why he'd always protect her. Molly shared his black hair, blue eyes, and love of mischief. But unlike Shadrach, the world of grownups did not await her.

A gentle breeze from the doorway tugged her hair, already loose at her temples, and she brushed it away with the back of her free hand. A well-known ache dragged across his chest like a rusty anchor tangled in a reef.

He saw it every day, but the scar from cheekbone to hairline shattered his heart each time he spied it. At fourteen, Molly still looked like the young girl he'd played with when they were children. He couldn't get her long black plait to sit like their mother used to, but given the number of sleepy-eyed-smiles she wore when he did it his way, he was doing something right. Most days he managed to keep her out of the well, the bush, and the sea. And that was good enough for him.

Mrs. Lawson arranged herself in a chair with an enamel pan in her lap to peel potatoes and carrots. "I best get a pot on to boil. Doctor may let George take a little vegetable broth."

Shadrach exhaled, his stomach fist-hard at the mention of food. How many times had he warned George about snakes in the bush? Had he ever told him they came right into the house? Mrs. Lawson peeled a potato in one unbroken curl and he watched mesmerized. Had he warned his friend properly? Had George even seen the menace at his door?

"Mrs. Lawson?" The doctor's low voice boomed from the bedroom. "I'm almost done. But our patient is making an almighty fuss about something. If that's Shadrach Jones we hear out there, you'd best send him in before our preacher boy crawls out of bed. If he comes looking for him, that'll kill him faster than the snake bite."

∽

Shadrach squeezed past the doctor, who took leave of the sick room with a cheerless shake of his head. The iron bed took up most of the floor with a large chest of drawers against one wall. Draped by a green velvet curtain, a narrow centered window faced the sea. Bloody cloths filled the corner washstand, and an acrid smell crowded Shadrach's throat.

"I hear you're converting snakes, now." He tried to smile.

George beckoned. "Help me sit."

Shadrach drew him up as if he were Molly's rag doll. Fresh vomit stained the preacher's shirt and sweat beads darkened his blond hairline. Shadrach dragged a chair closer to the bed and sat on its edge.

"Shad... you've got to get to Melbourne. My mentor, Reverend Mayfield, and his daughter arrive sometime today....tomorrow...." George winced and closed his eyes. "I wish I could go, but..." He turned his bandaged wrist over as if an iron manacle clamped him to the bed frame, to the floor, and to his fate.

Shadrach gnawed the inside of his cheek. Nothing would happen to George. Would it?

"Do something for me, will you? Open that trunk under the window. Get that wad of envelopes. They're letters from the Mayfields."

Shadrach found the parcel wrapped in a thin leather strap.

"Two years ago, when Rev. Mayfield's daughter turned eighteen, he suggested we correspond." George managed a half-baked smile. "Miss Finella was a child when I left Chingford Green. But she's not a girl I left in the village anymore and our friendship's blossomed to an agreement of marriage."

An unfamiliar blush pooled against the preacher's neck. "I thought it best to wait for her arrival to share our news."

Shadrach pressed his back against the chair. Since when did George have himself a girl? Any other day he would've slapped his friend on the back and whistled through smiling teeth. But not today. Not with limbs wrapped tight and hopes unraveling fast.

George closed his eyes. "They're coming," he whispered.

Shadrach leaned in. Was he delirious with fever? He looked down at the letters, unsure how to continue. "Now, listen—"

"I want to marry Finella." George ignored him. "But if something happens, I need to know they'll be cared for. Rev. Mayfield's frail. He's chosen Australia for the better climate. For the sun and ..." He looked at Shadrach, a newfound alertness in his eyes. "Please look after them, Shad. I think of them as family, and there's no one I trust more than you."

Shadrach hardened his grip on the letters. He didn't like where this was heading. "No need to trust them to anyone but your good self."

But George wasn't listening. "The top letter will tell you where to find them. In Melbourne. There's a photograph, too. Miss Finella, she's beautiful, and all you need to know is in those letters. Promise me you'll look after them."

"I won't have to, because you'll be—"

"Please, Shad." Their eyes locked. "Don't fob me off. I need to hear you say it. Will you look after Finella, as if she were your own?"

Shadrach stared at his friend. One by one he gathered the meaning of George's words, like a man forced to decipher his fate in a foreign language. *As if she were... his own?*

George extended his bandaged hand. "Promise?"

From outside the door, the scrape of Mrs. Lawson's footsteps pressed Shadrach to answer. His heart tripped, as if he were the one with venom in his veins. "There's nothing I wouldn't do for you, brother. You know that."

George relaxed his shoulders a little. "Good. Because, I especially mean Finella. Would you care for her, as I would?"

Astonished at the madness of such promise making, Shadrach grabbed the outstretched palm of his friend. Once again, he had no choice. And once again, he would promise. No matter what the cost.

"As if she were my own."

2

Finella slid the Everlasting into her traveling bag and breathed in something new. The ever-present smell of the sea held a hint of land today. Something earthy. Green and grassy.

Wind off the Australian coast gathered the memory of sickness from her father's empty cabin. It blew through the very chamber where he'd died and stormed the ship's canvas in a cleansing puff.

Finella would have liked to puff. Even just a little. To shake the grief from her frame and blame the sea for taking the only man she'd ever loved. Instead, she braved the arrival without him. Her neck held high. Her hopes a little lower.

Evidence of Melbourne-town buzzed against her borrowed mourning veil and dress.

"How many flies do you suppose we've swatted so far today?" She brushed her shoulder and picked at the faded folds of midnight silk, each flounce a painful reminder of the death she mourned each day.

Her cabin neighbor, Widow McLachlan, turned Finella by the shoulders to face Hobson's Bay. "Time to hide your grief away and take in this magnificent view. Look." The Aurora nosed her way through the bay along a coastline of timbered hills. "We're about to see the most splendid landing under southern skies."

The month old bruising in Finella's heart reminded her today promised very little of anything splendid. Not with her beloved father dead and buried at sea. "How do you know? You've never been here before either."

Mrs. McLachlan winked. "I've grandchildren to kiss for the very first time. That certainly makes it splendid."

"Yes, and you get to do it in your finest traveling dress." Finella eyed the older woman's periwinkle jacket and charcoal polonaise. In her simple bustle, the dressmaker looked every bit the elegant traveler. For the last month, Finella had looked every bit the dowdy blackbird in someone else's overly frilled skirt with crinoline hoop. And today, it swarmed with flies.

The dressmaker unraveled the twisted ribbons on Finella's bonnet, retied them and adjusted her veil. "Colonial customs may allow you to cast off mourning clothes sooner than you imagine. Your hem hardly drags now and the hoop wire's mended as best as I could secure it."

"I never imagined I'd arrive fatherless and in the borrowed clothes of a woman almost twice my height, and three times my age. I don't know how I'll ever repay you."

"By promising you'll not let grief mar this first meeting with your fiancé. Remember, this is your father's gift to you. You have the chance to honor him in the life you build with Mr. Gleeson."

Tears invaded Finella's vision and she busied herself with a fresh handkerchief. But nothing distorted the memory of her Father or his dying wish.

Make me proud, daughter, even if you find Australia untamed. George Gleeson will provide for your desires. And the Almighty will supply whatever else you lack.

Finella let the wind dab her wet eyelashes.

Mrs. McLachlan slid in beside her. "Mr. Gleeson will be all tenderness when he hears about your father. You may look less than a bride about to meet her betrothed, but frocks and such will disappear when he gets a good look at your brown eyes and lashes. That's what he'll notice, if you let him." She poked Finella gently with her elbow. "Once his eyes lock with yours, he'll be lucky if his tongue remembers his own name."

Finella pressed her hands against her ribs and breathed as deeply as her corset and crinoline straps allowed. She longed for Mrs. McLachlan to be right.

"Take a look at the future, Finella. One day your children will want to hear the story of the afternoon you sailed into their father's world. Take it all in, my girl."

Passengers jostled beside her at the railings for their first glimpse of Melbourne and Finella gathered her billowing skirt to make room. In minutes, the excitement carried the dressmaker further away, swallowed in the search for a better view.

She watched her go, glad for a moment to collect her thoughts. Isabelle McLachlan had cared for her since Father's untimely death only days after they'd passed the Cape of Good Hope. The widow had forced her to eat, altered the mourning clothes, and prayed with her every evening. But soon they would part, and Finella would stand alone on the sunny side of the street her father had so longed to see.

Her heart ruffled like a wind torn sail, held, yet ripped. She didn't relish the task of meeting her fiancé without Father to make introductions. But George Gleeson was a good man. He'd already shown his heart in their letters and he deserved her best attention.

Below, Queen's Wharf shimmered with a mess of people, garbage, and old boilers. A train line ran the entire length and pulley trolleys ferried cargo. Beggars, merchants and everyone in between looked up, and crewmen prepared to throw their ropes ashore.

"Please God. Let Mr. Gleeson be out there," she whispered into the bay breeze. "And don't let him notice my dress."

"A hideous sight."

Finella jumped and stood upright. "Pardon?"

The ship's surgeon, Dr. Saville turned his back to the pier. "Everything down there. Contemptible and hideous. Rotting fish, tallow. Melbourne's finest welcome."

He bowed and dropped his valise, and shivers flew all the way from the planks at Finella's feet to the frayed cuffs of her sleeves.

Not him again.

The sun reflected off the Soap and Candleworks factory roof, where its painted sign radiated in giant white letters. After weeks at sea, the sight of chimneys and gables held her interest. The rum-soaked doctor did not.

"Dr. Saville." She nodded in the direction of his scuffed shoes. "I expect you're eager to get ashore."

"And wade through that swill-drenched pier? I think not. In a week I sail for Tahiti. Until then, I'm forced to seek lodging."

The journey had shown her enough of the ship's doctor to dim her regard and fuel her disgust. Enough for her to abandon any good graces taught by Aunt Sarah. The sooner Finella bid him farewell, the better. "Well, Godspeed for your onward travels." She skirted around his valise, but he tapped it with his boot. It slid under her hem and nailed the hoop at its base.

"It's a shame your father dragged you on a voyage to Australia. You'll be wasted here on these rogues. What you deserve is a gentleman." He came closer and caressed her cheek with the rim of his hat. "What do you say? I could take very good care of you."

Panic rose in her chest. She stepped back and searched the crowd where porters negotiated the placement of gangways and gates.

"I've been watching you." He leaned against the handrail and stole a greedy look. "You're dainty, but the seasickness barely touched you. You'd make a first-rate wife on or off the sea. What do you say? We can settle anywhere you wish." He shivered as if a cold wind slapped him. "Anywhere, but here." His waxy mustache drooped under its own weight and brushed against his tongue.

Finella's throat filled with bile. She drew herself to full height. "You may think me dainty, sir, but I would sooner swim to shore than entertain a lifetime with you. Thankfully, my fiancé will be waiting for me to disembark." Her voice trembled and her words sounded less confident than she'd intended.

"I guess a respectable welcome will soften the blow." He toyed with his hat. "Out there, Miss Mayfield, you'll meet scoundrels you never imagined. Crooks, who've barely paid their debt to society before they disappear swifter than a pickpocket at work. Yesterday's convicts are today's businessmen and dirty constables." He wiped a drop of spittle from the side of his mouth. "I may not have the polish you desire, but there's even less on that shore, the one your father chose."

The speech was not a new one. Dr. Saville's scant regard for convicts was well known and he loved nothing better than to scare the women passengers with his tales.

Well, I won't be one of them.

Finella didn't need to imagine. She knew well enough they were out there, somewhere. Scoundrels. And thieves. But Dr. Saville was not far removed from that category, either. She squared her shoulders.

"You have no business questioning my father's judgment. Perhaps if you'd executed your duties as doctor instead of stirring up panic, my father might still be alive today."

Dr. Saville's eyes fixed on her like a seasoned surgeon locating a nerve. "Your father was not under the naive illusions of his daughter.

Evil is carried by the next generation, Miss Mayfield. The emancipated convict's blood is just as potent today as when he yanked the
chain."

He stepped closer. "Only now, his children carry the brand. Mark
my words. The blemish of the convict era hasn't faded and won't
anytime soon. Your father knew it. Why do you think he arranged
your marriage himself? For stain-free grandchildren, that's why."

Finella had heard enough. No one held the right to evoke her
father's memory. Or mention future children. Least of all this
grubby-handed, inept physician. She bristled and aligned her chin as
if Aunt Sarah herself propelled her to action.

"Good day, Dr. Saville." She kicked the side of his valise to remove it from under her hem.

It refused to budge, and even a second, firmer kick failed to dislodge it. Under a flood of heat she kicked a third time, only to be
rewarded by a wiry snap that pricked her calf.

The leather case came to rest beside the doctor who intercepted it
with his boot.

*Please God, I don't care about the broken hoop or the case. I just
want to get away.*

"Adapting already? I'm not surprised. Kicking and screaming is
the native language here. You're setting foot on dirty soil now, Miss.
And when things look sweet, you'll soon discover…the convict stain
has spread." He sneered and with mock gallantry stepped aside.
"Only then it may be too late."

"Is that ya sweetheart?"

"My… what?" Shadrach stuffed the sepia photograph into his
breast pocket. "No." He'd not noticed the beggar woman spying over
his shoulder. Where had she come from?

Afternoon sunshine bounced off the water and splashed onto the pier, creasing the hopeful corners of her eyes where weariness refused to hide.

" 'Course she is." She elbowed him in the arm. "I can tell from the way ya lookin' at her. Ya must have taken that envelope out of ya pocket a dozen times already. Don't blame ya though. She's a fancy one."

Shadrach leaned away but the beggar shuffled closer. She had more gums than teeth and her hair was as oily as the stained shawl hanging from her shoulders. For an instant he remembered a similar frayed shawl his mother once wore and pushed that thought away with the same haste he did the photograph.

"I could helps ya look for her if ya want. A pretty one like that shouldn't be hard to find. Wouldn't want her to get lost or anythin'."

Holding out a dirty hand she nodded in expectation of payment. Her fingernails were blacker than any he'd ever seen on a woman and the smell of fish guts wafted from her clothing. In this, she was nothing like his mother.

He stepped back. "I don't need help, thank you."

Her outstretched hand didn't waver. Nor did the pleading in her eyes.

"Here, then." From a paper cone he dropped three musk lozenges into her hand and crumpled the rest into his pocket for Molly. The beggar rewarded him with a radiant smile.

"Bless ya for that. I do love me a bon-bon from time to time. I'll shout out a cooee if I sees ya girlie." She jiggled the confections like coins in her fist. Hunched over yet nimble, she hopped away like a sparrow and blended into the crowd.

Against his better judgment, he'd lost half the morning in the careful study of the good reverend and his daughter. He'd seen a few beauties in his twenty-four years, and it took much of his discipline to look away when this girl, with the dark ringlets and large eyes stared back at him from the portrait. As if she knew his heart, Miss Mayfield looked directly at the photographer's lens, out from the card and right through him.

But she wasn't his to look at, no matter how much he wanted to. The photograph could burn a hole in his pocket for all he cared. He wouldn't look again.

Gulls screeched and hovered over a barrow of skipjack and a young boy zigzagged his catch out of their reach and across to the fish market.

"Oi," he yelled. "No pinching me fish."

The sun felt good on Shadrach's back, but promenading wasn't for him. Neither was waiting. Not with George waiting for him to deliver. A sick feeling pooled in his stomach. If the Mayfields didn't appear soon, they'd miss the last steamer out and be forced to stay in Melbourne overnight. That was not an option.

He'd not alarm them with the urgency of George's condition, but Shadrach would escort them to Phillip Island by sunset even if he had to bundle them on in a blind hurry himself. Nothing short of Biblical plague or pestilence would stand between him and his promise.

He scanned the crowd, again. So far, no traveler matched the likeness of Rev. Mayfield. Many sported the same walrus-style moustache the preacher favored but none with the clerical collar he'd seen in the photograph.

Shadrach heard the beggar woman yell before he saw her.

"Don't have a conniption, miss. I haven't a notion to harm ya, I promise. Ya just needs ta follow." She waved at Shadrach and picked her way across the train tracks.

"Found her." She sucked the confection in her mouth. "Didn't think I would be so quick, did ya? Looks nothin' like the photograph, but it's her, I'm sure of it. Those eyes." She sniffed. "I'm good at findin' things. Have ta if I'm gonna feed me grandkids."

"Where is she then?" Shadrach looked for Miss Mayfield.

"Right there." The beggar pointed to a shuffling woman, head bent over the tracks. "Came down a back gangway, with all them toff passengers from the fancy cabins. Walking slow, swishing her skirts, slow and steady."

"That's not her." Shadrach looked at the figure in black. "I'm looking for a *young* lady. That one's..." He stared at the figure in black.

She'd stopped right in the middle of the train track to tug at her dress. A horse-drawn trolley clattered down the line. Its bell clanged a furious warning, and passengers scampered around her to get out of the way.

Why was the woman dawdling?

"Ya better move lady or I'll plow you over," the red-faced driver yelled across the wharf.

Could the beggar woman be right? Was this Miss Mayfield?

The eyes he'd tried not to admire all morning looked up at him, wide and tearstained. Shadrach's heart galloped. Her ringlets were tucked away and she was all but swallowed in a wide black dress.

But it *was* Miss Mayfield. And she was thoroughly fixed to the iron track.

3

Finella yanked at the miserable hoop wire. Of all the places to snag, it chose a railway line along Melbourne's busy pier.

"Lady, did ya hear?" The driver bellowed over the roar of his horse and trolley.

Finella tugged again. The wire bent back but refused to let go and perspiration trickled into the hollow of her neck. Surely this wasn't happening. *Not now.*

"Come on…" The clang of the bell filled her ears with such a din, she could hardly hear herself. "Move!" She let out another grunt and rattled the wire, but silk gloves were not made for emergencies.

Two large hands pushed hers aside and snapped the coil.

Before she could identify the owner, the same strong hands hoisted her off the line, and deposited her on the other side in a vice-like grip.

Her feet touched the boards, and a wave of dizziness collected her in a blind surge. She closed her eyes. It felt as if the pier swayed underfoot, and she grabbed for whatever held her upright.

Her fingers tightened around the upper arms of a coarse coat, and she opened her eyes to see a man's collarless white shirt, open at the neck and black woolen waistcoat.

She lessened her grip. His remained fixed.

"Interesting way to step off a ship." His low voice wrapped

around her. Before she could properly raise her head, a grinning woman nudged her shoulder. Her musky breath hardly covered the stink of her hair.

"That was close." The woman chuckled and chewed at the same time.

Finella closed her eyes again and tried to gain her equilibrium. Not only was the pier moving, but a throbbing pain in her calf signaled more than a broken dress hoop.

"Told ya to follow. Lucky for you, ya boy decided to meet ya halfway."

She looked up at the man. Surely this was not Mr. Gleeson? Taller than her father had described him, with wide shoulders and a sun-touched face, he looked nothing like any preacher she'd seen. His shirt looked clean, but the stitching was frayed and unlike most men she knew, he was clean-shaven. Eyes a deeper shade than sapphires stared at her.

"You're not hurt are you, miss?" His hands let go but those eyes held on.

"No, I'm fine. Thank you." She glanced at the trolley track, and rubbed her shoulder. "Was that you back there?"

The beggar-woman chuckled. "Sprinted in like a trooper. Surprised ya both didn't end up under the cart." She chewed the side of her nail while she talked but pulled her finger out of her mouth when the man frowned at her.

"Well, I'm off then. I see ya both too shy for lovebird cooin' with me around."

Finella's head throbbed. What was the woman babbling about?

"Got ya'self a real hero here, miss."

The beggar pocketed a coin offered by the man and awarded them both a little curtsy. "May ya' days together be many and blessed."

Blessed? Finella shook her head. "I think there's been a mistake. I thought you were taking me to my fiancé. I thought you knew where I could find Mr. Gleeson. Mr. George Gleeson?"

"What'dya mean, luv? Ya boy's right here." The beggar woman gave the man a playful jab. "Been makin' eyes at ya photograph all mornin'."

The man shook his head. "Thank you. You're free to go." He forced his words through gritted teeth and Finella spied a hint of red in his cheeks. He lowered his voice. "Your help's appreciated. Your tongue is not."

With a mischievous wink the beggar took her leave.

"My apologies, miss. You are… Miss Finella Mayfield?" The tall stranger continued.

"I am."

An annoying slow blush crept into her own cheeks.

Surely this was not Mr. Gleeson? He towered over her with a head of black hair, a tad overgrown. For a brief second Finella thought she might have liked Mr. Gleeson to look like this. Blue-eyed, broad shouldered. Brash. In the same instant, she shook the wicked thought away.

"I'm Shadrach Jones. Mr. Gleeson sent me to collect you and your father." He drew a paper from his pocket. "I have Reverend Mayfield's letter to George with your arrival details. And this photograph."

Finella's heart matched the trembling of her hand. She reached for the photograph.

So, the old beggar hadn't been talking nonsense. Tears messed with the image of her beloved father and she caressed the card with her thumb. He'd wanted this new home for them more than anything. Now he was gone and she was left to…

Fear jabbed Finella in the chest. What if Dr. Saville's warning was true? What if this man picked the pocket of Mr. Gleeson with plans to defraud them? She pressed the card to the bony place on her collar, right where a beat trebled against her skin.

Was the beggar woman a part of this scheme? After all, she did wink like she knew something.

Even with her feet on the solid pier, the phantom swell of the sea caused Finella to sway. Her calf tingled, and if it were bleeding, she would need to attend to it soon. Tempted to fan her face with the card, she resisted, and slid it into her dress pocket. Aunt Sarah had words for less than appropriate gestures. Even if they served to hide even less than appropriate blushes.

"How do I know you're telling the truth?"

Mr. Jones frowned. "Isn't the photograph and letter enough? George himself gave them to me. *He* didn't think I'd need anything else."

His eyes darkened and his tanned face turned a deeper red. "I assure you, Miss Mayfield, I'm here on behalf of your fiancé whose instructions are to find you and your father."

Loss echoed in her core like a stored whimper. He waited for her reply. She'd not yet spoken the words, herself. Others aboard the Aurora had uttered the unutterable, sparing Finella the pain. But no one spared her now.

"My father is no longer with us, Mr. Jones. He took ill and perished at sea."

He rubbed the back of his neck, as if a muscle needed fixing, just out of his reach. "I am very sorry, Miss. I know Mr. Gleeson will be, too. He speaks of your father with the greatest respect."

"How is it you know Mr. Gleeson?" Finella had to be sure.

"I'm a member of his congregation. And a good friend."

"Why is he not here himself?"

"He asked me to escort you today because…" Mr. Jones stalled and ran a finger between his neck and shirt. "He's taken ill and thought it unwise to attempt the journey to Melbourne."

"What kind of illness?"

"Fever. The doctor was with him yesterday, and his housekeeper's there today."

Finella considered his words. If Mr. Gleeson were ill, it made sense to send a friend in his place. She tested him again. "Are you able to tell me about the woman who keeps house for my fiancé?"

"Her name is Mrs. Lawson. Susannah Lawson. She not only keeps house for George, but makes sure nobody else comes within inches of him while she does so."

Finella remembered now. George had written about Mrs. Lawson, the faithful housekeeper.

She searched the crowded pier. Where was her trusted friend, Mrs. McLachlan, when she needed wise counsel? Would it matter to wait in Melbourne another week or so until Mr. Gleeson could come himself? Recovered and robust?

"I appreciate you coming, Mr. Jones, but I'm not comfortable joining you on an unchaperoned journey. Perhaps I should stay on in Melbourne until my fiancé can collect me himself. I'm sure if he knew my father were not here, he would not have suggested we travel together. Alone." She tried to soften her words with a smile. "Surely another day or two will make little difference?"

A crowd passed by and two young boys knocked Mr. Jones' legs with the trunk they carried between them. He didn't appear to notice. His blue eyes held her gaze, and she squirmed a little to be so thoroughly stared at. Somehow he managed to look even taller than a minute ago.

"You should consider Mr. Gleeson's wishes. He's given instructions for your immediate passage home, and I gave my word I'd return with you. He's anxious for your arrival and you should make haste to accommodate him. I've done all I can to assure you I'm George's friend. Don't force me to deliver you against your will. You have to come now, or I'll—"

Finella stepped back. Breath bounced against her windpipe, like the burst of an oar from some cold depth. "You'll what, Mr. Jones? Tie me up, and row me there against my wishes?"

Shadrach Jones stiffened. "I'd never take you anywhere against your will, miss. But if we don't hurry, George will hold it against me for longer than you and I have to debate it. And I could never live with that. Now, are you coming?"

4

"That's twenty-three items, listed and corded, Mr. Jones. We sail in twenty minutes."

Shadrach thanked the steamer captain and gestured to Miss Mayfield to take the narrow stairs. Tempted to pack her in with her precious twenty-three crates and trunks, he relented, not keen to watch over her in the stuffy cargo hold. Eyes down he waited for her to complete the climb before he scaled the steps two at a time.

He found a seat for them on the upper deck, her sour mood rubbing off on him, now. It didn't surprise him the outdoor bench might prove uncomfortable. It shouldn't have been. With its back against the captain's room it offered a clear view ahead and down the pier to their left. But she ignored the sights around her and labored to tuck the rip in her skirt out of view. He leaned against the deck rail and wondered how to smooth things with her.

"Hungry?"

She shook her head, her sunken eyes tear-stained again.

"Are you sure? If you promise to stay put, I can jump off and get us something to eat."

"And where do you fear I would run to, Mr. Jones?" She pinned her back to the bench. "Sent away from Melbourne as I am, against my wishes with my belongings all stowed on this vessel."

He sighed and tried hard not to roll his eyes at the frightened twenty year old. "You were not *sent away*, Miss. You were sent *on your way*, to George. To where you belong."

His words sounded harsh even to his ears and he started again, this time a little softer. "Hasn't the captain settled your fears? Phillip Island is the next stop and then you're home."

Miss Mayfield forced a limp shrug, and looked to the pier where a saveloy cart and its owner greeted the hungry.

"All hot, all hot!" The vendor bellowed for customers.

"Throat cutter's here." Shadrach's belly rumbled. "Don't know about you but I can't wait another minute."

Her nut-brown eyes widened. "Throat cutter?"

"The pork and pie man." Sorry to have rattled her, he pointed to the pier and slipped away before she could protest. She may be too refined to admit hunger, but breakfast had been many hours ago for him.

He hurried over to the cart and quickly paid for two sausages. In a flash, the seller slit the saveloy with a long knife, slammed it atop a slice of bread and expertly sprinkled the lot with vinegar. A quick wrap of newspaper and the mouth-watering treats lay steaming in Shadrach's hand. He hoped the aroma would appease Miss Mayfield. There was nothing like food to coax a better mood from the sullen.

Back onboard, he settled onto the seat opposite her. She accepted the food parcel with gratitude and a dash more warmth but neither of them spoke while they ate. He munched on his saveloy and she nibbled on lady-like portions while the steamer cut a path through the bay and away from Melbourne.

The warm food and twinkling sun had their calming effect. Reflections danced off the waves and over Miss Mayfield who took in the sights around her. The steamer hugged the coastline and a brisk wind picked up. Miss Mayfield held her veil back with one hand while she ate with the other.

When she finished, she busied herself with the oily newspaper. Shadrach watched, lulled by the waves and mesmerized by the way she folded the ragged edges of the sheet to make a perfect square. A childhood image of his father fell into his mind, like a kite with a broken string, and Shadrach closed his eyes to let the waves rock him further. He'd promised to care for Molly and that meant he would. She kept him busy with today and tomorrow. And nothing worth thinking about would drag him back to the days of grimy newspapers and golden promises.

A moan broke into his nap. Miss Mayfield bit her lip and grimaced. She rubbed the back of her leg and the saveloy paper slipped to the floor.

"Cramp?" He stood to make room for her to flex her foot. "Hop up. Take my hand."

"It's not a cramp. It's the wire." She pushed the hoop to one side and tried to get comfortable. "It's been jabbing my leg all day. I think it may have broken the skin back on the pier."

Shadrach searched the deck for other female passengers. Two crewmen stood on the starboard side, but he didn't see any women. He sat back down and leaned toward her. "Do you want me to look—"

"No. I certainly do not want you to look." She stepped onto the underside of her hem and dragged it closer. "How can you suggest such a thing?"

Shadrach measured his reply. "I was going to say, for a woman passenger to assist you." Did she have to cut him off each time he tried to explain something? Tiny flecks of pink stained her neck. And possibly her face, but she kept that down and trained on her skirt. "There may be someone who can help you tend to your leg in privacy."

"I'll look at it later." Her folded hands landed in her lap in a dismissive flop, but it took some attempts for her thumbs to still. He waited until she gained her composure.

"There's amazing scenery coming up, at Cape Shanck. Not many people get to see it from the approach we're taking."

"Because you take them prisoner? With bound limbs and blindfold?"

Shadrach exhaled. She would hold a grudge all the way home. He looked at the coastline and hoped it would not be too long before he delivered her to George.

"For your information, the only other person I've escorted this way is my sister. She wasn't tied up, and I didn't hear a word of complaint from her."

"Did she have any say in it, or did you make that decision for her, too?"

"If you must know, Molly's lot is similar to yours. She's always lived with my mother but she died last month, and Molly's come to live with me." He said it as if it hadn't already toppled his world over. As if having Molly were as easy as adding another shelf to the wall. As if Miss Mayfield would even care.

But Miss Mayfield's eyes softened. "I'm sorry about your mother. How old is your sister?"

"Fourteen."

"Oh." Her shoulders lost a little of their starch. "I lost my mother at fourteen, too."

Heaviness lumbered into his chest, reminding him loss had followed Miss Mayfield all the way from England. And he had no idea what awaited them back at the island.

The vessel hit a wave and his stomach lurched in reply. He steeled himself to talk about anything but the loss of loved ones.

"Would be good for Molly to marry, someday, but that's not to be."

"She is only a child." Miss Mayfield almost smiled. "It's hardly too late."

"It's not her age. Molly's… a simple girl. Not suited to marriage."

"Oh." Miss Mayfield seemed to think about this for a moment. "Where is she today?"

"With Mrs. Lawson." Whatever had lumbered into his chest now settled there. He wondered what went on back at the little church house while they steamed toward it. George had better be sleeping and Molly had better be at Mrs. Lawson's elbow. Nothing else would do. Not with Miss Mayfield staring up at him.

"Does Molly enjoy living with you?"

"She's happy. I'm the one that's had to make adjustments."

"I guess Molly is the lucky one then, because you were certainly in no mood to make adjustments today." Her exaggerated smile reached no further than her lips and those brown eyes, warm only a moment ago, flashed resentment he knew simmered under the surface.

"Does Molly comply because you threaten to tie her up, too?" She brushed a breadcrumb from her lap. For someone with pretty eyes, she knew how to use them for fighting.

A prickle, like the burrs he sometimes picked up on his trousers, took hold in his chest. Or was it his heart? She had no business assuming anything about him, and certainly not about Molly.

"I'm not afraid to keep my promises, Miss Mayfield. My mother died knowing Molly would be safe with me. If I have to tie her up for her own good, then that's what I'll do."

Miss Mayfield's mouth dropped open. He wasn't sure if her eyes filled with tears or whether the wind made her blink. "You don't *really* tie her up, do you?" she whispered. "I can't believe an honorable man such as Mr. Gleeson would trust someone who resorts to cruelty."

He rubbed his knee and wondered how to answer. His *cruelty* had saved his sister's life. More than once.

If she baited him, Shadrach refused to play. She'd had a difficult journey and, with Phillip Island less than an hour away, she probably juggled a mess of jitters.

He stood to stretch his legs and murmured. "Let's hope you never have to find out."

∽

Finella imagined the sun threw golden ribbons across the sky just for her. Streamers of rust and purple festooned the horizon and for the second time in one day she stepped off a vessel and looked for her fiancé.

Dusk hovered over the wooden L shaped jetty; reaching out like a hook from the shore, ready to gather all that washed up into its neat hug.

"See that bunkhouse by the shore?" Mr. Jones pointed out a structure at the end of the jetty. "Jon Tripp lives there. He'll bring his horse and trolley down for your things. Most people come back next day to collect. Jon will keep it safe overnight." His words were kind but his eyes came nowhere near her. They scoured the village.

Finella regretted her biting words on the steamer but somehow he'd succeeded in crossing her more than once in their brief trip together. She didn't know how to offer an apology now and concentrated on making out the shape of houses among the trees. But the shadows matched the tides, and night lapped at the edge of the day.

She tucked a strand of loose hair behind her ear and peered at the sky. A low shadow of wings, a flock of some kind twisted against the sky and passed overhead.

"What was that?" Another stream followed, their path almost silent except for the long black wave they carved against the sunset.

"Muttonbirds. They come in every year. Most burrow on the other side of the island. Not many stop on this side." Mr. Jones answered with only the briefest look into the air. He kept his eye on the village.

Finella followed his gaze. The birds might not stop here, but she would have to. "Do you see Mr. Gleeson?"

"I don't see anyone. The house is only a few minutes up the track. Ready?" He picked up her travelling bag.

She considered her disheveled hair, puffy eyes, and ripped dress. She was hardly ready at all. She brushed the creases from her skirt and tried to ignore the vinegary smell on her gloves.

"I don't suppose it would make any difference to you if I said I am not ready, at all."

He looked her over.

"You're fine." His words scraped at her jangled nerves. "George wouldn't care if you arrived in sackcloth. You're here now. That's all that matters."

"To you, perhaps." She spat her words under her breath. What was wrong with her? Hadn't she learned her lesson already? Instead of composing herself, she let this man draw her into another argument.

Demure. She turned a deaf ear to the whisper in her mind, but Aunt Sarah's wisdom on greeting men snuck in anyway. *Demure* was the last thing she needed to hear. Shadrach Jones had served his friend well but he brought out the miserable worst in her.

"Thank you very much, Mr. Jones. You promised to deliver me and well… you have. Your job is complete. I'll find my own way from here." She collected her bag and marched down the narrow pier.

Too late. She forgot the blessed hoop slowed her down. Instead of storming off, the wire jabbed her calf with every step and she slowed to a limp.

In three, perhaps four strides Mr. Jones reached her. He snatched the handle and easily overtook her. His boots beat an angry tap against the jetty.

"You're in Australia now, Miss. Don't you forget that for one minute." He barely turned to address her, but she heard it all the same. "You know nothing about the bush you so bravely stomp into, so you'll follow me until—"

"Shadrach?" Voices and footsteps curled from the shore and two boys bounded toward them.

Mr. Jones dropped the bag and grabbed the taller boy by the shoulders. Both lads fought to catch their breath. Their chests rose and fell and they looked from Finella to each other.

"Who sent you, Jimmy?" Mr. Jones' voice remained calm and low.

"Mrs. Lawson. Said we had ta look out for ya… and let ya know ta hurry."

Shadrach Jones turned his back on Finella and drew the boy closer. Their whispers eluded her and she meant to elbow in when Mr. Jones faced her again.

"Jimmy'll bring your bag when he catches his breath." He frowned at Finella and rubbed his chin. Blew a quick breath through his lips and cracked the knuckles on his fists.

"What? What is it?" Her heart doubled its beat.

"Forgive me, Miss. I can't think of any other way to do this, with your leg."

"Do what? What's happened? Please, tell me." She shuffled closer.

He pinched his lips together and collected her up into the air as if she were a feed sack and flung her over his right shoulder. And then he ran.

Finella wanted to scream but her breath caught against her ribs. Blood rushed to her head and the wooden jetty boards turned into a sandy track. Sand turned to dirt and they followed a well-worn path to cover ground faster than Finella knew possible by foot. She closed her eyes and groaned at the churning of her stomach. She couldn't tell how many minutes passed before he eventually set her down. He with no breath, she with dizzy head.

A softly lit cottage sat in the shadow of a darkened church. Was this her destination?

"I'm sorry... I didn't know... how else to do it. George is fading and they—"

A whoosh filled her ears. A storm of blood and air she was not sure would ever return to their right place within her skin.

"Fading?"

Not fading. Surely he didn't mean...? She pressed her hand to her neck. To the wild slam of her pulse.

"Hurry." He gripped Finella's hand and dragged her faster than her legs had speed to follow.

Her garbled questions went unanswered and even with the prickle of the broken hoop, their speed never slackened until they reached the front door.

Mr. Jones burst in. Still holding Finella's hand he squeezed her into a small front bedroom.

They stood there, hand in hand, while George Gleeson, ashen and pasty, smiled at them from his bed.

5

Shadrach dismantled the trestle tables and slid the tops along the back verandah of the already crowded church house. Didn't these people have homes to go to? Horses to water? Hearts to hide?

The funeral of their preacher had brought every villager and farmer to the Cowes churchyard, but the food was all eaten now, and the bitter-long day ended.

"Excuse me." He returned to the verandah with the last of the tables. "Excuse me, please."

If they wouldn't leave, at least he could force their conversations to continue away from the house where he knew Miss Mayfield sat in the parlor receiving comfort from the womenfolk.

With the funeral over, he had to talk to her. But how foolish to ask a newly bereaved young woman to look at you as a suitable replacement for the man she's just buried. Shadrach let the trestle drop with an irreverent, ironclad bang.

"Shadrach Jones, do you have any idea where your sister is right now?" Mrs. Lawson yelled from the doorway where she shook a tablecloth.

"Not exactly." He hoped Molly sat inside the kitchen where he'd left her. "Why do you ask?"

"Not exactly means *not at all* in my book. She's in the room I gave Miss Mayfield. Won't come out for anyone's coaxing. You'd best get in there and rescue her before this day worsens, if that's possible."

Weariness washed over him. Molly could be curious but if Miss Mayfield saw her as a pest it would be another reason for her to keep her distance.

Not that he particularly wanted much to do with her right now. But a promise to a dead man was still a promise.

"I'll get her. It's time we were going home, anyway." He tried to pass Mrs. Lawson, but she yanked at his sleeve.

"And when you're done, I need to speak with you. In private." Her solemn face had not changed all day. Stoic and busy with endless teapots, she'd worked with a diligence like any other day in her service to George.

Shadrach nodded and stepped into the dark hallway leading to the second bedroom. A quick peek into the parlor rewarded him with no glimpse of Miss Mayfield, only the disapproving eyes of matrons who had, no doubt, tried but failed to draw Molly from her mischief.

Ivy Trilloe stood by the closed bedroom door. If meddlesome had a face it sported her eyes, ears, and nose. She eyed the door handle the way a gull might watch a forgotten crab basket. Greedy. Daring.

"It's a cruel thing to leave such a girl to her own devices when you so obviously have better things to do, Mr. Jones. Brother or no brother, Molly needs the care of a woman. Someone who'll devote their energies to keeping her safe and teaching her to be useful."

He tapped on the door, glad for a place to land his clenched fist. "She is safe. And useful."

"For how long? Do you think there won't come a day when your back'll be turned and she'll not wander further than you think she can? You already live too close to the sea and her eyes are charmed by every pretty thing that twinkles."

"You cannot have her." He wanted to yell the words but kept his simmering temper in check. "I know you're concerned for her welfare, but she really is fine. With me. Today's been… a trying day, for everyone."

He longed to be home and away from people. To grieve in a place where no one could find him. Where he could deal with life's knots and bruises his own way.

"Shadrach. You're a farmer. You spend hours outside. Surely you've already had moments of frustration with Molly at home."

"We'll work it out. My sister and I."

"Fine. Be stubborn." She threw her hands in the air. "But my offer remains open for the day you come to your senses and need a safe place for her to live."

"You mean work." His words came out low, and if she heard him, he was not sorry.

He would rather die like George than give Molly to the Trilloes. Yes, they were wealthy enough with their general store and bake house. Childless and comfortable. Molly might benefit with them as adoptive parents, but she deserved more than a life of floor sweeping, shelf dusting, and whip dodging. She deserved a brother who loved her. Protected her. Fought for her.

He ignored the retreating Mrs. Trilloe and tapped the door again. "Molly, it's me. Please come out. It's time to go home."

A key twisted in the lock and the face of his sister appeared behind the heavy door. Her hair looked more disheveled than usual. Tears stained her cheeks, but the crying was over. Perhaps she'd rested on the bed. Her dolly tucked under one arm, she let him take the other and usher her into the hallway.

"What were you doing in there? Did you touch anything you shouldn't have?"

Molly shook her head. If she'd broken or messed with Miss Mayfield's things he would have to make amends.

"I saw a mirror and brush. A pretty brush. So I..." She showed him how she tried to fix her hair to sit atop her head. Instead, it swung across her back in a thick plait.

Shadrach searched the room as best he could. The mirror and brush sat on a dresser and nothing appeared disturbed.

"Come on then. Let's say goodbye to Mrs. Lawson and get home before it's too dark.'"

A gaggle of wives dried cups and saucers in the kitchen. Mrs. Lawson hung her towel, squeezed past, and directed Shadrach and Molly to the verandah. If she had a stern word for him, she'd not be afraid to share it. Even today. But, her lectures came with a hint of care and, on occasion, even a smile.

Mrs. Lawson sat Molly in a chair on the now empty verandah. Dusk hovered over the village and a line of pink faded out of the inky sky.

"Sit here pet, while I fix your hair." She undid Molly's ribbon, finger-combed her long black hair and divided it into three. He did this too, every morning, but it took him longer. Mrs. Lawson collected all the fly away wisps he usually left untamed.

"Listen to me, Shadrach Jones. I've been meaning to say this all day." She kept her eyes on Molly and he strained to hear her whispers.

"I was a faithful housekeeper to Mr. Gleeson. Loved him like a son. Who could blame me with my own three babies in the ground?" She took a deep, sorrowful breath. "Some may think I overstepped my mark, but I knew what he needed and was pleased to make it my service to God. I am ashamed to admit I took it too far the day the two of you spoke last, before you fetched Miss Mayfield from Melbourne."

She peeked at him. "I didn't mean to. I was only coming to bring fresh sheets." She held the plait with one hand and wound the ribbon around the end with the other. "But I lingered where I shouldn't have and overheard words that passed between you."

Shadrach didn't know why she confessed this now. It was no news to him she was possessive of George. Perhaps this was her way of grieving.

"I know you'll miss him, Mrs. Lawson. He was lucky to have you."

She rested her fingers on Molly's shoulder. "Your bond with Mr. Gleeson was also strong, especially at the end there. Wasn't it? You of all people still owe him a service no other can fulfill."

With a sick twist to his gut, Shadrach leaned in. "What are you talking about?"

"You know very well what I'm talking about." She finished tying Molly's hair. "And it's eating you up. I can tell by the miserable look on your face. You haven't a clue how to keep your promise to George regarding Miss Mayfield." Her voice lowered. "Don't worry, I'll keep your secret. Mr. Gleeson knew nothing I overheard under this roof would spread thanks to me. But you..." she tipped an elbow his way, "have a girl to talk to."

Shadrach wanted the night to fall and cover him under a blanket of pitch. He'd made far too many promises for one lifetime. He was sure of that. First to his mother about Molly. Now to George about Miss Mayfield and with Mrs. Lawson in on the secret, he'd not be allowed to forget it.

"Not sure today's the best day for it. I'll take Molly home and see if I can come up with a plan."

"No need. I have the perfect one." She looked around. "Seems to me you've two problems. Molly could do with a mother or sisterly type. Don't look at me like that, Shadrach. You can't ignore the inevitable. Four weeks looking after Molly is just the beginning. You'll have all your spring chores upon you next. What do you plan on doing then?"

Shadrach leaned against Molly's chair and let his eyes close. Just a little. Enough to hint at total darkness. He was right. This day would not pass without another lecture from the good women of this village.

Mrs. Lawson patted him on the back. "You're good with her, to a point, and I'm sure you've agonized over this too. You don't want her growing wild out there without another woman for company."

He focused on the back of his sister's head. Mrs. Lawson's plait mocked him with tightness and precision. It never looked like that when he did it. Most days it flew around Molly's face. Loose, and … well, wild.

"And then there's Miss Mayfield. Only family left to her is an aunt in London and she'll be looking to get back there as soon as possible."

Shadrach swallowed. "She's not looking for marriage with a farmer. She came here to be the preacher's wife. Don't know why George made me promise foolishness."

Mrs. Lawson sighed. "Perhaps Mr. Gleeson knew more than we could imagine. You don't need to consider courting her right away. It's too soon to muddle with her heart. But you can offer work. Tell her you need a companion for Molly. For when you're not there." Mrs. Lawson stroked the girl's cheek.

"And pay her what?" Surely he was not expected to dip into his meager savings?

"A roof over her head and the type of work Mr. Gleeson would've encouraged her to do. Something to bless the people he loved. This house'll be empty soon enough and the elders will look for another preacher. She knows she can't stay here forever."

Mrs. Lawson tapped her temple. "Anticipate her needs, lad. Give her something to hold onto while she sorts herself out. If anything, she gets a chance to know you, and you her. Then… if you both like what you see…" She shrugged.

Shadrach could not hide the roll of his tired eyes. "Do all women plot the course of everyone else's future? Don't the menfolk ever have a say?"

Mrs. Lawson smiled for the first time that day. "Most times we aim to have you think it was all your idea in the first place."

6

_____

I have come for nothing. Let this book be a record of that. No father to watch regain his health in a climate promised to restore. No husband to honor and serve. Both are buried and lost forever. Perhaps only the loss of my mother can compare.

Of deepest sadness is the absence of words from my fiancé. His life, all but slipped away when I stumbled into his sick room. His first and last message to me, that haunting smile. And there in that clumsy introduction, George nodded and slipped into an eternity where only God chooses who will follow.

Now I have nothing of my own to sustain me. George's congregation cares for my obvious needs. They feed and warm me. They sit beside me and offer silent company.

I want to scream at the shallowness of their affections, yet I know they are sincere. And I am ashamed. I cannot receive them, and wish for all to leave me, yet when they do, displacement threatens to undo me.

The small house has throbbed with mourners all day. This house, which should have been mine to make into a home, is now a false promise, and I desire to leave it as soon as possible. Mrs. Lawson has ordered me to bed. She's prepared a tea tree poultice for my leg and insists I rest here with it plastered to my calf.

I will write to Aunt Sarah and make plans for my return to London.

How I longed to stand with my back to the wind and yell over the sea until my voice carried to where Father is buried. To tell him, with George's help, I'd discovered what we always searched for. That the unknown is no more, and I can live the life he desired for me. With the freedom only knowledge brings.

Without George's help, how am I to find what will restore me? And why would God allow this journey to end in twofold death... and nothing more?

⌇

"Five shells, Missy. No more. Leave some on the beach for someone else." Shadrach called from where he leaned against a moonah tree and watched Molly add to her collection of sea treasures.

The tide crept up the shore and the sun dipped in the west, bathing Cowes in fiery sparks. Was it only a week ago he'd brought Miss Mayfield to a similar sunset only to present her with more loss?

Shadrach kicked at a crusty mound of sun-baked sand and watched it crumble over his shoe. Like an hourglass time moved on, slipping their days forward into whatever it would look like now, without George.

Miss Mayfield would've made the preacher proud. She'd held herself together well during the funeral. Dignified, her silent weeping hidden behind that mourning veil.

She should have been a preacher's bride. She'd brought honor to the funeral of George Gleeson and now it was his turn to act honorably. He shook the sand from the bottom of his trouser leg and kept an eye on Molly who balanced at the edge of a rock pool.

If he ever took a wife, she'd have to share in his poverty and hard work. Finella Mayfield was not used to that kind of life and perhaps never would be. Other than Mrs. Lawson's plan, he had nothing else to offer, and a part of him was glad. Turning down an offer of work was not nearly as bad as turning down an offer of marriage. Even if it were for clumsy convenience. He joined Molly where she poked at the seaweed with a long twig.

"Look, Shad." She hooked a strand of green pearl-like tendrils and held them high. "Jewels." She swung like an angler with her find.

"Very pretty." He admired her catch.

A blackened piece of driftwood bumped the jagged edge of the rock pool. Too weak to push the displaced branch into the embrace of the little pool, the gentle waves only lapped so far.

Shadrach climbed onto the rocks and tapped the driftwood with the toe of his boot. It plopped into the shallows with a splash. Molly squealed with delight and urged Shadrach to repeat the fun.

"More, Shad? More?" She let the twig slide into the rock pool, dipped her hand into the water and fished out the driftwood. It landed with another plop near Shadrach's foot. "Again?"

Shadrach laughed at her childlike game, this time exaggerating the kick to create a bigger splash.

Molly didn't hesitate to thrust her hand into the water once more. Only this time her fun met with a sharp scream.

"Oh, Shad. Bad thing." She brought her fingers to her mouth. "Something… bit me."

"Let me see." Shadrach pulled at her hand. "That's not a bite. It's a splinter. Look." He cradled her little finger and showed her the small fleck of wood wedged in her skin. Molly drew her finger away and tucked it back in her mouth.

"I can get it out if you'll let me." He held out his palm and waited.

Molly backed away.

"I have to take it out. It'll hurt more if we leave it there."

"No. Don't want you." Molly ran along the shore and up toward the sand dunes.

"Molly, come back!" Shadrach sighed and followed. He should teach Mrs. Trilloe a real lesson and lend her Molly for a day.

But he could never use his sister for fun. It would take every ounce of patience, but he would do whatever it took to ensure her safety and happiness. And if his plan worked, keep his promise to George at the same time.

He quickened his pace to reach her. To reach for all it meant to love Molly Jones.

"No, no. I said *No*."

From the top of the dunes, Finella heard the sound of someone crying.

She juggled the shell she'd been admiring and raised her hand in a friendly wave, eager not to scare the young girl who slid down the sand in her direction. The girl's crying gave way to a hiccup and then she stopped to stare.

"Molly, isn't it?"

The girl sniffed and nodded.

"I'm Finella. Is something wrong?"

She nodded again. "A wood bit me." Her teary reply came from a finger stuffed mouth. "Here." She pulled out the wet finger.

Rugged up against the wind, Finella guessed she was the last person anyone would expect on this beach. Instead of the parlor in the little white house, where she'd sat in polite quiet for days, she now perched on an old fishing blanket of Mrs. Lawson's. "Go exhale your sorrows and breathe in some hope, girl," the housekeeper had encouraged. "When you're this close to the sea, you might as well let the wind soothe the aches, even just a little."

Finella pushed the shell and aches aside.

"You mean a splinter?" she patted the blanket beside her. "Come, sit by me. I'm sure you'll feel better once you catch your breath."

Molly sank beside her and their shoulders rubbed together when she nestled into the sand.

Finella dug into her pocket and from the cluster of her chatelaine, extracted a miniature magnifying glass. She lay it flat in her palm.

"Have you seen one of these before?"

Molly shook her head.

"No? Well, it's a very clever glass. It helps us see things which are tiny, by making them bigger. See?" She peered into the glass and held it over Molly's hand by the mother of pearl handle. The tiniest sliver of wood had pierced the skin, and hung there by a thread. Molly pulled away a little.

Finella dropped a purple scalloped shell into Molly's curled fist. "What do you see now?"

The young girl extended her fingers to hold it better, allowing Finella to scrape the splinter away with her nail.

"The shell. I see it!" Molly marveled at the magnified distraction. When she remembered to look for the splinter, all that remained was a red pinprick.

"All gone?" Her eyes lit up to match her grin.

Finella grinned back. She opened her mouth to confirm the good news but Molly held her hand high and spoke to an unannounced third in their midst.

"Look, Brother, all gone."

Finella turned. Shadrach Jones stood behind them, his hands jammed in his pockets. But surprise swam in his smile. How long had he hovered there, watching them? Watching her? A quick thud found a way to her throat.

"I don't know how you managed it, but I think you may have done the impossible. I couldn't even catch the minx."

He crouched by Molly's feet and eyed them both. But those blue eyes, bluer than the sea, flickered over Molly for an instant. When they were done, they settled on Finella and took her in.

"Well." Finella fiddled with her chatelaine. "We had a few tricks up our sleeve, didn't we, Molly?" She shifted back a little on the blanket. Aunt Sarah would have words to say about accidently brushing against Mr. Jones' long legs and bent knees.

"Good tricks," Molly agreed with a slow distracted nod, still absorbed by the glass.

"I see you two have become acquainted, then." Mr. Jones anchored his feet in the sand.

"We have. And we also managed to put the splinter problem behind us."

His smile faded to match the cloud cover overhead. Finella wondered if she'd done something wrong. Perhaps she should not have touched the splinter.

"Miss Mayfield..." He faltered. He looked at Molly who examined her fingernails with the glass, then back at Finella. He looked like a wave that couldn't make up his mind about running in or rolling back.

"I wanted to speak with you the day of the funeral but you were being cared for by so many." He pressed one knee to the sand. "I know it's been a difficult time for you."

Instinct reared its head and hummed a warning. He was on his knee. Right in front of her.

"I'm hoping you'll be receptive to a proposal I'd like to make."

His voice carried a cautious edge. A trepidation of heart both foolhardly and brave. As if he'd pushed himself up a slippery hill, one he'd rather slide off. And yet, he hung on.

She clenched a handful of blanket in her fist. Surely the man did not mean to propose marriage? Was she not to have one simple day in this country without the assault of the unexpected?

She brushed at a dusting of sand on her sleeve. Her answer would bite, even if she delivered it with the pinch of regret she tried to ignore.

"I would not…be receptive." If his sister were not sprawled against her skirt in such comfortable fashion, she might have said more.

He refused to look away. "But… you haven't heard it yet. How can you say no when I've not yet made the offer?"

Her cheeks flamed and she hoped the wind were the culprit.

"Mr. Jones, with my father's encouragement, my correspondence with Mr. Gleeson lasted two years. I agreed to our engagement after much gentle courting, and even then with the knowledge I was agreeing to marry a man I hardly remembered. You cannot suggest I make another, less agreeable arrangement, with him only just buried?" She let her voice soften a little. "I'm not so lacking in choices I would agree to a marriage of convenience. I am not a young widow with children hanging off my apron." She hoped to convince herself as equally as she hoped she might convince Mr. Jones.

He frowned and opened his mouth to continue but Molly turned to Finella.

"Our George died." Molly's words pressed at the wound they all carried. "So did my mum." She turned her cheek away and found a resting place for it in Finella's lap.

Her words and warmth proved Finella's undoing. With trembling fingers she found Molly's hair and stroked the wind chased strands off her pretty face. And to her horror, right there on the sand with a perplexed Mr. Jones staring at her and Molly pressing her to the blanket, Finella began to cry.

∾

Shadrach had no idea how it had gone so horribly wrong. He stretched his legs in front of him, careful not to touch her. Were all attempts at conversation with Miss Mayfield to end in misunderstanding and tears?

False as her assumption of marriage may be, it came with a stab of rejection.

Less agreeable arrangement, she'd called it. Well, for her information, he wasn't offering marriage.

At least, not today.

The temptation to tell her exactly what George suggested occurred to him, but only for an instant. He wasn't that cruel. Being parceled from one groom to another would not bode well for any girl, and right now he needed to set her straight.

Molly comforted her the only way she knew how. By resting in Miss Mayfield's lap. Or was it Miss Mayfield who comforted Molly? Something about the way they slumped together stirred a new hope in him. Deep in the chest where she'd just kicked him.

"You have no fear of a marriage proposal from me, Miss Mayfield." *Not today, that is.* "Mrs. Lawson told me you were on the beach and I came looking for you."

He waited for her to look at him but she kept her eyes on his sister.

"I'm offering a position as companion to Molly."

Her fingers stopped moving and she stared at Molly's shoulder. If she saw the scar, she didn't ask questions he was not prepared to answer.

"In the month she's been with me, we've worked out an adequate daily routine, but it would be better for her to have the guidance of a woman. Someone to teach her how to manage. To take better care of her own needs." To show her how to live.

He let his words trail off. Was she even listening? Red blotches stained her face, but those lashes, heavy with tears, barely moved until she looked from her hands to Molly and finally to him.

"You're offering work?"

"I am."

"As companion to Molly?"

He nodded. "And teacher. Not school work. Household tasks."

Until such time I can honor my promise to George and convince you to look at me as a more 'agreeable arrangement.'

"Where would I live?"

"With Molly. In my house. I've a skillion next door. I built it last winter for storage. I can throw myself a bedroll on the floor. I'm gone most of the day so I'd expect you to teach Molly the duties of keeping a home. She's capable of learning but I've not had the time to show her yet."

Miss Mayfield blinked against the wind. "How is it your mother didn't teach Molly?"

"Our mother worked for a Ballarat laundry business. As a washerwoman she could only afford to live in a boarding house."

He stopped. Miss Mayfield's mouth had slipped open, as if he'd confessed they'd once lived in the Tower of London.

"Ballarat? You mean the goldfields?"

"Yes. But not during the rush. Later, anyway…" Why did that even matter? Shadrach focused back on Molly's story. "Simple meals were part of their boarding fee. Molly knows how to scrub clothes but there are many things I've discovered she doesn't know. Mum kept her close, in a way I can never do and work my farm."

Miss Mayfield swallowed. Hard.

"I can't offer paid work. My farm is only starting to yield a living. Enough to keep us fed and warm, but you're welcome to share in whatever we have. I know you can't stay in the church house much longer, and I need someone for Molly. I thought perhaps we could be of help to each other."

She looked to the sea. "I've already written to my aunt in London. I've asked her to come and get me as soon as she is free to travel." A fresh wind played over the shore and Miss Mayfield shivered in its path. "I never wish to journey by ship alone again."

Shadrach nodded. He must have said something right. So far she hadn't said no.

"If I were to accept, it would be a temporary appointment. I suppose I could teach Molly, but you must know when Aunt Sarah arrives, I shall leave. If all goes well I expect that will be in three months. That's all I can promise."

Shadrach unwound a smile and hoped it stayed put. If George believed Shadrach had it in him to *look after Miss Finella*, then three months under his roof should give him ample time to convince the lady herself.

"Agreed. Until your aunt arrives." He tapped his sister's shoe with his knuckle.

"Miss Molly, we have chores waiting for us." *And three months to keep a promise to George.* The terms might be hers today, but he'd work to change all that.

"How about we collect you from the church house tomorrow afternoon?"

Miss Mayfield breathed in a deep, slow breath as if she gulped for the antidote to dread. "I'll need to help Mrs. Lawson pack the last of George's things, but we should be done by then." She brushed Molly's shoulder and his sister stirred.

He would've offered his hand to the two young women but they helped each other stand. Molly silent, just when he needed her to cheer, and Miss Mayfield, equally thoughtful.

"Molly and I are grateful you've agreed. You may have come along just when we needed you most. Isn't that right, Sunny?"

Poor in enthusiasm, Molly had little to add. Even after he used her favorite pet name. Lost in her own thoughts she stretched and looked beyond his shoulder to the sea.

The notion of Miss Mayfield coming to live with them had not landed in Molly's heart the way it did his, and he tried to ignore the small thrill spinning in his chest. But it rattled, all the same, like a prized jack-bone he'd won as a boy and toyed with in a loose fist for days.

Miss Mayfield shook the blanket and folded it. When it sat neat and straight in the crook of her arm she turned to Shadrach, her eyes wide, her breath short, her voice a whisper.

"Sunny?"

"Our mother used to call her that, sometimes." He reached for his sister and brought her closer. "She drifts easily. I use whatever I can to draw her back."

Miss Mayfield nodded, but her fingers trembled and she buried them in the blanket.

"I know what it feels like to lose a mother at fourteen. Unlike Molly, I had my aunt and father to keep our home as I'd always known it."

She straightened her shoulders, much like the blanket she folded into readiness for whatever service it might offer next. "So, I agree to be a teacher and companion to your sister, Mr. Jones, because I believe God is offering me the chance to lift someone who needs me. My aunt taught me there's always someone who needs us. If I didn't believe this was my calling I would never have agreed to come to Australia in the first place."

Molly screwed her heels into the sand and Miss Mayfield steadied her with a touch to the arm. "Perhaps, for a season, that someone is your sister."

7

October 4

I have cast away my mourning clothes. Locked them away in a trunk and I am not ashamed to have done so.

Not to mourn any less, but to offer some gladness to Molly. Besides, I cannot suffer that crinoline hoop a moment longer and I swap it for a simple white shirt and lavender skirt to please the young girl.

Sometime this afternoon, Molly will become my charge, to be cared for as one of Mr. Gleeson's lambs. I will do this in tribute to him.

To mark this day I add to my Everlasting its first bloom. Petals from the Little Noonflower. Mrs. Lawson tells me it's common in these parts and grows well in sandy soils. I fan open its tiny purple petals and hope God will see in me the same desire to open my heart to Molly.

I have stood where she stands. Motherless girls should never be alone. Least of all one such as Molly. It took her one afternoon on the beach to wriggle into my lap, and further still, into a crevice in my soul I didn't know existed.

No one comforts me the way she does. She offers no words to dismiss my sorrow. No instruction to put away my tears. And I hear no mention of the will of God.

Instead, she lays her head against my knee and without shame cries and stays there, pinning me so I have nowhere to run or hide and I find

myself wrapped in God's comfort anyway, and with a heart full of
tenderness for Molly Jones.

∾

Finella helped Mrs. Lawson pack George Gleeson's remaining belongings. Together they braved the threat of rain to add them to the items in Mr. Jones' already crowded wagon. He'd collected her trunks from the jetty, and little room remained in his wagon for what they crammed under a dirty oilcloth.

The good people of George's congregation deemed it only right his possessions should pass to Finella. But even greater generosity prevailed in the heart of Mrs. Lawson who wrapped two loaves of her own bread, along with a pan of lemons and a jar of honey. A final wink from her as they pushed off failed to reassure Finella.

"Huddle under the oilcloth." Shadrach Jones covered his sister's shoulder and beckoned for Finella to take the corner. "There's a dumping of rain coming."

Finella shivered, and as if by instinct, Molly snuggled into her under their makeshift tent. But it was not the cold which shook Finella.

The fault lay firmly on the soles and sides of Molly's shoes. Slippery roads and pathways did not make for a warm welcome and Finella's heart churned at the sight of Molly's well-worn boots, encrusted with a generous slap of mud. Red mud.

Their house must be surrounded by it. Finella's heart skidded.

Caked with a thick layer, Molly left a rusty smear wherever she set foot. Finella imagined Mr. Jones did the same. If their shoes carried inches of farm dirt, Finella's first task would be to scrub the front step and teach Molly to wash the door from lintel to stoop.

"Good thing, this rain. Most folks 'round here just seeded their fields. Last night's downpour was heaven sent." Mr. Jones didn't seem to mind not sharing their oilcloth. Instead, he looked very pleased with himself. Against a grey sky, his blue eyes flashed at her like gems. She looked at them for a moment longer than she should. Long enough for him to grow his smile into a grin.

Oh no you don't.

Finella buried her head under the cloth and determined to keep it there. Was Shadrach Jones looking for smiles? While they dodged a slow but persistent rain and his horse negotiated the slippery road ahead?

The track became a water-filled ditch and her stomach dipped when the wagon rattled ahead with a huge splash. Molly drew closer.

"We've got mustard," she whispered. "On our farm. And chicory."

Finella smiled. How long had it been since she'd shared a secret whisper under a cover like this?

"Do you?" She whispered back.

Molly nodded. "And I've got shells."

"You must be a very busy girl, Molly. Are you ready to learn a few new things?"

"No." She shook her head. "Shad said I didn't have to."

"I said nothing of the sort." Mr. Jones snapped the reins and hurried them through a puddle the size of a duck pond. "Don't let her tell tales, Miss Mayfield. She knows you're here to keep her company and that includes learning a few things, too." He leaned into Molly, "And you'll learn them with none of your mischief."

Steady rain set in and Molly drew away from her brother while Finella pulled the oilcloth even tighter.

"You don't spin tales do you, Molly?"

Molly smeared mud on the board at their feet and shook her head. She nursed her lie as if it were a newly hatched gosling, impossible to hide in her lap.

"I hope not. My Aunt Sarah says, the truth is a heavy load to carry, but those that do are free."

A drip of rain fell from the tarp overhead and landed on her nose. She wiped it away with her wrist before Finella could remind her to use a handkerchief. If indeed she even had one. Right now, she sucked on the end of her braid, the tip lodged in her mouth.

First thing I'll teach you, Molly Jones, will be to wipe your shoes clean on wet grass, at our earliest opportunity. All other good manners will follow on those clean heels.

Rain dribbled through the eucalyptus branches. With the neat wooden houses of Cowes behind them, they now passed freshly plowed fields. Clearings where wet animals huddled together in soggy pastures gave way to thick groves of tea tree and the smell of camphor filled Finella's lungs. That and wet earth, fresh mud, and damp oilcloth.

Soon, Mr. Jones turned his horse onto a narrow red track. It wound under trees Finella didn't recognize. White bark with a pink underbelly hung in strips from the trunk.

They stopped for him to open a farm gate. The simple entrance marked by a rough hewn crossbar on a homemade hinge.

She tried to spot wildflowers for her *Everlasting*, but nothing caught her eye. They must all be ducking the weather. She was not surprised. She had deliberately kept her head down for most of the journey and even with eyelids half closed all she saw was the rain and the road ahead.

And Molly's dirty shoes.

"Go straight in. I'll load these things into the skillion." Mr. Jones jumped into a large puddle. Splashes of mud didn't slow him down and Finella found herself roused from her huddle with Molly, and deposited on the ground.

She lifted her boot to the squelch of brick-red putty. The pull of the fat clod matched the sinking of her expectations and repulsion raced through her body. She inched her way along the wagon to a drier patch of earth. It wasn't a puddle but it was no cobblestone pathway either.

A wattle and daub hut sat in the midst of the same mud which lapped at Finella's hem. Mr. Jones must have thought it much grander than that. He called it a house. He urged Molly to take Finella in and they both slipped through the mud to lean on the outside wall and secure their slow steps. Finella's fingers touched the same dried mud which now clung to the sole of her shoes. It was everywhere. Underfoot at every step, and in every horizontal crevice of every wall. Only the wood shingled roof escaped the same treatment.

Already she loathed the L shaped dwelling that sat in a bog. This was no cheery white-clad weatherboard, the likes of which she'd seen in Cowes. Instead, a layer of red dust on her gloves confirmed her worst suspicions. Molly and her brother lived in a mud hut, surrounded by mud, and if she were not careful, she would be wearing this same mud before she completed the short journey to the front door.

If the house could boast anything, it probably fell to the two mud free doors made of woven saplings. Here, long straps of tree fibers and young branches wove together in a tight construction bound by rough twine. She hoped insects didn't make it their home, too.

"Come on." Undeterred by the mud, Molly beckoned and made her way across the courtyard.

Aunt Sarah might have called it a pigpen. Mr. Jones called it a yard and warned Molly not to slip in it.

Conversation had fallen to silence during the journey from the church house, and that was fine with Finella, for she wrestled for balance most of the way.

But, Mr. Jones issued no word of caution and to Finella's regret, he did not issue any words of welcome, either.

She passed the door which lead to his skillion. His coat dripped from where he'd thrown it on a nail in the wall. Broad shoulders flexed under his damp shirt and he worked quickly to move Finella's things out of the rain.

"Excuse me." Head down, he hurried back to the wagon. Finella let go of the doorjamb and slid to where Molly waited for her at a second door. She scraped her boots as best she could before entering. Molly bounded right in.

Larger than the skillion, at one end a stone chimney begged a good clean. A beaten table and roughly made chairs filled the middle. Against the walls, long strips of timber shelving held an unmatched collection of plates, cups, and crocks. As endearing as the grin of a toothless drunkard, they did nothing to warm Finella's heart, nor did the welcome of dust on every surface. She looked for something to make her glad.

Beside the door, a small window let in only enough light to hide the true condition of the packed earth floor. At least the roof held the rain back. Was that the one good thing? That rain would not trickle down their necks while they slept?

At the opposite end of the room, two plank beds sagged against the wall. Her heart joined in this sagging at the thought she would sleep there tonight. Even more of a surprise was Molly's quick scramble to get out of her shoes and lift the covers.

Mr. Jones arrived at the door with a crate. "She sleeps a lot. Especially in the afternoon."

He too entered without wiping his feet and dumped the box on the table. "My only instruction is she's never to be left alone. If she knows you've gone off somewhere, she'll follow, get distracted...," he grabbed a wooden pail from the floor, "and most likely become lost."

How dim-witted did he think her? For longer than what Finella felt necessary or proper, he looked at her. Cold and unfriendly, his earlier smile now almost replaced with a frown.

His fingers tapped the side of the bucket.

"You have no need to concern yourself with Molly's safety, Mr. Jones. Her welfare is my responsibility now. I'm fully aware of that." She lifted her chin despite the heavy ache in her neck from the jostling ride. What had made him so mad?

From the shelf, Mr. Jones lifted the lid off a saltcellar and plucked a fistful for the pail. "She already knows it, but now it's full of your crates and my bed, you might as well remind her there's no sneaking into the skillion, either. She's a nosy magpie."

A trail of grains spilled onto the floor and peppered the toe of his shoe. He filled the pail from a ceramic water filter and turned to the shelves again. Tucked high where Finella suspected Molly couldn't reach, lay a knife. He threw it in the bucket and headed for the door where he stopped and turned back.

Finella didn't move from beside Molly's bed where the fully clothed girl no longer fought sleep's pull on her fluttering eyelids. Mr. Jones watched his sister with a strange tenderness. It bore a hole in Finella and she longed for her own lost family.

"She tires easily. Needs her naps. I know it'll be hard to teach her. I'm not too fussed how much she learns, as long as she's safe." Softness stole into his face. "I shouldn't be long." He closed the hut door with barely a sound.

Through the dirty window, Finella watched him trudge across the yard and into the bush without a backwards glance. And something about that bothered her.

8

Shadrach lay down his hunting knife. Crouched beside his traps, he turned his back to the biting wind. He normally did his butchering at home, but today he kept it far from the house. The open field would be dotted with another shower at any moment and already the yard around his house filled with more puddles than he liked.

Miss Mayfield had screwed her delicate nose at his yard the minute she'd sunk into the mud. She hated it all. He knew it and it annoyed him more than he'd expected.

He tried to tell himself it didn't matter. His mother's pouch of gold dust had paid for his land and there was still something in there for a proper house. Someday. When he'd place an order for a plank delivery from Melbourne. But Miss Mayfield didn't know that and her obvious distaste wounded and silenced him.

He'd done his best to tidy inside before she arrived, but who would've imagined he'd need to give thought to the muck by his front door. She'd said little about that but her tiptoeing across the yard shouted disgust. He made sure he was not there to see her reaction when she stepped inside. Some things he didn't have to see.

He wiped his bloody fingers on the wet grass before he touched the rabbit fur again. At least there'd be fresh meat for the pot tonight. With two small rabbits from his traps there'd be enough for the makings of a meal and two more pelts to set aside.

If she had not deboned a rabbit before, surely Miss Mayfield would appreciate him doing it for her today. It might make up for her disappointment. Then again, she may dislike even this attempt at a welcome. He had no way of knowing how to please her. Yet.

He reached into the already gutted cavity of the first rabbit and tugged at the tiny heart. Still warm, it slipped into his palm with ease. It didn't take much to rip it out. When all the innards lay in a pile at his feet, he sliced the second one and with care tore the skin off that carcass, too.

Stripped of her mourning clothes, an image of Finella as he'd found her this day hit him afresh. A skirt the color of a violet dusk. The fragrance of lavender. A collar of something soft and lacey at her throat.

For a man used to gutting rabbits, you'd think the sight of a beautiful woman wouldn't displace him. Yet his stomach flipped like a stranded fish in a shallow pool.

But even in different clothes, her haunted eyes remained the same. Still wide-eyed and often startled, they only held warmth for Molly and even though her fresh appearance lifted her mood, she appeared to fight it with every breath.

"Ah, George. What have I done?"

He tried not to see it, but his mind's eye couldn't shake the vision.

Twice he'd caught her with a scowl on her face while he labored to unload her crates. Tomorrow, Shadrach's muscles might burn from carting them, but right now he burned with a humiliation he hadn't felt before.

Into the bucket of salted water he dropped the quartered pieces of the saddle and all the rabbit legs. The brine would draw away any bitterness. Pity he couldn't dunk himself in the ocean and deal with his mood the same way.

He set the bucket aside and stood to stretch his legs. Raised his arms high above his head and held them there while the kinks stretched in his shoulders.

An angry procession of clouds filled the heavens and he breathed a heavy sigh. He'd brought a woman into his home who despised being anywhere near it. Or him for that matter and she made no disguise of either. Having her close was going to make keeping his promise to George all that more difficult, not easier.

He prayed for patience. For God to help her grieve and settle. For him to keep a cool head.

He crouched again and caressed the soft downy rabbit pelts. He'd need many more to make a blanket for Molly, but he'd find them. He'd make his sister the best blanket he knew how. He'd promised, and nothing would stop him keeping his word.

I write by the light of the lamp. I sit at the table and the fire waves and keeps me company with short crackles. I am in a hut, no better than the crudest shepherd's shelter. My heart withers to find there is no oven or range. A naked fire, medieval and unbridled is all I have for cooking.

I wish to fling the door open, let in light and toss every dirty item out. To boil water and scrub until each surface is rid of its filthy layers. Instead, I listen to Molly's soft snoring and the scrape of my pen.

The tabletop is naked and badly scratched. If I had to guess, I would say Mr. Jones cleared it of everything and rammed each item on a high shelf.

What Molly does not learn in cleaning tomorrow, she will learn as the days go by, for I do not intend to live with dust, grime or sour bedding.

And I will, under no circumstances, live surrounded by puddles and mud.

∽

From the open barn door, Shadrach watched his house, lit from within. The small window spilt a honey glow into the night.

How much longer before he headed in? It felt like hours since he'd handed Miss Mayfield the pail of rabbit meat.

Molly would eat bread and jam for every meal if he'd let her, and the temptation to give in and dish up her favorite after a hard day meant she'd eaten her fair share of hasty offerings at his table. He hoped Miss Mayfield's cooking would put an end to hurried meals for Molly and if he were honest, his own stomach anticipated something warmer and savory as well.

The salt he rubbed into the rabbit skins hardly stung his fingers. Tough and calloused, they stretched the pelts over wire cones to dry and when secured with dome pins, he hung them on an overhead beam.

"Well, they've had long enough." He spoke to Old Lou, but suspected his words were more to convince himself than his horse. "If they haven't set something out to eat by now, they never will and I'm about ready to grab jam and bread if the cook pot's empty."

He washed up in the barn and ran his fingers through his hair. He sloshed across to the door where he tapped lightly before entering. Silly to knock on your own door before entering, but after a few hours away he figured he'd do all he could to smooth the way with Miss Mayfield.

Molly beamed at him from the table and grinned when he winked at her. Her rosy cheeks flushed with something he hadn't seen. Before he had a chance to discover more, a wave of aromas collided with the night air. Onions and meat simmering in the Dutch oven mingled with smoke and fire from the hearth.

And a sweet aroma all-together unknown in his house wafted across the room to assault him. A perfume he didn't recognize but knew must be some kind of flower water.

Miss Mayfield rose from a chair nearest the fire.

"Just in time. Our rabbit curry is hot and ready to serve."

She dished up their meals onto tin plates and set them down, steaming and pungent.

"I washed the cups, Shad. And plates and forks and spoons." Molly reached for a slice of bread. This was not the damper he normally set out for them.

"Did you now?" He couldn't help sneak a look at Miss Mayfield but she'd turned to place the lid on the pot. His belly did another fish-flip. Drawn to her waist, his eyes took in her apron strings pinched and tied in a neat bow.

She was here, at his table, dishing up his evening meal. A loyal memory of George washed over him and like a traitor, he nudged it away to make room for an altogether new hunger.

"Yes. All by myself. And tomorrow, we wash the sheets." He'd never heard Molly delight in housewifery. Ever.

Miss Mayfield's face matched Molly's pink one. She fixed her eyes on the table and he blessed the food. It looked as good as it smelled and his stomach growled to sit down to a meal twice as abundant as their normal fare.

Steaming rabbit curry pooled in his plate against a mash of potatoes and boiled carrots, with slices of bread on the table beside the butter crock. With no encouragement, Molly busied herself with the goodness before her.

"If this is what Molly learns to prepare, then our arrangement will prove a very happy one." It hadn't escaped him the table itself shone and a hint of lemon bruised his palms where he rested them against the edge.

He wanted to compliment the cook more, but wasn't sure how she'd receive his words.

"Molly's been the most trustworthy washer today. She scrubbed the table until I thought we'd need another top for it altogether." A fresh twinkle lit Miss Mayfield's eyes and fell on his sister. "She did all she was told to do, and didn't budge from where I set her."

Shadrach thrilled at the light in her eyes. "So, it's been a good start then. I'm pleased for you both." He brought another fork full to his mouth, eager for more. Much more.

"Mr. Jones…" Less interested in her food, Miss Mayfield poked at a piece of carrot. "I think it's fitting we start with spring cleaning, tomorrow. A deep clean." Large brown eyes blinked at him. "Do you have a wash-house?"

A wash-house? Here, among the rough structures he called house and barn? He stopped chewing.

He did not. He had fields sown with crops, and saplings which promised fruit a few summers from now, along with a milk cow and chickens. But not a wash-house. Nor a smoke-house or a boat-house. Not even a birdhouse. Or maybe he did, if you counted the chickens…

He reached for a slice of bread. "There's no wash-house, Miss Mayfield. The tubs hang out back. I'll bring them around and build a fire before I do anything else in the morning. I'll also carry up as much water as you'll need." He fought the bitterness which tainted the good food.

"Thank you." She set her fork down. "I… Perhaps you could tell me where you'll be building the fire. For the washing.'"

Another question? He swallowed again. "Same place as I always do. Out front."

"And… the lines?"

"The lines…?"

"The washing lines? Will they be near the house too?"

The nearest tea tree served him well enough. He'd never needed a line.

"I'll string something up in the orchard. There's a good wind there for drying. If it doesn't rain."

"So, I'll have to work out front and walk through the muddy yard with every basket of wet washing?" She frowned, as if he'd suggested she take it on a barge to Melbourne.

"Same as I've always done. I can help if you need me to."

Redness filled her cheeks again. "That won't be necessary. Molly and I will manage."

Shadrach mopped his plate with a chunk of bread. It wasn't his fault there was no washhouse. A man could only do his best, and right now it was all about crops. Everything else came later. Didn't she know that?

He steadied a rise in his temper and eyed the pot. Surely there was more in there. He cleaned his plate with the last of his bread and hoped she'd notice.

She did and reached for it. "Let me fill that for you again." It returned to him as generously heaped as the first time. He couldn't remember when he'd last eaten two servings of anything.

"You're a good cook, Miss Mayfield." He turned to his sister. "Are you watching, Molly? You've good things to learn in the days ahead."

He continued eating until his plate emptied and Miss Mayfield looked up once more. "If I may ask another question, Mr. Jones? I was wondering how I might bake bread? Without an oven."

Shadrach shifted his chair from the table with a scratch against the hardened floor, and stared.

First, she wanted a washhouse. And now an oven? Wasn't a stone hearth good enough? He'd carried those rocks for miles and heaved them into a working chimney. He never thought to build an oven. He didn't need one.

"We make damper, Miss. In the same pot you used for the rabbit. I'll teach you when this bread, I assume from Mrs. Lawson, is almost gone." At the rate he ate it, that would be soon.

"Yes, it is Mrs. Lawson's. She packed two loaves in with her lemons."

"Day after tomorrow, then. Worry about the washing for now. We'll sort out the bread later."

Little pink dots deepened in her cheeks but she didn't look away. Irritation vexed him, and his own house, the room he'd built for himself, suddenly crowded upon him like a sinking roof.

"Thank you, Miss Mayfield. For the meal. I'll leave you to your chores, and attend to my own." He pushed away from the table and stood.

"One last thing, Mr. Jones, if I may?" She rested her wrists on the table, either side of her unfinished meal.

Shadrach had no time to hide his clouded face. His jaw hurt and his teeth could not be any more clenched. And he wasn't about to unclench them. Had she not exhausted her list of inadequacies? Was she looking for directions to an icehouse, now?

"Yes. Miss Mayfield."

If she flinched at the rumble in his voice, he didn't see it.

"Before I retire, I wish to secure the door. How do I do that, without a key?"

Heat rushed through him like a firestorm and he almost let the temper fly. Instead, he swung the door open with a boot shove. Molly sat upright, her bread-filled mouth open mid chew.

"There is no lock here, Miss Mayfield. No fancy latch either." He slapped the string he'd fixed to secure it. "The door is made of sticks and wood and rope. Much like everything else you see here, for which we're grateful and I suggest, before you go finding fault with your bed, or the fire, or the roof above your head, you remember I built all this from nothing. With the help of no man. For myself."

He knew his face flamed and regret would eat him later, but now he needed to say it. Tell her exactly what simmered under his breath all day.

"I didn't expect a sister to join me here so soon. And not even in my wildest dreams did I think a third occupant, used to life's fancies would also take residence."

He shouldn't have spat the word *fancies* like that. He would have to add that to his list of regrets, too. He yanked at the rope loop and dragged the door to his shoulder.

"If my home displeases you this much, then leave it. I didn't ask you here to be reminded of every inadequate plank and stone. So don't go asking for a replica of the home you came from."

He stepped out, one hand on the door. "Because here, we have a yard full of mud, no oven, no fancy wash-house and when night falls we shut the door and say goodnight."

He could have pulled the door clear off its crude hinge. Instead he shut it as hard as it took to rattle every timber in his house. *His house.*

The walk across the yard to his skillion resembled more of a military stomp than a man retiring to his quarters. With equal force he shut that door, too. Pity he couldn't deal with the bristle in his chest with equal measure.

He fell back onto the pallet he'd set up that morning and jammed his fists behind his head.

His home. Purpose built. A temporary structure to keep the rain away while he grew a farm from nothing into something. That's all he wanted. A working farm.

This was never meant to be a boarding house for girls, and, as Miss Mayfield made perfectly clear, certainly not for ladies.

9

Molly had no trouble falling asleep shortly after she'd washed their dishes and laid the breakfast table. Even here, in this crude hut, Finella determined she would follow Aunt Sarah's rules. Especially here.

Tables should be set early. If possible, breakfast tables should be set the night before. Admonitions brimmed in Finella's mind like a swell of waters.

"If we lay the table now, in the morning when we need it, the work's already done."

Molly had set the table with three plates and three tin cups. Aunt Sarah had things to say about naked tables too, and Finella reminded herself to look for a suitable cloth among her packed linens in the morning.

Neither she nor Molly spoke about Mr. Jones' temper-fuelled exit and each time his anger blazed through her mind, Finella pushed it aside and concentrated on Molly.

Molly washing tin dishes. Molly drying and putting them on the freshly scrubbed shelves, like dented tin soldiers in a row. Molly obeying while Finella instructed, until all chores were complete and one tired girl lay in her bed. Tucked under her chin, Molly's ragdoll kept her company.

For Finella, no one offered solace. The evening faded and the kettle hummed on the fire for one last pot of tea before bed. Struck by the loneliness of the months ahead, she slumped on the edge of the second bed.

Weariness needled her bones, dragging her down with a weight she'd never before carried. She rubbed her eyes with red raw fingers. The smell of soap and lemon did nothing to disguise the unwashed quilts covering Molly, and no doubt, the ones on the bed reserved for her, too.

A soft cry escaped her before she could stop it and she slumped on the bed. She pressed her palms to her eyes. Her head throbbed and the longing to escape to Molly's dark world of sleep beckoned with the strength of ten men.

She shifted her weight on the lumpy mattress. Until last night this bed belonged to Mr. Jones. No doubt, so would the bedding. She chided herself for not remembering to collect Aunt Sarah's lavender scented sheeting from her trunks in his skillion. She couldn't fetch them now, but neither could she sleep under someone else's bed-clothes. She peeled the covers back one by one.

A coarse blanket, then a light quilt. Both needed airing, if not deep soaking. A soft knock on the door broke the silence. Finella wiped her eyes and gathered her shawl closer.

Mr. Jones stood outside. Raised and messed, his hair looked as if the chickens had combed it for grubs.

Good. Perhaps he'd come to apologize. She mashed her lips together and waited.

He rubbed the back of his neck. "Thought I'd check on Molly before she fell asleep." His frame had lost its soldier-like stance and from somewhere within, Finella was sure she spied the unwinding of a small smile. Perhaps Molly alone brought that out in him.

"She's asleep." Finella kept her hand on the door. A tiny thought, smaller than a tick bite, gnawed at her conscience. What if he hoped for a cup of tea before bedtime? It was his home, and he had every right to the fire, his table and its provisions. Would it be so bad to share a pot together at the end of a trying day?

He shuffled from one foot to the other. "She does a lot of sleeping but I guess the excitement of you being here knocked her out even earlier." He cleared his throat. And that annoying tick sunk its teeth a little deeper.

"She'll sleep the whole night through, too. Never gets up 'til you wake her. Unless she has a fright in her dreams, but that doesn't happen much. It's during the day she needs watching. If you're still planning to wash, you'd best give her a chore where you can keep your eye on her all day long."

Finella nodded and crossed her arms, the fringe of her shawl caught in each fist.

Mr. Jones didn't look like he planned on moving on in a hurry. His eyes searched her face and even with a swirl of cold night air in the small mud hut, a twinge of heat stoked her cheeks.

"Well, I don't mean to disturb, but I need to collect something from…" He pointed to the empty bed.

Finella backed away and he inched past, crossed the small room and knelt on the floor. From underneath the sapling base, he pulled a thick Bible. Loose papers stuck out at all angles and he pressed it to his chest to fish for something else. When he stood, his other fist clenched a black velvet pouch. He took a quick look at the blankets she'd tossed to the end of the bed and ducked into the night.

"I'll leave you to your rest, then. Goodnight."

Finella couldn't tell if a sad smile crossed his face, but his words held a hint of tenderness. He jumped over one large puddle to cross the yard and slipped into his room.

From its place over the fire, the kettle hissed at her and spat reproach, completely drowning out Finella's attempted reply.

She would not have dared speak it too loud, but a sorry whisper directed at the shut door of the skillion would have to do.

"Goodnight to you, Mr. Jones."

〜

"I'm hungry." Molly grumbled for the third time from her place at the breakfast table.

"We're waiting for Mr. Jones." Finella stirred the porridge pot but nothing worked on the lump in her throat. If Molly were to learn anything, it would have to be by example. "It's good manners to wait."

"Mr. Jones, Mr. Jones…" Molly sang to her dolly. "Mr, Mr, Mr. Jones." A garbled tune rang out with a string of words Finella didn't understand.

There was not much she did understand these days. She was sure she did not understand the man Molly sang about. Or the unrefined ways of his Australian home and she barely understood her own deep conviction to stay in it with Molly.

But here she stood; ready to teach the things Molly's mother had never been able to share. The very thing Aunt Sarah had done for her. And it felt good.

She banged the wooden spoon on the edge of the pot. Mr. Jones wouldn't bully her into leaving. Not when Molly needed her the way she did.

"No, not Mr. Jones." Molly shook her head. "Shaaad-Raaach." She sang his name like a sweet lullaby. As if it were her favorite song. "My brother. Shad-Rach."

Finella turned from the fire. "Yes, your brother is Shadrach. I call him Mr. Jones. It's my way of being polite. You do the same with Mrs. Lawson."

"I like Shadrach." She tapped her chest with her doll. "My Shadrach." Molly's blue eyes flashed with deep love for her brother. He must have done something right, to make his sister defend his name with such tenderness.

"Of course, he's *your* Shadrach." Finella drew the boiling kettle away from the fire and muttered into the steam. "He's certainly not *mine*."

"Miss Mayfield is correct. I belong to you, Miss Molly and don't you ever forget it."

His deep voice invaded the room. Had the whistling masked the sound of him opening the door? Finella dropped the kettle on the iron trivet, but her heart continued to drum, drum-drum.

"Mr. Jones. Good Morning. I'm just about to make the tea."

"Miss Mayfield." He squeezed Molly's shoulder and took his place at the table. "I've a fire outside. For your washing. Water's almost boiled. And you'll find a line down by the orchard."

Molly leaned across the table. "Finella slept on your bed, Shad."

He glanced at Finella before turning to his sister. "Well yes, we… talked about that before Miss Mayfield came. Remember? She sleeps here with you and I've a bed in the skillion, now."

Finella looked away. If her face matched the flush creeping into his, she didn't want him to see it.

"Did you sleep well, Miss Mayfield?"

In that sapling bed of sour linens? She blew out a quick breath and turned to face him.

"*On…* your bed." Molly slid her doll across the table and a fresh tide of nerves filled Finella's stomach. The kettle weighed twice what it should have, but she carried on filling the teapot, glad for even the thin veil of steam.

"Not how we sleep, Shad. Not under the covers. *On them.*" Molly bumped his arm with the doll's round head. "With her shawl for a blanket. On the bed, Shad." He covered her hand with his and silenced the raw babble.

"I heard you, Molly." His words came out low and measured. "I heard you."

Two sets of blue eyes pinned Finella. Shame washed over her, like a hot dousing of pickling liquor. Surely he could understand she would not sleep underneath a heap of dirty coverings? And when had Molly spied her sleeping? She had risen a good hour before the young girl first stirred.

Finella placed a steaming cup of tea in front of Mr. Jones.

Eyes fixed on her, he dragged the cup closer. "I expect, dear Molly, you'll find Miss Mayfield will have no trouble sleeping *under* the covers tonight. A day of scrubbing will thump the starch out of anyone. Even the high and mighty." He mumbled *high and mighty*, but Finella heard it. She handed him his porridge dish and clenched her fists behind her back.

"You're right, Molly. I did not sleep under the covers." She looked from brother to sister. "I normally do and as Mr. Jones has pointed out, I probably will tonight after we've aired the blankets and washed the sheets."

She couldn't think of a reply to his *high and mighty*. At least not one she cared to speak in front of Molly. She looked away, but not quick enough to miss him sling one arm across the back of his chair. A smile pulsed at the corner of his mouth. Subtle. Slow.

"I'll pray. I'm hungry." Molly laid her doll in her lap and bowed her head.

But the child's prayer did not draw Finella. Against every fiber of her well-tuned judgment, she stole a fleeting look over Molly's bowed head.

And then she saw it. Satisfaction played across his face in an inescapable symphony of creases and twitches and twinkling blue eyes.

∽

Finella smacked the soggy sheets with a wooden paddle. Steam burned her eyes and scorched the back of her mouth. Grated soap did little to mask the odor of sour washing wafting into her nose.

Molly sat on a sawn log and scrubbed equally hard at the contents of a tin bucket in her lap. She poked her tongue out the side of her mouth in deep concentration for the task. And today the task would be huge. Every stitch of bedding needed boiling and not even the threat of rain would hold Finella back.

Against the side of the mud hut, two thin hay-filled mattresses aired in the morning sun. Finella prayed it would bless them all day, for if she were to experience anything near a good night's sleep, she needed to have everything dry and on the beds by nightfall.

Already, the promised line fluttered with the few blankets and quilts she'd stripped from the beds. Mr. Jones hadn't been seen since breakfast. She did not fancy entering his skillion without permission so she left his bedding where she guessed it lay, on the floor.

"You're doing a fine job, Molly." Finella wondered if the pillow-cases would survive Molly's rubbing. From the looks of her red knuckles, Molly was a keen washerwoman.

The girl nodded but her focus remained on the tub. What she lacked in cooking skills she more than made up for in sheer strength at the washtub.

"Blankets are dry." Molly sniffed and looked at the motley coverings fluttering nearby.

"Well, yes. We hung them dry. Remember? To air them. We'll have to wait until summer to wash them properly. Quilts need air and sunlight every week to keep them fresh and a long soak in summer." Finella marveled to think about the turn of the seasons.

Her next summer would collide with a bush Christmas, the likes she'd only heard about on the ship to Australia.

"Finella?" Molly disturbed her wandering thoughts. "Brother's making me a rabbit blanket." Molly looked up. "He promised."

"For you? You're one lucky sister."

With wet fingers Finella collected flyaway curls from her neck and face and dampened them back across her head. She stretched her arms over her head. If Mr. Jones kept his temper in check, she and Molly would spend a pleasant enough time together. Even if it did mean an upside down Yuletide.

"Brother made a promise to George, too."

Finella wasn't sure she should ask what it was. Perhaps Molly would keep talking and tell her anyway. For a few moments both young women wrestled with their tasks until Molly looked up.

"On the day the snake came." Molly nodded. "Mrs. Lawson told him he has to keep it now. That's what happens when you make a promise." She looked at Finella.

"I see." Finella reached for the washing bat, not exactly sure what Molly prattled on about. "And have you made any promises Molly?"

"Only to Shad." Molly blew a stray hair from her forehead. "I promised to be a good girl and obey you. If I'm good then you stay. And brother can marry you."

Finella let the paddle slip into the wash trough.

"Marry me?" She stared at Molly, whose bent head gave nothing more away than another quick nod.

Finella's head spun like a newly cranked mangle. "I think you're remembering the story backwards. I came to marry George." She took a deep breath and tried to wind Molly's thoughts the right way. "But now he's gone, I'm here to keep you company until my Aunt Sarah arrives from England."

Poor child must have blended fact with circumstance. Finella could see how she made the mistake. Hadn't she herself jumped to the same wrong conclusion that day on the beach when Mr. Jones offered this position? She fished for the paddle.

"I'm here to be your teacher and friend. And right now I see you don't need me for washing lessons. You're the best scrubbing girl I ever saw."

Molly grinned. "I like washing. I washed everyday… before." Her pink tongue poked out the side of her lip. Finella watched her a while longer. No different to any fourteen year old girl at her chores. But she was no ordinary fourteen year old, and that played tricks with Finella's heart.

"What is it you wish for the most, Molly?"

Molly looked into the sky. "Hmm." She licked her lip for a moment until her eyes filled with a spark normally reserved for Shadrach's winks. She turned to Finella.

"Fancy things."

"Fancy things?"

"Yes. Like your …glass."

"My magnifying glass?"

She nodded. "And your brush." She swept at the left side of her head with the back of her soapy hand. A tiny bubble stuck on her temple just above an old scar. It slipped down her hairline almost tracing the same path to Molly's earlobe.

Sadness stabbed at Finella. She wondered how many feminine accoutrements the girl went without. Her simple dress lacked length and she determined to let the hem down as soon as she could. Her new home screamed bush bachelor, and who knew how long she'd worked beside her mother, hunched over a washtub with little else to fill her days?

"We could look for something pretty for the house each day?" Finella remembered her hunt for wildflowers. "And in my boxes I have a few fancy things you may like. How about a cheerful cloth for the table? We could start there." A rumbling of storm clouds threatened from overhead but she would not be thwarted. "And tonight we'll have sweet smelling pillows on our bed."

Instead of eyes filled with anticipation the young girl looked up with tears and shook her head.

"Shad doesn't like fancy things. He says fancy things bring trouble. To run from the tem...tem..."

"Temptation?" Finella finished off her sentence.

Molly nodded.

Finella returned to her sheet stabbing. What could be so tempting about a cloth square on a tabletop? Surely his hut wasn't so austere because Mr. Jones believed simple comforts a sin?

"Perhaps we can show your brother not all fancies are terrible temptations. He may even learn to like them for himself."

Molly shook her head. "Don't think so. Shadrach knows lots of things."

"I'm sure he does." Finella yanked at the sheet with the paddle and lifted it high to let the steam escape. "But he may wish to learn something new from time to time."

She dumped the dripping sheet into a tub of fresh water at her feet, and smacked it so hard, the rinse water splashed onto her neck. "And you Molly dear, will be just the one to teach him."

IO

*I*f wood chopping best suited those stewing over a hurt, shell shoveling won second place. Shadrach hoisted dripping spadefuls of shells into the wicker basket he'd already filled too many times to count that morning, and the ache grew with each basketful.

He sliced the blade of his tool into the wet sand underfoot and rested his elbow on the handle. Salt and sweat clung to his hair and plastered it to his neck. He shook his head like a dog and flicked the ends away.

One more trip to Rhyll beach and he would have enough. He'd incinerate the shells and grind them into the perfect additive to improve his clay garden beds. Thinking of beds reminded him of Finella. Again.

He dragged the overflowing basket along the shore to Old Lou and his dray. Shells spilled over the top, adding to the trail already there.

"I shouldn't have laughed at her, I know," he told his horse. "She needs time to get used to her surroundings and I don't want to add to her aggravation. But sleeping *on* the bed? With last night's chill? She deserved that."

Old Lou kept her counsel.

"Gonna take her side, hey girl? Should have figured.'"

He lugged the basket to the edge of the cart and tipped its contents in. He had nothing more to offer than what Finella had already seen. And it didn't impress her. He understood that now. Under his roof, her expectation for fineries meant disappointment would be her daily medicine. Surely George knew that about his bride-to-be.

He tapped the bottom of the basket to dislodge the last of the shells.

"No doubting it. Life would've been sweeter for her with George." He plucked a tangled piece of seaweed from the wickerwork and tossed it away. "Can't be easy when so many of her expectations have been buried with him." He pitched the basket onto the shells and headed back to the water.

By week's end, he figured she'd come down from her lofty aspirations. Hard work would dull that in her. Either that, or she'd balk at the foolishness of being out here, demand he reload her things and drive her back to the pier for the next steamer out.

Who knew for sure? He certainly didn't. He wiped the sweat from his eyes with the back of his hand.

"Who am I fooling?" he muttered under his breath. "My farm's no stop for a lady." He knew it as certain as the sun rose each day over Rhyll beach, but he'd let persuasion and honor sway him. Not to mention those eyes. Tear stained and brimming with care for Molly.

A fellow could get used to those eyes.

Looking at him. Looking for him.

Shadrach shook his head at whatever tried to take root. He was no George Gleeson to have Finella look his way. He'd best remember that.

He returned for the spade. Signs of his industry littered the beach. The wide groove his basket drew in the sand would soon disappear with the afternoon tide, and there'd be no evidence he'd raided the shore of her wealth.

Would Miss Mayfield vanish from their home the same way? Last night, thanks to his pride, he'd hoped she would. This morning, the unfamiliar sight of blankets snapping in the wind between his fruit trees served as a poke to the ribs.

He'd brought her here. And for reasons he didn't fully understand, he liked it that way.

He leaned on the dray to wipe his cold feet. The wet hem of his trousers rarely bothered him, but today, the nagging thought of getting near the fire she tended, persisted.

"Hard work and plenty of it for us, Old Lou, my girl." He led his horse across the island tracks to home.

By the time he got there he'd almost convinced himself. Better to concentrate on the brush timber he needed to collect. The seaweed and sod covering for the pyre. He could almost see the barrows of crushed cockles he'd use to dust his fields.

With hard work and a long list of chores, he might even convince his heart to steer away from the washing that waved at him from the orchard hill. And the brown-eyed woman standing there, hands on her hips, surveying his farm.

❧

Finella could see clear to the beach, but she cared little for its vista. She searched the young orchard on her right, where barely a leaf obstructed her view, all the way to the sandy slope, which wound through the tea trees to the water. On the other side, the generous market garden of red earth held the green fuzz of new crops, but not the object of her search.

Her heart slammed like a roller on a reef. How could she see so far and so clearly, and not find her?

"Molly." She called for the girl and her throat thickened. "Where are you?" She tugged at the washing line, heavy with bedding. Had the girl slipped behind the blankets in a game of hide-and-go-seek?

"Molly, please come out if you're hiding."

A lonely wind ripped through the clothes on the line, but no muffled giggles pierced the air.

From under a canopy of low trees, the sound of horse hooves snatched her attention. *Not now.*

Finella swallowed her panic. Mr. Jones guided his horse toward her. She stepped in front of the string of quilts and prayed under her breath.

"Please God, let Molly somehow be with her brother. Please. Please. Please." She tucked her hands beneath her apron and clenched them into fists.

Old Lou labored with a heavy load and Mr. Jones whistled a tune. He nodded when he saw her and turned toward the barn.

"Good thing the rain's held off." He looked at the sky. "Better day for washing than most this month. You must've done some prayin—"

"Have you seen Molly?" Finella could no more stop her words from spilling than she could keep the wind from beating at her side.

Mr. Jones reined Old Lou to a stop.

"What do you mean, have *I* seen Molly?"

Low words, each one spoken with deliberate lag slowed the passing of time. Fear boiled in Finella's chest and she ached to yell at him. To shake him down and everything else in the world until the missing girl rattled at their feet like a lost marble.

"Molly is meant to be wherever *you* are." He ripped the brake as if he planned to dislocate it, and jumped down. "Are you telling me she's not?" His voice remained low but the look in his eyes curdled her blood faster than any scream.

Finella pressed her knuckles to her mouth. If only she could make sense of it. "She's been beside me all morning. I... I made sure of it. We washed there, together." She pointed to the tubs and smoldering fire. "And she helped me with the hanging... and then we went inside for lunch."

"I don't care what you did. It's what's you didn't do that's my concern now." He cupped his hands around his mouth.

"Molly. Molly." He yelled toward the sea. Toward the house, and even up into the sky.

"Where did you see her last?"

"Inside, with me. I sliced bread and she sat at the table to eat." Finella breathed hard. Her words would not come out as she wished them.

"Then?" Mr. Jones seized her by the shoulders. Finella knew she must tell the truth. She studied his muddy shoes.

"I needed the... out...house."

She looked up. He looked away and ran his fingers through his hair.

"I was gone less than two minutes." She pleaded. "I left more than enough bread and jam to keep her busy until I got back. She must have followed me, and now..."

I can't find her.

Finella wished to finish her sentence but a lump the size of her own fist squeezed at her throat.

"Where've you looked?" Mr. Jones stomped through the puddles to the house. "Did you look in the beds? Under them?" He threw the door open and saw for himself the stripped sapling bed frames.

"Did you try the outhouse?" He bolted past her and Finella ran to keep up. "Perhaps she's hiding there."

Finella hadn't, but his search only served to discover an unoccupied privy. A flutter of clothes on the line mocked them with nothing more than an empty yard and orchard.

"Molly." He called again. This time louder and with a desperation to outdo even her own.

"If she's heard me yell from the bush somewhere she may try and find her way home." He scanned the afternoon sky before stomping back through the mud to the house.

"I'll grab a blanket and get down to the beach. You," he pointed with a trembling finger at the door of the hut, "will stay here. Understand?"

She nodded through fresh tears. He didn't have to yell at her. She was not unaware this was her fault.

"I'm not surprised at Molly." He marched across the yard to his room. "The girl's got no sense when it comes to time or weather. But I thought you would've been smarter than this."

Finella picked her way behind him. Her heart plummeted to think he could be right. She was smarter than this. So how could she have let it happen?

"If she's at the beach it won't be the first time. Last time she slipped into a rock pool and sat there, shivering, 'til I found her." He pushed on the door to his room.

Against the backdrop of Finella's trunks, his pallet took up most of the floor with a large basket tipped beside it on its side. A mess of linens and cloths littered the floor and in their midst, almost hidden in a sleepy tangle, lay Molly.

II

Shadrach crouched by his sister and tapped her shoulder.

"Molly. Wake up."

She licked her lips and a soft moan escaped them. He tried again with a harder poke.

"Wake up. Do you hear me?"

Molly opened her eyes. "Brother?"

He caught the roar before it took hold. He wanted to yell. Demand a reason for her stolen nap when she knew she was not allowed in his skillion.

Instead, a wash of relief swayed over him, as close as the gentle swing of Miss Mayfield's hem against his leg. He knelt on the ground.

Jet-black hair covered Molly's face and he tucked a strand behind her ear to see her better. Her scar carried the added creases of sleep where her cheek had crushed her ragdoll.

"Molly." He measured his words to slow his racing heart. "Did you hear Miss Mayfield calling for you? You promised to always stay where she could see you."

He didn't know whether to tug at her unraveled plait or wrap her in a fierce embrace. With Miss Mayfield at his heel, he figured he'd do neither.

"Here." Molly blinked and offered him a cloth. "Finella wanted something pretty for the table. And ...I remembered Mum's old sewing basket. And this one. With the strawberry stitches..." She smiled and looked up from him to Miss Mayfield.

"Then, I saw your bed, Shad. And, I wanted to sleep somewhere. Because my bed's in the sun."

He cared little for her reasons. How much more mischief would she toy with before real harm found her? Shadrach caught her chin in his hand. "You disobeyed, Molly. You ignored more than one instruction."

Her blue eyes settled on him. He searched them for a sign, any sign to tell him she really understood but her attention fell to the tablecloth and he let her go.

With one finger she traced a curling green vine until it reached an embroidered cluster of rose-colored fruit. His mum's tea cloth. Molly must have remembered he'd crammed it here in a basket of useless items their mother had collected over the years.

He rubbed her cheek with his knuckles, and stood. Miss Mayfield stepped back but the skillion offered little room between them, and the wall at her back soon stopped her from moving further away.

She kept her face tilted to the floor. Hard work at the washtub had loosened her hair and it curled around her neck. Her cheeks held the rosy slap of wind, and she chewed the edge of her chapped lip while her hands rummaged in her apron pockets. She pulled out a handkerchief and held it there.

Determined to secure her attention, even if he could not hold Molly's, Shadrach kept his silence until those brown eyes inched their way up from her hands and met with his.

The mark of wide-eyed panic from earlier had disappeared. Instead, her long lashes held tears. His heart cracked a little but he couldn't let it sway him. She owed him an apology.

"Do you now see why I insist she be in your sight at all times?

Today, it was a silly tablecloth. What if she decides to bring you a feather for your hair? Will you turn your back while she climbs a tree for a nest, or wades into Saltwater Creek?"

Miss Mayfield's mouth snapped open to make an O but he cut off her attempt to speak.

"What if she decides to please you with wildflowers? Are you going to let her wander through snake-filled gullies?" He knew he sounded unreasonable, but he had to make her understand.

Miss Mayfield squared her shoulders.

"Mr. Jones." She angled her chin and her hands disappeared behind her back like a schoolgirl about to recite the Lord's Prayer. "In the one day I have cared for your sister she's worked beside me at every turn. True, she slipped away. To the safety of your room."

This was no apology.

"In your care I believe she almost fell in the well, and by your own admission, ended up in a puddle on the beach. And let's not forget our first meeting on the sand dunes where we enjoyed several minutes together before your arrival."

Each word hit him like the arrow of an expert marksman.

"Where were you then, when Molly wandered the beach alone and distressed with a splintered finger?"

The woman had a point. She had a few points and wasted no time making them.

Unlike Molly, her shoulders did not slump when he reprimanded her. And even when she returned accusation for accusation, her left eyebrow stayed perched above her eye, defiant and hooked.

He mirrored the lift of her chin with his own. "The matter remains the same. We can be nothing less than vigilant. I don't expect anything more from you than I expect from myself."

"Good. Well, I guess we carry on then." She helped Molly stand. "If you'll excuse us, we're going to see if our washing's dry and remake the beds."

She tucked Molly's arm in the crook of her own. Together they picked their way across the well-used courtyard. Miss Mayfield lifted her skirt and wiped her shoes on the long wet grass. At the coaching of her new friend, Molly did the same.

As if it were not enough to contend with Miss Mayfield's fancy ways, now he'd have to deal with Molly's attempts to match them.

He followed them out and shut the door on the mess in his room. It was not as easy to bar the protest of his heart.

How would he ever find it in him to court a woman so clearly charmed by the very things he loathed?

And why, knowing the strife this would cause him, had George ever thought he was the man to do so?

❧

Finella breathed deeply. This was no lavender perfumed bedroom of Aunt Sarah's making. But bedding kissed by a few minutes of sun brought welcome freshness to the small farmhouse. Every stitch of clothing that could be spared had found its way to the tubs, and even though her arms ached to unpin her hair, Finella knew it was worth the day's labor.

Glad for her bed, she climbed under the newly laid covers. Aunt Sarah would have much to say about unironed sheets on beds. Finella ignored this. Each crease, proof of diligent scrubbing, outweighed Aunt Sarah's strictest demands. Today's sheets couldn't appeal to Finella more if they'd arrived wrapped in tulle ribbons from the Royal Laundry.

The weight of her body gave into the mattress and she stretched into a sigh. How quickly her perfect schedule of preacher's wife chores had tipped upside down. There would be no tea making for a husband who poured over sermon notes. No dusting of his library shelves. No lectures to attend on his arm with lively discussion afterwards.

She rubbed her cheek against the pillowcase and closed her eyes. The day flashed before her, like pictures from a book. Fluttering blankets filled her mind. Steam, from the washtubs. Molly's pink tongue poking. And then, sparkling blue eyes.

Was it Molly or Mr. Jones who stared at her while she fought her way to sleep? Wide as a grave and deep as a pit, blue eyes condemned as they traipsed the farm in a frenzy.

She pulled the covers closer. She didn't want to think about what they'd been spared. Enough misery had visited her in one lifetime. She pushed aside the memory of Mr. Jones' stern words, but nothing budged the vision of the man himself. Arms crossed, farm gate style, angry and afraid.

"Miss Mayfield?" A soft bump on the door prodded her sleepy thoughts. "Do you have a minute?"

Finella untangled the grip of dreams and wrapped her shawl round her shoulders. She didn't fancy opening the door in her nightdress, but with the lamps out and the fire dying, she cracked it open. She poked her head past the door and hid most of her body behind its planks.

Mr. Jones held a swinging tin lantern.

"I didn't think you'd be in bed already. It's earlier than when I knocked last night."

"It's been a long day, Mr. Jones." *And I wish to sleep and put images of you and your blue eyes out of my mind.*

He juggled something against one arm and held the lantern higher.

"I untied the washing line." He dropped the coil of rope at her feet. "I've used it a few times to keep Molly in one place when I..." he paused, "couldn't take her with me."

He kicked a loose end from where it dragged in the red mud. It flicked across the threshold and landed with a thump against Finella's foot.

A muddy splatter stained her hem and dribbled onto her naked toes, like the raw chill that kicked at her stomach.

She dragged her foot into the shadows. No sooner had she expelled dirt from his home, he swept it back in. And with the washing line no less. Had the man gone mad?

"You expect me to tie her up?" Finella whispered. "Like an animal?"

"No. Not like an animal." His shoulders rose and slumped with a deep breath. "It's for her own good. For when you need to visit… another part of the farm."

He looked at the rope as if it needed further explanation. Finella didn't need another lecture. She knew what a rope did.

"If you tie it to the leg of the bed she'll lay there 'til you get back. There's plenty of length for her to get up and walk around but not enough for her to escape. She might even nap."

He had done this before. Many times, probably. "I can't believe you would tie your own sister to the bed."

Finella shook her head at him.

He frowned back. "Why not? You saw what happens when you turn your back for a minute. Isn't it better to know she can't run off? If you're… outside, there's a tree beside the hen house. If you tie her there she'll watch the chickens and you can…" He stopped short of answering.

Finella could see how a man might need such a plan, but that didn't mean she did. She'd rather squeeze Molly in the outhouse with her than bind her to a tree. "I'll store it under the bed for now."

"I'll do it." he passed her the lantern and gathered the rope. "Her bed or … mine. I mean, yours?"

Even with the draught from the open door, heat wrapped around her neck.

"Hers, I guess."

Mr. Jones dragged the rope in. It took some shoving but he finally crammed it under Molly's low bed.

"She worked hard today, little imp." He stroked his sister's forehead and looked up at Finella. "You both worked hard."

From behind the door Finella had remained partly hidden. But now, she had nowhere to hide her bare feet. And her loose hair. She gathered it in her free hand and brought the mess over one shoulder.

Midnight blue, his eyes snagged on her own and took her in. Her eyes, her hair, all the way to her toes and back up again.

An eternity passed and she burned in the shadows. Her hand trembled and the lantern cast a twinkle over the room. He'd finished his errand. Stored the rope. Why wouldn't he leave?

He crouched beside Molly and brought his lips close to her ear. At first, he hummed a tune. Then words, like a low prayer filled the small room.

"Jesus loves me, this I know,
For the Bible tells me so.
Little ones to Him belong,
They are weak but He is strong."

Not even the cramp in Finella's arm could make her lower the lamp. She stood, rooted to the packed dirt floor, while the well-loved chorus washed over brother and sister. But Mr. Jones didn't stop there. He sang another verse, one Finella had not heard.

"Jesus loves me, loves me still,
Though I'm very weak and ill.
From His shining throne on high,

Comes to watch me where I lie."

The refrain gathered wing in Finella's heart and fluttered, like a finch she'd once found, newly born and spilled from its nest too soon.

For a moment her own loss and Molly's mingled into one. Mr. Jones touched his cheek to his sister's, and stood.

Heat pricked Finella's face as if he'd touched her there too and for a second she let her eyes close to hide the scene before her.

A flood of longing crept into her heart for the tenderness of childhood days. It more than matched the ache of washday.

Had her father wrestled with the burden of a motherless daughter? She had no idea. Aunt Sarah had stepped into the void even before Mother had passed away.

She lowered the lantern a little and blinked into the shadows. She wanted to forget the haunted look in Mr. Jones' eyes. To break the silence he cloaked her in while he stood there like a sentinel over the bed.

She wanted something that had no name.

"Does Molly miss her mother?"

"She mentions her. But she lives in the moment. Doesn't visit the past too much, doesn't look forward either. Enjoys the day for what it brings." He smiled down at his sister. "Knows how to teach a fellow about living, this girl. Wish more people had her spirit."

Finella set the lantern on the table. "Molly's a brave girl."

"We're all brave, Miss Mayfield. Perhaps, you and I more so than Molly." He gripped the back of a chair. "You're brave, to take on a task completely different from the one you expected."

His tone pinned her and she couldn't look away.

He took the lantern off the table and ripples of light danced around the room. Held high, a wild beat flickered through the flame.

"And you, Mr. Jones?" Finella sucked in a fortifying gulp of air. "How can you be more courageous than Molly? You have control over your life. What you do, and say. Where you go and how you do so. No one's tethered you to a tree."

He watched her, as if looking for something she meant but hadn't said.

"Don't be so sure of what you can't see, Miss Mayfield. Some battles are fought against unseen tethers." His voice remained low, but soft. Soft enough to creep through the shadows and deep into her.

He'd loosened the end of a coil she'd pressed to her ribs since the day they'd met.

Not enough for the coil to unravel.

But just enough to start the damage.

12

"No more bread." Resting her head on the table, Molly pouted at Shadrach who shouldered his way into the house with the morning's eggs. "All gone."

He wanted to laugh at the crease in her forehead. When had he ever let her go without bread?

"Then it's time for us to teach Miss Mayfield how we make bread. Bush style. Soon as I've finished up outside."

Molly laid her doll in her lap and clapped her hands at Miss Mayfield.

"And not a moment too soon. Molly's been fretting all morning." Miss Mayfield reached into her apron pocket for a faded green ribbon. "Let me tie your hair Molly. My Aunt Sarah says baking begins with the most secure of hair braiding."

Shadrach's heart twisted at the mention of Aunt Sarah. He cared very little for the old woman's wisdom, not to mention her intrusion into his world. Wasn't it enough she would arrive one day soon and open the way for Miss Mayfield's departure?

He had until Christmas to find his way to Finella's heart. Lord knew, she already had a hook in his. If he cared to admit it, she may have managed that the moment he laid eyes on her photograph.

Or was it when she looked at him all tearstained the day he'd rescued her from the pier trolley? Perhaps, it happened when he first saw her hanging blankets between the saplings in his orchard. Like she always belonged on this island with him. On his farm. In his life.

Maybe he couldn't say for sure when it happened, but he knew one thing for certain. Every time Finella Mayfield cared for his sister, every time she spared a smile for the little girl he loved, she stole a piece of him. And that was a new kind of heart plummet.

Eyes closed, Molly sat still at the gentle fixing of her hair while a storm rose in Shadrach's chest. Who was he fooling? He couldn't leave it to the last minute. He had to secure a promise of marriage sooner than Christmas. And to do that, he had some Old World formalities to knock over.

∽

"Molly, you won't be able to see from there." Finella called to her young charge who sat on the bed, back turned to the goings on at the table. A collection of shells jangled across her blanket, sorted into groups.

As promised, Mr. Jones had returned midmorning for a lesson in damper making, but with Molly in a world of her own, this left Finella his only student.

"Sunny." He called her this time. "Come help us make bread."

Molly ignored him.

"She does this sometimes." Mr. Jones rolled up his shirtsleeves. "Disappears and won't come out for any coaxing."

"Not even for bread?" Finella raised her voice for Molly to hear. The girl shifted closer to the wall.

"Shall I try and bring her over?" she whispered.

Mr. Jones dumped a sack of flour onto the table. "Leave her for now. She might join us if we don't press her."

He poked the embers in the fire with the poker. "Perfect. Now...this couldn't be easier, and after that delicious rabbit stew I'm sure you'll master damper with your eyes shut."

He winked, and Finella held tight to her breath. She focused on his sun-browned hand, his strong wrist, stronger knuckles, his cup-grabbing grip, the quick swing of his thumb, the slick command of everything at his fingertips.

Into a basin he tossed three cups of flour. He leaned across the table for a pinch of salt and sloshed in a generous amount of water. With a wooden spoon he mixed the ingredients and then dug his fists in to pummel the mix.

"See? Nothing to it." He grinned. "A simple bread. Fresh from the fire, it'll match and beat any oven baked loaf."

Ignoring his handsome smile she concentrated on the lump he hoped might become bread. Until a glossy ball formed she knew it would not pass Aunt Sarah's test.

With flour-covered hands held high he stepped back and pointed to the wet dough with his elbow.

"Have a go."

Finella tapped her fingers to her throat. "Me? But you're already—"

"Come on." He hooked his little finger around her thumb. A sticky clump of dough glued it to his. "Get into it. If you do it wrong, we'll tell you. Won't we, Molly?" He raised his voice but no words came from the girl.

He smiled and drew Finella closer until her fingertips hung over the pan.

She wasn't sure if something else held her there. Something more than his grin. Where was angry Mr. Jones? Or sullen Mr. Jones? He was easier to fight.

Something played around the corners of her mouth, a smile to match his own.

"Surely you don't suggest I am new to bread making Mr. Jones? I assure you, I am familiar with the skill and your attempts are certainly not—"

"Call me Shadrach."

His voice lowered to just above a whisper. A hush enveloped them at the exclusion of all else and he tugged her hand. Finella's heart thundered and she hoped he couldn't feel it in her pulse.

"I'll be Shadrach," he pushed her left fist into the sticky dough, "and you can be Finella." He added her right hand to the mess and let his hands rest on hers. Finella shivered, and he let go.

He rubbed his fingers together and tiny bits of dough fell on the table.

Finella opened her mouth to speak but the words stuck to her tongue, as sure as the dough clung to her fingers and she looked down at the table to hide the flame in her cheeks.

This familiarity must be the Australian way. She'd been warned life would not be what she thought. She guessed it made sense to call him by his Christian name, if nothing else for Molly's sake.

He nudged the pan closer. "You do know how to knead bread dough?"

She licked her dry lips. "I know enough about kneading to inform you this mix is not even a proper ball yet." She lifted her fingers from the pan and the tacky dough slid off her fingers.

"Oh, you know enough, do you?"

Finella could hear the laughter he held back.

He leaned against the table. Sure and tall. "Show me how it's done, then."

She wouldn't be baited by his teasing. But, perhaps… with the loosening of decorum, she could give him a bread-making lesson of her own.

"Aunt Sarah says dough is ready for baking when it's silky smooth. And this will never be silky because you have added too much water."

She reached for the flour sack, but he snatched it away and held it to his chest.

"Need more flour, do you? Well, if you ask nicely, I might let you have some."

Finella tried not to smile at his antics.

He opened back the folds of the sack, leaving the top of the flour just beyond Finella's reach. "Just say… please, *Shadrach*." He sang each word, like a magpie's warble, and Molly hopped off the bed to watch the fun.

Now two sets of blue eyes waited for an answer. Molly sucked on the end of her braid. Shadrach smirked.

Finella rested her wrists along the edge of the pan and looked to the ceiling.

"Please. May I have some flour?"

He drew the sack away. "I'm sorry. Did someone say something?" He sat down in the nearest chair and balanced the bag on his knee. "Do you hear anything, Miss Molly?" He winked at his sister.

Molly nodded. "Brother. Brother's got the flour." She looked from Shadrach to Finella and pointed. "It's here. See?"

"Oh, this flour?" He pried the top open some more. "But, I'm not Finella's brother. Am I?" He closed his eyes and stretched his legs, lofty-like and lazy. "If only there were some way Finella could get the flour she needs to make us all some damper." Molly hopped from one foot to the other, waiting for Finella's reply, and giggling at her brother's trap.

Tempted to laugh along with Molly, Finella shook her head at the man with the closed blue eyes. If she could steal from under his nose, a large fistful was all she needed.

Seizing her opportunity Finella dug her hand into the top of the powdery bag.

He clamped his fingers around her wrist and opened one eye. "You have to ask. You have to ask, *me*."

Fingers stuck in the flour, Finella stood there, pinned by more then his hand. If she didn't look away now, his gaze might hold her longer than she dared. She knew she had to give in. And what frightened her the most, was the desire to give in completely.

"I would like some flour please. *Shadrach*." Flame fired her cheeks.

"Did you hear that, Molly? Finella wants some flour. Should I give it to her?"

"Yes." Molly hugged her doll and laughed. "Give it to her."

Shadrach grinned. "Oh, I'll give it to her." He pulled down on Finella's hand, and hid it all the way to her wrist in the cool powder of the flour bag.

A thrill of alarm snapped in Finella's stomach. He held her by the other elbow and from the smirk on his face, planned some slow mischief.

Well, two could play his game. And this game was not over yet, *Shadrach Jones*. He loosened his grip, and Finella seized the opportunity.

One swift flick of her fingertips delivered a flour dusting to his face and neck. Not much, but enough to make him cough when he breathed it in. He dumped the bag onto the table and stood.

Somehow, he still managed to hold onto her wrist and he yanked her closer with it. Molly's laughter filled the room.

"Why, you little minx." He rubbed one eye and blinked at Finella. "You best be ready for your punishment."

Finella wasn't sure if he continued to jest and her tongue thickened with a jumble of excuses. What had come over her?

"You... you baited me. You can't say you weren't ready to do the same. Besides, there's nothing wrong with you... nothing a little brushing won't fix."

The upturned corners of his mouth betrayed him. "Perhaps. Perhaps I did bait you. But you'll pay for it, either way." A slow smile returned to his white face.

Finella's cheeks blazed with another flush.

This was not how Aunt Sarah baked bread.

Molly giggled at their antics.

"Think it's funny do you, Miss?" Shadrach brushed the tip of her nose with the back of his floury hand. "Now who looks like she's been kissed by cinders?"

Eyes crossed, Molly looked at her nose. "What about Finella?"

Shadrach wiped at his chin. The scraping of his fingers against day old bristles sounded a warning.

"Miss Finella will have to wait for her fun. She's got a damper to finish. I'm thinking I'll reserve my revenge for when she least expects it."

He hoisted the bag of flour onto the table and sat down. "Take what you need, Miss Finella."

"How can I be sure I won't end up wearing the flour the minute my back's turned?" She dipped an enamel cup into the sack and sprinkled a liberal amount over the dough. "I'm not sure I can trust you."

He leaned back into the chair with a deep smile and let Molly brush at the mess on his shoulder. "I'm not sure you should."

Finella's heart skittered with every pull of wet dough. She'd have to watch him or her moment of fun would come back to bite her. "This is better." Her rhythmic twisting pulled the lumpy dough together. "See, Molly?" She worked to bring it together and the supple mix obeyed and drank in the added flour. She mashed and molded with the heel of her palm until a smooth ball emerged.

"Shall I shape a loaf?"

"It's fine as it is." Shadrach took the lid off the cast iron pot. "Dump it here."

Finella eased the ball in.

"And now, you will see why there is no need for a fancy brick oven."

Shadrach knelt by the fire. A strand of hair covered his eyes. With a quick puff from his lips he drove it away and placed the pot directly into the coals, banking it well with ash all the way to the lid. "Thirty minutes, Miss Molly, and you'll get your damper."

He sniffed, and a sneeze shook his whole body. Ash flew around the hearth and the coals glowed under the urging of his breath. He rocked back on his heels and covered his face with both hands for a second sneeze.

He stood and a third sneeze burst before anyone had a chance to speak.

Molly pointed at a long smudge of flour along Shadrach's left eyebrow. "Oh, Brother." It gave him the look of a wizened old man. His cheeks looked much the same. A bubble of laughter escaped her, and Finella covered her own mouth with her knuckles.

"What's so funny?" He wiped his chin and nose.

"You are." Molly gathered her skirt and stepped onto a chair. Using her thumbs she smoothed his eyebrows and wiped the flour away. "You're funny."

"Is that right?" He snatched Molly by the waist and swung her round before tossing her on the bed like her rag doll.

Floppy with laughter, she lay in a merry puddle of fun. Her giddy giggles flooded the room and lit it from within like a shower of stardust. "Again, Shad. Again."

"You'll have to wait 'til later, Miss." He rubbed his knuckles against his chin. "I'm heading out to shave. I plot my best revenge when I shave and I've got to come up with something worthy of Miss

Finella's mischief now, don't I?"

Something bloomed in Finella. A blend of fear and thrill.

"Spin her too, Shad." Molly pleaded. "Spin Finella."

He wouldn't dare. Would he?

Instinct screamed at her to flee. Instead, she clung to the edge of the table and wouldn't think twice about reaching for a panhandle, if he tried.

"I'll think on it, Miss Molly." With a slow nod he directed his words to his sister, but his eyes sought out Finella. "You can be sure of that."

Finella loosened her grip on the table and pressed a hand to her belly. From the way her pulse pounded in her ears, one would think he'd already given her a thorough spinning.

13

For the next three weeks, heavy rain pounded the island. The swollen Saltwater Creek lapped at the bridge and surrounding tracks, and tucked the isolated household in their tiny world.

All three farm occupants ducked the weather and busied themselves with indoor work. Finella produced damper after damper, and a secret bubble of satisfaction kept her smiling, but Molly would not join in any of the cooking. The young girl's disinterest bothered Finella almost as much as Shadrach's promise of revenge, which failed to materialize.

Needles and threads proved equally troublesome. Finella kept at their mending lessons, but only dish washing drew Molly from her bed. At this rate, the sleepy girl would never move on from expert washerwoman.

"Do you hear that?" Finella looked up. The roof song they'd become accustomed to had softened. "I think it's stopped raining. Shall we walk?"

With warm wraps secure, Finella and Molly picked their way down the slim track, past the drenched chicory and mustard fields and into the tea tree scrub. They traipsed through wet sea grass and by the time they reached the open sand, their hems dragged against their heels.

Eager to keep away from the water's edge, Finella managed to

convince Molly they might find wildflowers among the spinnifex at
the edge of the sand hills.

The wind pushed them from behind but a wisp of yellow caught
Finella's eye.

"Over here." She held her hand out for Molly who already carried
a fistful of shells. Glad to have spied something for her Everlasting,
Finella knelt beside a tuft of dense green leaves and daisy shaped
petals.

"Do you know what these are called, Molly?"

The young girl shook her head.

"Me neither. Maybe it's a buttercup?" She picked a bud and
examined the stem. "If we collect enough we could make a daisy
chain for our hair"

Molly wriggled into the sand beside Finella. "What's a daisy
chain?"

"You've never made a daisy chain?"

Molly shook her head.

"Well, we shall remedy that, right now." Finella showed her
where to pick, at the base of the short stems.

Molly soon set aside her shells to gather more flowers. Finella
wondered about the girl's early years, afraid if she asked, she might
hear a story she didn't want to know. Instead, she asked about
Molly's new life on the island.

"Why doesn't Shadrach have any dogs? Most farms I know have
at least one?" Finella held out her apron and Molly tossed another
handful of flowers her way.

"He had a dog. Before I came. But he was old and died. He's
afraid to get another one."

"Afraid of dogs?" Finella couldn't believe that.

"No. Afraid the dog will run away and take me along."

Finella smiled at the upside down way Molly understood her

brother.

"Have you ever run away?"

Molly shook her head, stopped and gave in to a slow nod.

"I wanted to see the water," she pointed with her elbow but kept her head down to reach for another flower. "Shad wouldn't take me."

"Do you remember what happened?"

"I got wet. All over. And Shad got so mad he…" Molly stopped.

"What did he do?" Finella crouched beside her.

"He…" Molly scooped a handful of sand. It trickled through her fingers and returned to their feet by the wind. "He yelled. A lot, and cried. And said if Mum knew she would be cross."

Finella couldn't imagine Shadrach crying. Perhaps Molly embellished her story.

"When Mum was happy she called me her *Sunny Sunshine*. But she never got cross. She said I was the only sunshine our house ever needed."

Finella helped her stand, burdened by loss, not knowing how to fill it. They continued walking, their aprons round with flowers. "My mother died, too. You must miss yours. I know I did. I still do."

Molly nodded. "Are you the only girl, too?"

"Well, not exactly. Aunt Sarah lived with us after Mother died. She's my father's sister. But now," she shrugged, "I guess since she's living in London, and I'm here, I am the only girl left, too."

A wind tore across the shore and whipped at their skirts, snatching Molly's ribbon from the end of her plait.

"Oh no! It's gone." Molly tried to follow the ribbon caught in the clutches of the wind but her hair wrapped around her eyes and mouth.

Carried on a gust, the frayed scrap flew beyond their reach. It settled on the water of the Saltwater Creek, where it met the beach from its long neck in the bush. A wave of sea foam rushed in and collected it together with a twisted mess of seaweed.

Molly frowned and stepped back. "We don't go there. That's the snakey creek."

Finella looked to where she pointed. The swollen creek twisted its head into the bushland, as if it were a wide silver serpent.

"Don't fret now." With one free hand, Finella gathered Molly's hair from her face and held it at her nape. "I have some ribbons in my sewing box. You may choose a new one from there if you like."

"I can?"

"You can. I promise. And in return, you must make me a promise."

"To obey you?"

"You've made that promise already. To your brother. You can promise *me* something now."

Finella threaded her arm through Molly's and they turned back to face the wind head on. "You can promise to help me cook."

Molly pouted. "I don't like to cook. It's too hot."

"Too hot?"

"I like to wash."

Finella already knew the girl liked to play in the tubs but even dish water started out hot. "Do you think you could peel some potatoes? You'll need to do that with a basin of cold water."

Molly poked the tip of her tongue out the side of her mouth. The wind made her blink and for a moment she looked like she contemplated the world's most difficult question.

"Peel potatoes? With water?"

Finella nodded.

"And I can have a ribbon?"

"You may choose the fanciest one."

Aunt Sarah always said it was easier to catch a fly with honey and although she had not deliberately set a trap, Finella could see how persuasion and sweet incentive were good friends.

Molly smiled. "I'll peel."

Shadrach's shells sat in his field like a human sized honeycomb. Layers of wood, oyster shells and cockles rose from the ground ready for burning, but this dome-shaped pyre would see no flame today. Or tomorrow. As much as Shadrach welcomed the watering of his crops, he lamented the downpour on this stack.

"What's a man to do?" He spoke into the wind. "I keep busy, work until I collapse each night and God toys with me. *I've other plans for you Shad. No shell burning this week. Again.*"

He kicked the base.

"Why would I not be able to light it today, Lord? Do you really care if a lowly farmer gets to burn a pile of shells or are you needing it for something else?"

One fat raindrop fell onto his forehead, followed by a second on his cheek. Shadrach shook his head. Who was he to question God? Had God ever failed him? He hung his head and made for the house when low grey clouds opened their arms and showered his fields again.

Sloshing through the yard he contemplated his course. He could retreat to the barn. A leak from the roof needed attention before it became a problem. Or he could slip inside and find a chair beside the fire. But with Molly and Finella already bumping around the small house, he needed a better reason to be there. If only he had something to take inside. Something he needed to bring in from the rain. Other than his own drenched self, nothing came to mind.

No, if the Lord did not want him burning today, there must be a reason. Perhaps it was to spend time with Finella. Show her.... Shadrach ran his fingers through his wet hair. Show her what? He had nothing. She'd seen it all. She knew his fortune lay wrapped in a small farm years from its true potential. She knew his sister needed more than he could give of himself. How much more was left over for a woman like Finella?

A woman like Finella. He walked through his fields with the words ringing in his ears. How could he reach a woman like Finella Mayfield? George had managed it from across an ocean with a courtship that grew over years. And with the persuasion of her father.

Shadrach stopped at the skillion door. What help did he have?

After examining every length of trim in Finella's sewing basket, Molly chose a thin length of red velvet. Nothing caught her eye like the vermillion remnant braid. Even the yellow daisies, one tucked behind Finella's ear, the remainder left outside in a basket by the door, lost their shine in the presence of Finella's fancies.

Molly's blue eyes shone. "So pretty." She ran her fingers through the ribbon like a much sought after sea treasure.

"Aunt Sarah used a length on one of my skirts last winter. I wore it to church on Christmas Day."

Molly's eyes widened even more. "Oh, I know about Christmas. Mum found a card one time and showed me the picture of a pretty table. And happy people eating good food." She touched her cheek to the soft pile of the ribbon.

An ache settled in Finella's chest to see a simple remnant stir such longing. Those deep blue eyes on the other hand, larger than two bottomless rock pools, made up for what Molly's lips kept in. Instead of the comb Shadrach used on the girl, Finella now shared her own silver hairbrush set. Mirror in hand, the young girl watched Finella's slow gentle brushing.

"We can have a beautiful Christmas, Molly. Would you like that?

With our very own decorations."

Molly turned to face her. "Here, in Brother's house?"

"Right here, this December. If you can promise to peel potatoes, I can promise you the finest Christmas we can make together."

Molly turned back and smiled into the mirror. The smile of a girl with something to look forward to. It thrilled Finella just as much to be the one to promise it. And she would do it. With all the fancies she could find.

She worked each knot out of Molly's hair with an extra measure of kindness, careful not to go near the dimpled scar on the left side of her face.

"I have a box of Christmas things we can explore, one day. Decorations and embroideries, I think there may even be part of a costume in there." Finella fastened the ribbon into a neat bow. But her busyness with Molly's hair didn't keep her heart from remembering Mother's hand stitched napkins. The ones Aunt Sarah always set in mother's memory on their Christmas breakfast table. The incomplete set of six, now only five, but still well loved. Like all of mother's well washed and faded stitch work.

She let the pang of loss float for a moment before sending it back to where she kept it locked. "You'd like to help me set a Christmas table, wouldn't you?"

Molly nodded, but the hair brushing had caressed her well. Sleepy eyed, she slipped her boots off and got into bed. Finella kissed her cheek. The girl would be no good for a lesson in potato peeling until she'd woken from an afternoon nap.

Finella collected the muddy shoes and stepped outside to tap them together. A stream of sand trickled from each one and pooled at her feet.

From nearby, the low clearing of a throat startled her.

Shadrach leaned against the doorway of his skillion.

Her face flamed to think he'd been watching her, and her heart raced to know he still did.

He tossed a wad of papers onto his pallet and shut the door. "New game?"

Finella tapped Molly's heels together. "Old shoes." She tilted them the other way and another sprinkling of sand spotted the damp ground. "Molly will need a new pair soon. I think your sister hasn't had new clothes or shoes in some time."

Shadrach came closer. Close enough the heat from his arm touched hers like a warm breath.

"I see you've been paid a visit by the blue wren."

"Blue wren?"

"It's about now the males start courting the females with fancies they find in the bush. Anything bright, mostly feathers or flowers. Like this." He stroked the petal behind her ear. "They like to put on a display. Flap their wings around and get a pretty girl's attention."

His words squeezed her breath, just beyond her grasp. "Molly and I gathered some flowers, that's all," she whispered. Her blush deepened and spread like fast growing ivy. She plucked the flower and threw it with the others.

"Cape Dandelion, if you must know." He looked away. "Pops up every spring, in time for the blue wrens to impress."

"Thank you." Now she knew what to write beside her next Everlasting entry. Cape Dandelions. And Blue Wrens. "And while you're being helpful, could we talk about Molly's clothing? What she has is woefully inadequate for a growing girl."

He scratched his eyebrow. "You're probably right. Our mother couldn't afford much. Worked hard just to pay their boarding house fee. Plan was for them to come and live here once I had a larger house built. Here, let me…"

He took the shoes and pulled a small knife from his boot. With one shoe tucked under his arm, he picked at the other with the point of the blade, scrapping off bits of red dirt. When he finished one, he swapped and worked on the second, leaving only a smudge of dirt for Finella to polish off with a damp rag. He handed the shoes back.

"Want me to do yours now, Dandelion?" Blue eyes teased.

"I can clean my own shoes, thank you." She pointed to the soggy courtyard. "But, there wouldn't be a need if you gave thought to…" She stopped and looked at him.

Head down he wiped the knife clean along the sleeve of his shirt. Long red smudges, bloodlike and broad, stained the light blue chambray cloth.

"Gave thought to what?" He tucked the knife back into his boot.

Finella let her hands fall to her side.

How could he not know what she meant? "Your house sits in a bog, Shadrach. Every time we come or go, we stream across puddles and bring half the mud indoors."

He shrugged. "So? There's worse things for folks to get upset about."

Finella squeezed her nails into the leather of Molly's shoes. "Do you have any idea what a slippery yard can do? How much danger there is when a simple pathway doesn't exist for safe travel to the…" She pointed in the direction of the outhouse.

A rumble of thunder growled from above. Shadrach leaned over, just enough to make Finella wish she could shove him into a cold puddle.

"There's nothing wrong with the yard a little summer sun won't fix. Trust me, by then you'll be moaning about the dust. Or the flies."

He pushed off the wall and crossed the yard. Each long stride fell with as much determination into the mud as Finella employed in avoiding it. When he was halfway gone he turned around and walked backwards, arms outstretched to embrace another fresh shower. And he grinned.

He closed his eyes and stuck out his tongue for a mouthful of rain. Finella's blood simmered as surely as if he'd ordered a torrent to annoy her from the Almighty Himself. With little thought to the undoing of all his good work, she tossed a shoe right at him.

It missed and landed with a plop in a puddle, overshooting her mark.

He opened his eyes, laughed and took another backwards step. Her simmer rolled to boil. With a high pitched grunt she chucked the other shoe with greater force, and with remarkable accuracy hit him in the chest. He caught it and held it there against his shirt before collecting the one at his feet.

"I don't control the rain, Finella." He yelled above the raindrops as if he'd read her mind. "That's God's business."

Finella screwed her fists into tighter balls, and thank God she did. For if she'd allowed herself one sinful luxury that day, it would have been to toss every dandelion petal in the basket by her feet, across the mud, and probably the basket itself, directly at his stubborn head.

14

Shadrach tossed the papers aside.

Who cared about the hyacinths her aunt forced to grow on their windowsill in winter?

He stretched his legs along the pallet and lay on his back in the cold skillion.

His feet cleared the end and hit the floor with a thud.

Reading Finella's letters was like eating an unsalted egg. Wholesome and bland, her correspondence with George held very little tenderness.

Instead, she wrote about her Father, his work in Chingford Green and the parishioners they served together. Most of what she wrote consisted of her duty to her father's village. Where were Finella's dreams and desires? He knew what she didn't like. *That* she shared freely. He needed to know what she longed for. If he was going to do anything about it.

He smoothed out another paper and followed the flowery copperplate through yet another letter.

Dear Mr. Gleeson,

I enjoyed reading about your early days at Phillip Island. There is much to be gained by sharing oneself with those in need. My Father's encouragement in this has helped me look beyond my own loss.

Yesterday, I visited the spinster sisters, Miss Matilda and Miss Jemima Grace, the busiest of Father's elderly parishioners and quite possibly my favorites. For years they've cherished three old mulberry trees beside their family home. They've tended silk worms and sold their thread to a nearby mill.

Last week a strike of lightning destroyed a tree in a burst of fire. Even worse, the flames spread to their house and only the two dear ladies escaped the catastrophe. Home and possessions all burned to a sorry crisp. Everything. Including the old trees.

They will move on to live with a nephew, also in Chingford Green, but I fear they will never be the same. Decades will pass before a new grove of mulberries flourish. And they will not be there to see that day.

I'll miss the jams they gave Father each year, but even more, I'll miss the shade of those trees. They remind me of a day Mother and I visited there together. I don't remember why we went, but we all sat under that canopy and drank mulberry cordial, fragrant with cinnamon.

And now, I have one less place to remember my mother, but these dear women have even more to count as loss.

Shadrach put the letter down. Always counting loss. Had she counted much true happiness in her days before she left England? He knew her days since held more misery than she cared to revisit, and he couldn't blame her.

Tucking his hands beneath his head he looked at her trunks, pressed against the wall.

Locked and fastened, many of them with leather straps, they shadowed his room with a presence he couldn't fight. They loomed above him while he slept and reminded him each morning they sat in storage under his nose until he made good on a crazy promise to a dead friend.

He closed his eyes and tried to imagine Finella as his wife. Under a mulberry tree somewhere in his yard, drinking tea in the shade.

His yard? Unlikely.

❧

"She is not going to church like that." Shadrach slammed the door shut and crossed the room to where his sister stood by the bed. Mirror in hand, Molly admired herself from every angle. "You've dressed her like a hussy."

"Surely you're not serious?" Finella's pulled on her gloves, and a little crease appeared on her brow.

"My sister will not go to church dressed like that. Anyone with half a brain will wonder what you've done to her."

"Done to her? *Done to her?*" Finella repeated his words as if they were new to the English language. "And what exactly have I done to her?" She rested her hands on her hips.

His good shirt choked him and Shadrach ran his finger between the stiff collar and his neck. What had she done? He wasn't sure exactly, but his sister had a look about her. A fancy look, and he didn't like it.

She wore a chocolate colored woolen skirt with red trim along the bottom and a white shirt with shiny black buttons. He only recognized her old tan shawl and shoes, now rescued from the mud and polished.

But her hair stood out more than anything. He knew it had something to do with the rags Finella tied there last night. He had no idea it would turn out like this. If he had, he would never have allowed it.

Curls fell around Molly's face, like a twist of bean shoots. Some of them gathered at the back with that new red ribbon, in a style very unlike her somber plait.

Finella waited for his answer.

"You've dressed her up… like a doll. That's not what you're here for. You're supposed to teach her what my mother didn't get to. This…" he struggled to find the right word, "is not what I meant when I asked for your help. I never asked for anything fancy."

Like Molly, Finella looked different too and he tried to ignore the snap in his chest that brought. A small hat perched on her head, under which similar curls to Molly's escaped from where she'd piled them all up in a loose knot. A matching dark blue skirt and jacket replaced her work dresses and aprons. She stepped beside Molly and took the mirror from the girl's hand.

"You may not have asked for anything fancy, but Molly did."

"Molly did?" He found that hard to believe. The girl hardly knew what day it was. "Molly doesn't know what she wants. She's perfectly happy with simple hair and simple clothes."

"Shadrach, I assure you, this couldn't be any less fancy. Molly's wearing an old skirt of mine I altered to fit her. The shirt is mine too, but look…" She patted the girl's arm and smiled. "She looks different not because the clothes are *fancy*. She looks beautiful because she looks like a young girl, and that makes her happy."

Molly looked at him. "I'm the only girl now, Shad."

She was the only girl. His mother's sunshiny girl. "I don't like it. Not one bit."

"I told you." Molly slumped onto the bed and lay on her side. "He doesn't like fancy things." She pouted and closed her eyes.

Finella pulled her back up by the arm. "Oh, no you don't. You'll crush your beautiful curls. We've waited long enough for this rain to ease and we're going to church looking our best. Now, sit up, love."

Shadrach tapped his hat against his leg. He'd not taken Finella to church once since she'd arrived, and while the bad weather would excuse their past absence, they had no real excuse today. They'd have to leave in the next few minutes or face being late.

Who knew if any of the tracks ahead were still water logged? There was no time to get bogged on the road. Or here in his own home.

"Wagon's hitched and there's no time to argue. You'll both be seated in less than five minutes. Do whatever needs doing so we're not late."

He slammed his hat on and with equal force slammed the door behind him. Heaviness in the pit of his stomach slowed his march across the yard. It had nothing to do with the hurried breakfast he'd eaten or the strong black tea he'd gulped.

It had everything to do with the way Finella worked her charm on Molly. What was so hard about teaching a girl how to cook and sew, anyway? Why did she insist on fancies that didn't belong in the bush?

He checked the harness again. Was it fancies that didn't belong or Finella herself? He dragged his hand through Old Lou's mane, smoothing it down. If only the tangle in his stomach were so easily unraveled. He needed the comfort of scripture and hymns to quiet his soul, not the mess of thoughts he mulled over each day. The grief of George's loss hit him afresh and he wondered who would do the preaching that morning.

The sound of the door opening drew him from his thoughts.

Molly held her shawl close and Finella shut the door behind them. Both stood still and surveyed the yard.

He hadn't noticed the large puddles on his way in or out. But he saw them now. Finella looked down her nose at them and up at him as if he'd put them there on purpose.

"Come on!" He yelled. "Time to go."

Molly stepped out first. Schooled by Finella, she collected a chunk of skirt with each hand and lifted it high. She looked different in a longer skirt, older somehow, and he'd never seen her walk with such deliberation. She picked her way through the puddles and a coil of impatience sprung in his chest. This would take all day.

"You're doing fine, Molly." Finella followed behind her, each ginger footstep placed to avoid the worst of the mud. "Just keep that hem up."

Molly's tongue poked out the side of her lip but her eyes remained fixed on the ground. At this rate they would get to church in time for the benediction. Shadrach contemplated walking over and scooping her up in his arms.

"My shoe's dirty." Molly lifted her foot to lament the muck at her heel.

"It doesn't matter!" he called. When had it ever mattered? She could wipe her shoes later. "Just keep moving."

"But Shad…" Molly came closer. "I don't want dirty shoes." She placed her foot down and inched forward in a quick slip. Her arms swept the air and she fought for equilibrium, stopping in one less then elegant pose.

She looked at Shadrach, feet akimbo, eyes wide, mouth open. "Nearly," she breathed in a whisper.

"You're fine. Just jump over this last big puddle," Shadrach encouraged, and in three more steps and one leap she crossed to where he waited.

"Good girl." He lifted her into the seat and turned for Finella.

Frozen in the middle of his yard, the ever-proper Miss Mayfield searched for a way out. Molly's slip had left a long trough of mud right in front of her, erasing her best option.

She looked at Shadrach with the same eyes he'd seen that first day at Queen's Wharf, when she wrestled with the iron track for her snagged dress. He'd seen it then, the look that begged for rescue. He saw it now; in eyes so deep he wondered if he could ever look away.

She needed him. George was right. She needed Shadrach as much as he needed her. A finger of something hot and cold pressed his ribs. Like an I-told-you-so from the other side of eternity. Right into his heart. What he felt for Finella Mayfield had little to do with Molly. Or George. It had everything to do with how she fit into his world. Even when she fought it.

"Wait there. I'll come for you."

"I didn't ask for your help."

"Yes, you did." He held out his hand. "Your eyes said it. *Please Shad, come get me. I'm stuck in all this mud, with my fancy hat and I need you to get me to the other side.*"

"Nonsense." She took a tiny step. "I didn't ask for help because I don't need it."

He came closer and reached out. "Grab on and hop over that puddle. There's no trolley coming this time."

"Jump, Finella!" Molly yelled from her seat on the wagon. "It's fun."

Finella dipped her toe into a shallow puddle.

"Come *this* way." Shadrach warned and pointed to where he stood.

Finella pushed her other foot forward, but instead of stopping on solid ground, it slipped like Molly's had. Her long slide and scramble did nothing to keep Finella upright. Her foot lost ground to a flurry of skirt and petticoat, and Finella Mayfield landed on her back in the mud.

"Oh dear!" Molly whispered and stood up.

"Keep your seat, Molly!" Shadrach hoped his frantic heartbeat would follow suit. With quick long strides he splashed through the puddles to Finella's side.

She opened her eyes and closed them again. Moaned softly and tried to move. Her hands, palm down in the mud reached up. Cold and gritty, they wrapped around his.

"Are you hurt?"

She opened her eyes. "Well… my pride didn't escape, unmarred." Lost in the tumble, her hat also lay in disgrace, crushed against her shoulder and newly decorated with the signature red mud of his farm.

But her hair bore the full brunt of the fall. Loose and wet, it dripped round her face and onto her shoulders. She blinked and tried to sit up.

"Are you sure you're not injured? How's your head?"

"I'm not sure." She let go of one hand and rubbed her neck.

Shadrach guessed puddle water found its way through the layers of her church clothes.

"I'm taking you in." He scooped one arm under her legs and the other around her shoulders.

"Into the house?"

"Of course, the house." He lifted her out of the mire. "I haven't yet built an infirmary, so yes, into the house it is."

"Please, Shadrach. I don't want to bring mud into the house."

He cradled her in his arms. Water dripped from her skirt onto his trousers and a long strand of her hair fell loose from where she'd secured it. He avoided more puddles between them and the door. His hold on her a little firmer, a little closer.

He tipped her against his shoulder to reach for the latch. Another strand of hair slipped from her temple, its end slick with mud. It drew a brown line along her cheek and fell with a soft slap to rest under his chin.

It drew his gaze to her as surely as if she'd reached for him. If she had caressed him herself with her very own fingertips, it would not have burned any less.

A small cry, the protest of one freshly bruised, escaped her lips, and breath, sweet and warm touched his neck. Elbowing his way in, he hooked a chair with his foot and dragged it over.

"Sit here. Anything broken?" He knelt beside her.

She shook her head.

"Are you sure? Sometimes these things take a few minutes to show up."

She touched the back of her head, then examined her dirty glove.

"I don't think I'm bleeding."

Blood was the last thing he needed now.

"There's a…" he reached with his thumb, "small splash of mud just here." He rubbed under her right eye. "And… here."

Drawn like a moth to its fate, he touched her bottom lip. Its pink flesh marked by the rust of dirt. His dirt. The soil of his farm. It touched her. And so did he.

He wiped at her mouth and her whisper scorched his hand.

"Shadrach." She withdrew her head to where his reach no longer found her.

"I'm sorry." He stood upright and searched for a breath deep enough to lift the weight off his chest. The longing he could no longer ignore.

Head down, Finella pulled at her soggy gloves. Her fingers trembled on the buttons and no amount of fumbling peeled them off. She dropped her hands into her lap with the same defeat he saw in her shoulders.

A tear, and then a second one fell into her limp palms.

There would be no hymnbooks today. No verses for strength, just when Shadrach needed them most.

"I'll bring Molly in. She'll help you get cleaned up." He hovered, wanting to scoop her up, until she nodded and tucked a strand of hair behind her ear. Earthy smudges marked her beautiful face. Like words on a page, they dotted her neck.

He glanced her way once more, lest she faint or take a turn. But he knew for certain now, it was his own breath that had been knocked clear from his chest.

15

For as long as Shadrach remembered, Sundays had never been for baths. Not even on the goldfields where the rush for riches watered down man's civilized rituals. But here, in his own home, long after the church bell stopped swinging, Shadrach carted water bucket after water bucket to rival any Saturday night bath-house.

He wished there were more he could do for Finella, but she assured him all she needed was to wash the mud out of her hair. But he could not ignore the way she protected her elbow. And the tears she wiped when she thought he wasn't looking. And finally the door she fastened to keep Molly in while she bathed.

Shadrach returned to his skillion. He'd met there with God enough times to know a man didn't need a pew on a Sunday to turn to Scripture. But the Psalms soon gave way to Finella's letters, stacked less neatly than when he'd received them, fattening the pages of his well loved book.

It didn't escape him. The temptation he hid in the pages of his Bible. But he figured with George's permission he had every right to sift through her letters.

Tired of reading the same pleasantries about the summer heat at George's end and windblown tales at Finella's, Shadrach skipped ahead to what passed between them just before her departure.

June 12, 1875
Chingford Green

My dear George,

Father has sold the piano. And my mother's mahogany chiffonier she inherited from Great Aunt Anna. Our little parsonage grows empty and more hollow as the weeks pass.

And there's an echo here, now. It pushes us out, as if we were in a nest no longer ours.

Aunt Sarah keeps me busy filling trunk after trunk. Everything of my mother's which can be transported, we shall pack. And somehow, I feel Mother's arm over us while we dig into her cupboards and empty her drawers.

She's here, not like a specter from the grave, more... a treasured fragrance. A caress to the cheek, like her embroidered pillow shams. The happy weight of Mother's handmade lace stitched onto my wedding dress by Aunt Sarah. Her Christmas linens.

Dear George, do you suppose Mother's arm is pushing me closer to what I've always searched for? Do you suppose her memory, dimmer with each year, might sharpen now that I am to see you again?

You must know how much your promise to help means to me. If Aunt Sarah knew, she'd chide me for foolishness she forbade years ago. But you know from my last letter, I cannot stop. How deep the root runs and how heavy the longing for that name. Just one name. I need to finish what my mother uttered on her deathbed. And your promise to help, fortifies my resolve and convinces me Father chose well when he matched us together.

If I am to walk away from my mother's grave forever, then perhaps God will allow me to put all this to rest. With your knowledge of Australia to decipher what I never could, I'm cheered to contemplate this torment might finally end. Your assurance we will do this together is the best wedding gift. Far beyond any other token you could offer.

I remain sincerely and affectionately yours,
Finella

The loose sheet pulsed in Shadrach's hand. What was she talking about? Unlike Finella's early letters, this one breathed an air of intimacy he wasn't sure he cared for. When had her words with George taken a turn toward the familiar? And why was his heart thundering at familiarity they'd had every right to?

He sat on his bedroll, surrounded by a mess of correspondence out of sequence, and very much out of his depth.

A thousand soldiers marched across his chest and drummed up fresh trouble. "What are you looking for, Finella?" He addressed the air. "How was George meant to help you?"

The empty skillion offered no reply on her behalf, and Shadrach stood to face the wall of trunks. He planted a hand at either end and leaned in. Hard, but not hard enough to extract anything. Her well packed cases remained tight lipped and Shadrach rested his forehead on the brass lock of a small case jammed between two others.

"Locked, tied, and latched."

He didn't know who was more tethered. He or Finella.

Jealousy crammed his throat like a thumb to the neck. He wished he'd never seen the letters. He'd only read what George asked him to. It's not as if he pried into business that wasn't his.

George made sure of that when he made him promise. And for his troubles, Shadrach had more questions than when he started.

He rummaged through the pages, casting aside those too old, those too bland. But nowhere in the mess could he find another letter as direct as the one he'd just read.

"You're still cornering me, George. With as much clarity from the grave as you did on your deathbed, Brother." He flattened the papers into a loose wad. "Her father may have matched her with you, I'll give you that. But *you* matched her with *me*. And whatever it is Finella's looking for, I'm going to be the one who hands it over now."

⸙

There was no question in Finella's mind. She would not spend another day on Shadrach's farm.

She sat by the late afternoon fire and finger-combed her freshly washed hair. Molly had been a fine helper and considering the day's dramas and hasty meals, Finella was not surprised the girl now slept. The familiar sight of her dream-lit face galvanized Finella's resolve.

She had to get out. And she would do it fast. No more thinking or praying. Her gut told her all she needed to know.

With a light tap at the door, Shadrach let himself in.

"Better?" He stood on the threshold, hand still on the door latch.

Finella nodded, but her gesture hardly matched her mood.

Shutting the door to a new wave of rain, Shadrach pulled a chair for himself and sat near her.

"I'm guessing the bath revived you and sent Molly scrambling for bed."

Finella nodded again. A lump the size of a goose egg crowded her windpipe.

"Shadrach, I want to leave. Tomorrow morning. And if you'll let me, I want to take Molly with me." She caught her fingers in the loops of her crocheted shawl.

He stared, mouth open. Then shut. He sat back and looked at her sideways.

"You did knock your head. Are you dizzy?"

"I'm not sick, Shadrach. I'm scared." She gathered the shawl closer and dropped her hands into her lap. "I won't stay here another day. And I don't think Molly should, either."

"Because you slipped in the mud? You want to leave because of a simple fall? And take my sister with you?" He shook his head, disbelief in his voice. Even to her ears it sounded a little mad, but she would not be moved.

"I can't live here. I know that now. To you, it's … it's only a puddle of rainwater. A small hiccup the sun will fix, someday. But to me…." She bit on the tremble in her lip, but even that could not keep her tears from falling.

She fought against the flood which threatened to shame her and focused on his fists where they tapped against his knees.

"Tell me." His low plead resonated against the sound of rain on the shingled roof. "Why is this all so hard for you?"

His blue eyes didn't accuse or force her. His confusion deserved an answer. With her hand still caught in the fringe of her shawl, she brushed at her tears. Could she tell him? Would he care? The fire snapped and so did a floodgate deep within her, long held back by weariness and Aunt Sarah's version of decorum.

"The winter I was Molly's age, my parents visited the family of Ben and Alice Brown. They'd had scarlet fever in the house and lost their baby son. It wasn't far from our parsonage so my parents walked there. Alice was George Gleeson's sister, and he was visiting too that day, although I hardly knew him, back then."

She shuddered and the well-known story came to life from where she kept it hidden. "On the road home, two men stopped to ask for directions to an inn just past Chingford Green. Father said they looked like they'd been on the road for days. One was only a youth, the other much older. Both unshaven and dirty. Father pointed them in the direction of the tavern, and the men started on their way but turned back."

Shadrach leaned in and pressed his lips together, as if to keep his words in, and hers flowing.

Emboldened by his attention, she continued.

"Mother had already delivered the meal so her basket was empty, but the younger one plucked it from her anyway. The older man teased him for grabbing nothing of worth. He said, 'Watch how it's done, you whip-shy baby.' He tried to snatch the brooch at Mother's neck, but my father fought him off and told Mother to run, and that's when the thief knocked Father to the ground."

Flames from the fire rose and tangled with the story in her mind. The heat, already pulsing in her head, grew. She'd never shared the account in such detail. Not with someone outside the family.

But sitting beside Shadrach's fire, with him sinking into her story, Finella let the words land where they might.

"Mother ran to a nearby cottage. Mara Green lived there then. She never cared for her own person, let alone her house. Birds nested in the roof and the pathways lay in a twist of thistles and puddles."

Tears filled her eyes and the vision of Shadrach blurred, but not the events of that day.

"Poor Mother must have slipped on her way down Mara's path, because when Father found her, much later, she was unconscious, the brooch ripped from her collar, a gash in her head so deep they would not let me see her for hours when they brought her home."

Finella shook her head, still unable to reconcile her heart with her mother's fate. "She lay on her bed for two days, gray and clammy until life drained out of her completely. All she asked for was his name. The man who robbed her."

She didn't dare close her eyes for fear the bandit might appear before her. Like every nightmare in which he'd appeared that winter. "George Gleeson recognized the younger man. He'd been a suitor of his sister's but had run away to Australia to make his fortune. I remember people whispering he'd come back too late, too drunk, and too poor in the pocket for Alice Gleeson. When no one could tell Mother who the other man was, she whispered, 'If only we could name him. God have mercy on the unknown soul.' And that's when we lost her."

The fire spat and hissed but Finella's shoulders shivered with a chill no flame could ever slake. "We lost her. Because a lazy old woman couldn't keep her yard safe."

Shadrach cleared his throat but kept silent until Finella looked up at him.

"Finella." He cleared his throat and tried again. "I'm so sorry you lost your mother like that. I can only imagine your grief."

"Then you can also imagine how I never want to see another person snatched the same way." She tapped at her chest with her fingers. "Nor be that person myself."

"That's not going to happen here. I promise." He gathered her hands, fringe and all in his own and held them tight. "Your mother was running from an evil man. There's no need to run here. Why, you saw Molly herself, hop and skip across the yard with ease."

"You can't make that promise." She shook free. "What if Molly decides there *is* a reason to run. You and I both know, anything can happen with her. In a heartbeat. It happened to me."

She rubbed at the bruise on the back of her head.

"Finella." He pleaded and leaned closer. "This is different. So many things are different here. Please, don't go. Molly needs you."

"That's why I want to take her with me. Mrs. McLachlan might take us in. I can find work in Melbourne until my aunt arrives."

"And then what? Take her back to England with you?" He shook his head. "I promised my mother I would take Molly. Not give her to strangers."

"I'm not a stranger, not anymore. She trusts me. And I have a soft spot for her, too. Please, Shadrach. Think about it for a minute. You can work here unencumbered, and Molly can mix with other people, learn to fend for herself. I would never put her in harm's way."

He rested his elbows on his knees and pressed his forehead to the tightly coiled fist of each hand.

"No." He looked up again. "Absolutely not. I won't allow it. We had an agreement. You and I. Until your aunt arrives, you will teach her, here."

He scraped the chair back a fraction and let his pointer finger rest on the table beside them. "I never offered anything else but work for you *here*. If you want to leave, I won't hold you to your promise. I'll drive you into the village as soon as the rain stops."

Molly mumbled and nestled into a new position, gathering the covers closer.

"But you can't have her," he whispered.

Finella expected the fight.

She'd lined up her arguments hours before like ammunition, yet still, the thought of hurting him slowed her down. But she couldn't let it stop her.

"She needs a woman more than she needs you. Not because you don't care for her, but a young girl needs a woman to help her enter the years ahead. Believe me, I know this bitter lesson firsthand."

"Then stay here and be that woman. That's always been our agreement."

"I never agreed to live in a bog. My shoes are wet all the time, Shadrach. Our hems forever damp and now I have a lump on the back of my head. I don't want to face anything worse."

He straightened against the back of his chair. "Would you still feel like this if the rain stopped and everything cleared by tomorrow morning?"

Finella played with the button on her sleeve cuff. "That's not going to happen though, is it? You're the one who told me the rain is God's business."

"And who better than God to sort it all out, then?" Half a smile played on his lips, but Finella would not let him sweeten the argument with talk of God. Where had God hidden deliverance when her own mother lay in the mud with a cracked head?

"I'll wait. Another two weeks. If there's still a mud pit every time I step outside that door, then…"

The soft tap of rain filled the silence and the unspoken settled around them.

"So it's two weeks, now?" He knotted his arms over his chest. This tall farmer, who was used to swinging his farm gate open or shut when he pleased.

Finella tried not to look at him. "Or, you can let me take Molly to Melbourne sooner. Give her a finer future than she'll ever have here alone with you. I'll write you letters every week and tell you how she's faring. And you won't need to tie her up to do your chores when I'm gone."

She knew it sounded harsh, but her head throbbed now and she was in no mood to look for kinder words. She rubbed at a bruise on her elbow. "We both know I'm not here forever."

He exhaled softly. As though he might start with a fresh argument. Instead, he stared at her until it almost hurt as much as the bruising.

He stood. "Two weeks then. Unless God intervenes." He tucked the chair back under its place at the table where it scraped like an angry groan against the packed dirt floor.

"Let me know if your head hurts. I keep some powders in the skillion where Molly won't find them."

And with that he slipped into the steady rain leaving Finella to finally understand what her aunt meant by a *hollow victory*.

16

---

*D*ays of constant rain kept Finella and Molly indoors and trips to town or church remained well off the calendar for another fortnight.

Trapped by weather determined enough to lift an ark, the ever-growing pools outside their door grew, and kept Finella and her young charge busy with the lessons Shadrach required. Finella carried too many bruises to forget how much trouble she'd faced the last time she ignored his instructions.

Not that he issued many more. He appeared at the table for hurried meals, his hair often plastered to his head from working in the rain.

How the man dried without a fire, Finella could only guess. Blue and shaking, he sought the hearth each time he came indoors, but hardly lingered once he'd finished his food.

They spoke no more words about Finella leaving, but the sky whispered the inevitable everyday in sheets of misty rain.

While Molly still refused to cook by the fire, she no longer avoided the vegetables Finella brought her to dice and chop, and so food preparation delivered the girl to her seat at the table, where she now peeled apples.

Against a steady stream of rain to lull the senses, drowsiness stole into the hut each afternoon as sure as the overflowing gullies and tracks which gurgled through the farm.

Finella paced the one room house, littered with drying washing. Thunder rumbled overhead and she pressed articles of clothing strung above their heads to her cheek to feel for dryness. She hung a shirt over a chair again and stood with her back to the fire.

Something sounded different. More than rain. A noise she didn't recognize spilled into the yard with a whoosh and crash.

She opened the door. Shadrach stood shovel in hand before a pile of white rocks. Water cascaded from the top of his head, down his neck and into his soaked shirt. Old Lou and the wooden dray stood not too far off with a larger load of the same rocks.

He straightened and arched his back. "Did I wake Molly?" he called.

"No. She's peeling apples."

He flicked the hair from his eyes. "I might make more noise the closer I get to the house." He had to yell to compete with the downpour. "Go back in. You'll get wet standing there."

Finella squinted against the spray. Had he gone mad to work in a flood of rain?

"What are you doing?"

"I said, go inside." He motioned with his hand for her to get back. "Can't a man do his chores without having to give reason? Beside, this is between me and God."

Finella pushed at the door until only a crack remained. The cold wind bit into her cheeks but curiosity kept her watching. Shadrach jumped onto the bed of the dray and scraped the contents onto the ground.

Molly snuck her head under Finella's arm.

"What's Brother doing with shells?"

"Shells?" Finella peered. "I thought they were rocks."

"No, that's shells."

Perhaps the man had gone mad. Why else would he work in drenching rain? But *shells*? She shut the door. Had her request to leave with Molly pushed him so far? Is this why he hardly spoke to her anymore?

She knew people who lived in the bush could lose their minds for lack of someone to talk to, but surely this was not happening here? Was it?

She opened the door again. "Shadrach."

Crashing shells fell with the rhythmic dig and toss of his spade. Chalky colored mounds littered the yard like anthills, and still the load in the dray looked like it had hardly been touched.

She cupped her hands and screamed into the cacophony. "Shadrach!" How could she compete against wind, rain and… shells?

Either he couldn't hear her or didn't want to. With his back to the house he continued to work until Finella shut the door and faced Molly.

"If he's not already sick, he's going to be. Very soon." She banked the fire, thankful the farm's stack of kindling and logs kept dry under an oilcloth. She snatched all of hers and Molly's damp things from where they hung and brought anything of Shadrach's closer to the hearth. Finally, she pulled the kettle over the fire and prayed it would not take an eternity to boil.

"Do you know what he's doing?" she quizzed Molly.

"Maybe he's bringing me more shells. He only lets me take a pocketful each time. Maybe he wants me to have more."

A louder crash and rumble sounded from the yard, this time just outside the door. Molly dragged the chair to the wall and pushed Finella's newly hung lace curtain aside.

Finella followed, but she couldn't see much. Tempted to look out again, she squeezed at the latch and inched the door open.

From the other side, Shadrach threw a spadeful of shells in her direction. They crashed just short of her feet.

"Shut the door, Finella." Water dripped off his trembling lips and chin but he didn't break his shoveling. Another scoop landed in her direction.

Finella slammed the door shut and backed into it for good measure.

This wasn't a simple bad turn. This was delirium.

Shadrach shoveled as if fuelled by a furnace. He'd mourned the loss of drier days, more suited to burning and crushing his shells into dust, and wrestled with God, the giver of rain, for too long.

No, he would not be fixed with misery a moment longer.

If she wanted a yard where she could walk from one end to the other and not risk even the tip of her shoe on one blade of wet grass, he would give it to her. Or he would die trying.

At first he wanted to rip shell pyre apart and snap each timber into splinters. It did him no good, sitting there soaked and useless. Then he saw it for what it could be.

He'd pulled each branch out, collapsing the structure he'd labored to build, until a small mountain of shells remained. Not enough to fill the yard, but enough to make a good start.

But he wanted more than a good start.

So he'd visited Rhyll beach again and filled the dray with more. Days of driving rain slowed his efforts but failed to hamper his resolve.

With Old Lou now in the barn, he swapped his shovel for a rake and drew the shells into long lines. Wide paths he'd give her, wide enough for her and Molly to walk side by side. Arm in arm, if she wished. And if he were lucky, she might even take his arm as well.

From her door a path would snake to the left, all the way to the garden, the outhouse and down to the beach track. One to the right would pass his skillion, all the way up to the barn. And one more would lead from the house, across the yard to the orchard where, if the weather allowed, she could hang the wet clothes that filled the house today.

He added another generous spadeful to the puddles nearest the door and watched the rain wash every trace of red earth off the shells and back into the clay below.

He tried to focus, but the paths blurred. He blinked away raindrops that clung to his lashes. Tomorrow he'd walk Old Lou over each pathway and crush it down.

Today... a wave of dizziness washed over him and he grabbed the rake to keep steady. Today, he just needed to sit. Today, was all he had left.

✍

"Brother? Wake up."

"Molly, don't poke him. Here, put this on his brow." Finella handed Molly another cool cloth. "Is he still hot?"

Molly touched her cheek to his. "Burning."

Finella turned to the fire where a pot of broth simmered. She didn't know what to do if he didn't wake soon. No matter how much she stirred the soup, it did him no good if he couldn't eat it.

She'd done everything she knew. Dragged his body in with Molly's help and stripped every piece of soggy clothing off him, covering him in great haste with a dry apron from her makeshift indoor washing line.

In a frenzy she'd pulled her own mattress onto the floor, dragged it by the fire and lugged him onto it.

Covered with her quilt he lay there for hours, under the vigilant watch of his sister. If he did ever choose another dog, it would never love him as faithfully.

"Is he dead? Like my Mum?"

"Of course not, dear girl. He may be ailing but he's very much alive. See his chest rise with every breath?"

Molly pulled the quilt down to his belly and leaned in. Any closer and she'd rest her chin on his ribs. Finella looked away from his naked chest.

"How long before he wakes?"

"Not long. I hope."

Finella had no idea, really. She prayed warmth and shelter would bring him 'round soon. There was nothing else she could do for him, foolish man. Fancy working in the rain until completely exhausted and gripped by fever. What possessed an individual to do that?

"Will he sleep here all night?" Molly tucked the quilt under his feet. "Where will you sleep?"

Finella shrugged. She didn't know that either.

She didn't know why he'd brought the shells into the yard, didn't know why he labored with a task that made no sense, and didn't know when he'd wake to explain himself.

She had about enough strength left to settle into a chair to keep from falling onto the floor herself. She pushed the lamp to the centre of the table and laid her head on her arms. Just for one minute. Enough to close her eyes and let her shoulders slump a little.

Murmuring voices woke her much later when firelight illuminated the room. At first, Finella fought to understand where she was. She opened her eyes to see Molly's bed, empty and missing not only an occupant, but its blanket and pillow. Whispers came from near her feet.

"So, you weren't dead?"

"No, silly. Nowhere near dead."

"But, we carried you in. And took off your clothes. Like when Mum died."

"You did? You and Finella?"

"Yes. And she made soup, but only I ate it."

Finella's face burned and she was glad for the shadows where she hid.

"Finella didn't eat?"

"No. Her stomach has a headache."

Shadrach chuckled softly. "Where is she now?"

"Sleeping, up there."

Finella imagined two sets of blue eyes looking at the underside of the table and folds of her skirt. She kept her feet rooted to the floor.

"Will you still sleep here? Your face is cooler now."

"No, I'll sleep in the skillion. Soon as I get myself there."

He moaned, and the sound of shuffling soon faded into a soft grunt and thump.

"Which, I don't think I can manage tonight." One more rustling noise and she hoped he was on his back again. "But I wouldn't mind a cup of water. Can you get it, Molly?"

Finella squeezed her eyes shut. In no time Shadrach gulped his drink.

"Thank you. You're a good girl, Sunny."

"Want soup, Shad?"

"Maybe later."

The cup clunked and came to rest on the tabletop before more shuffling and then another long silence.

Had brother and sister fallen asleep together? Should she risk a quick tiptoe to Molly's bed? Finella bit her lip and waited.

"Shad?" Molly snuck in with another question.

"Mmm," he replied after a long silence.

"Why did you bring shells? Are they for me?"

He drew a long, deep breath before answering.

"For you, Miss Molly. Always for you."

"Hmmm." Molly sounded satisfied. Perhaps she would drift off to sleep now.

Finella waited for longer than she thought a person could sit slumped at a table. Until she could not bear the tingling in her frozen feet another minute. She wriggled her toes and knew unless she traded the chair for a bed she would be no good to either Molly or their patient in the morning.

With only the faint crackle of the fire to mask her movement, she crept to Molly's bed, grateful the child had left behind a thin quilt.

With Shadrach in the room, she would remain dressed but she slipped out of her shoes and into the vacant bed. Who knew what urgency might call her in the early morning hours. With Molly and Shadrach nestled together, she'd snatch an hour of sleep and check on them soon.

Under the cover of dark she heard Molly's soft snoring.

A log slipped in the fire and hissed.

And then silence, until Finella heard a short, deep sigh.

"Molly can have a pocketful. The rest are for you, Dandelion."

17

"Cooee!"

A knock on the door tossed Finella from her sleep. She turned her feet for the floor and hit wall. Where was she? She turned the other way, and tripped over her shoes.

"Coming," she shuffled to the door and blinked at the figure standing there, a wicker basket on her hip. "Mrs. Lawson?"

"Let me in, girl. Rain's let up but my core is ice frozen."

Finella swung the door open. "What a surprise."

"For you, or me?" The older woman stomped her feet and shook her shoes clean. "What happened out here? Did you people have a sand storm?" She took in the room. "Or should I ask about in here first?"

Clothed yet disheveled Finella knew her hair hung round her shoulders in its usual morning mess and a quick glance of the room told the same story.

Mrs. Lawson's widening eyes roamed from one unmade bed to the other, stripped of all its bedding. It didn't get any better at the table, with its tangle of half dried clothes. Above the fire, a rope sagged with Shadrach's shirts and trousers.

Mrs. Lawson bent at the waist. "And what have we here?"

Naked to the chest, Shadrach lay in a twist of quilts right where Finella had left him, on his back beside the fire.

Or what should've been a fire, had Finella not overslept. She died a little death to see what surrounded her in the cold light of a new day.

Mrs. Lawson tilted her head and shoulders to peer at Finella. "I'm sorely interested to hear what's going on at my feet here, but first, I want to know where Molly might be."

Molly?

Finella spun back to Shadrach. Molly's blanket lay wrapped around his bare feet.

"She was right here, all night." Finella's heartbeat roared in her ears. She searched the room in vain.

If Molly were not asleep beside her brother, where was she? She sidestepped Mrs. Lawson and opened the door.

"Molly," she yelled into the morning mist. "Molly!"

She stumbled back in for her shoes.

Shadrach sat up and rubbed his eyes.

"Um…" he looked from one woman to the other before his eyes rolled back like one not meant to be awake from whatever malady had caught him. "What…?"

"If you're not fully dressed, my boy, you'd best stay put." Braver than Finella, Mrs. Lawson spoke first. "Looks like our Molly's gone for a morning stroll, if I'm not mistaken."

Shadrach's eyes flew open and shot blistering inquiry at Finella.

She fumbled with her laces. "Molly was right here." *Of all days to sneak out.*

She grabbed her shawl, as well as Molly's, and ran for the skillion.

Shells snapped under her feet, breaking into smaller pieces on her way across the yard to Shadrach's door. She flung it open, hoping the girl would be asleep on his pallet or busy nosing around.

Nothing.

The cold room offered boxes and the unmade mess of Shadrach's bed.

She ran to the outhouse, kicking the door open with ease.

Empty.

"Molly. Where are you? Do you hear me?" She pushed her voice to its limits. "Molly!"

She followed the new gritty path through long grass to the hen house. But only chickens squawked and peered at her for scraps.

Where else then? Puffing, she ran past the house and beyond. She'd never been this far before. A deep puddle had separated the house from the barn since the day she'd arrived.

But today, a long stretch of broken shells fanned out from where she stood, all the way to the barn door. Tiny shards stuck to her shoes, but not once had she stepped in mud in her search of the outbuildings.

The barn door opened and Molly tiptoed out, the end of her messy braid in her mouth. She clutched the front of her dress, bulging with what Finella imagined a generous helping of shells.

"Didn't you hear me?" Finella doubled over for breath.

"Shad said they're for me. The shells. Look." Hands already occupied with her loot, Molly pointed with her toe. "They're everywhere."

Newly laid tracks glistened like foam washed up from the sea. As if woven through, seaweed and sand made up the other elements of the tracks, but it was, in essence, a walkway of shells, designed to link every door on every building of Shadrach's farm.

No thin smattering, sprinkled in haphazard fashion. These paths lay thick and wide. The puddles filled, the long slip marks completely erased. Shadrach must have worked for days collecting all this. Had he left even one shell on the beach?

"I went all over," Molly marveled. "The outhouse, then the hens. I found a purple one there." She rummaged in her stash and held up a scrolled shell with mitered point. "Then I came here, but only Old Lou's in the barn."

Finella draped her with a shawl.

"You went too far, Molly. Without proper clothes and without permission. And you mustn't suck your hair." She looped a finger at her cheek and gently pulled the hair loose.

"I played a game, to stay on the river of shells. Look," she raised her shoe. "See, no mud. I didn't slip."

Nor had Finella.

At least her foot hadn't.

She pressed her hand to her heart. "Well, let's follow your river back to the house, shall we? We have a patient and a visitor waiting, and I don't think either are happy with me."

∽

"Are you telling me you carted all this from Rhyll, in the rain, yourself?"

Hands on hips Mrs. Lawson stood with her back to him and looked across the yard.

"I did." Shadrach buttoned his shirt. The warm serge felt good against his chest. He'd have to hunt for long johns later. He grabbed a pair of trousers from where they hung and fumbled his way in.

"And you spread it all the way up the hill, and down past the outhouse?" She turned to pierce him with a look reserved for the worst larrikins she caught messing with the church bell. "How many trips did that take?"

"I... don't remember, twenty, maybe thirty."

"Thirty? No wonder you nearly did yourself in." Her voice softened a little.

Shadrach wasn't convinced he was altogether in the clear, yet. Climbing into his clothes was about all he could manage. A dizzy head forced him to slump in the nearest chair and he wiped a line of perspiration from his forehead. He needed to look for Molly.

"And all to keep Finella here?" Mrs. Lawson shook her head. "You've lost your mind. Or something."

He didn't like her looking at him. She was too good at extracting secrets he didn't know he had.

He shrugged. "I had a shell stack ready to burn. Rains kept me from lighting it. I got an idea after she fell, that's all."

"That's all?" She echoed his words. "That's why you're slumped here, all hollow eyed? That's more than an idea, my lad. That's desperation." She peered at him and gasped. "You love her. That's why you did this. Don't deny it, there's a thousand muddy shells out there singing your affections."

Shadrach closed his eyes and wished the woman would back out the door and leave him to sort it out. He didn't need her voicing the tremble of his heart.

"I'll talk with Finella when she's ready to hear it. For now, she needs to learn to trust me."

The old woman smiled and tapped the table with her palm in one triumphant slap. "I had my doubts you were listening when I planted the seeds for this. But now I see some of my words fell where I intended."

He shook his head at her in what he hoped looked like admonition, but let a slight smile follow in reward. If anyone was to blame, it was Finella.

For how she made him feel, and for the things he did to show her.

"*You,* will keep out of it." He tried to stand and she pinned him down with a gentle prod to the shoulder.

"You're not fit for outside today, Shad."

"But, Molly?"

"Molly is right here."

His neck ached to twist around and he let his eyelids close for a moment, relieved to hear Finella's voice at the door.

"Brother, don't be cross." Molly knelt beside him, her face split by a huge grin. "I didn't run away. I looked at the long, long shells." She made a snaking motion with her hand.

Her delight did nothing to stop the steady throb in the base of his neck, but it felt good to hold her hand.

Thank God, she hadn't gone far. It killed him to move but he had to look at Finella. To know what she thought about the yard.

But Finella busied herself at the fire. "We've had a rough night, Mrs. Lawson, and you've found us somewhat unprepared for company."

Shadrach wasn't fooled by her good manners. A tremor in her hand gave her away. Not one for disorder, a surprise visitor may have rattled her, but add a lost girl and sick farmer to the mix, and she'd be close to tipping over.

Finella brushed against his leg to reach for the mattress.

Mrs. Lawson grabbed the other end. "There's nothing here Molly and I can't fix. We'll straighten the beds. Finella, you get the breakfast. When everyone's been watered and fed you can tell me why you're planning on leaving, while this foolish man courts death to make you stay."

Finella turned to Shadrach. "You told her I'm leaving?" Deep pink spots freckled her face.

"Finella's leaving?" Molly frowned at him.

"No." Shadrach patted Molly's hand. "Well, I don't know, but..." he looked from Finella to Molly and then Mrs. Lawson. They all stood there, looming, demanding. Mrs. Lawson cocked her head in Finella's direction and urged him on.

Only, he couldn't remember what it was he had to say. Or do.

He didn't know how a low mist rolled in from outside or how the room swayed and lapped around him. He only feared what might be said over his head when his chin came to rest on Molly, only a moment before he sank to the floor.

∽

"I've seen foolishness before, but nothing equals this." Mrs. Lawson backed into the skillion, and Finella and Molly followed. Between them they carried Shadrach to his bed.

"Fevers and such come and go without much help. But when a man's completely spent, dragging the ocean floor across the entire island," they lowered him onto the pallet, "that's crazier than howling at the moon."

No one needed to tell Finella.

There'd been no howling. But it felt like the moon had rolled out of the sky and now sat on her chest.

Molly lay on the pallet beside him. "Wake up, Brother."

"He will, Pet. He's tired and poorly from working in all that rain. You be a good sister now and watch over him. If he starts to burn, you call Finella." She looked the room over. "Won't overheat in here in a hurry. If he's covered and looked in on, he'll pull through soon enough."

She gathered her skirt and sidestepped the patient and his companion on the floor. "Finella? You and I have some visiting to do by the fire."

∽

"There's no crime in changing your mind. You're as free as I am to come and go from here. I'll take you back myself if you desire, this very afternoon when Mr. Lawson collects me." Mrs. Lawson sliced a loaf of her bread into thick chunks at Shadrach's table. "Seems mean spirited to leave now, though. When both of them need you."

Finella leaned her elbow on the table and pressed her knuckles to her mouth. Not much made perfect sense anymore. Not since the day when he brushed her lip with his thumb. She'd tried to shake the thought from her mind, erase the treacherous tingle she still felt there. But it lingered. Blossom heavy. Like a balm.

"I promised to look after Molly until my aunt arrives. And I can do that in Melbourne as easily as I can here, maybe even better. I can find work, for both of us."

"And why is here so bad?"

"Here… it's always wet and outside there's…," Finella stopped. Even with the rain, her excuse had been dealt with by Shadrach. Washed away by his labors.

"He's paid you a great compliment. Don't be afraid to accept it for what it is. I don't know another man who would fight so hard for the girl he loves."

Finella's pulse tripped and quickened. "Do you mean Molly?"

"No doubting he loves Molly. But she's only some of what he's fighting for." Mrs. Lawson pushed the plate of bread towards Finella. "I saw it in his face the minute you walked into the house today. Sometimes… men don't know how we'll take their words. They stumble over them in their own minds and wrestle with what they can't say. It's much easier to fill a barrow and push it in the rain. He's laid the path for you, Finella. Question is, will you follow it or go your own way?"

"Am I meant to follow a path simply because a man lays it down and dares me to?"

"Didn't you follow a path when your father set one down? Didn't he chart a course long before you could object?"

"I trusted my Father."

"And now it's time to trust yourself. Shadrach's an honorable man. There's no way I would've allowed you to come out here in the bush with him if I doubted that. Remember, I knew the man you were going to marry. Shadrach is no less worthy."

Finella closed her eyes. "What would George make of all this? Isn't it a great wickedness, with my own fiancé in the ground such a short time, to even entertain thoughts, of..." Her words jammed together.

"George had a servant's heart, Finella. I see that in you, too. Wouldn't he tell you to search your own heart for the way ahead, if he could?"

Like the dawn already running into day, the blush of promise rose over her.

If she dared, what would she find in the searching of her heart?

Mrs. Lawson smiled, as if she knew the answer. "Heartfelt gratitude unlocks the goodness of life, my girl. Love, is the key."

18

Shadrach rests for a second full day. The rest of the weary. No longer tossed by fever, it's now the replenishment of strength his body craves.

And so he sleeps, with Molly at his side in the skillion. I have no fear she will wander. She could not be more attached if I employed his rope to keep her there.

The rain hems us in again. Less furious than in days just passed, but equally determined. It seeps from heaven, everyday. Floods his crops and trees, and turns tender green shoots into emerald leaves. The rain barrels overflow and trickle into streams which find the sea.

And here underfoot, we tread on broken cuttlefish. On cockleshells and mother of pearl and other extravagant gifts, for which I have not yet thanked the giver. Instead, I watch as he pays the price for his extravagance.

"You look like the Queen of Sheba." Finella teased.

With her back against the open skillion doorframe, Molly reposed across a threshold of rolled blankets like a blissful regent. Feet up against the jamb, she picked from shells nearest the doorway, scooped handfuls into the length of her apron and examined her favorites in the welcome sunlight.

Finella sat against the outside wall on a chair. She had to jiggle its legs into the ground under the path of shells to set it straight, but when she did, it was the perfect place to sit and trim her hair. She untangled its knots, and exchanged her brush for scissors.

Short snips dealt with any split ends, and a breath of wind blew the wisps away. They danced across the yard and disappeared.

"I think this is the first day since I've been here, we've had such a warm afternoon. I could get used to this." She stretched her legs and crossed them at the ankles. Sunshine splashed off the shell path and warmed her from her scalp down to the toes she wriggled in her shoes. Clean shoes. If she didn't count the crushed shell fragments on her soles.

"Look at this one." Molly held her palm to Finella. "There's a rainbow inside."

"That's mother of pearl. What are you going to do with them all? Your collection's outgrown your tins."

Molly shrugged. "I just like to have them. They're pretty."

"Not as pretty as you." A raspy voice from the skillion joined their conversation.

"Brother!" Molly tumbled from the door in a spill of skirt and shoes. "Why did you sleep so long?" She crawled to him faster than Finella could stand up and lean into the doorway.

She poked her head in, not surprised to see Molly draped across her brother.

"I slept so long because I knew when I woke up, I'd get a sweet *good morning* from you." A weak smile lit the face they'd watched twist and turn for days.

"Silly. It's not morning. It's afternoon."

"It is? I slept all day?"

"All day and all night. And all day and all night." Molly counted using her thumb and three fingers.

"That long?" He scratched his chin. "Really?" He looked around the room to where a jug of water rested on a crate near his feet. He peered at the ceiling and then turned to the doorway. He squinted and blinked at Finella.

She remained in the doorway, rooted to the spot by the goosewing that banged in her chest. "Welcome back. You left us there for a few days."

"So I'm told." He coughed, and Molly sat up to pour him a drink. A cover of bristles darkened his face and a pillow crease marked his neck.

Finella had watched that same spot on his neck for days. Watched it pulse while he slept. She couldn't do that anymore, not with him staring back at her as if he knew all along.

"I'm glad you two were here to look after me." He took a long gulp but kept his eyes on Finella.

"And look, Shad." Molly pointed to the door. "There's sun today. No rain."

"So I see, Miss Molly." Stuck on Finella, his gaze pushed. Like a finger on a day old bruise.

"Does your head hurt?" Finella stepped closer, dropping the scissors into her pocket.

"I could do with some of that damper of yours, Finella."

A tremor caught in her throat. He did it to her every time he said her name. Spoke it like a question. Like a hook that dangled between them.

"There's damper and soup and Mrs. Lawson's scones." Eager to give him anything they had, Molly made a list. "And tea."

"Mrs. Lawson was here?"

"Don't you remember?" Molly scrunched her nose at him. "She

helped us carry you. She left after Finella promised to stay."

Shadrach stood. He arched his back and rolled his shoulders. And came to life right there where Finella had prayed he would.

"Finella said that, did she? Promised she'd stay?"

He looked at her as if he'd woken with the sparks of life in his possession. He may as well have gathered her by the shirtwaist and nicked the rib under her skin with something beautifully dangerous she hadn't felt before.

She ignored the sensation but it trembled inside her with a will all its own. Half fear, half delight, she juggled them both.

"Come along." If she weren't careful Molly would fill his head with all manner of nonsense. "Come, sit outside for a spell."

He took over Finella's vacated seat. Eyes closed, he sighed. "With all this sun, a fellow would think he'd died and woken up in heaven."

Molly united her apron. "Want me to get you a scone? They were good. We saved one."

He opened an eye. "Only one? Poor old Shadrach, sleeping off a fever and nightmares. And you only save me one?"

"We…" Molly didn't really have an answer. She shrugged and looked to Finella.

"What she means is, we needed to keep our strength up. So, we ate them all. Except the one we saved for you." Finella smiled.

Satisfied, Molly nodded, and ran across the new shell path to the house. Finella watched her every step. Watched the door bang behind her. Studied the shingles on the roof for longer than necessary.

When she looked back at Shadrach, he'd opened both eyes. They rested on her face and followed strands of her hair where the wind teased it from her shoulders.

She had to say it. Couldn't keep it unsaid any longer. She crouched beside him, balanced on the balls of her feet and gripped the leg of his chair.

"You could have died." She whispered, hoping Molly would not bound out of the house too soon.

"And you, look so good with the sun in your hair."

"Shadrach." She took a deep breath. "Listen. I'm trying to tell you something."

"Tell me."

He crooked a finger around her freshly trimmed hair and twisted.

"You worked until you collapsed. Completely. Do you know how dangerous that was? What would Molly have done if I were not here?"

"But you are here." He wound his finger a little more and drew her in. "So, I guess it was worth it."

Finella's legs trembled. She grasped his trouser cuff to keep from overbalancing.

"What I'm trying to tell you is, this…" she looked over his new paths, so much more than a gentleman's coat to soak up a puddle. "I never expected this. It's so, it's such—"

One more corkscrew turn and he brought her forehead to his.

Her breath snatched and she pushed against his knee, ever so lightly with her fingertips and backed away. "Thank you, Shadrach. You more than made the courtyard safe. You made it a place Molly will never tire of exploring."

He let go of her hair, but his face didn't change expression. His eyelids lowered. A beat slammed in the hollow of his neck, and she couldn't tell which ran faster. Her pulse or his.

Molly returned, tin plate in hand with the prized scone. Broken in two she'd crowned it with more plum jam than a scone ever needed. Her lips glistened with signs of the same treatment.

"Mmm…" Shadrach dipped into the ruby pool and licked his fingers. "I could get used to this. Eating outside, with the sun on my face."

"Just like Finella." Molly dragged her blanket and set it down beside him. "She said the same. In the sun."

Lifting her head to the sky, Molly closed her eyes and flung her arms wide. "I could get used to this. You said it, Finella."

"I never opened my arms like that. I sat perfectly still with my hands in my lap and held onto my scissors." Finella stood and straightened her back.

"Perhaps you should try opening your arms, someday." Shadrach wiped his mouth with the back of his hand, winked, stretched his arms and locked them behind his head. "You should try lots of new things, Finella. You never know what you might like."

She shook her head, afraid her blooming smile would match his if she were not Aunt-Sarah-careful.

But she'd all but given up that kind of careful, hadn't she?

And so, her smile took root.

~

"Is Elijah Moore our new preacher?"

Shadrach tightened the reigns on Old Lou who carried them away from the little white church to the soft track home.

"No, Molly. He's a visiting reader. From Melbourne. Until we find a preacher of our own."

"Good." Molly sounded satisfied. She wriggled on the wagon seat between him and Finella. "He talks like his name. More and more."

Shadrach laughed. "Perhaps you would like a new preacher with the name John Little-John or John Quick-Sticks?"

"Quick-Sticks." Molly clapped. "Can we get him?" He leaned into his sister, glad to make her laugh in the dappled sun under a canopy of blue gums.

"We should never talk about God's servant like that." Finella ducked an overhanging tree branch, but he saw her smile. "Mr.

Moore spoke very well."

"Have you heard his wife? No wonder the poor chap talked without taking breath. Probably never gets a chance to utter more than three words at home before Mrs. Moore'n'Moore takes over." Shadrach nudged Molly for more giggles.

It felt good to be out. After weeks of being shut in by rains, a trip to church buoyed his spirits.

Even Molly's altered Sunday clothes didn't bother him so much. While still not impressed with her curled hair, he did give in and allow some fussing. It was the least he could do for the pair after their days of caring for him. But he did prefer Molly's hair braided.

Finella's he liked anyway she thought to fix it. Even better unfixed.

"Well, I have news regarding the position of preacher." Finella interrupted his thoughts with melancholy voice. "As it turns out, Mr. Spencer pulled me aside this morning and told me there's a young preacher from Sydney who's applied for the position. He wanted me to be one of the first to know." Her words faded.

Shadrach looked at her over Molly's runaway curls. "He did?"

Mr. Spencer normally slaughtered meat in his butchery, but today the chairman of the church board offered a juicier morsel to chew on.

"He did. He said the church elders received a letter and they're keen to meet with this candidate. Apparently his references have impressed already."

Shadrach's jaw tightened as if it had a will of its own. "Does he have a family?"

"Mr. Spencer didn't say."

He thought of all her boxes. Unpacked and waiting a suitable home, and the empty church house she thought would be hers.

That's all he needed. One suitable preacher had almost married her, and that would have been fine with him. He smacked Old Lou from her meandering with a smart flick. But not anymore. And not while he could do something about it.

19

"We have too many eggs." Finella cradled the day's offerings. "Let's make some batter puffs."

Molly didn't budge from the bed where she sat sorting shells. She divided them into color groupings, and the blanket sparkled with blue mussels, sandy colored cockles, and her most precious, a line of delicate sage and pink sea urchin shells.

"Come see how I cook them, Molly. It's not hard at all. Have you eaten batter puffs before?"

The young girl shook her head. Remnants of yesterday's church curls flopped against her shoulders with each shake.

"If you love jam, this is what you need to mop it up."

Molly's legs slid to the floor at the promise of jam.

Finella kept her smile in check. She placed a pan over the fire with a measure of water and butter.

"Why don't you stir this with my wooden spoon while I get the flour?"

Molly pressed her lips together and turned her head away.

"All you have to do is stir." Finella dangled the spoon over the pan.

"I like to wash."

Finella dipped the spoon into the frothing mixture. "Yes, and it's a sterling job you do at the basin. How about I lift this from the fire, and you can stir it over here?"

Finella swung the heavy pan to a small trivet on the table. Closer than she thought, her knee bumped the table leg, and the three eggs she'd set aside rolled toward her. They stopped at the edge of the trivet where Finella labored over it with her pan.

"Oh, oh." No good smashing the eggs, even if there were too many. Finella swung back to the fire.

The weight of the pan dipped and twisted her wrist. Iron clanged against iron. The base of the pan hit the fire cradle with a thud, and scalding butter-water splashed out, onto her apron, her thumb and the fire itself.

"Ouch." Finella ignored the rude hiss of steam and brought her hand to her lips. This was not how to deliver a cookery lesson.

She dipped a corner of her apron in a jug of water. "I think I may have shown you how it's not done, Molly." She wrapped the red skin with the cold hem.

But Molly was not even watching.

She huddled between their two beds, shoulders trembling, arms wrapped around her knees.

"Molly?" A jolt, like the stab of a hot poker pushed Finella to reach her. "Did the boiling water splash you, too?"

The girl rocked from side to side, her eyes shut tight.

"I'm sorry I frightened you with the pan." Finella pulled her close. "Look, my hand burned a little, but I've dabbed a wet cloth on it. Please don't be afraid anymore."

Molly rocked faster. She hummed a soft wail, wordless and mournful and no amount of coaxing prized her from her spot.

Eyes scrunched, she sat on the dirt floor and rocked until the light faded, and Finella's legs cramped from sitting beside her on the cold clay.

There would be no batter balls today. Shadrach would have to contend with a hasty supper of eggs and bacon and perhaps, Finella prayed, console poor Molly from whatever tipped her into quiet agony.

Molly refused to eat at the table.

Finella passed Shadrach a plate of toasted bread and wondered how he could squeeze into such a tiny corner with Molly.

But only for a moment.

Either one of them would crimple and pucker anywhere they had to, to comfort their girl. Shadrach folded his legs and shared the small space beside Molly, who sipped on a mug of tea between gulping hiccups.

When she was done, Finella helped her into her nightdress and tucked her in with a quick prayer. Only then did they sit at the table for their own meal.

Finella's stomach had little room for food. She'd even forgotten to throw a cloth over the table. She passed Shadrach his food.

Weariness etched his face in shadowed lines. "Some days she does so well, I forget what she's been through. Then she has these moments, where she slips into her own world." He twisted his neck to look at her where she slept. "She may not even remember this in the morning."

Finella hardly bothered with her plate. Instead, like Molly, she sipped on sweet hot tea.

"I shouldn't have pushed her. She was happy with her shells."

"Don't blame yourself. You weren't to know."

"I want to know. So I don't tip her over like that again."

He pushed his plate aside and laid his fists on the table. They flexed and relaxed a few times before he eventually left them as fists.

"She was only four. We lived on the Ballarat goldfields, then. If you think this place is bad, you should have seen that tent city."

He shook his head, and Finella's mouth dried at the mention of Ballarat. The infamous gold town where those who lusted for gold were often sent home empty handed, lusting for more.

"Our dad had been gone for a few months. We had no idea where he disappeared to most times. He left Mum with just enough gold dust to feed us on next to nothing 'til he turned up again. When he felt like it. We always hoped he'd arrive with a sack full of nuggets to buy us real food. But he never did."

He pulled his tea closer. Finella didn't dare imagine Shadrach as a hungry boy. The grown man, broad shouldered and long limbed had already hollowed something out of her. He wrapped his palms around the mug and she concentrated on his words, wishing she could ask questions of her own.

"One night, our father came back full of drunken stories. His mates knew of a lucky strike further north. Wanted us to pick up pegs and move off. Again. My mother'd heard it a hundred times before. But, she'd buried my brother, Daniel, in Ballarat and she wasn't budging, not for any whisper of gold."

"Did your father get mad?"

"He yelled and kicked at the floor 'til he choked on the dust. Said we'd go if he had to yank her hair and drag her all the way."

He looked into his mug.

Icy shivers crawled over Finella's skin. What kind of monster had they lived with?

"You have to understand, my dad was always trying to outrun his own memory. I once heard him tell another miner he'd been transported from England at seventeen for larceny. That's the day I learned for sure he'd been a convict."

Shadrach's father? A convict? She cupped her elbows but no matter how she folded her body, she couldn't escape the cold.

Shadrach stared into his mug. "Dad promised fineries we never saw. A real iron bed for Mum. Velvets and laces and other nonsense. He was fixated on a mourning pendant she'd seen once, and wanted something like it, in memory of our Daniel."

His eyes deepened from dark blue to just dark.

"That night, I was still at the table. I had a pocket of beans given to me by Jimmy Narong. He had the best market garden near us. I would count those beans each night and dream about being as far from a goldfield as I could get. Even then, all I wanted was my own farm."

He let the tin cup go and leaned back in his chair. A catch in his breath stopped the flow of words, and he exhaled in one long deliberate breath.

"It was late and Molly'd been asleep for hours. Dad woke her with his foul screaming and she started to cry. She wasn't used to seeing him. Didn't trust him, I guess. Who could blame her? Each time he opened his mouth, the place shook like a wind ripping at the canvas roof. When Molly got out of bed, he…"

Shadrach grazed the edge of his chin.

"He'd roughed us up with shoving before, but this night something else got hold of him."

He gripped the edge of the table. "Two wooden cross beams held our tent up. We used them for shelving. Gold panning equipment, baskets, lengths of wood for mine shafts. Dad wanted to know why no one listened to him. Only his mates were good enough 'cause they all stuck together. He was so angry, he grabbed a poker and pushed the kettle into the fire. Before we could work out where the steam and hissing came from, he scraped the poker across the table, right under my nose."

Finella sucked in her breath. She didn't want to hear what came next, but Shadrach held the corner of the table like a drowning man, and she wouldn't let him sink in the memory without her.

"I let my body slide from chair to floor. Landed under the table like a puddle in a mess of beans. If I hadn't, that poker would've wrapped around my head. He was so enraged he'd missed, he must have raised it and swiped at the rafter because next I knew, everything from the beams above crashed around our heads with a roar I've never heard since. Shelves fell, tins rattled into every corner. By the time Dad dragged me out by the elbow, Mum was crying and Molly was bleeding."

Finella covered her mouth with both hands. The start of tears filled Shadrach's eyes but he held them off. Like anyone who'd been thrown around from an early age, he probably kept his crying for when no one could see him. She hardly knew who she hurt for the most. The mother, young Molly, or Shadrach, still shattered by the events of a night so long ago.

"Did he strike Molly, too?"

"No, an empty vinegar flagon fell and shattered all over Mum's shoulder but Molly took the brunt of it. Split her head open from temple to ear."

Finella flinched as if it happened right before her eyes.

"Oh, Molly," she whispered into her fingers.

"I thought he'd killed her." Shadrach toyed with his cup, twisting it one way, then the other. "Don't remember who came first, but someone helped us bandage Molly's head and clean up all the blood. A mate of Dad's took him away to simmer down and by the time the troopers got there, Mum had little to say. It had all been an accident..." He shrugged and tapped against the side of his cup with his thumbnail.

Finella waited for him to continue. Could her words ever soothe the ache?

"Soon enough, folks came with medicine and food. When Molly

finally woke up, she didn't speak. For weeks. Just sat there, following us with her eyes. And she never came near the fire."

"What happened to your father?" Sickened, Finella needed to hear he'd been thrown into the foulest jail.

"He disappeared. Turned up four years later. By then Mum was working in a laundry in Ballarat. The gold boom had fizzled and only the big mining companies were striking it lucky. And Dad knew it. He'd changed. He looked harder, if possible. I think he'd had his nose broken in a fight. I couldn't stand the sight of him and I left for Melbourne soon as I could."

"How old were you?" Questions tore at Finella.

"Eighteen. I'd worked odd jobs for the boarding house owner where we lived 'til I found work with a carpenter. But what I really wanted was my own farm. I saw a job in the newspaper for farm hands on Churchill Island and next I knew I was shoveling manure with two other lads. Made my way here two years later."

"What about Molly?" Finella quaked to think of her little friend, broken and afraid.

"She didn't talk for a full year. Then one day in her sleep she called for Mum. Just like that. Next morning, she said 'hungry.' After that, it was small words. One by one. Then short sentences. But she never went to lessons. Never really grew up as we would've liked. Lived in a world of her own, but I think she was always happy alongside Mum. No one troubled her."

He twisted to see her again. Wrapped in innocence and secure in the embrace of her rag doll.

The horror deepened and seized Finella like a bandit by the back of the neck. "What happened to your father?"

Shadrach turned back. "Eventually, he left and never came back. Mum got a letter from one of his mates saying he drowned in a river one night after a fall."

Finella's heart held no sincere condolences. So she left them unsaid. "What happened to his body?"

"Got washed away, I guess. Not that we cried any for him." He dug his nail into a long chip in the table. "This is where the poker hit. Didn't do as much damage as when he lifted it up and brought the roof crashing on our heads." He rubbed the table with his palm. "Mum kept it. All these years. I shipped it here with her things after she died. And every time I look at it, right here," he pressed his fist across the worn top, "I remember it was me who slid under like a snake and let someone else take the brunt of the old man's fury."

Finella reached her hand for his. "Shadrach."

He wouldn't look at her. Kept his eyes on his fist.

"You were just a boy. A terrorized boy who'd already lost a brother. No one could blame you for wanting to protect yourself."

"*I* blame myself." His fist came off the table to pound his chest. "I should've had that poker in my hand long before he did. Should've held it in his face and told him to get out and never come back. Before he ruined my sister's life." Blue eyes flashed at her. Dark and tortured, they barely restrained his torment.

"I should've defended them. Risen. Fought. Instead, I cowered under the table." His words held a resignation she'd heard before.

She reached for the teapot and refilled his mug. The aroma seeped into the room like a salve, gentle and smooth. A small dose for a deep wound.

"My father often said the same. Wished he'd fought harder against my mother's murderer." Finella refilled her own cup. "He died on that ship, holding a grubby newspaper clipping one of the thieves dropped in the scuffle for my mother's brooch. He never let Aunt Sarah burn it. A ragged article, on how getting the right amount of sunlight makes people happier. None of us could ever explain it. A dirty thief held a pure ideal close to his heart. And he still stole away the sweetest light from our lives before Father had the chance to stop him. My father wasn't a child, Shadrach. He was a grown man who lived with regret all his life."

She set the pot down but kept her fingers curled around the handle. "Don't make the same mistake. Be proud. Dwell on how you've taken Molly in. How she's safe in your home, now."

He watched her for a very long time, his face so drained of color she feared he'd slipped into the silent place where Molly found comfort. A place where thoughts and memories burned at their most fierce.

But some color returned on the tail of a smile.

"I always knew I'd end up with her. Didn't realize it would be this soon or how much trouble she'd be." He twisted his lips. "I bet you didn't either."

Finella stirred sugar into her tea. The only real trouble around here was the way he held her with his blue eyes. She set the spoon down. *Think of Molly.*

"I didn't realize she would be so reluctant to cook, but now that I know why, I can work around it."

"How?"

"I'll let her get over her fright, first. She was almost at the fire when I dropped the pan. Deep down, I think she wants to try. We'll work on it together." She sipped her tea, hoping she sounded confident. "By the time I'm ready to leave she'll be stirring the pot like a seasoned cook."

"You don't have to leave us."

Finella blinked hard and searched for the right reply. One they could all live with. "Well, if I don't leave, Molly will never get the chance to do things for herself. That's what you wanted all along wasn't it?" Her voice sounded too cheery. Too much like a strangled attempt at steering this from where it might go.

He ignored her chatter. Pinned her with a look that had nothing to do with Molly. Her heart skipped a row of beats.

He'd already managed to unnerve her with words. Now he came at her with a look, and it snagged.

"Molly's future is not the sum of all things I want." His eyes pleaded with her, and Finella lowered hers to the blue vein in his neck.

"I have to leave. Eventually."

"No. You don't. You can stay here with us. With me."

She stood to let her lungs take in air. Turned to the fire to do something. Anything, but see the way he looked at her. She put her hands on her hips and looked at the flames where they played.

The scrape of his chair charged the air with a crackle sharper than the fire's spit. Heat from the hearth stole wisps of her hair and blew them against her neck.

"I don't want you to leave." His voice came in a whisper from behind her. Soft and hard all at once, it grazed her skin, carried on a breath so close it rivaled the sparks of the fire.

A gentle tug of her hair made her shiver. She knew not to turn around. He stood right at her shoulder. Like the day she'd thanked him for the shells, he wound his finger through a fallen curl.

He did not insist.

Although she imagined he loomed closer than he should, his reach for her served more to fix her course, until she could not resist the pull. A gentle sweep she wanted, and could not fight.

First her chin tilted, then her cheek.

"Finella…"

She allowed her neck and shoulders to turn, carried by the coaxing of his voice until she faced him and he released her hair to rest his hands on her shoulders.

"I want you to stay. You don't have to leave." He repeated his words and she felt them, each one, land on her heart like drops of rain on his roof.

"I do. I'm only here until Aunt Sarah comes, and then I—"

He cupped her chin and raised it up. "You don't need Aunt Sarah. You're not Molly. You can decide for yourself where you belong."

She couldn't look away. Her heart bounced against her ribs to a beat stronger than any fear she'd known. And more compelling.

"Let me help you work it out." He leaned in, unhinging his eyes from hers. They roamed her face, and settled on her mouth, followed in a heartbeat by his lips.

Warm and soft, he tasted like sweet tea and Finella closed her eyes, overwhelmed by the scent of earth and smoke. Lost in a sensation too frightening to be good, too good to be real.

His thumb caressed her cheek and when she pulled away, he slid his hand behind her neck and drew her back.

She wasn't sure the wildness in her heart could take another kiss.

"Are you telling secrets?" Molly stared up at them.

Blush swept over blush and Shadrach released his hold.

"Never you mind, Miss Molly. What are *you* doing?" He guided her back to bed.

"I wanted to hear the secret, too."

"There is no secret. Other than if you don't sleep you'll be all grizzles in the morning." He gathered her quilt and held it up. "Hop in."

"Is it the secret about Finella? The one, you promised George?"

"I told you. There's no secret. Now, sleep."

"Night, Brother." Still puffy, her eyes held affection for Shadrach, but he patted her cheek and she let her lids slip back to sleep.

He stepped away from the bed.

"Pity she woke." A smile played with the corner of his mouth.

Finella's blush simmered. "What secret about George? And me?"

"About you? No, She was... talking in her sleep." He stumbled over his words and eyes which only a heartbeat ago sought hers, now studied the door.

He held the latch. "Better watch it. Molly might have tales to tell at breakfast." He opened the door and chuckled, but the smile wasn't fixed to his face anymore. He lingered, his hand on the rope.

"You shouldn't have done that." Finella spoke first.

"Done what?"

"Kissed me. There's no place for that Shadrach. We were talking about Molly, and her welfare."

"No, we'd moved on, to yours. And pretty soon," he snuck a look at Molly and lowered his voice, "I'm going to make sure we get to *talk* about it some more."

His whispered promise sent a thrill into Finella's belly. It toppled there alongside the flicker of uneasiness Molly had thrown into the mix. Confused, she turned to object, but the last word belonged to Shadrach.

"Goodnight, Dandelion."

20

November 3

One violet noonflower and one cape dandelion is all I've added to these pages. My feeble attempt to make an Everlasting. It hardly rivals Aunt Sarah's.

I don't dare read the words already here. I dare not look back. And even looking forward causes something to churn inside me, now.

My heart aches for this motherless girl, lost in a world I cannot reach. She is there. And she is not. I can help her. And I cannot. The day will come when I will be forced to leave her to her own devices and I fear for her then.

Once, the promise of an unknown name, a deep-rooted misery, kept me under its thumb. But Shadrach Jones has snatched a portion of my heart, and I add to my fears a new companion.

My own sorrow at leaving what has already won me.

I long for russet. The absence of bramble leaves and hawthorn berries reminds me I watch the seasons upside down. Or am I the one displaced? I can hardly tell these days.

Would the Finella who once wrote here, have let the son of a convict steal her heart? Would she have turned for his kiss? Would she have laid aside the dying wish of her mother, the deep-seated desire of her father, their collective search for a name?

What has happened to her?

Instead of autumn, we skid into the last days of spring and with it, a flush of growth; it threatens to overtake my senses. Shadrach's crops beckon in the wind like dancers on a stage.

Molly sits on the edge of his chicory field sorting shells in a tin lid. Behind her the cornflower blue of the chicory crop soaks up the sun.

This hint of blue has fallen on the muddy landscape, as if God himself tipped the sky at my feet. But I am not surprised.

Blue has followed me from the day the sea and clouds delivered me here. Landed me so close to the water's edge I cannot escape it, not even for one day. Deep marine skies hem me in beside waves of turquoise, and even when it all hides beneath midnight blue, I still look into the sapphire eyes of Molly, and Shadrach Jones.

And now, behold a blanket of blue takes hold of the earth, as well. Invites the wren with its puffed chest to pluck and bring gifts to its mate, while I watch, and tremble at the ancient game of courtship before me.

Shadrach whistled a tune he'd not heard before. It came completely out of his own good cheer and he didn't mind it one bit.

He tethered Old Lou outside Trilloe's General Store and Bakery, tapped his breast pocket to make sure his list had not flown away, and bounded inside.

The smell of fresh bread gathered him in, and he drew a deep breath. Not just bread, but something sweet and fruity beckoned from the baker's cart. He made a mental note to find out what before he left.

"Shadrach Jones. We were only now talking about you." Mrs. Trilloe beckoned from behind the counter. She lowered her voice and mumbled to the stranger. "She lives with him and his sister. For now."

A punch to Shadrach's jaw would not have felled him any quicker. Did she think he couldn't hear her? He eyed the stranger.

A tall fair-haired gentleman, neatly dressed in crisp white shirt and rolled sleeves turned to Shadrach. Relief swept over the man's face. He stepped away from the counter and offered his hand, almost too quickly.

It wasn't often Shadrach needed to look up at another man. "Shadrach Jones."

"Goliah Ashe. New preacher."

Already? Weren't there any grey haired preachers out there looking for a church to shepherd?

"Goliah?"

The man laughed. "Most people get stumped by it. I just finished telling Mrs. Trilloe here what I may as well tell you, too."

Mrs. Trilloe nodded. She already knew more about the new preacher than most would for days, and wore the pleasure on her face like a country fair blue ribbon.

"I was one of those big babies. Looked three months old the day I was born. My parents knew little about Bible stories and thought Goliath was a giant hero. So they named me in his honor, not realizing they'd left out a letter. Anyway, here I am, Goliah Ashe, at your service." He bowed a little and shrugged.

Shadrach guessed Goliah Ashe had made peace with his name long ago and wasn't afraid to share the tale. He liked that.

"I guess anyone who's weathered life with a name like Goliah's got a bag full of good sermons. Welcome to Phillip Island. Moved in yet?"

"Just pulled in this morning from Melbourne. Crates are lined up on the verandah at the church house, with more due on the steamer tomorrow, but I thought I'd secure a fresh loaf for my lunch before I did anything else. I imagine with aromas like these you'd sell out before noon. Is that right, Mrs. Trilloe?"

She beamed. "We do most days. Bread's our specialty you know. I'm sure it wouldn't be prideful to say we've the best oven on the island."

"Not prideful at all." Goliah placed his hand on his chest. "If your heart's clean."

Mrs. Trilloe blushed and turned to grab a loaf, leaving Goliah Ashe to raise a conspiratorial brow. Shadrach looked through the shop windows to the twinkle of the sea and chuckled.

Undeterred, the woman kept talking. "I've just been telling our new preacher here about Molly, and in particular dear Miss Mayfield."

Shadrach snapped his head back. *Neither one is your concern.*

"About her terrible loss, and how frustrating her days must be out on a farm when she should be serving beside a preacher. As her father intended."

He tapped his thigh with the rim of his hat and kept his attention on the way she wrapped a length of brown paper around the bread. She handed it to Goliah with a sugary smile.

"A welcome gift. For your first meal here."

"I'm most grateful, Mrs. Trilloe. Batching's not my gifting you know, so any help from a wonderful cook is always appreciated."

"It's a pleasure. I'm sure you'll find the women of the island eager to add to that bread as the days go by. Won't he, Shadrach?" She didn't stop for a response. "Will Mrs. Lawson be working for you, Mr. Ashe? She was our last preacher's housekeeper."

Goliah frowned. "I had a housekeeper, once. On my first placement. Vowed to never find myself at the mercy of a controlling woman again. Know what I mean, Shadrach?"

Shadrach couldn't stop a grin from sneaking onto his face.

"I do."

The preacher tapped his bread. "Mrs. Trilloe, many thanks for the bread." He turned to Shadrach. "I guess I'll see you and your sister, and the famous Miss Mayfield, on Sunday."

He hurried away, leaving a path Shad longed to follow. To catch up to him and tap the good man on the shoulder and tell him not to look forward to anything more than preaching the Word and keeping his eyes to himself.

"Quite the handsome one, isn't he?" Mrs. Trilloe busied herself with rearranging the remaining loaves. "Old enough to command the respect of any congregation, but still young enough to make the perfect catch for any refined young woman, wouldn't you say?"

Shadrach examined the shelf behind her. What would he say? Nothing she poked him for, that's what.

"I'll have a seed cake and a bread loaf, please." He hoped his teeth didn't crumble into his gums with each forced word.

Mrs. Trilloe's eyes remained cold. "Indeed you will." She wrapped the loaf and cake into a bundle and set them aside. "And if you care to give me your list, I'll fill it for you while Mr. Trilloe gives you a letter."

He fished in his pocket. "A letter came for me?"

She held out her hand and lost no time flattening the list against the counter. "No."

She ran a finger down the paper, and when she made it to the end slapped her palm against the counter and looked up.

"A letter has arrived for Miss Mayfield." She mouthed the words to him as if he were deaf. "From her Aunt Sarah."

He was sure that was none of her business. She turned to reach high on a shelf for a tin of raspberry jam. She'd probably read the letter right through. Steamed the envelope open and sat by the lantern all night to memorize every line and now waited to deliver something he didn't want to know.

She set the tin on the counter with a thud. "Are you going to shadow me, or go get that letter? Unless you want us to speak about Molly working here. Summer's coming and we're bound to get busier with all the guesthouse holiday trade."

He stepped away. "Not talking about Molly with you," he muttered into his collar. How had the day turned grim, after such a sunny start? Goliah Ashe hadn't yet stepped into the pulpit and the storekeeper was plotting to match him with Finella. Plotting a way for Molly to be in need, and him to not meet that need.

He reached the other end of the counter where Jack Trilloe sorted mail.

"She sent ya over, didn't she?" Mr. Trilloe's chin wobbled against his neck in thick folds. "Been bustin' a gut to get ya here, for this." He slapped an envelope into Shadrach's hand. Mr. Trilloe didn't bother with a greeting. He just did as his wife instructed. Shadrach stuffed the letter into the pit of his pocket, wishing he could do the same with Aunt Sarah, meddling storekeepers, and handsome new preachers. He tried to remember only a few short months ago when all he had to think about was his crops and animals and how much rain he might get the next day.

When had it come to this? That his thoughts were for a girl in dark plaits he would always fight for, and a young woman whose lips he wanted to taste again.

So help him God in heaven, he would do what it took to keep them both.

"Jon Tripp's unloaded a market order from Melbourne, yesterday. Steamer's brought in something of yours, too." Mr. Trilloe pointed to a printed sign on the counter. "Oh, and the Egging's coming up. You planning on beating your record from last year?"

Shadrach stared at the paper. The Egging? He'd won the annual egging contest two years in a row, but hadn't given it much thought these last few weeks. Or the order he'd placed with an orchardist in Melbourne.

"That time already?"

Jack laughed. "Every year, my lad. Last week of November. One more week and those bird burrows will be gold mines, waiting for the long arm of anyone game enough to hunt for eggs. I thought you of all people would be dusting off your gear."

Shadrach mulled over his chores. He hadn't forgotten the Egging. He just hadn't realized how fast the month of November raced by. Soon enough it would be Christmas.

"Thanks, Jack. Glad you reminded me. I got lost with my farm work there."

A roar of laughter rocked the room. "Who are ya fooling, Shad? It's not farm work that's got ya all lost. It's ya bleeding heart." Jack slumped onto a chair behind the counter and his thickset frame gave way to waves of laughter and a phlegmy cough.

Shadrach let him chuckle. Let them all snicker and plot. He had plans of his own to make.

"Mrs. Trilloe?" He turned back to her counter. "I need to add to that list.

21

"No more glue." Molly held her hands up and spread each finger wide. "All gone."

Finella tasted the gravy in the stew pot and reached for the saltcellar. "Don't tell me you've already used it up?" She wiped her hands on her apron and looked over the girl's shoulder.

"Molly. This is exquisite." A tingle crept along her arms. On the back of an old postcard, Molly had pieced a delicate flower of tiny shell fragments.

"You have a rare gift, Molly Jones. That is God's honest truth, my girl." She kissed her on the head.

Molly beamed and rubbed at a blob of glue on her chin. "Will Shadrach like it?"

"Like it?" Finella returned to the fire. "He'll swing you round 'til your head spins and insist you make one just like it for him. Because this one," she pointed with her wooden spoon, "stays in here with us."

"But I'll need more paste."

"Indeed, you will. And how might you get some while I keep my eye on our stew?"

The girl shook her head. No answer came from her lips, and Finella guessed one did not enter her head, either. She would have to prod a little harder.

"Why don't you put another cup of flour into the glue pan while I stir the stew? Unless you want to cook while I make the glue."

Molly frowned at such nonsense, and Finella pressed her lips together to smother a smile.

The girl eyed the cup. It sat in the flour sack, its handle angled within her reach. She crooked her finger and scooped out a cup full.

"And now?"

Finella hovered over the well-stirred stew pot.

"Now, add a third of a cup of sugar to the pan."

Molly filled the cup and showed her.

"Less. Take out a spoon full. Now pour water from that jug into the cup until you reach half way."

Molly poked her tongue out and did just that.

"Mix it with the flour. It will be lumpy but your spoon should take care of that."

Molly worked at the lumps until Finella saw the paste form.

"Now, add another full cup of water, all the way to the top. And then one spoon of vinegar and another good stirring."

Molly fetched the vinegar bottle from the shelf. Dribbles landed on the table and her wrist, but she kept her eyes on the task.

"Done."

"Good. Now bring the saucepan to the fire."

Molly dropped her spoon into the pot and backed away. She shook her head. "You do that."

"I can't." Finella turned her giggle to the fire. "I'll help, but you must bring it to me." She peeked over her shoulder.

Molly pincer-gripped the saucepan and extended her arm until the base of the pan neared the flame.

Finella made room. "Set it here. It shouldn't take long. You'll need to stir it or your paste will burn."

Molly scowled, and stirred like a restless boy aiding his mother to wind wool.

Finella took pity on her and rescued both glue and stirrer, and poured the mixture into a basin. She'd secured a precious victory, but some triumphs were best left to glow without too much pressure on the warrior.

"What splendid cooks we are. My stew can sit on a trivet now and your glue needs to cool. Fancy a walk along the road?"

Molly had the door open before Finella could say more.

"Where shall we go?"

"I saw a wild rose for my Everlasting near one of Shadrach's fence posts. Let's go that way."

"Why do you press flowers?" They walked into the sunshine.

"Well, my aunt thought it would be good to look for the beauti-ful things God grows and take a few petals for my book. It's called an Everlasting because when the flowers dry, we can still look at them in the pages, even years later when the ones in the meadows have long gone."

"Is that because you're going to leave?" Sadness framed Molly's face as sure as it did Finella's heart.

"Shadrach and I agreed I would stay until Christmas. Remember, that day on the beach?"

"Where will you go? Does another girl need you?"

No one else needed her.

Of all the people in the world, she could only name one person who truly needed her. No, two. Tears filled her eyes and Finella pushed the thought away.

With each step along Shadrach's red boundary, Finella counted all the reasons her aunt's ship might arrive later than expected. But she would arrive someday, and bring with her every reason Finella could not stay with Shadrach and Molly. Reasons she knew by heart.

She'd been raised to be a preacher's wife.

Matched to a man chosen for her. For a life in service to a congregation, like her mother, whose role had been cut short.

What would Father say if he knew she wrestled with affections for the son of a convict? If only he knew she'd let their search for her mother's assailant dim a little, in the sunlit world she shared with Molly and Shadrach. Finella didn't need to wonder. Soon enough, Aunt Sarah would deliver exactly what her dear Father and Mother would say if they saw the life she contemplated.

They reached the rose, growing wild up a post and through the wire fencing. Tiny pink buds opened to the sun and their fragrance hit Finella with memories of home. Long lost vows she'd made to Father, to help him find the name of the man who robbed him of a wife. To honor her mother's deathbed request.

"Aunt Sarah makes the best rosehip syrup for cordial in late summer." Finella dragged her thoughts from one faded past to another.

"Can we?" Molly pleaded. "Can we make it, too?"

"After watching you cook up that glue, I think you could make anything you put your mind to. It will be a while before there are any rosehips, but we could brew a rose petal tea."

Finella braved the thorns and showed Molly how to twist the roses from where they belonged.

And perhaps, one day, her sweet girl would return to gather rosehips for cordial. When summer had ended...

Shadrach hooked his elbow over the back of the chair. You'd think a fellow could bring a girl a trinket without the kick of two and a half dozen grasshoppers in his stomach. Chatter hummed in the yard, then a crunching of shoes on the shell pathways. And then their voices carried into the house.

"Brother, you're home already?" Molly pouted.

"What kind of a welcome is that?" He frowned back.

"We wanted to make rose tea before you came back."

Finella followed, with the fragrance of summer in her basket and Shadrach guessed in her hair and probably every fold of her dress. "Why don't you show Shadrach what you made today?"

Molly scrambled for the hearth.

"I made a flower. And I made a pan of flour paste. On the fire." She beamed and handed him a card.

Shadrach stood and tilted the rosette of tiny pink shells.

"You made this?" His heart swelled.

"And this." She grabbed a basin from the table. "On the fire." Her eyes twinkled, and she waved it under his nose. Vinegar wafted from the mix.

He sought Finella. *The fire?*

"It's true. She stirred that pan right over the flames. Measured all the ingredients herself." Finella winked and his gut double fish-flipped.

"Then you most certainly deserve your reward." He pointed to his packages on the bed.

Molly wasted no time and peeled at a paper parcel to reveal two black shoes. She held them up to the light and touched every loop and line of stitching. "For me?" She asked, and he grinned at her delight. But it was Finella's reaction he longed to see.

"New shoes for church and old ones for everyday." *That's a start, right, Dandelion?*

But Finella wouldn't look at him. She gathered Molly's discarded paper, her eyes no longer bright. What happened to the winks they'd just shared?

"I know how well you look after your shoes, Finella. I figured you'd like something… different. Go on. Open it." His fingers itched to nudge her closer. Instead, he tapped his knuckles together until Finella unwrapped the pieces of her gift.

"So pretty." Molly peered at the four glasses and jug.

"It's a lemonade set." But the frosted grape vine detail didn't thrill him as it had in the store. Not with Finella setting the glasses down on the table as if they belonged to someone else. "I know we make do just fine with our tin cups, but I saw them and…" He shrugged, confused as to why he'd bought it in the first place, now. Did he really think he would win Finella over with trinkets, the way he did with Molly?

Still, he'd wanted to bring her something beautiful. Give her more than what he'd offered so far, which wasn't much and not likely to be more than trinkets and saplings for a while to come.

"We're going to make rosehip cordial. To drink, after the flowers are gone. Can we drink it from these glasses?" Molly pretended to sip.

Finella traced the pattern on the jug. Her fingers trembled and she set it down.

"What's wrong? Don't you like it?"

She pushed away from the table and pressed her hands to her stomach.

"I like it very much." She whispered. "Perhaps that's what's wrong."

"It is?" What did that mean? He tried to reach for her but she waved him away.

"Don't you see?" Her voice teetered on something raw. Wounded and breathless. "Everywhere I look, something's muddled. It's warmer when it should be cooling down. The stars are in the wrong place. And roses, that should be dead by now, are budding in disregard to everything God intended."

She sidestepped Molly. "And now you're bringing gifts you would normally despise, right into your home like treasures. What am I supposed to think when you turn everything upside down?"

22

Finella raced along the familiar track to the beach. Through reeds and seas bushes, she gulped in air like someone who'd held their breath too long.

The sea lapped at the shore, lazy and still, and she pressed her fists to her side. Nothing ever happened the way she needed it to anymore. Even the water was not churned up today. Where were the frothing waves, the roaring crashes to match her mood?

She dug her nails into her palms. She would not see the rosehips dry. She would not show Molly how to turn them into syrup. She would not pour their drink into beautiful etched glasses which now sat out of place on a scratched and dented table.

Didn't Shadrach see how foolish a lemonade set looked in his mud hut? What place did it have against crude beaten furniture and sapling doors?

Finella quickened her pace until the sweat trickled down her back. Until her sprint lost steam and her legs outran the dismay of not knowing where she belonged.

She sat on a rocky mound exposed by the distant tide. The cry of a gull hovering nearby pierced the air. It too, searched for something but flew away at the sound of voices from the beach track. Shadrach emerged first, with Molly just behind. She plopped onto the sand, but he continued on.

Dread rolled around her chest. Shadrach deserved a proper explanation. But she hardly understood the tricks being played on her heart.

In a few long strides he perched on her rock. Close enough to press the warmth of his arm to hers. Grass and roses mingled with the smell of the sea.

He didn't say a word. Just watched the same patch of sand where Molly played. At their feet a pile of black rocks slumbered in a silent bath. So clear, it would have been easy to think the water was not there at all. Shadrach dipped his hand in and pulled one out, shaking seawater off his fist. He held the rock in the palm of his hand.

"Forget the lemonade set. Let's pretend I never bought it."

"You want to give me a rock, instead?"

"Not any rock. A piece of volcano. Been here for thousands of years but it didn't start off like this."

He reached for her hand and prized her fingers open. The rock tipped into her palm.

"See any edges?"

She did not. It was as smooth as every other round rock at their feet.

"This rock probably started out as jagged as the top of that outcrop behind us. Pointy and sharp, I'd say a pounding wave gave it such a walloping, it broke off and fell into the sea, to be sifted on the ocean floor against all the other rocks."

Finella held the weight between them.

"Point is Finella, you may not think you belong with us, but you have to trust God to show you whether you do or not. This rock fits this beach. Looks just like the others beside it, because it's been shaped that way. By life. By the storms and the crashes and the beating sun, and now it's perfect. And it belongs. It has a purpose and it would not fit anywhere else as well as it does here."

Slow tears fell onto her dress. She hoped they told him what her voice could not.

"We want you here. Molly needs you, and I don't want to imagine life without you. That's what muddled would look like."

Her chest tightened. Still, she said nothing. What could she tell him? That she feared the love for him in her own heart? That she feared Aunt Sarah more?

She wrapped her fingers around the rock. He covered her hand and stroked it with his thumb. A gentle caress, firm enough to let her know he wasn't going anywhere.

"You don't have to answer right away. But you need to understand, even if Molly were a million miles away, I would still want you to stay. I would still want you."

He tilted her chin and brushed his lips across her cheek, through her tears until he touched her mouth with a tenderness she never expected.

"And, if glasses and rocks don't bring a smile to your face I may have one more thing up my coat sleeve."

"What's that?" She dared to breathe the words.

"A letter from your aunt. I dumped it in the skillion when I threw my coat in. Shall we go find it?"

A letter? Word from Aunt Sarah would bring counsel, wouldn't it? Wisdom from a level head. She could only hope for something less crazy than the notions of her wild, wild heart.

⁓

They walked together, like they'd never walked before. Shadrach's arm brushed hers, and every so often he held branches back for her to pass through the gully.

"It's true. What I said about Molly. She needs you now more than anybody, but if my mother walked out of that thicket alive as you and me, wanting Molly back, I'd still plead with you to stay."

Finella breathed in the eucalyptus. It no longer filled her chest as it did in the rain. It washed over her now, through the bush on a wisp of air, still pungent. But no longer heavy. It had become a fragrance to enjoy and she realized it also had become a comfort. Like the steady brush of his sleeve against hers when they ducked the tea trees. Like the tug of the black rock in her pocket.

At the open door of the house, Molly threw off her old shoes.

"Now can I try them on?'"

"Yes, you may." Shadrach called back. "I promised she could walk around in them when we got back."

"Brother, these laces are different." Molly's voice carried through the open door. "Come help."

Shadrach made a face at Finella.

"My coat's on the hook just by the door. Why don't you take a few minutes to read your letter?"

Finella nodded and let him go on. Reading Aunt Sarah's letter would be the closest thing to speaking with a loved one since Father died. She was glad to read in peace.

But the wall in Shadrach's skillion held no coat. Finella searched the floor, and found it right where it must have slipped from the nail. She scooped it into her lap and sat on his pallet.

My dearest Finella,

I could not imagine a letter worse than the one you sent about your father's death at sea.

But I weep with you to read the sorrowful news of Mr. Gleeson's death. My dear girl, I have prayed and agonized over this tragedy for days now, wanting to help you as best I can.

And so I have secured passage on the Golden Empress, Aus-tralia bound. It leaves late next week, God willing with me

aboard. The ticketing agent assures me the vessel will sail into a
southern summer and deliver us early in the New Year.

I anticipate I will not be far off by the time this reaches you,
and I encourage you to hold steadfast the calling shown to you by
your father. There may be no Mr. Gleeson to marry, but there
will be a man worthy of you, someone honest and faithful to
God's word.

Remember the legacy of your dear parents and their shaping
of you for the days ahead. Whatever temporary amusement you
may enjoy at Phillip Island, I am sure will equip you for the life
God has chosen for when we return to England.

My prayers and courage for the days ahead.
Aunt Sarah.

Finella's gentle sobs ruffled the pages, but they didn't go far. Her
tears made sure the letter remained weighed down and fixed to her
hand.

Aunt Sarah was right. Two losses in as many months, and now
two other hearts called her.

And what of the man Aunt Sarah believed she should find? What
had she written? Finella looked for the words. Honest. Faithful.
Devoted to service.

Wasn't that Shadrach? If he wasn't devoted to Molly, then Finella
had never seen true devotion. Was he not honest? Had he ever caused
her to doubt his integrity or roused her suspicion? He hadn't. He'd
told her all there was about his sad childhood, his longsuffering
mother, his often absent and violent father.

He couldn't furnish the answers George might have found for
her, about the thief and his unknown identity. Shadrach's memories
of Ballarat were crowded with the specter of his cruel father, and
Finella wouldn't press him to share more of that misery.

But perhaps Shadrach Jones had something else for Finella. A different kind of freedom. One wrapped in the love only reserved for a man and woman. Could he truly be that man? For her?

She cradled her head and searched for a prayer. How much truly passed from father to son? Dr. Saville implied the children of convicts grew worse than their parents. Was it true? Even Shadrach? Surely not. And certainly not Molly.

Through the open door a gust of wind snuck in, and Aunt Sarah's letter floated away. One page fell at her feet, the other stopped beside the crate Shadrach used for a table. A table where his weathered Bible sat, on top of papers she'd held... in another lifetime?

Her stomach fluttered. Was this the paper Father had given her in a letter set for her eighteenth birthday? With her own words drawn across the page? Had they tumbled out of one of her trunks?

The flutter in her stomach kicked harder. She gulped hard and snatched the book.

Page after page, she pulled out letters she'd sent from her girlhood home to George Gleeson. They pooled in her lap like the loose threads of a long lost diary, creased and well read, and in the possession of a man who had no right to them.

23

"Find your letter?" Shadrach mopped up stew with Trilloe's fresh bread.

"I found it."

Strangled words snapped at his ears, and both he and Molly looked up.

"Aren't you going to eat with us?" He didn't like the way Finella stood there, papers in hand. "That must have been a mighty long letter. You've been gone ages. Did she write you a book?"

"Not exactly. Two pages. Enough to say how sorry she is for the loss of my fiancé, and let me know her arrival date. First week of the New Year."

Finella stood straight as a needle and stared at him. He didn't like it. "Looks like more than two pages you've got there. Looks like—"

Finella pressed a page to the table. "This is my aunt's letter. Page one." She rummaged through her stack. "And this, is page two." It floated onto the first as if it were a feather.

A piece of stew stuck in his throat like a fishbone he'd once almost choked on.

"This page, belongs to another letter. Written to George. A private letter to my dead fiancé."

"Finella," he stood, letting his napkin slip to the floor.

"And this," she rifled through the papers, "also belongs to another letter. The writer is also me. The recipient once again, not you."

"I can explain. Please—"

"And here, we have letter, after letter, oh and look, more letters. All from me to my fiancé. Private words I wrote to him. Not to you." She let them float from her hand until they littered the floor. Some fell under the table and one came close to the fire. He snatched it away and laid it with the others.

"Don't touch my letters." She slammed her hand on top of the pile to match the rise in her voice. "I don't know how you came to steal them, but you had no right to take them. Or read them. You, who have always told us to keep out of your skillion, have the nerve to hide something that is not yours in there?"

"Finella, please sit down. Let me tell you how I got them." He slid a chair out for her.

"I'm not interested in your tales. It's clear you took these from George before I cleared his things. I always thought my letters were among his other papers. I never thought they were stolen."

"They were never stolen. Stop saying that." He fought to keep exasperation from rising.

"What should I say? The letters got up from wherever George kept them and hid themselves in your skillion?"

She pressed trembling hands to her red cheeks. "I can't even re-member what I wrote in half of them. Some were written just after my eighteenth birthday. How could you read them and not know it was wrong?"

"Listen, I'll tell you, but you have to calm down." He patted the chair back. "Will you sit?"

She sank into the seat.

He licked his dry lips. "George gave me your last letter. Do you remember me having it, at Queen's Wharf? I had a photograph of you and your father, too. You know he gave me that letter, and photograph. You believe me about that, yes?"

"Yes." She nodded. "It was a means of identification."

He knelt beside her. "George gave me that photograph, along with *all* your letters. In a bundle. He wanted me to have them. All. Don't shake your head. It's the truth."

"Why would he do that? Why wasn't one letter and photograph enough?" Her eyes demanded the truth he was not prepared to admit. "Shadrach?" Her voice softened. "Tell me."

He looked away from her tears. "George gave them to me so I could learn more about you."

Neither of them spoke.

"Why?" she finally ventured. "I didn't come here for you. I came here to marry George." Wrapped in pain her words came at him like an arrow to a target. Still, he knew *his* words would inflict the worst pain.

"He knew he was dying. He did it to protect you. Thought if someone stepped in to care for you and your father…"

She recoiled. "He knew?" she whispered. "*You* knew he was dying?"

She flattened her hand to her chest. "You all knew?"

"I knew." Molly joined in from her place at the table. She'd long stopped eating. "And Mrs. Lawson. And about the promise to get married."

Finella's face caved. "Married?"

"Molly, hold your tongue." He rolled a look at his sister that would have silenced any fourteen year old. But Molly wasn't looking at him.

"What do you mean…get married?" Finella's angry flush deepened. He wanted to take her hand again, but she twisted them into fists and pressed them to her lips.

"I guess people have inklings when death approaches. George

asked me to care for you. And your father. If anything happened." Shadrach cringed at the awkward way he said it.

"George passed me off to you?" She labored to breathe. "And you… accepted? Just like that?" She leaned as far from him as the chair allowed.

"George was a good friend. He showed me more about God's love than any man ever had. Or probably ever will. He had time for me when others thought little of the poor farm hand with nothing to his name."

"Still, who makes a promise like that?" Her voice quivered. "All these weeks, I thought I was here for Molly. Now you tell me even she knew the real reason. To keep a promise to George?" She shook her head. "Who gives away the girl they were going to marry?"

She stood and searched the room. There was nowhere to hide. For either of them now. She swung back.

"All this time, you've been reading my letters to get to know me better? To find out ways to tip me into a marriage you and George devised while the man fought delirium? Are you as crazy as he?"

He'd heard enough. "What's so crazy about it? You didn't think it was crazy an hour ago when we talked on the beach. What's so crazy about opening your mind and heart to a possibility? Yes, I agreed to help George. Out of loyalty to him. It was crazy. But it isn't anymore. Not to me." He let his words simmer down. "It's some-thing more than crazy, and if you stopped long enough to think about it, you would see the gift George gave us."

She blinked through tears. "I thought you were a man I could trust. Someone who didn't stoop to deceit. I was warned this country echoed with cheaters and thieves. I didn't think you were one of them. But now, I'm not so sure. Not when I discover I was a mere possession. Secretly passed from one man to another."

He wanted to stem her pain but his words failed each time. He reached for her but she pulled away, breathing harder.

"You knew George was dying and kept it from me. And conspired to get me here and somehow, I don't know how exactly, use whatever childish thought I may have expressed in old letters to get into my head and …what?" She pointed to the lemonade set. "Win my heart with trinkets and fancies you detest anyway?"

"Finella. Please, listen." He heard the pleading in his voice, and hoped it would speak through her anger. "This is so much more about what I love now, than what I ever detested. Can't you see that? You're twisting it the wrong way."

Her fists hung by her side. "How did you and George plan to twist it? Was this discovery part of your plan? Did you think I'd be pleased when I found out your scheme?"

"You didn't mind when your father made plans. You were pleased to marry at his suggestion."

"I was a child, trained to obey. And as you so rightly told me yourself, I have a mind of my own and I don't need anyone to plot my course anymore."

"Your father loved you and wanted the best for you. So did George."

She dug into her pocket. "George marooned me here under false assumptions. I have him to thank for being laughed at behind my back, and you for toying with my affections right under my nose."

She tossed his rock onto the table where it toppled the lemonade jug with a sickening splinter and crack, right there on the tabletop with more scars than a table should ever hold.

24

Finella's heart didn't normally slam in church. She preferred
the calm of sliding into her seat and resting in the prayerful
solace only Sundays brought. Today, she battled a prickle of nerves.

Shoulder to shoulder, the little white church crammed with parishioners, some she'd not seen before. Upright and alert, perhaps the
entire district sought to allay their curiosity, and take a long look at
the new preacher.

He bellowed the hymns as if he'd penned the words himself. But
when the hymnals were laid down, he leaned into the pulpit, long
arms draped over it as if it had always been his.

"My parents hated God. He was nothing more than a curse word
most days."

Less heat would have flooded her cheeks if Goliah Ashe upended
a sack of unwashed pantaloons onto the church floor.

"They encountered Him when they were only a few years off
meeting their maker." His voice did not waver.

"But they lived most of their lives ignorant of God. Most of what
they'd heard was wrong. At best, inadequate." The new preacher
introduced himself. His voice resonated off the timber walls, and not
one sleepy head dipped at the sound.

"That's how I ended up with my name. They thought Goliath
was a giant hero. Someone mentioned him in a tale and they figured

it would be a good name for a strong boy. Problem was, they didn't know the whole story and saddled me with something I have to explain each time I shake a stranger's hand."

A chuckle from young Simon Callahan didn't stop the preacher's stride.

"But I can tell you my name is one of the greatest gifts my parents gave me. It made me want to know the real Goliath. And I was not impressed." He fingers tightened around the pulpit.

"However, I was impressed with David. Soon I became impressed with David's God. I found myself wanting to know more." He speared the youths with a look. "What I'm trying to tell you, good people, is God draws us to Him in different ways. But He does draw us. He calls and invites, but He never insists. Your name, your background, your circumstances, none of these things matter. What matters is how you're going to respond to God's love and forgiveness. Where you'll let him direct you in the days to come."

Like a cool wind, his words draped Finella with an unexpected freshness, and all eyes remained focused on Goliah Ashe, the man who stood in the imprint of her George.

Even Molly did not fidget. She listened to the man's story, woven with words of scripture and somehow by the end of the morning, a sermon on God's love had been delivered, couched in the story of the man with the foolish name.

For a few luxurious minutes Finella forgot how many churchgoers might know about Shadrach's promise to George. Instead, she let herself concentrate on the echo of the new preacher's words.

"God's rewarded me for seeking Him. In that search I also found my real self, and in doing so became the man I've been able to offer to this beautiful woman you see sitting here. May I introduce my dear wife, Agatha Ashe."

He beamed and she stood and bowed before quickly resuming

her seat. "My wife would've arrived with me earlier this week, but remained in Sydney to attend to her younger sister who became a mother for the first time last month. I am indebted to her for following me here when she would have liked to stay longer, but she believes as much as I do, this is where she belongs."

He may have said much more. Or nothing at all.

Finella closed her eyes against the sting to her cheek, and her face radiated with the double-sided slap of loss and replacement. Even with her lids closed she could still see the back of the elegant head to which Goliah Ashe cast a fond smile. Blonde, like her husband, the object of his affection wore a small elegant hat of velvet sage and matching dress.

Finella opened her eyes for a better look. *He had a wife.* Not that he shouldn't. The man was entitled to a wife. Did she expect him to be a bachelor? She examined her gloves. No, she'd known for weeks someone would eventually take George's place. But it wasn't confirmation he was already married that made her stomach twist.

Mrs. Ashe offered the touch of a woman. The perspective and tenderness only a wife could add to her husband's duties. Finella swallowed the bitterness in her throat. It refused to budge. Like a messy knot, it filled her chest and stole her calm.

A preacher's wife says as much with her presence, as he does with his words. Aunt Sarah had much to say about the life of a preacher's wife. She'd probably wasted more breath on the subject than any other.

Too bad for Finella, the instruction she'd held onto for so long, now amounted to nothing more than beautiful disappointment.

"You're not coming, Finella." Shadrach leaned over the wagon and pulled tight on a cord around his largest canvas roll. Any tighter and he'd be nursing rope burn. "You are to stay home and look after

Molly."

"Please Shadrach, I don't see why we can't join you. If it's an island tradition, Molly and I shouldn't miss out," Finella followed, her begging the first real conversation they'd had since she'd found her letters in his skillion. And while he'd even settle for her sour company, he had much to accomplish this day, and none of it included her.

Even in the morning shadows, her doe eyes found him. A pull in his gut warned him to look away. If she didn't get out from under his feet he'd undo the rope and use it to tether her to his nearest fencepost.

He reached for the last of the hay filled crates and held it between them.

"You're an islander now?"

"I live here, don't I?" She lifted her chin but in her eyes he saw the offering of something she'd held back for days. Something mellow, light, and amiable. "I guess I am an islander, now."

She guessed? He didn't care for guessing. He wanted her sure as the ropes he tied to his gear. He wanted her. Absolutely and unconditionally. But she wasn't even talking to him. Not properly.

"I said 'no'. Now move." He shouldered past and dumped the crate into the dray with a dawn-breaking thwack.

"We won't get in the way." She matched his steps to the barn, where Molly whispered to Old Lou. "We could help you."

From the rafters he got his spare lanterns.

"How? Until yesterday you didn't even know what an Egging was."

He waited.

"I know now. Thanks to your very hesitant explanation."

Shadrach reached for two coiled lengths of fencing wire and a long sapling rod. "I didn't think it would interest you. And frankly, didn't think you'd care to spend your time in a tent or scramble the Woolamai hills for muttonbird eggs."

"I. Well…" Hands on hips she tried again. "For starters, I thought I could cook for you."

He marched to the door. "We camp round the fire. For a fistful of coins, Old Man Sharpie does most of it for us anyway."

"I could guard your eggs." She followed. "Make sure no one steals them when you bring them to camp and you're off hunting again."

"Steal them? Everyone's too busy at the burrows. Who would think to steal someone's eggs?"

"*You're* stealing them. From the muttonbirds."

For a second he tried to dismiss how right she was. He brushed the thought away as quickly as the pink in the sky chased the blue dawn.

"You're not convincing me."

"Shadrach, please? Molly and I would like to be a part of the Egging party." She took a deep breath and continued. "If we can help, we want to. If there's nothing we can do, then so be it. We'll gather wildflowers."

As if to compete with the waking day, she prattled on. "We won't interfere with you. I heard from folks at church yesterday, you won last year. You'll want to win again."

She was almost right. Two years in a row he'd claimed the winner's crown, but it was the money he made from selling muttonbird eggs he counted on.

"I know it will be different with Molly along, but it would be so good for her to see it. And me."

The lanterns bumped against his shin. He couldn't think of one single thing he wanted less than to worry about Molly wandering the cliffs. A breath of wind caressed the loose hair at Finella's neck.

And he certainly couldn't think of one single thing he wanted more than to spend time with Finella. If she were willing.

He juggled the sapling and wire.

"Woolami's a rough beach. There's wind and cliffs. It's nothing like Red Rocks. Most likely one of you, or both knowing my luck, will get blown away."

Finella stepped back and held her hands up in surrender. "'We shall remain wherever you think it's safe.'"

She complied all too soon and too eagerly. Shadrach pushed the thought of kissing her far from his mind. If she really wanted to be safe, she should have stayed in England.

"Why do you want this so much?" He tossed the coils into the wagon and secured the lanterns and rod. "And don't tell me it would be fun to camp in a tent at the edge of a cliff because I know you." He turned to face her. "Camping's a step down from this farm. You do realize that?"

She dug her hands into her apron pockets and shrugged. "I didn't get to talk to Agatha Ashe as much as I'd like at church. She and Mr. Ashe will be there, too. They invited me to take tea with them, at the camp."

"Agatha Ashe?"

Finella nodded. He could almost see her hold her breath.

Goliah and Agatha Ashe were her sort of people. Refined. Dedicated to the kind of life she'd hoped for. No wonder she was ready to trade a bed for their company.

Light spilled into the sky through the beach banksias where blue wrens shared their morning song. Shadrach shook his head. He should have known something fancier beckoned. Not that he blamed her. He and Molly had been her only company for months now. But that didn't mean he would give in without a trade of his own.

He crossed his arms. "If I let you two come along, it will be on my terms."

Her eyes lit with a glint he hadn't seen in days.

"I accept."

"You haven't heard them yet."

Hands still in her apron pocket she twisted them in the folds. "You won't tie us to a gum tree while you hunt?" The glint grew into a tease.

"Not quite." He kept his voice low and hoped the pounding of his chest stayed well hidden. "You will stay at camp. The whole time. And you get to come only if you promise to spend half an hour with me each evening."

Her smile faded.

He hurried on.

"One quick beach walk. Every sunset. For both nights we're there, starting tonight. The rest of the time is yours to do whatever you and Molly wish as long as you stay safe."

"That's a little unfair."

"No." He dragged an oilcloth over the wagon. "Unfair is being accused of stealing letters when you didn't. Of bumping against a wall of silence when you try to explain yourself."

"You don't think we've had this talk enough already?"

"I think you've had your say, and plenty of it. But you've not let me reply."

She smoothed her apron. "Fine. I agree. One half hour each day. For you to talk." She turned toward the barn. "Molly, he agreed. Come help gather our things."

Molly appeared like a loyal pup.

"It won't take us long to pack." Finella rested her arm on Molly's shoulder. "Were you planning on leaving soon?"

"I planned on leaving an hour ago, but your pestering slowed me down."

The girls hurried to the house. The wind whipped at their skirts, and the crunch of their footsteps softened to a faint crackle before the hut door closed with a soft bump.

"Then again, a small delay might be a fair price to pay, Miss Finella. If we get talking time. Question is, will you be listening?"

25

Finella searched the cluster of tents. An icy blast of coastal wind hammered the campsite and she laced her fingers through Shadrach's taut tent ropes for balance.

Through the trees and beyond the low hills, cliff tops gave way to the ocean drops where huge waves smashed in a wreck of foam. Cape Woolamai might be the island's highest peek, but even from her vantage point Finella couldn't find what she looked for.

No other skirt thrashed against the wind this morning. She hoped Agatha Ashe might brave the gusts and arrive soon. Her tenuous, unpacked truce with Shadrach hadn't delivered all she expected. It had delivered more. And she needed to divert her mind from the walk she'd promised, or suffer a belly of nerves the rest of the day.

"Mrs. Ashe isn't here." Shadrach threw the last of the blankets into the tent. "I just heard. The Ashe party arrives tomorrow."

Finella tore her eyes from the pink cliffs.

"Tomorrow?"

He nodded. "Agatha's sick. I heard they're coming tomorrow now."

His hair stuck up from where he'd run his hands through it after he'd finished pitching the tents. One large enough for her and Molly where he also jammed all his egging gear, and a small one on the other side of the tree, only wide enough for his bedroll.

"Where's Molly?"

"Here." Molly inched out of his tent backwards. "Smells funny in there."

"Good." He helped her up. "Stay in your tent then and we'll both be happy." His face matched the cloudy sky.

"I think tea's a very good idea." Finella rummaged through a wicker basket for the billy to steady her jittery hands. With an absent Agatha Ashe, she'd have a long day to sit through before sunset. "And if I can find where that pan of batter balls is we can have a bite to eat as well."

"When do we get the eggs?" Molly tapped Shadrach's odd assortment of gear with her toe.

"You don't get to hunt for eggs, Miss." He tugged at her braid. "You're only here because Finella thought it might be good for you to watch. I never agreed to either of you getting in the way. There's people here from all over the district. So stay put."

He took the billy from Finella. "That log will make a fine enough spot to sit. I'll get this on the boil while you make yourselves comfortable. There's nothing you won't hear about if you sit near the cook pots. Sharpie's just setting up now. Don't get in his way."

He moved toward the fire.

"He's mad at someone," Molly balanced her foot on a rock and tried to see beyond the tents.

Finella found the tin cups and jar of sugar. "You and I will explore when the egging starts. Until then, we'll do what Shad wants and not bother him."

And hope dear Mrs. Ashe arrives in time to make this trip worth the effort.

Finella folded their quilts as best she could and laid them at the foot of the tent while campers milled and helped each other stretch canvas into makeshift shelters. Some she knew from church, but many faces she hadn't seen before.

Soon enough Shad returned with a bubbling billy.

"When does the Egging start?" she ventured.

He filled her mug from behind a coil of steam.

"This morning is for setting up camp. Someone'll ring a bell soon. Then you won't see much of me around here until the sun goes down." He filled another cup and handed it to Molly.

Finella's heart plummeted at the mention of evening. The thought of walking with him along the beach did not appeal to her now, anymore than it did this morning. He and George had negotiated about her as if she were a chattel. Couldn't he see why that would make her mad? How could he expect her not to find that deceitful?

She blew into the hot tea and wrestled with how much grief he'd caused. Or was it how much she didn't trust him?

She didn't know anymore.

Molly leaned into Shad's shoulder. But his eyes soon found Finella.

She cradled her cup like a shield, but he watched her with a long dark look, enough to shower her in his misery. Enough to reflect her own.

She tried to look away, but it was as if there were nothing between them. Nothing but the promise of sunset.

"Ladies and gentlemen. Hooks at the ready." Perched on an upturned crate, the man they all called Sharpie held a bell above his balding head.

Finella kept her eyes on Shadrach, poised with a crate of his own in one hand and the long sapling pole she remembered from this morning. It now sported a mean looking wire hook. If a photographer were to capture the scene before her, he'd have trouble getting them to stand still. Grown men to school lads and every age in between jostled like horses about to bolt.

With iron and wood, wire and twig, the motley group stood armed for the hunt. Youths hopped from one foot to the other, eyeing the bell then each other to make sure no one stole a head start. At the sound of the clang, the campground almost emptied, and dust settled on those who remained.

Molly clenched her dolly to her chest. "Where will they go?"

Finella drew her closer and they linked arms.

"Over to the burrows, I think." She tried to remember what Shadrach called them. "Rookeries. Where the birds keep their nests."

They followed the newly vacated path for a clearer view of the sloping hill.

"And where are the chickens?"

"You mean muttonbirds? They live way out there." Finella pointed to sea. "If you look as far as your eyes let you, you'll see where the sky meets the water. That's the horizon. Somewhere out there, is where the muttonbirds fly. When the sun goes down, they come back to their nests."

"What do they do all day?"

"Well, I guess they eat fish."

"And where is their house?"

"Their burrow is their house."

Molly busied herself with her doll. "I had another house. With Mum. Now I have one with you and Shad."

Finella tried to ignore the ache that brought. She could not be a part of *you and Shad*, and Molly should not become used to pairing their names. Especially with Aunt Sarah so close to arriving.

Finella pointed to a group thrusting rods into the side of the hill. "See how they drag their hooks out? Oh, and look. There's an egg, now. See?"

She turned Molly's shoulders so she could peer down on the first jubilant find, egg in the hand of the finder, held high while his group cheered him on.

"That must be the first one of the day. My, that was quick. I can't imagine they'll whoop and whistle for every one."

"Where's Brother? Does he have an egg?"

Finella searched the rookery. Shadrach had started his hunting further away. Squatting at the opening of a burrow, his arms and shoulders worked to a rhythm. Each time he found an egg, he placed it in his hay filled crate and moved onto the next hole in the hill. Reach, drag, scoop. Reach, drag, scoop.

He worked fast. She'd give him that. No wonder the islanders knew him as the best. Try as she might, she couldn't help but puff a little with pride.

They strolled to the end of the track along the cliff edge, where a good vantage spread before them.

"This is as far as we can go, I guess."

At their feet, Finella recognized a ground cover of little noon-flowers. So far she'd collected pink and orange varieties. Today, waves of purple lay strewn across the hill as far as the eye could see. Islanders called it *pigface* but she preferred the little noonflower. Aunt Sarah would, too.

"Here's a new color for my Everlasting." She knelt and patted the grass for Molly. The girl flopped onto her back and closed her eyes against the afternoon sun.

Finella sat beside her to examine the tiny petals. Like many of her seaside succulents, these too held water in their leaves. She pinched a leaf and snapped it in half with her thumb.

Molly wriggled for a soft spot in the side of the hill. Their day had started earlier than usual, and Molly would be looking for her nap soon enough.

"We should keep walking or we may end up napping on this bluff and not be able to sleep tonight. Who knows what noise there'll be around the camp fire and for how long."

"I'm already tired." Molly closed her eyes against the sun shifting from behind a cloud.

Finella peered at the men on the rookery. Was she thinking of Molly's wellbeing or her own? Surely she wasn't planning a smooth bedtime for Molly. For what? Her walk with Shadrach?

She played with the succulent leaf until its juice dripped into her palm. The sun still hung in the heavens, and while it did, she'd ignore the worry she nursed for the end of day.

༄

"We've walked a long way." Molly puffed and sat on a large rock. "Did Brother say we could come this far?"

"We can still see the egging. And tents." Finella shaded the sun from her eyes and hoped seeing the camp, also qualified as still being at camp. "I thought this track would take us back the long way. I guess I took a wrong turn."

"Can we go back please, Finella? I'm tired. And I want to know how many eggs brother caught."

Wind burnt cheeks and loose hair were not the only telltale signs of fatigue. Her eyelids drooped and Finella recognized a sleepy Molly when she saw one. She poked a flap of grass against a mound in the hillside with her toe. "Is this a muttonbird house?"

Finella inspected the gentle rise. "Is there an opening?"

Molly knelt and thrust her hand in. "I think it is!"

"Molly, don't. You can't hunt for an egg without a hook." Finella pulled her back.

"Eggs don't hurt. Our hens leave them for me at home." Molly leaned closer.

"These eggs are cared for by a mother and father bird. I expect they may not like you disturbing them." Finella held her hand out. "Up you come."

"If there's no bird in there why can't I put my hand in? You said they fly over the ocean."

"What if it's not a muttonbird at all? What if it's a snake? Shad told us to be careful."

"It's not a snake. I can hear something. A bird." Molly pressed her cheek to the burrow entrance. "A chirp! Can you hear it?" She poked at the grass until it parted like a curtain. "It is a bird. See?"

Finella gathered her skirt and perched on her toes. Her foot slid and a quick wobble toppled her into Molly's back. Neither of them had time to regain their balance before they fell into a heap.

Molly laughed at the undignified upending. Finella joined in.

"I guess you're meant to have that lie down, after all."

"You pushed me." Molly accused with justified surprise.

"I didn't mean to, Love. I slipped and you were a soft place to fall."

Molly's face crumpled and she let out a high-pitched wail. She yanked her hand from the ground where it had broken her fall and shook it. "Ouch. Oh." She twisted her mouth, and turned to Finella, eyes wide open as if she'd been slapped.

"What's wrong?" Finella knelt beside her.

"Bad thing. It stings. Like fire." She jumped to her feet and flicked her hand against her skirt, as if to rid herself of whatever had sunk it's teeth or tail there.

Finella held Molly's other hand so she wouldn't run off and wrestled with her own skirt to stand up. *Please God, don't let me see a snake.*

On the ground, giant ants the size of a grown man's thumb,

scurried in all directions from where Molly lay only moments before.

Molly let out another shriek. "Make it stop." Tears spotted her cheeks and she shook in an awkward dance, while Finella brushed wildly at the girl's sleeves.

"We need to get back to the tents. Someone's bound to have packed a lotion for stings." A louder wail drowned Finella's suggestion and she held her breath while Molly crouched and hid her sore hand in the pit of her arm.

"Let me see."

Molly could barely stand still long enough for Finella to spot the angry welt on top of her hand, already red raw and puffed. The poor girl shook like a marionette on a string. Her shrieks carried over the hilltop to the egging parties, where some lifted their heads at the sound.

Finella pulled her into a tight embrace, and whispered in her ear. "I have something to make you feel better, back in our tent. But we must go. Now."

Between gulps of breath and sobs, Molly shook her head and inspected her hand. And nothing moved her on until a familiar voice carried over the hill.

"I knew it. I knew something like this would happen. I knew it in my gut." Shadrach stormed across the cliff, each foot stomp in time to his aggravated words. His voice silenced Molly's crying and sent a racket of quivers through Finella.

Jaw fixed, eyes narrowed, his handsome face flashed a mix of anger, impatience, and loyalty to both her and Molly, and it carved a path right to them.

He knelt in the groundcover and snatched a handful of leaves. "Show me." He reached for Molly's trembling hand and snapped a leaf directly above the bite mark.

Clear juice dribbled onto Molly's fingers. He snapped leaf after leaf and doused her hand until she blinked at him through her tears.

"Fire's... gone?"

He pulled his hat off and fanned her with it.

"Should be." Clipped and cool, his words hardly matched his mission. "Takes no more than a second to soothe with pigface. If you know what you're doing"

He turned to Finella. "Anything bite you?"

She shook her head. "I saw them, though. Biggest ants I've ever seen."

"Jack Hoppers, probably. Jumping bull ants. Take a running leap to get at you if you're in their way." He let go of Molly's hand. "You've scored yourself a lovely bite mark for your troubles. But if you take a bunch of pigface back to camp, Finella will dab more on when you need it."

He stood and turned to Finella. "Think you can manage to follow *those* instructions?"

She nodded. She'd only played with the same leaves herself a little while ago with no idea they were good for anything. What else had she misjudged?

"Did you get many eggs, Brother?" Molly sniffed.

He ran his hands through his hair and shook his head.

Finella waited for him to cross his arms over her chest, farm-gate style. But he didn't.

"Not enough. Jack Trilloe's nephew, Tom Darley's breathing down my neck. Last year, he was just playing at this, but he's matching me egg for egg now and if I have to leave my spot to rescue you two again he'll take me over, good and proper." He fixed Finella with a stare. "So make sure I don't have to."

"Shadrach, we didn't mean to stray. I thought a nice long walk ..." Finella didn't know how to finish her sentence. *I thought if Molly slept soundly, you and I could walk the beach and, maybe, unravel the ache we're carrying.*

Even in her head that made her squirm. His fierce march across the cliff wasn't for her. He'd abandoned the hunt for his sister. Their agreement had always been Finella would care for Molly and Shadrach would be free to work, but most days those lines blurred. Naturally.

Why was it so hard then to believe Shadrach would naturally cross over whatever lines George had established? That his feelings for her went beyond his promise to a friend.

"Look, you need to take Molly back to camp and let me do what I came to do." He slapped his hat back on and marched across the hill. Long strides put distance between them until he stopped and turned. "And I mean it Finella. Get moving. When I see you next it had better be outside your tent."

Finella watched him leave, and a new ache grew in her heart.

She had agreed to care for Molly. And their arrangement included nothing of love.

But her love for the child had grown without slackening, and was greater than she could ever have imagined.

Arms wrapped around each other they walked back to camp. Two companions, thrown together by life's misfortunes.

Why was it easier to love Molly than Shadrach? Both were children of the same convict. Both had changed her heart so deeply she knew she'd never be the same.

But where Molly asked for nothing, Shadrach asked for everything.

And that would change her destiny.

26

"69, 70, 71. Pathetic." Shadrach pushed his crate of muttonbird eggs to the foot of Molly's bedroll.

"Is that enough, Brother?"

"Molly? I thought you were asleep." He stuffed the last layer of hay over the box. "Did I wake you?"

"Not you. The music's too loud."

He lay beside her and looked at the sky through a small rip in the canvas ceiling.

The egging party gathered by the fire for a singsong under a canopy of burnt orange and dusky pink.

"You don't like the accordion?"

"I do. But I'm tired." She turned her cheek to his shoulder and closed her eyes. "What's your number?"

"My number…? Oh you mean egg number. 71." It killed him to think he'd brought in less than any other egging day.

"Is that bad?"

"It's not wonderful, but I have tomorrow to catch up. Is that hand still throbbing?"

"A little. My eyes are sore, too."

"No wonder, with all your wailing. Nothing a good sleep won't fix. Let's make plans for a better day tomorrow. Agreed?"

"Agreed."

Her breath warmed his neck and he knew if he didn't get up he'd fall asleep right there on the edge of Molly's bedroll.

"You're the best hunter, aren't you?" She whispered, and he knew if he waited another minute she'd be fast asleep and he wouldn't need a reply.

But he wasn't that kind of man. He'd promised to care for her and that meant answering her questions. He sat up and rolled his tired shoulders.

Was he the best hunter? Last year he'd secured over one hundred eggs in his tent by the end of day one. But this year Molly slept in his spare tent. And out by the fire, a certain Finella Mayfield messed with his thoughts. Right now, they had nothing to do with muttonbirds or their eggs.

"Time will tell how good a hunter I am, Sunshine." He kissed her forehead. "Time will tell."

∽

Twilight settled over the camp like a blanket. Unfamiliar and mournful, the song of the concertina whimpered, and folks who'd long ago left England for Australia lamented in a blend of wistful harmonies. A snap of timber underfoot announced a footstep and Finella felt a hand pull her close.

"Time for our walk." Shadrach was not asking. He was telling.

"I thought you might wish to stay for the singing."

He didn't even glance at the gathering. It was as if there were no other beat.

"You thought wrong."

He laid his hand on her back. "Now, watch your step, and follow me."

The steep path wound through beach scrub and with each turn the sound of the ocean grew louder and clearer. They reached the bottom in a hurried slip of shoes against sand, to the smash of waves against the shore.

A furious wind struck Finella's ears. It whipped her skirt. Wrestled her hair and wrecked her well-hidden discord.

She pulled her shawl tighter. "I didn't know about this path. I thought the one we were on this morning lead to the beach."

"You weren't meant to go to the beach. Or the cliff edge." He frowned.

"Well, we didn't make it to either, so you needn't worry."

The sun kneeled on the horizon. A fiery ball at the edge of its end. Shadrach stuck his hands in his pockets and walked. Finella followed.

"I shouldn't have spoken harshly today." He kept his voice loud, but it held some resignation. "I panicked when I heard Molly cry. Happens to me whenever she's distressed."

"Is that an apology?"

"Is that what you need from me, Finella?" He stopped and tugged at her elbow. "Do I need to say I'm sorry to make things right between us?" Wind gusts pushed against his trouser legs but he ignored the sandy tempest around them.

"Are you sorry?" She wasn't sure he was. Offering an apology was not the same as meaning it.

"About the way I spoke today, yes. I'm sorry and ashamed. But we know there's more than that between us."

She lifted her hem a little, just enough to keep the froth in the end of the waves from touching her.

"You stole my letters. You took pieces of me I never intended for you. Not accidently, but on purpose and in order to manipulate me."

He moved between her and the wind.

"I never saw it as stealing, Finella. Never thought you would see it that way, either. You have to understand I made a promise to a man who gripped my hand on his deathbed. Not to just take them, but to read them. Would you have denied him?"

He grabbed her hands. "Like this." He squeezed hard. "George made me promise to look after you. Why does that make you so cross?"

Fire spilled across her chest and up into her cheeks. She shook her hands free.

"I'm cross you made plans for me. You and George. Even before I'd ever set foot in this country, you altered plans my father made." She pushed against his chest. "Was there ever a time when God thought my days should not be decided by dead men?"

Aunt Sarah would have much to say about her raising her voice, but Finella didn't care. She would scream if she had to. No one else could hear them.

"There's no dead men deciding for you now." Shadrach yelled back and sidestepped a long piece of driftwood at their feet. He dragged it across the wet sand until a wonky line appeared. "Make your choice Finella."

He threw the wood away and stood on one side of the line, arms spread wide. Finella couldn't tell if it was defeat or defiance.

"There's only you and me, now." He poked the sand with his foot. "I'm here. The one George thought, no *knew*, would care for you. If you're not afraid to let me love you."

He motioned with both hands to where she stood. "And you're there. Just you. No man, dead or alive, is deciding anything for you anymore."

Her heart beat louder than the crashing waves. If only he knew how much this frightened her. How the thought of being a farmer's wife and loving him in return rubbed out all her father's dreams, and Aunt Sarah's years of training.

Not just any farmer. The son of a convict.

She blinked against the wind, or was it her tears?

Shadrach waited, fists clenched, but Finella's words caught in a place she couldn't dip into. Not without letting go of more than she knew how.

As if nailed to the sand, her toes stood just shy of the groove he'd made. A push of the tide splashed over her shoes, and filled the line with sea foam. Trickles ran back to the sea, while the remainder soaked into the sand, erasing his mark.

Neither of them moved. Only the sun dipped and fell like a curtain onto a darkened stage.

"I guess our time is up, then." Shadrach ushered her to cover the steps they'd already taken, his anger gone as sure as the setting sun. "Let's get back to camp. Before it's too dark to know what either of us is doing."

Under the hem of another dusk, Finella stepped alongside the man who'd taken her to the brink. And almost pushed her over.

November 25
Cape Woolamai

Agatha Ashe plays the role meant for me like a freshly tuned pump organ. Pressing through whatever ailed her yesterday, she carries on beside Goliah and warms the heart of everyone who sees her. It's not her smile I envy so much, as her attentiveness to Goliah Ashe and his congregation. The way she anticipates his move and follows his lead. She is so suited to the task. I wonder why God chose to take that from me and it shames me to wrestle Him for what I've already lost.

Isaac Sharp lumbered into the campsite with another load of wood. Each time Finella saw the man, he was either hauling logs or burning them.

He poked at an iron grate laid over the fire pit. "Not running a restaurant Miss Mayfield. Breakfast comes at the bell. Not hours after."

Finella's cheeks flamed to match the pit, and she grimaced at Molly. Agatha Ashe, standing just behind the young girl, mercifully adjusted her hat and kept her eyes on the cliffs.

Finella tucked a loose coil of hair behind her ear and hoped the hasty pinning would not unravel alongside her own internal dishevelment. "I'm dreadfully sorry, Sharpie. Molly overslept and I've only now managed to rouse and dress her."

Truth be told, she hadn't cared to bump against Shadrach so soon after yesterday's walk. The ring of the bell had only served to keep her where she lay, staring at the canvas, listening to Molly's deep breathing.

Sharpie fussed with the fire. She came at him from the other side, hoping rumors about his quick temper remained untrue.

"I don't wish to trouble you when you're already so busy. But I would work quickly if you let me make us a pot of tea."

"No one touches Sharpie's fire. Don't care what the rest of ya do back home, but out here, I'm the cook and if ya don't like it, then you're welcome to eat plum pudding in your tents."

Finella backed off and bit down a smile. She'd seen Sharpie pass treats to Molly all afternoon yesterday, with the barest nod and wink. If his bark was not worse than his bite, she didn't know another soul who could best him.

He wagged a finger. "*I'll* make the tea if you don't mind, and you can take it over there where I won't have to listen to ya babbling." He pointed to where a cluster of chairs and an old trunk served the men who'd played cards the night before, not far from where the singsong had taken place.

Finella exchanged sheepish grins with her companions. "You're the boss."

"Too right, I am," he muttered against a clash of lids on pots.

Finella thanked him and moved away.

"For all his sharp edges, I think Sharpie's more of a soft one," Agatha Ashe whispered. They settled into a dappled spot near the burnt out logs of last night's fire.

"Now, that was a quick observation." Finella smiled at her new friend.

"Well, Goliah has asked me to observe. To see people as they really are. Because sometimes we all appear less or more than who we think we should be."

"Sharpie's the boss." Molly joined in. "He told me to talk to him whenever I'm hungry."

"Ah, but you're hungry almost all the time, aren't you, dear girl?" Finella pulled the end of Molly's thick braid from where it had caught in her collar.

"I am right now." Molly rubbed her belly. "I wanted breakfast Finella, not just tea."

"Well, here ya go then." Sharpie arrived to rest a plate of buttered damper, three tin mugs and a steaming billy on the trunk.

"And you'll get your other meals along with the rest of them if ya turn up when the bell rings." He jabbed Molly's jaw with a pretend blow.

"We promise to be here, Sharpie." Agatha Ashe helped with the cups. "Especially if it looks as delicious as this." She offered Molly a piece of damper.

Finella poured the tea. "I don't know why this tastes so good, perhaps because we're taking it outdoors."

"Or the company." Agatha smiled. "I've wanted to get to know you since Goliah told me you arrived here for your wedding, only to meet with something altogether different."

Finella's smile slid into a sigh. "I guess it's a strange predicament to be in. A bride arrives to no husband, but stays on anyway."

Agatha nodded. "I've always loved Goliah. I wanted nothing more than to marry him from the day we met. So when I heard you were still here on this island," she shrugged, "I suppose I got curious. Wondered why you wouldn't go back to life among your own people?"

Finella blew on her tea. Her people were not where she could find them anymore. She wondered how much she could tell this warm stranger with the green eyes.

"I couldn't imagine another sea voyage on my own. Coming in was the worst ordeal I've ever endured. Losing my father and burying him at sea." Her stomach tipped at the memory.

"Poor Finella." Agatha set her cup down on the ground and pulled her chair closer. "How ever did you manage?"

"I kept thinking about George and my life here with him. George promised he'd help me find the name of a man. A thief, who dropped a tattered Australian newspaper page when he ran off with my mother's brooch and knocked her to the ground. She died wishing she knew the thief's name, and George thought, maybe…if he saw the scrap he might…"

Gum leaves danced in the tree limbs above them, but all Finella heard was the memory of a prayer she'd offered each day on a ship between the world where her life had altered forever, and the world where she hoped a remedy might be found in a name.

One name. That thief's name.

But that possibility had been buried with George, too.

"I thought about it everyday. As soon as we would wake, I'd pray God would keep me safe until I reached Phillip Island. And each night, I'd plead with God for a dreamless sleep and good speed to shorten our journey. I knew if I could hold myself together until we sailed into these waters," she pointed to the horizon, "I'd be where I was always meant to be."

She tried not to look at the fold in Agatha's forehead. Didn't want to remember how it felt to be pitied as the groomless bride.

"What a horrible double blow. To lose so much. And there's no one in England you can return to?"

"My aunt used to live with us, but moved to be with her cousin in London." She tried to imagine Aunt Sarah at this crude camp taking tea from a blackened billy. "Her ship's due sometime after Christmas. And then, we'll return to England together."

Agatha's frown deepened. "And that's what you want? To return with her?"

Finella set her cup down beside Agatha's. Molly poked at the cold charcoal of last night's fire with a long twig. Finella had never seen her venture so close to a fire, dead or roaring. Not by herself. Not even on the coldest night. Her heart soared at the sight.

"I promised to look after Molly until Aunt Sarah's arrival. I need-ed to be useful, and somewhere to lodge. Shadrach needed help with his sister." She shrugged.

For a long time she'd though their pairing had been inevitable, for Molly's sake.

"Perhaps he'll listen to reason and let me take her. With me. I'm wondering whether God allowed me to come all this way to rescue *her*. For years, I imagined I'd help George with his congregation, but perhaps, that's why you're here Agatha, and I'm here with Molly." She searched the preacher's wife for affirmation. For approval and blessing.

"You think you're here to rescue Molly by taking her away from the only other person she loves?"

Tiny flames seared Finella's insides. "Is that so wicked? To want to care for a motherless girl?"

"It's not wicked, Finella. I'm sorry. I didn't mean to imply that." Agatha pressed her hand with the lightest of touches. "I've heard a story about Shadrach Jones and a certain promise to Mr. Gleeson. I don't take words of gossip to heart, ever, but I do watch people. And I'm very good at it. What I've seen of his interaction with you hints at a man already very much taken by the woman caring for his sister and home."

Finella wriggled on the uneven chair. What did church-folk see when she and Shadrach sang hymns together, with Molly between them? Surely not the looks he sent her way when they were alone? She looked away to cool her blush.

The chair listed like a ship and she wished she could right it before it slipped on the soft ground. But Agatha Ashe had her fixed as surely as a sailor with his winching ropes. And she worked those lines with a well held pinch.

"And in case you're wondering about my observations of you, I'll tell you this much." Agatha's frown lines set into the warm creases of a smile. "It's no longer about what George Gleeson could offer you. Or what your father wanted for your future. There's something else to consider now. Much bigger than all of that. And you're fighting so hard against everything Shadrach Jones represents, if you're not careful, it will cost you both him and Molly."

27

The egg gatherers finished their outdoor supper under the warble of magpies and the clang of forks on tin plates.

Finella played with her food, certain she ate less than a magpie ever could. The knot in her throat, and matching one in her stomach, only grew with the passing hours. She watched the sky where the sun teased its imminent dip. And still, Shadrach did not appear.

"I reckon he's found a new rookery. One further off." Sharpie considered Shadrach's absence. "I'm not surprised he worked through lunch, having to catch up after yesterday's delay, but I didn't think he'd last 'til sundown. Must be determined to win, no matter what."

Agatha had no trouble finishing off her meal and Molly's plate must have been generously served because she'd eaten it all and shook her head when Finella offered her the remainder on her own plate.

"Are you sure you don't want it?"

"Brother should have it."

"He *can* have it." Finella set the plate in her lap. "If he ever gets here."

"Why don't you take it to him." Agatha winked. "It's obvious he's making the most of daylight hours. Why don't you bundle up some of Sharpie's bread as well?"

Finella cocked her head at her new friend. Preacher's wives weren't supposed to make mischief, were they? A twitch in Agatha's mouth did little to allay Finella's doubts.

"If I did something like that, he'd misinterpret my actions and think I was pining for him back here at camp. I'm here to care for Molly. If he wants to miss his meals for a crate of muttonbird eggs, that's his folly."

"It may be *your* folly." Agatha leaned in. "What would George want you to do?"

"George would say to go." Molly nodded.

The lighthearted ambush came at Finella from both sides.

"You're using Molly and a dead man to make your point?"

Agatha laughed. "It's a plate of food, Finella. Not your heart in a velvet box." She pointed to the sky. "There's about an hour left of good light before he'll be back. By then, the food will be stone cold. Do the man a favor. He did stop his work to help you yesterday."

"He helped his sister."

"Who would not have been here if you didn't pester him to allow it. Didn't you say Shadrach let you come so we could become acquainted?"

Finella stared at her and hid her smile. "Yes, a little too closely I see. You've used almost everything I've told you to support your argument." She collected the plates and stood. "If Sharpie's agreeable, I'll take a portion to Shadrach and be back to help Molly into bed."

"No rush. I'll settle Molly to bed. That's just enough time to find him before he whisks you away for your sunset walk."

Finella's skirt sliced through the dusty air on her way to Sharpie's fire. How had Agatha armed herself with such an arsenal in one afternoon? One minute they'd been talking about the Women's Missionary Union, and the next, Finella found herself spilling far too many details of her life with Shadrach and Molly. Agatha certainly knew how to dig for truth. That was a gift. But returning that information with such precision was a craft Finella hadn't anticipated.

"Here you are." Sharpie met her with a cocky grin and cloth covered plate. "Take this to Shad and tell him the day's hunting was the best ever. Cape's teeming with eggs this year."

He winked at her and swapped his heavy plate for her half empty one.

Finella looked over her shoulder at Agatha. The preacher's wife ducked and turned to Molly.

"Did Mrs. Ashe put you up to this?" She snapped back and fixed a stare on Sharpie.

"Just thinking of Shad, that's all."

Finella lifted the edge of the cloth. Steam rose from the serving, and a big piece of damper soaked up the juices of the stew.

"'I'm sure Shadrach will be pleased you've thought of keeping food for him. Even though he *missed the bell*."

He handed her a fork. "Get. Going."

She awarded him the briefest of smiles, snatched the fork and walked away before he could boss her around anymore.

Crowded by the schemes of others, it felt good to walk alone. Along the narrow track, tall grass brushed her knees and she took care to negotiate the slippery path to the burrows.

With her back to the sun she scanned the wide hills for Shadrach. Nothing caught her eye in the open ruggedness of this side of the island. To her right, the ocean rumbled below. To her left, tussock grasslands pelted by ocean winds welcomed only the hardiest of creatures. And these, she knew, bunkered into the earth.

She shivered and searched the hills. She'd hate to walk all the way up again if he were not there.

Where is he? How do I find my way to Shadrach Jones?

Step by hesitant step, she descended the hill. She didn't need to see him up close to know for sure he sensed her approach. His head snapped and his shoulders turned to her.

Did she even want to trust him? Is that why she tramped her way through muttonbird burrows? Was she looking for a sign from Shadrach, or a sign from her own heart?

Shadrach juggled the last dozen eggs into a bundle he made out of his coat, and peered at Finella. What on earth was she doing away from camp, sliding down the hill? And whose eye was on Molly because it sure wasn't Finella's? She picked her way down the hill like a skittish billy goat.

Fear kicked him in the stomach. What if Molly needed him again? But no. Finella was in no real hurry. He imagined she might wave and yell out if some urgency brought her down.

But down she came. He would've liked to watch her all day, but he searched for a place to set his eggs. She'd chosen her side of the line last night. She may as well have signed her name in the sand with that long stick and poked him in the eye with it for good measure.

But this island had a way of erasing marks in the sand. Perhaps, tonight's sunset...

A long whoop interrupted his thoughts. Still clutching the eggs in his coat, he rose to his feet.

With a louder scream, Finella slid down the steepest section of path, tripped on a long root and raced down faster than a girl ever should.

She held something to her chest and her feet moved as if they had a mind of their own.

"Careful," he swung his bundle to one side and raised his free arm like a rail, hoping she'd grab for it.

It did neither of them any good. Momentum carried her into his embrace with full force. Together they took a few steps in a clumsy dance, and he steadied them both by bringing his other arm around and holding her tight.

Eggs smashed and trickled between them. First his coat fell away, followed by the clang of tin and the slop of something fishy.

She tried to step back but he held on. "Interesting way to step off a cliff." Wide brown eyes looked up at him. He tried not to smile. "This isn't the first time I've rescued you from yourself. You're making a habit of needing me."

For a moment, he didn't care how she got there. Just that she was, and unlike their introduction on the pier, she held her head high.

"I brought you your supper, but I think it's on my shoes." Her face crumpled and he loosened his grip.

"Fork?" She offered the cutlery on her palm with a twisted smile. He took it. Anything to hold her hand, even for a second.

She brought him his supper? It killed him to look away, at the mess of stew and bread that lay between them in the dust. Along with his last dozen eggs, scrambled and soaking into his coat.

"I am so sorry. I didn't mean to…" Her apology faded. He dragged his coat up by a sleeve. Broken shells and yolks dribbled into the creases of wool and slopped onto the ground.

She'd brought him his supper.

"I did wonder what I'd do with this last dozen. Crate's already too full but I see that's been sorted for me now." He tapped the fork against his leg. This could be fun, if he played it well.

She wiped her shoes on the nearby grass. "I'm sorry, Shadrach. I really do feel like an uncouth bull in a china shop."

She looked anything but. Almost undone by the wind, brown locks framed her red cheeks, flushed by her sudden catapult down the hill and the loss of his supper. He wanted to lift her up and swing her around, but he held his ground.

"I don't know, Finella." He shook his head in mock disappointment. "You'll have to make it up to me."

She flushed deeper and he moved away to shake the remaining eggs from his coat. And hide his smile.

"A man works all day. Then loses his dinner and precious eggs all in one quick slip down the hill. You'll need to make amends."

Finella picked the plate off the ground and wiped it on the grass where she'd cleaned her shoes. "And how would I do that?"

He stole a quick look at her but she wasn't looking back. "I'll have to think about it while we take our walk. You do remember you owe me one more?"

She straightened. "I remember."

She held his eyes a little longer but before either of them could speak again, a spill of sand hissed from the track Finella had only moments ago slid down. It crumbled and took with it the thin walkway and some of the surrounding scrubland.

Shadrach pulled her close.

"Did I do that?" Breathless and unbelieving, her voice held a measure of panic.

He didn't like the look of that slope. He'd seen sand drifts before, but never this wide and he had no idea how far across the hill the danger hid.

"It's my fault just as much as yours. I probably got it started and you may have set it off when you tripped over that root." He scanned the rookery. "No one comes this far. I can see why. There weren't too many burrows here anyway."

"How will we get back?" She stayed where he'd pulled her. Close.

Nothing on either side of the lost track offered a foothold now. The surrounding slope even less of a possibility.

"Not the way we came. We'll have to walk along the beach."

"Can we do that?"

"If you're game to risk the tide?"

He picked up the egging crook from where it leaned against a rock. "Come on. Let's head back to camp along the shore."

Finella added the plate to the already overflowing egg crate and gathered the twine loop from one side.

He took the other loop. "No need for me to tell you to be careful where you step now, is there? With your ability for dramatic entrances."

They fell into step together, juggling the load between them.

"No need. But you'd best be on your guard, Shadrach Jones." She smiled, at last. "Because you never know what might come next."

28

$\mathcal{F}$inella wasn't sure why she teased. But it felt good to match him while they walked the beach with their shared load. She remembered the ribbons of purple and scarlet that first evening when Shadrach brought her to Phillip Island. How she thought the sunset welcomed her home, to a husband and future. Had she been wrong to think that? For months she thought she had. But now…

She readjusted her grip on the twine handle.

"Too heavy?" Shadrach asked.

"No, I'll be fine. I had no idea you would collect so much today."

"I don't much like losing. Anything I believe I should win, that is."

She liked the way he looked at her when he said that. The way he spoke about one thing when his eyes meant another.

"Did you find out all there is to know about your new friend, Mrs. Ashe?" Shadrach pushed a drift of seaweed out of their path with his crook.

"She's too clever, I know that much."

"Why doesn't that sound like a compliment?"

"Because in getting to know Agatha Ashe," Finella grinned, "I discovered she's quite astute. For every detail I learned about her, she extracted five about me. She's the possessor of an uncanny way of unearthing more than you intend to admit."

"Sounds like Mrs. Lawson. She knows what you're thinking because she plants it in your head."

"Has she been a stand-in mother to you and Molly?"

"Mother-hen, busy-body, keeper-of-secrets, fuss-pot…" He listed the roles Finella knew well. Hadn't Aunt Sarah assumed them in her own life?

"Ah, but we all need someone to fuss over. We can't blame Mrs. Lawson for wanting to do that. At heart, we're all a little like your muttonbirds. Nest making and burrowing for warmth. Why, even you find yourself making Molly a *fancy* rabbit blanket."

Shadrach's pace slowed. "Muttonbirds don't fuss as much as you think they might. They let their young fend for themselves. For weeks on end."

"Yes, but they're away. Getting food. And they bring it back to the young. Don't they?"

"Well, in the beginning they fly back to their chicks."

"You see. Feathering their nests. It's as natural for birds of the air as it is for us. And you, Mister Blanket Maker, are no different."

"Muttonbirds eventually leave, Finella." His words filled the space between them. "They leave, when their time is up."

"They're migratory birds. I know. They have another home, somewhere." She cocked her head. "Is that so strange?"

"They don't all go. The chicks don't leave."

"They don't?"

"They don't." He shook his head.

"You mean the young stay and the parents fly away? Even the mother-bird? How does that work?" That made no sense. "How do the chicks manage without their mothers?"

He looked at her with sadness. As if the price were his to pay. "They just do."

"Are they ever reunited?"

He shook his head.

Finella fussed with the hair at her nape. Her mind scraped to make sense of what pounded in her heart. Mothers should never be taken from their little ones. "I can't believe they *choose* to leave. What happens to the chick when the mother leaves?"

He took a deep breath. As if the open sand and wild sea did not offer enough air. "They're safe in the nest, until hunger drives them out. They rummage around and if they survive long enough outside the burrow, they fly off in the direction of their mother and father."

"And when does this happen?"

"Mature birds leave at the end of summer. The young fly off a few months later, when instinct tells them to."

Finella looked away, nailed by the emptiness of cruel separation. A cruelty she could not afford to taste again.

"I remember what it felt like to really know my mother would never come back. It's the darkest, most hollow place for a child, even with an aunt nearby. No one should live like that. Not even a baby bird."

"You don't need to tell me." He forged ahead, but Finella stopped. Up ahead, the sand shimmered. Shadrach's end of the crate pulled at her wrist, before he too, stopped.

She pointed to the stretch of beach. "Look."

At the other end of the cove, the sea rushed in like a river.

"It's not as bad as it looks. Just the tide swelling." He gave the twine a light tug and coaxed her along, a fresh cheeriness in his voice. "Before the sun sets."

"But how do we get past?" The cliff offered no way up and if they didn't hurry, they'd be locked in. She quickened her steps.

Soon enough, they found the source of their trouble at the end of the cove. An estuary filled as quickly as the day closed upon them.

Shadrach put the crate down and tested the water's depth with his crook. "Deeper than it looks," he mumbled.

Finella didn't like the way he said that. He scanned the cliff face but with his back turned she couldn't tell what he thought.

"Shadrach?"

He kept walking, testing the water's depth every few paces. Each time the crook hit sand, the water deepened.

"I reckon it's just above my knee at the lowest point."

"Your knee is significantly higher than mine. Are you suggesting we wade through?"

"What if I wade and carry you? I'll come back for the crate when you're on the other side."

"You're going to carry me? Across there?" She looked at the widening stream.

"It wouldn't be the first time. That I carried you."

A flame lit in her cheeks. She hadn't forgotten the way he galloped along the pier with her across his back. Or how he'd carried her into his hut when she'd slipped in the mud.

"I was injured then. You don't suppose I could manage on my own this time?"

"You could. Or you could learn to trust me."

There it was again. Another poke with his words. Scarlet swipes deepened over the sky and soon there would be no light left at all.

"I promise not to rush through the water. You won't even feel a drop."

"A drop of water, or a drop *into* the water?"

"Neither." He said it with such tenderness she could hear the promise in his voice. And in that moment, Finella dared to believe this convict's son could fix all that was wrong in their world.

With a scoop she hardly saw coming, he whisked her off the sand. Finella gathered her skirt in one hand, and secured the other around his neck.

"Are you going to walk through with your shoes on?" She tried to angle her face away from his, but thought better of it. There was no sense in upsetting his balance by throwing herself too far in the opposite direction.

"Better for me if I keep them on. Don't know what's under there."

Another step and he had both feet in. He closed one eye and looked at her with a scrunched up face. "I hope you're considering how cold this might feel against a fellow's legs?"

Finella smiled. "I hope you consider how desperate I am to not share the experience."

He took another step and she felt his body sink further.

"You mean slip and fall or deliberately dunk you?"

"You wouldn't let either happen, would you?"

"As I remember it, there's always been a moment I've looked for as payment for the face full of flour. Remember that, Miss Finella." He stopped in the middle of the stream. "Remember when I said revenge would find you, somehow?"

His breath tickled her chin. Sent a posse of shivers up her nape and through her hair and they had nothing to do with the freezing waters swirling around them.

"Keep walking."

"I will." He answered, as if he lazed against the garden gate. "When you pay your passage across."

She stared at him. Stared hard and wondered how she'd not seen this coming. Blue eyes flashed at her, daring her with a deepness she cared for more than her desire to escape an ill timed ocean dip.

He let his grip slacken a little. Enough to warn her to hurry up. Enough to make her hold tighter. She leaned in, close enough to leave a tentative kiss on his rough cheek.

"Call that a kiss?" he asked with a low rumble.

"From where you stand, Mr. Jones, you've not completed our crossing. You get part payment here and full payment when we're clear."

'He sloshed his way across in five large steps. Quicker than she imagined, her feet landed on a low spread of rocks jutting out from the cliff.

Shadrach shook his legs free of cold water and climbed the rock to stand beside her.

He bowed and with one arm, scooped her into his embrace again. Only this time they met with all four feet on the ground. Finella wasn't sure how long hers would stay there. He ran his other hand along her cheek and pulled her close enough to whisper against her lips.

"Pay up, Dandelion."

Finella trembled. He'd stolen a kiss from her before, but now he demanded what she'd just promised. And she'd have to give it. She'd meant to add a quick kiss to his other cheek but now...

"In full." He closed his eyes and waited.

Finella leaned in and pressed her lips against his. He did nothing in return. This was not like last time. This was like kissing a fence post.

He cracked an eye open. "Like you mean it," he added, and closed his eye again.

The swell of life bubbled up in Finella's chest and she fought hard to find just the right place to balance her toes.

A flicker of the sun's last rays bounced off his dark hair, and she pushed it with gentle strokes off his face with her fingers. The tightness in his eyes faded and he opened them to watch her.

Emboldened by lengthening shadows, she wound one hand behind his head and cradled it against her palm.

And right there, with the sun and all its ribbons playing in the sky, Finella thanked Shadrach Jones for carrying her along the pier, over the puddles, and across the stream.

29

―――――――

"*Y*ou did *what?*"

Shadrach ducked Sharpie's laughter. It roared across the campground drowning out the music until Shadrach elbowed the guy in the pouch with a soft blow.

"Enough, old man. Ever thought I might not want an audience?"

Sharpie sucked in gulps of air and doubled over to laugh some more. "You've got no choice there, Shad." He wiped his eye with the heel of his hand. "Get prepared to become the laughing stock of the district." He dissolved into another round of chuckles, and hunted in his pocket until he produced a crumpled handkerchief.

Shadrach shot the man a look he hoped said, move-or-I'll-give-you-a-real-reason-to-need-that-rag. He picked up his empty crate and egging crook, and moved off to his tent. It would only last until morning, but at least the cover of darkness saved him from further disgrace.

For while he'd enjoyed his sunset walk with Finella more than he'd imagined possible, he hadn't factored the tide would slip in and steal his crate of eggs.

"Shadrach? Is it true? Did you really lose your whole day's catch?" Goliah Ashe sidled up to him.

" 'Fraid so."

"How?"

How indeed? He fumbled in the dark with wet boots.

Inconceivable as it sounded, he knew this wouldn't be the last occasion when he'd have to explain the misfortune. He'd better rehearse the shortest version.

"Finella slipped down the slope where I worked part of the afternoon." He tugged a stubborn wet knot. "Between us we disturbed some sand and well, we had to come back through the cove and along the beach. Tide had come in at one spot and I carried her over. Didn't get back for my eggs until it was too late."

Was that short enough? The preacher kept his face hidden in the shadows.

"By the time I went back the tide had carried everything away. Lucky I found the crate and crook, floating nearby."

He tossed his shoe against the empty crate. Silence, less than golden, filled the space between them.

"You… you forgot your crate of eggs?" Goliah's voice trembled but to the man's credit, he didn't guffaw.

"I didn't forget." Shadrach yanked at his other bootlace. "I just didn't get to them in time. That's all."

Because kissing Finella was better than almost anything else I could think of. "Could happen to anyone, couldn't it?" He turned to Goliah.

The new preacher coughed. It sounded more like a stifled chuckle.

"It could. Why not?" He didn't sound convincing. "I hope your empty crate means you caught another prize."

Shadrach threw his other boot down. He didn't care much where it landed. Dizzy with hunger and hot with fury at himself for letting his egg catch slip away, he needed a way out of this mess. But it was more than eggs snatched by the tide. It was what had happened next that filled him with shame. But he wouldn't think about that now.

"Do you know how much Melbourne bakers pay for those eggs, Goliah? How many Christmas cakes they make each year with eggs from this island? They're mad for them in town. They sell faster than goose eggs." He hung his head. "If you've got any to sell."

Goliah sat on the ground beside him. "That's some loss, Shadrach. I'm sorry to hear it. What do you have from yesterday's hunt?"

The accordion cried in the night.

"Half a crate."

"So, you missed out on your egg money this year. My wife tells me there's something else you've been hunting."

Shadrach shrugged. Yes, he'd managed another kiss from Finella, but the walk back had been marred by their shared disbelief and disappointment at losing the eggs. And the annoying tap of the empty crate against his wet trousers. Neither one said much along the bush track, the lost eggs extinguishing the sweetness their kiss had delivered.

Shadrach blew out a puff of air. "I ruined something I've waited for a long time." He looked up at the stars and the knots in his neck crackled.

It pained him to admit it. To remember the frenzied way he'd trampled eggs in the shallows. The disbelief that tipped him over. The anger that pushed him to nearly split the crate into a million splinters on the ragged rocks.

"I clammed up pretty good after I found that empty crate. Lost the mood." He dug his elbows onto his knees and looked at the preacher.

"There's always next year. Folks will enjoy your story for a few days, but they'll forget about it soon enough."

"Question is, will Finella?"

"How did you part?"

"She couldn't scamper away fast enough."

The preacher tapped him on the back. "Fresh trouble always looks worse than it really is. I'll help you pack up in the morning. I'm thinking you'll want to move off early."

"Is before dawn too early?"

"If you've still got Finella on your side, you won't care about the eggs by nightfall tomorrow. I promise."

Shadrach hoped the man knew what he was talking about. Right now he had a sinking feeling lost eggs were only the beginning of his troubles.

∽

Shadrach circled the house like a speared bull; steaming mad for reasons even he didn't understand. He pocketed a quick breakfast when he knew Finella and Molly made a trip to the chickens, but other than that, steered clear of the two of them.

He didn't need reminders of his quick-tempered outburst at the shallows when he lost the eggs, and probably Finella's respect.

Probably?

He scoffed at his own logic. Not probably. Definitely. Absolutely. And any other word that meant she was most likely in his skillion right now, balancing on a chair to reach her bags.

He hunkered down in the barn and threaded a long needle. He'd not made a blanket of rabbit before, and hoped his attempt would make Molly happy come Christmas day. He remembered how he'd ignored her this morning and dread squeezed at his core. Dread and shame and the knowledge by dusk tonight the entire district would laugh at his misfortune.

And tomorrow? He didn't want to think about facing the village when he took his eggs in for sale.

How had he gone from champion one year to laughing stock the next? He pierced the rabbit skin with such force his own flesh paid the price.

Goliah Ashe had better be right in thinking people would forget. He sucked the blood from his palm. The sooner they had something better to talk about the better.

But what about Finella?

He dropped the skins and paced. Stretched his arms over his head until they met with the rafters of his barn. His fingers grazed the rough boards he'd nailed there himself. Flashes of his father and the night he brought their tent crashing around their heads, chipped at Shadrach's thoughts.

Have I turned into him?

If Finella hadn't held her ground, he would've smashed that crate into sawdust.

Turned into him.

Shame folded around him and he gripped the rafter with one hand. Finella deserved to be with someone who wasn't going to turn into a monster. Wasn't a big part of her fear the convict legacy? His gullet brimmed with hot gall and he let go of the wooden plank to kneel in the dust.

I've held it back long enough, but is one wrong move enough to turn me into my father?

"Will Brother ever cheer up?" Molly asked from her bed where she lay like a cat in the sun.

Finella measured oats into the porridge pot. "He will. In time."

"He's cross about the eggs."

"He's cross about many things, the eggs being one." Finella poured the milk.

"I like Brother when he's laughing."

Finella considered much of what she'd been thinking on the

silent ride home. "Me too."

She banged the pot over the fire. Her kisses were not for any charmer who came along. And if she was going to kiss someone, he'd better not be grumpy about it afterwards. Even if all the eggs in creation washed away.

But Shadrach Jones was not any old charmer. And she'd not soon forget the look on his face when she pulled away from their kiss. The rough scrape of his hand on her chin. The way he drew her closer for another kiss, and then another.

"Is my debt paid?"

"Not yet." He'd whispered. "You still owe me." More and then some more, until the cold shadows of night pulled them out of where nothing should have found them.

Only calamity was a good hunter and had snuck in with great reward. Just when she found herself wanting him to ask again, questions about their future remained unexplored. Robbed in more ways than one, they'd returned with less than they imagined. Not even one egg remained at the end of a fractured day.

In a way, she understood his brooding last night. But to remain silent all morning when they drove home under the morning fog? Even with Molly?

No. An ember lit in Finella's stomach as sure as the flame at her side. She ground the wooden spoon through the thickening oats.

No one would steal from her again. No thief, no sickness. Not even the deep blue sea.

30

*H*e didn't consider it stealing, but eating a slab of damper and two pickled cucumbers in such a hurry at his abandoned table, almost came close. Shadrach didn't know where Finella had taken Molly, and if that were his only bothersome thought, the pickle may not have caught in his throat like a thief's reward.

But the empty room was only part of what grieved him. He scraped his hand along the stubble on his jaw. Where had they gone? He should have sought them out, but he'd been too busy. In his fields, in his barn, and in a self-made pit where he'd stewed all day. And he had no mind to climb out, just yet.

He pinched another pickle. Sour deserved sour, didn't it? *And that's why Finella doesn't deserve you.*

He wiped his vinegary hands on his trousers, and ground every boot-step back along the shell path to the barn. Even his rabbit pelts came in short. He may as well grab the blanket from his bed and measure how much more he'd need for Molly's gift.

Unlike the empty house, his skillion chimed with laughter.

"Now, you put it on." Molly's voice held the sparkle of someone who'd been tickled.

He peeked into the room where they sat on the edge of his bedroll. Finella and Molly. Shoulder to shoulder they looked like the best of friends, one of Finella's trunks open at their knees. Finella tried on some kind of crown and made a face at Molly who giggled for more.

He warmed to see them so close. He'd done the right thing by Molly in bringing Finella here. What he wouldn't give for his mother to see this.

"Brother?" Molly reached out. "Come and see.'"

He let Molly take his hand and squeezed into the small room. The ache in his chest pressed him from within, while the overcrowded room closed in from every side.

"And what am I looking at?" He peered at the box. He was in no mood to be drawn into their fun.

"Christmas." Molly beamed.

"In there? All of Christmas?" He knew he should smile, but he didn't have the heart for it.

"And look at Finella." Molly pointed with two hands.

Did he have to?

"She's wearing a hello."

Finella grinned at him, but her smile didn't reach her eyes either. "A halo, actually." She lifted it from her head and long ribbons of gold and silver pulled at her hair.

He couldn't help himself. "Travel with your own halo?" He leaned back against the doorframe.

She wrapped it in a piece of tissue paper and laid it back in her box of fancies.

"I wore this when I was Molly's age for a Christmas pageant at church. It's all I have left of my angel costume. My mother made it before she…"

She slapped the lid on the box and looked up at him.

"Molly and I shall be adding some of these trinkets to the house over the next few weeks. Christmas preparations." She held his eye with a pained look. "If you agree."

Christmas. Aunt Sarah. She didn't need to tell him anymore. He filled in the gaps. *Her ticket away out of here.*

He shrugged, but it did nothing for his sinking heart. "If it makes Molly happy."

"Really?" She sounded surprised. "You won't mind if we decorate the house?"

"Do what you have to."

"Even if we use *fancy* things?"

He knew she tried to draw him from wherever she thought he might be. Truth be told he had no idea *where* he was. Only that it was no place he enjoyed.

He yanked the blanket off the bed. "I don't care, Finella. Hang every last one of your fancies off the shingles."

He walked past Molly who scowled at him and probably past a deeper frown on Finella's face, but he wouldn't turn to look. It was enough to know he'd hurt them both. The best thing they could do was get used to it.

○

The barn offered no peace. Or light. He dumped all his pelts into the blanket and dragged the bundle outside, behind the barn. Facing west, he crouched and spread out his skins.

He was right. No matter how you lined them up, the pelts only made a lap blanket at best. He sat with his back against the barn and threaded a new length of cotton onto his needle.

"Did you think I wouldn't find you hiding back here?" Finella turned the corner, steaming mug in hand.

"Who said I was hiding?"

She sat down and her skirt brushed his leg. "Oh, you're not hiding from us today? My mistake. I thought you might like a cup of tea."

He let the point of the needle touch his thumb.

"Where's Molly?" He took the tea.

"Washing angels. She's got a tub on the table and she's washing a Christmas apron, embroidered by my mother. We only ever used it once a year. Molly's quite taken by it. She couldn't wait for washday to freshen it up." Her lips formed a baby smile. She baited him for something, but he wasn't sure what.

She ran her fingers through the nearest pelt, a light brown piece. "So soft."

A slim thread of silver from her Christmas decorations still caught in her hair. Yesterday he would have pulled it out. Maybe brushed her cheek as he did it. Today he chose to look away.

"You'd better get back. Molly's probably run out of water and on her way to the well for more."

Finella rested her shoulders against the barn wall. "I tied her to the chair."

A splash of hot tea burned his chin. He spluttered and wiped his mouth with the back of his hand. "You did what?"

Her smile widened. "I tied her up."

He stared at her. "How?"

"You should know. You're the one who showed me." She threw the brown pellet back in the pile. "I tied the rope around her waist and the chair. I explained how it's good for her posture to sit up straight while she scrubs. You should come in and see her. She's so proud of her washing she hardly knows the rope's there."

He tried another sip. "I thought you were against that."

"I was. But, I've discovered Molly doesn't care about the rope if she's doing something she enjoys." Her face clouded over. "And I guess, you forced me to consider it."

"I did." He repeated her. "I did force."

The orange sun shot through the scrub right into her face and she closed her eyes.

"Shadrach, we've hardly talked since last night. I can't pin you down long enough to say I'm sorry."

When he didn't answer she peeked at him through one eye. One beautiful golden-brown eye. How had he not seen those honey flecks before?

"*You're* sorry? What for? *I* lost the eggs."

"Were you walking alone?" she demanded, both eyes on him now. "Perhaps if you were, then it would be all your fault. But you weren't. We were there together." Her words settled on him with a tenderness he couldn't afford.

"Look, I should have gone back for that crate the minute I set you down. It was my responsibility and I'll have to wear it. You don't need to worry. These things happen." He put the mug down and reached for his needle.

She beat him to it and snatched it away. "Then why are you still vexed?"

"I'm not vexed at you." He held out his hand. "Now, give me my thread."

"I think you are."

He rubbed the back of his shoulder. His muscles ached, he was sure his tongue was burnt from the tea, and a weariness pinched a nerve so far into his soul, he hardly knew where that was.

"I'm not angry at you. I don't blame you for the eggs. Now give me the thread."

She wound the cotton around her finger. "Then who are you angry at, and could you please fix it? Because we have other things to talk about, you and I. And I don't like it that we're not."

Blood colored her skin where she wound the cotton. It matched the red in her cheeks and a sick feeling filled him. He'd kissed her. And she'd returned the kiss. And he'd rewarded her with raw silence.

"I'm angry at myself. And tomorrow when I take that little crate from the first day's egging to the village, everyone else will be there to watch me sell the smallest amount I've ever handed over to the Melbourne traders."

She lifted her head and waited.

"But I'll get over all that. It's…" Did he want to uncover this nest of maggots he wrestled? How could he tell her? He blew out a trapped breath and let some of his fury take sail. "I'm furious at myself for the way I almost smashed that crate." He rolled his fingers into fists. "If you hadn't been there to take it off me, I surely would have."

"If I'd not been there, there wouldn't have been occasion to walk the beach with a heavy crate of eggs."

He looked away. She didn't understand. But she'd asked and he'd be heartless to let her think it was her fault.

"If it didn't happen at the beach, it would have happened somewhere else. I didn't react how I should have. I'm ashamed you saw it, but the sooner I get a proper grip on it the better. You did me a favor."

"What favor? What are you talking about?" She let the thread unravel against her palm.

He took it from her. He would rather sew his mouth shut than say it. He hardly knew how to explain it to himself.

"You helped me see something. About myself." Still warm from Finella's hand, he twisted the thread into a knot. "I'm just like my father. And he was a monster."

The sick feeling he'd kept down all day threatened to boil over. But he swallowed and looked beyond the tea tree scrub. A flame of sunset dragged the blue out of the sky.

"You're no such thing." Soft words hung between them like down. But he refused their cover.

He wouldn't look at her, either. Whatever face she had for this was one he didn't want to see. He turned his back on her to sort the pelts.

A hard thump pushed against his shoulder.

"Did you hear me?" She poked again.

He picked two pieces and pressed them fur side together. "I heard you."

"Good." She stood. "Then you can hear this too." Her words came out clipped. "You are not your father. If you had been, I would've left months ago. With Molly in tow, whether you liked it or not."

Months ago, he'd been a different man. But he loved her now, and would fight himself to protect her.

Copper and sparks shot from the flyaway wisps of her hair. She turned to go and in the same step turned back.

"I saved my kisses for a fine man, Shadrach Jones. You best be sure of that. And I won't have you turn me into a liar."

December 1

Aunt Sarah believes her ship will arrive in the New Year. For weeks I've watched the horizon and wondered how many miles she's already put behind her.

But her journey here is only the beginning. After that, there's much to be seen. Most of it I dread.

But I'm at a greater loss to know what will fix the drift between Shadrach and me. And that is not something I wish to explain to Aunt Sarah. Shadrach hints at Molly's future. He skirts around the subject with veiled reference to her and me. Molly and I. But he's not in the picture he alludes to. And I do not know how to convince him we all belong together. That he is his own man, and not a replica of his father.

I always thought if I could alter the course of time I would have

begged God to put that wretched thief on another road, far from my
parents on that day he killed my mother.

But now, I find myself pondering the morning I begged to go to
Shadrach's egging, and how he gave in to me, despite his doubts. How
tangled he's become since, in his own misery. And how I wish I could
change that.

I have nestled in a groove not of my making, and find my heart
turned to it. If only he still felt the same.

Shadrach wiped his hands on his shirt. Long streaks of chalky clay
striped not only his torso, but his trousers as well and mud clods
clung to his boots.

He pushed his barrow over slimy wood planks to the other end of
the clay pit, where a wide parcel of his land now held close to one
hundred bricks.

Imagine Finella having to wade through this mud.

Good weather meant his bricks would dry well and early summer
filled his chest with a shaft of hope he'd not felt in days. All he had to
do was ignore the rain clouds in the distance.

If he could make another few hundred bricks to sell in the village,
he would make up for the lost egg income. People paid good money
for bricks on the island. If word got around he had some at a fair
price, he was sure they'd sell faster than Christmas geese at Spencer's
butchery.

And he needed the sale. Not for the seed he planned for next
year's crops. Nor for the timber he wanted to order for a large
farmhouse on the hill. Every last penny would go toward his sister's
future. And if Finella wanted her, he'd give her over. And all the
money he could earn in the meantime for her support.

The barrow squished into the ground. He rubbed his hands together and mud flakes crumbled like confetti onto his shoes. Yes, Finella wouldn't set foot in this quagmire if he begged her. And those days were gone as sure as his egg money.

∽

"I think we should have pie for Christmas."

"Pie?" Finella tapped her pencil on Aunt Sarah's recipes, spread all over Shadrach's beaten tabletop. Most of her Christmas favorites needed an oven. A pie might not be as easy to deliver as damper. "And what pie would you like, Molly dear?"

"Jam?"

Finella drew the girl's shoulders into a tight embrace. She wouldn't let tears smudge her view. All scrubbed and clean, with a fresh apron on, it didn't take much for Molly to pull on Finella's heartstrings. The young girl pressed against her with the warm crush of a sleepy toddler.

Finella dragged her thoughts back to the Christmas menu. A meal to make a dear one happy, and take away the sting of loss. She unbuttoned her sleeve cuffs and peered through the window at the movement outside. Shadrach pounded his feet in the yard.

Transfixed by the churning of her heart, she stood still while his blue eyes stared back at her from the other side of the clear glass. For blue was the only color she saw, other than his head to foot covering of mud.

"Open the door," he called, and she swung it open. "I know, I know. You'll skin me, if I come closer." He raised his palms in defeat but Finella heard the teasing in his voice. She leaned against the doorjamb.

"Why are you here, then?"

"Just wondering if a man could ask for an outdoor lunch today. It'll save me from getting out of these." He slapped at his dirty trousers.

Finella made room at the door where Molly joined her. "Looks to me like you found Jimmy Callahan and his mudslinging gang."

He smiled, and the white of his teeth shone out from his dirty face. She hadn't seen that smile for days and it couldn't have smacked against her any harder than if Molly had elbowed her in the ribs.

"No. Just me, out there." He rubbed at a spot on his cheek. "I need to get a few things from the barn, but if I could trouble you for my meal now, I'd be happy to take it with me."

Finella nodded and he hurried for the path up the hill.

"Brother needs a bath." Molly watched him go.

"And food." Finella couldn't tell what made him happy after so many miserable days, but she didn't stop to wonder. He was smiling and that was something.

"Why don't we pack Shadrach's lunch and eat ours with him, too? Here," she spread a cloth on the table. "Wrap the last of the damper." She grabbed a coarse towel from where it hung by the fire. "And some apples and I'll take our bean stew off the fire and carry it myself. Can you manage?"

Molly nodded, already selecting the apples she fancied best.

"And some forks too." Finella reminded. Whatever drew Shadrach's smile was worth seeing for herself. Even if he hadn't invited her along.

31

"Brick making?" Finella stood on the slope and looked past his last chicory field. "Since when?"

He hurried on, careful not to nudge her with his dirty sleeve. "Since last year, when I thought I'd dig a second well for my crops and found clay instead."

He hoped she followed. His stomach rumbled and he wanted to get back to work while the day hung with sunshine. "Always meant to turn it into bricks one day. When I had the time." *Or needed the money.*

He put the stewpot down under a blue gum. "This spot's shady enough. Finella?"

She wasn't watching. Her eyes remained fixed on the stack of bricks drying in the midday heat. "And you're going to sell them all?"

"Already good as sold. Every one of them. Spencer put me onto a fellow who wants to build a kiln for his chicory crop."

He untied the knot in Molly's bundle. "Might build a kiln for myself, too. If this clay pit is kind enough to supply it."

Finella spread a blanket and settled on the ground with Molly. She dished up the stew and Shadrach's mouth popped in anticipation. He blessed the food quickly and devoured it a little less so.

"We have apples, too." Molly handed him a red one. "I polished it."

He wrapped her hand with his and squeezed.

"And I trust you to look after it for me." He wiped his mouth. "I'm going to make another row and then I'll come looking for that apple." He winked at her. With a full belly and a pit full of bricks, it came easier, somehow. Until he remembered why he needed the extra money.

"Thanks for the picnic, Finella." He stood. "Stay and enjoy the day if there's nothing pressing back at the house." He slapped his hat back on his head, "I'm gonna make bricks."

◌

Finella sliced an apple and held a piece to Molly on the tip of her knife. Aunt Sarah would have a royal conniption to see her offer food like a barbarian.

Surely you could have used a plate, Finella dear. You've turned into a savage already. She could hear her now. Finding fault with the table setting, the crude utensils, Molly's manners. In another month they would hear it all for themselves.

She leaned against the blue gum, and somehow, it mattered less and less. Molly munched on her fruit and Finella joined her, and together they watched Shadrach lug another barrow of clay.

A long sweat stain lined the back of his shirt, and the mud from this morning, lighter and dustier than when he'd eaten with them, now hid behind a layer of wet clods. He wiped his palms on his trousers before grabbing the barrow handles, and tipped the lot into a large mound.

He squatted to dust a wooden trough with sand. Finella craned her neck to see more. He dusted his hands the same way, and formed a warp of clay into a brick shape before pressing it into the wooden mold. With an implement she didn't recognize, he scraped the excess, tapped the side with a small hammer and pulled the whole mold up, leaving one more brick in step with the others.

Again and again, he worked with a rhythm until another ten or so bricks appeared.

Finella picked up her knife. "Molly, let's take Shad his apple and see what he's up to."

"But we'll get dirty. We hate mud, remember?"

"We're not going to make bricks, dear. Only look at them. We'll watch from the grass, near the edge."

By the time they reached the small clay pit, Shadrach leaned against his shovel.

"Come to help?"

"I thought you might like your apple." Finella offered a quarter on the tip of her knife.

Molly squatted along the edge of the grass and pressed her fingertip in the top of a freshly made brick.

"They'll take about a week to dry." Shadrach reached for the apple and took a bite. "If the sun stays out long enough."

"How many bricks do you have?" Finella tried to count them.

"Over a hundred." He tossed the shovel into the barrow. "And, if you will excuse me. I'm about to make another hundred."

He tried to pass but she stood in his way.

"When will they be ready?"

"I need to fire them. Another two weeks, I guess." He shrugged and tried to weave past.

She moved with him, blocking his way further. "Will there be any left over?"

He let the handles go and the shovel bounced against the barrow.

"You're in my way."

She held her ground, but sliced another quarter off the apple and held it out. "If you have enough bricks left, would you consider building a proper brick oven?"

He eyed the slice as if it were poison. "What are you talking about?" He took the fruit.

"An oven, made of bricks. Nothing nearly as tall as a kiln would be, I imagine. You could sell what you can and keep some for a baking oven."

"And why would I want to do that?" He swerved the barrow past her.

"So we could have something other than damper. So I can cook a real Christmas dinner."

Molly joined her. "So I can have pie."

He sliced his shovel into the bog like a spear and held the top for ages before he turned. Long and measured, his footsteps trailed back to where she stood.

He unrolled his shirtsleeve, now crumpled past his elbow and refolded it to sit around the muscle in his arm.

"You want me to give up my income, so you can bake a pie?"

"Not just any pie. A Christmas pie, with currants. And perhaps we could even cook a goose."

He worked on his other sleeve.

"Molly won't be so scared if the fire's contained in an oven. It doesn't have to be anything…" She stopped. She wanted to say *fancy,* but they'd fought over that word enough. "Elaborate. A simple bread oven." She handed him the last apple quarter.

He shook his head. "There's no time. I'm going to have to work 'til there's no light as it is just to make this order. If I take any bricks out for myself, there won't be enough for anything."

"What if we help?" The words hurtled out before Finella knew she'd said them. She held up her chin and tried to belong to the offer.

Shadrach pointed at her with the fruit. "You… would dirty your fingernails and drag your shoes through this?" He cocked his head at the pit behind them.

Finella slid the knife into her deep pocket with a slow unconvincing nod.

"You wouldn't last a half hour here. Why..." he laughed, "I'm sure you wouldn't make one solitary brick, and do you know why?" He leaned closer and whispered. "You hate mud." He straightened and walked away.

"I don't like it on my doorstep, but I like it enough to make an oven for your home." She wouldn't back off. The pit held hundreds of bricks, and it would take him days to make them all. But if she, and Molly, who already poked her fingers where she shouldn't, helped, perhaps they could have an oven for Christmas after all. She had nothing to lose by begging. "Please, Shad?"

He filled the barrow with heavy slops and wobbled back across a plank. "You want to play in the mud, Finella?"

With a slow squelch, and under a growing smile, he slid the shovel out of the clay and handed it over as if it were the finest silk parasol. "As you wish."

32

"It's cold." Molly squealed like a baby pig, lifted her skirt and inspected her wet toes.

"At least your shoes will stay clean." Finella returned from where she placed Molly's shoes and stockings beside their picnic things. Her own shoes would not fare so well.

"If Molly gets to stir the clay, what do I do?" She undid her cuff buttons. Shadrach added water to where Molly worked sand into the mix. He pierced the ground with a long stick and showed his sister how to hold it to keep from slipping over.

"You, Miss Mayfield," he pulled at the string of her apron, "will fill the molds while I bring more clay from the pit. Unless you'd prefer to push the barrow?"

He couldn't be serious? Not with that glimmer in his eye. Finella had neither pushed or emptied a barrow of mud in her life.

"I'd be happy to press bricks for your new oven, Mr. Jones." She mirrored his playfulness. "And you will not have time to draw breath to thank me, when you taste your first mouthful of cake."

He laughed and pushed off. "Make ten before I'm back. Then you can brag."

Ten bricks? Just like that? She hurried to the pile of sand, thankful the ground underfoot was not the quagmire where Shadrach and his barrow sank.

"Well, Molly, you've been watching. Let's see if I do it right." She crouched at ground level and looked for something to scoop up the mud. A *C*-shaped sapling with wire across the open end was all she could find. That wouldn't do. That was for shaving excess mud.

"Ten bricks, Finella." He called from the pit. "How many have you made already?"

"None." Molly called back, and a long chuckle wound out from the pit like the clapping of a child about to win a prize.

Finella balanced on her haunches. "Molly, if you're going to take sides, would it be too much to ask it be mine?" She wriggled for a firmer footing. "I would have made a start if I could find a trowel."

"Use your hands. Like Brother."

Finella bit the inside of her cheek. "He did, didn't he?" She closed her eyes and ran her palms over her hair. Secured any curls behind her ears and pushed her rolled up sleeves even higher.

"He's coming back." Molly whispered.

Finella plunged her hands into the cold, sticky mix. She wriggled her fingers. Oh, and she'd forgotten to dust them first. Would it matter? She gathered a thick lump and let it fall into a mold.

It landed with a slop, and a drip of mud bounced up to her forehead. Half in, half out, she pushed the mud back into the frame and wiped the overflow with her palm.

"He's coming." Molly whispered again.

Finella tried to lift the frame but it wouldn't move. She tugged and tapped the side, but the odd shaped brick refused to fall.

"So, ten bricks is it?" Shadrach stopped the wheelbarrow right beside Finella, nose to nose with her failed attempt.

She raised her hands in the air, a mess of mud stains clear to her wrists.

"I can't get it out."

"Why not?" He pressed one knee in the ground beside her.

Stuck out at an angle as it was, her elbow came perilously close to his chin, and for a moment, she thought about how she could poke him with it. How good it might feel to push him right into his pile of mud.

"Perhaps you can tell me what I've done wrong." The balls of her feet flamed and a slow wobble took hold in her ankle.

Shadrach massaged her hand. "Did you dust your hands and the brick mold with sand?"

Finella shook her head.

"Well, there's your trouble." He dragged another mold through the sand and like a conjuror, scraped mud and tapped the box to release a perfect brick.

He slapped his hands together. "Now you make one."

Finella didn't know how she would stay upright a moment longer. Her legs trembled and she leaned into the dirt with one hand.

"Let your knees keep you up. You'll never manage like that." He rested his other knee in the mud to show her.

The smell of earth and sand filled her mouth. Mud dried in her fingernails and splotches already stained her apron. What difference did it make now if she rested one knee in the dirt? She could dream about honey cakes when she next labored over the washtubs.

She copied Shadrach's stance. It felt good to change position. Good to not tremble. On the outside at least.

On the inside, it felt good to kneel in the dirt with Shadrach Jones. To work beside him with Molly laughing at her attempts. To have him tease her while they made brick after brick after brick, until another five rows emerged from the ground.

"You see." He stood and pulled her up. "Mud really is your friend."

She stretched her arms above her head. "Are you sure you don't mean that about Molly?" They laughed at their girl, ankle deep in the mire.

"Can I stop now?" Molly rested her chin on the balancing stick. "My feet hurt."

"If you can get there, you can have a rest at our picnic spot." Shadrach helped her out. "Wipe your feet on your way across."

Molly moved away to nestle in the perfect place for an afternoon nap.

"Normally it's me telling her to wipe her feet." Finella picked at her nails. "Sounds strange to hear you say it."

Shadrach fixed a fresh smile on her. "Stranger than you making bricks?"

Finella rested her hands on her hips. There was no keeping dirty fingers from smudging her clothes now. That battle was already lost. "Ready to make more?"

Wider than a country mile, his smile engulfed her. "How about I race you? First one to twenty bricks."

A fresh smudge colored his cheek. Flecks of mud littered his hair, but it all disappeared against the drag of his eyes. They tugged at her heart, until bricks and ovens and honeycakes faded from her mind, and all she remembered was Shadrach Jones.

She pulled away, afraid of what it meant to see him and nothing else. She searched the trees for Molly who stretched out on the blanket with another apple. She'd be asleep before the second bite.

"Too much?" Shadrach pushed against her with his shoulder. "Not up to it? Shall we say fifteen and make it easier for the poor English lass?"

She poked him in the arm. One long bony poke she knew would hurt.

"Oww. What's that for?"

"That," she said, shoving him away, "is for me to get a head start.

Twenty bricks and not one less." She pressed Molly's stick in the ground as a marker. "You put your bricks there and I'll stack mine here. No cheating." She wanted to laugh at the look on his face.

Open-mouthed, he watched her for a second, and then hurried to reach for the second brick frame.

Finella knew he would beat her. Knew from his long steps and swift maneuvering of clay she didn't stand a chance. But good-natured banter while they worked filled her with something she couldn't help savor.

She peeked at his progress. For her three bricks he had six.

"Come on, Finella." He coaxed. "You spend too much time watching and not enough time slapping mud."

True enough.

She watched his broad shoulders flex against his dirty shirt.

Taking aim, she tossed a handful of wet clay at his neck. Remarkably, it slapped where she wanted it to.

Shadrach froze, and the clod dribbled down the inside of his collarless shirt. She bit her lip. Oh, she'd pay for it, but slowing him down was worth the damage.

"You mean like *that*?" She dared him. "That kind of slap?"

He rubbed at a pink welt on his neck and raised one knee. Like a lever about to spring.

"Do you know… what happens to people…who toss mud?" He spoke in a low rumble.

Finella threw a trembling wad of clay into her mold. "They hit their target?" Pretending to work, her fingers achieved even less than before.

"Is that so?" Shadrach pounced. He flattened her hands down in the clay with one of his. He brought his cheek against hers to whisper.

"You don't fling mud, and pretend it never happened." Tingles exploded where his voice brushed her neck.

"I'm busy, can't you see? I'm going to best you at brick making." She shoved him with her shoulder. "Move away and let me finish."

He didn't budge. "What I see, is a face about to become messier than it already is."

"Now, Shadrach…" She wriggled but it made no difference.

"Now, Finella," he echoed, and pointed one dirty long finger. "You're about to learn more than brick-making today, so sit still."

"Shadrach, I—"

"Shh." He almost touched her lips. "Lesson one." He drew the back of his hand along her cheek forcing her to close her eyes against the wet brush of soiled fingers. "Never, ever poke your teacher. That's disrespectful."

She had never shown disrespect to a teacher before and she was sure no teacher had ever caressed her in return. His fingers sent out splintered rivulets in every direction and her shiver deepened.

"Lesson two." He marked her other cheek with his dirty palm. "Never throw mud at a fellow unless you're prepared to receive in good measure what you give away."

She opened her eyes. He brought his other hand to her cheek, and she grabbed a fistful of his shirt to keep from toppling over.

His eyes found her mouth, just as quickly as her heart found a new beat. Fast, like the beat she supposed took over when ground turned to quicksand.

"Every time I want to kiss you, you're almost drenched or covered in mud." His grip tightened on her face.

"Not fancy enough for you, Mr. Jones?" Finella wrestled with the air around her. Surely some would fill her lungs.

"Fancy enough. For me." His hands took the back of her neck with a shaping better than any brick making he'd do that day, and his lips did the same. Better than any mark, his kiss stamped an earthiness she needed more than London's best row of pastry ovens.

Shadrach pulled away before she'd savored enough. He stretched his legs and found a place beside her on the ground where she'd sunk. Both of them in a muddy tangle.

"How did this get so messy? I want to keep kissing you. I'm not going to lie. And I forget until I'm half way lost that I can't do that." He bent his knee and brushed the wet spot where he'd kneeled.

"Shouldn't I have a say? Aren't you the one who's said all along I need to make decisions, too?"

"That was before. There's more to be considered now. I'm sorry. I shouldn't have teased you. I…" He rubbed at his face, as if he could erase her by tearing at his skin.

Finella covered his hands with her own. "You don't have to fight me."

"Don't I?"

"No, you don't. You're not your father. No matter what you think. You're a different man and I wouldn't care to be here, in your bog, with you, if you were someone else." She let her voice soften. "But you're not. You're Shadrach Jones."

"Son of a temper-fuelled man." He searched her eyes. "A man who tore his own house apart 'cause he couldn't keep a lid on it."

"Just because you lost your temper at the beach doesn't make you him." She moved Molly's stick from between them. "Didn't he run off, when you and your mother needed him the most? When Molly needed him? I don't see you running away. You're here, caring for a sister who needs you and a woman who…" she stopped.

"Are you going to tell me you need me, too?"

"Would you recoil like your father if I did, or take the risk?"

He reached for a curl that brushed against her neck. He coiled his finger in it and let it bounce away. "Can *you* risk it?"

"What do you think I'm already doing, sitting here with a clay hem?"

He smiled but his eyes held onto pain. "What if you're wrong?"

"I have to trust my heart. Isn't that what you told me?" She leaned her face into his palm. "I didn't come all this way to consider a future with a monster like your father. If you were anything like him, my footprints would've already washed out of the sand on my way home." She pulled away a little to see him better. "You might be covered in mud, but you're full of courage. Nothing your father has ever done could take away from who you are."

Spots of rain hit the fledgling brickworks, but Finella didn't care. She leaned against the cup of his hand, and into the fold of another kiss.

33

Shadrach urged Old Lou on. Up the hill and over the yard to the barn and its welcome roof. The dray held the last load of bricks. After this, it would be mud he'd cart from the pit. Shovels full. Barrows to the brim. No threat of rain would keep him from turning his barn into a covered brickworks.

He had hundreds more to mold. A sale to secure. And an oven to build. He shook his head in disbelief, but his heart surged on.

An oven for Finella. Perhaps his farm had something to offer, after all. Even now, she worked to move bricks in from the rain. She lined them into rows on the ground, even dragged some planks together in a crude sawhorse she preferred for a brick-making bench. Better for the back, she'd said. And the knees.

He wasn't used to having someone work beside him. And he liked what went on under his nose. Gulped it in with the same ferocity he felt in the wind when it buffeted the trees and swirled around him. Finella no longer twisted her nose at him or his mud. She was knee deep in it now, and nothing thrilled him more.

Shadrach rummaged through his nail and screw tin. "Time for a break. You'd think someone had cracked a bullwhip in here." Finella and Molly turned to face him. "No use making a ton of bricks and not having a little fun."

Finella and Molly joined him at the trestle where they'd worked to shape the morning's bricks. Side by side for three days, and he'd not heard one complaint from Finella.

He poked at a brick. "Good, still soft. We're going to scratch our names on three of the best shaped bricks. And when we build that oven, they'll be front and centre."

He held his hand out for them to choose a nail each.

"But I don't know all my letters. I only know the M." Molly's arms fell at her side.

"We'll do it together." Finella selected a nail. "Put your hand over mine. It will be as if you've done the writing."

Shadrach steadied a brick and Finella and Molly's fingers brushed against his own. Molly poked her tongue out and Finella sounded out the letters.

"M-O-L-L and a Y." She finished off the tail with a flourish. They all peered at the brick. The delicate scroll of Finella's handwriting, against the soon to be rough texture of the brick.

"Looks good." Shadrach kept his eyes on Finella, his heart clanging in his chest like a pair of brick and comb hammers.

He set Molly's brick down to dry.

"Your turn." He held another one for Finella who slipped her hand under his. Did she steady it against his shaking or her own?

She smelled like lemon balm and earth. A mixture of who she was and who she'd slowly become. He wanted to let the brick go and scoop her up.

"There." Finella let the nail drop onto the bench. "All done. Now let me hold one for you."

Shadrach scribbled his name, etching out the letters with deeper scratches than Finella's.

Three bricks, one for each of them. Next week he'd build a clamp to fire the lot. Some wouldn't make it. He already knew he'd have cracked losses to count. He hoped these three would not be amongst them.

"Your name's on the brick now, Miss Finella. Means you have to stay here, forever. It's like signing a pledge," he teased.

"I might have to see where you lay that brick first, Shadrach Jones. You might choose to put yours and Molly's where they'll be admired by all, and brick mine in at the back. Right at the bottom. Facing inward." She pressed dirty fists to her hips but her brown eyes sparked.

"No chance." Now it was his turn to convince her. "Once these bricks go through the fire, they'll sit in a row. Side by side. Feel free to choose the order and position. I don't care much where they sit. As long as your name is there, beside mine." He dared voice the words he hoped she needed to hear.

A blush along her cheekbones told him she did.

"Let me see." Molly shoved Shadrach aside and rested her chin on the trestle. Crouching, she peered at the bricks. "What happens now?"

What did happen now? Shadrach would have liked to carry on the conversation he'd started with Finella. But Molly had other ideas.

"Well, when they're dry, I'm going to lay every brick on a bed of coal and slap the whole thing over with more mud." He winked at Finella. "Finella can help, seeing she's so good at throwing it around."

Finella puckered her lips and nodded. "I am good at that, aren't I?"

"And then?" Molly continued.

"Then, we'll light a fire and bake these bricks for a whole week. When they're cool, and make a lovely chinking sound when we take them out, we'll have bricks to sell and some left over for Finella's oven."

Molly frowned. "In the fire? Even the one with my name?"

"They all go in the fire. That's how they become strong enough to hold together. No use making a cottage or kiln out of bricks which haven't been fired. It would crumble at your feet in no time."

Molly didn't seem convinced. "I don't want mine to go in the fire."

"If it makes you feel better, Shadrach and I will be in there too. Well, our bricks will. Right beside yours. One on each side."

Molly turned and faced them. "Promise?"

"We promise." It pained Shadrach to see her blink against a long forgotten fear. A seared childhood memory of fire, smoke, and temper rose in his nostrils. "Best way I know to make oven bricks, Miss Molly is to cook them in the fire. It's the only way Finella can ever make you a pie." Shadrach nudged her and Molly ran her arm through the crook of his.

"Promise nothing bad will happen."

Shadrach pulled her close. He was getting good at making all kinds of promises. To George. His mother. Mrs. Lawson. Now Molly asked him for something he had no real control over.

Chances were, any one of these bricks would not make it. But he had to hold onto his faith. Faith that the three named bricks would come out stronger than they went in. Faith that God would hear his prayer for courage. And faith to believe Aunt Sarah wouldn't ruin it all.

Two sets of eyes waited on his answer. One wide-eyed and blue as his own. The other, deep brown and sweeter than any pie he craved.

"I promise. Nothing will happen to our three bricks. They're going to stand together on our oven front for many years to come."

34

December 12

Molly and I soak our fingers in lemon juice every afternoon. We scrape our nails and knuckles free of mud and wake each day to play in it once more.

No longer the threat under my feet, it is now the source of everything I have come to love. The shaping of what Shadrach and I have fought to hold onto. For so long we remained where we'd slipped, crippled by fear and blindness. Now, we pull the earth from its foundation and lay new hope for the days ahead.

Aunt Sarah forges on. Each night, I pray the journey would be sweet, knowing her arrival will not only bring the unlacing of her dreams, but some of mine.

No doubt the vessel plows deep and I feel her approach in my bones. She's in the gale that lashes the bay. The shadow in every dark cloud. But Shadrach is all else. And I am no longer afraid.

Shadrach couldn't smell any worse had he fallen into a festering cesspit. Smoke drenched and sweat filled, his clothes already carried more filth than he cared for. But the last two hours of carting and shoveling manure over his crops, sealed his fate. He wore the essence of his farm on his sleeve, in his hair and in a thick glob at the bottom of his shoe.

He scraped the last dredges of manure from his cart. The sun still hung high enough for a quick poke around the brick clamp. By tomorrow, it would be ready to crack open. He pushed the empty barrow along the last row in his chicory field and headed back.

He thought of the mulberry sapling he'd bought and hidden in the barn for Finella. A Christmas gift, hidden alongside Molly's rabbit blanket. He needed to water it. But he didn't mind being extra busy, if it meant being extra happy.

"He won't agree." Shadrach heard Finella's voice before he saw her. She and Molly sat on a wooden bench under a quince tree, with newspapers in their lap and scissors in hand.

"But what if we smile?" Molly snipped at a long strip of newspaper. Her tongue poked out whenever she wasn't talking.

Finella lay her scissors down and unfolded the sheet to reveal a pattern of Vs. "He's the boss and he'll do it when the time's right."

"Do what?" Shadrach stepped closer, but not too close.

"Brother." Molly dumped her papers on the seat and jumped over to where he stood. "Open the bricks. There's not much smoke today."

"And how would you know that?"

Molly stood still. "Um…" She picked at a sliver of paper from her skirt. "I, ah.."

"Your sister decided to take a wander without me this evening." Finella weighed the papers down with her scissors. "I found her by the brick clamp, stick in hand. She's eager to get it open and I figured she'd be better employed making a Christmas decoration for the mantel." Finella smiled.

Molly scrunched up her nose. "What's that I'm smelling?" She pinched her nose with two fingers.

"Sorry Sunshine, that's me. Been playing with manure. Not as much fun as making bricks with you two."

Molly pulled at his hand. "Then let's open the bricks. I want to see my name."

Shadrach held her warm fingers in his. He was already dirty. And it wouldn't take too long to crack them open. "I was planning on doing it tomorrow. But if you can stand the smell of the chicory field—"

Molly ran off without the risk of being called back.

"You've been gone all day." Finella came close and stepped back with equal speed. "And I can smell why from here."

"So it wouldn't be a good time to tug at one of those brown curls?"

"Not unless you want me to pick up my skirt and run like Molly."

"Maybe, I'll risk it." He reached for her apron strings.

Finella smacked his hand but her eyes shone. "Mud farm I'm learning to live with. Manure is not so endearing, Mr. Jones."

With a chuckle he let her go. She wasn't going far. He would make sure of that.

⌒

Even through oversized gloves, the bricks shared the glow of the fire straight into Finella's palms. Shadrach tossed them her way and in turn, she caught them and passed them on to Molly. Eager to find the brick with her name, the young girl blew on each one with care then stacked it in a row.

"Well, well. What have we here?" In the fading light, mischief played in Shadrach's blue eyes, and Finella's stomach dipped at his smile.

He held the brick high, away from Molly's flapping hands.

"Now, now, Miss Molly. Remember your manners."

"Is it mine?" She swiped at the air. "Give it to me, Brother."

He lowered his arm and Finella stepped closer.

"It is mine."

Molly cradled the red brick in her hand like a chick and Finella rested her chin on Molly's shoulder.

"No cracks. No bumps. One perfect brick."

Molly moved away, still holding the brick to her heart. "It's beautiful. And warm." She sat on the ground, crossed her legs and rocked like a mama with her baby.

"I'm not sure you're getting that brick back, tonight." Finella nudged Shadrach. "I wouldn't be surprised if it replaced her dolly."

He laughed and slipped off his gloves. "If she wraps it in a blanket, it'll be safer than out here."

"Do you think our bricks are nearby?"

He squatted and pulled two from a pile at his feet. "I found them first. But I wanted to keep looking until I had Molly's." He held one in each hand and blew where the groove of their names held the most soot. "Perfect."

Finella's heart tripped and tumbled. She ran her fingers over the bricks.

Finella and Shadrach. Shadrach and Finella. They'd survived the fire.

"You've a spot on your face."

"I do?" She looked up at him. "Where?"

"Under your eye." He rubbed at her skin. "No. My mistake. Must have been the shadows. Oh wait." He tilted her chin so he could see her other cheek. "I thought I saw something here, but no. It's nothing."

Finella giggled. She knew what he was up to and her face tingled where he wiped his dirty fingers and left a deliberate smudge. She remembered their kisses in the clay pit as well as he might. "You're one to talk. You've more soot and manure on you than anything else on this island."

"And for my troubles, I now have well covered rows of chicory, a market garden about to explode with summer vegetables, and right before Christmas, it seems I will have me a newly built oven right on my doorstep. What else could a man want?"

"Probably pie, or cake."

"Pie." He added their bricks to the others. Straightened and licked his lips. "And cake." He swallowed. Hard. "Finella, the other day, when we wrote our names on the bricks. Well, ... you know you have to stay with us now, don't you?" He teased, but his words wavered a little.

"You're not going to tie me up, are you?" Finella whispered.

"If it means keeping you here with us. With me." He reached for her hand and winked at Molly. "There's not much *miss* over here isn't a part of. And you know she and I are a special pair. But we don't want to stay at two. I don't."

Finella's cheeks flamed under the breath of his words. "I want us to be like these bricks. Molly in the thick of trouble, you and me on either side. Me looking over her shoulder at you. You, looking back. What do you say, Finella?" He squeezed her hand.

A bubble built in her chest and she wasn't sure she could say anything. But her deep fondness cracked and widened, and she squeezed his hand in return. "I know for certain you'll like my baking, Shadrach Jones. Question is, can you love it enough to live with it forever?"

He gathered her other hand. "Finella Mayfield, I like your cooking enough to want nothing else on my plate ever again. But I love *you*. If I had to live on Sharpie's cold fish stew for the rest of my life, I would still love you and want you for my wife. Will you say yes?"

The trembling in her shoulders raced along her arms and into her palms. There was no use hiding it from the one who held her hands. He'd already captured her heart.

He'd dug the beach for her shells, dug the earth to make her bricks but now, now it was her turn to answer with a gesture she hoped would mean as much to him as his had to her.

She pulled her hands away and cupped his dirty, unshaven cheeks. "I don't just want my name beside yours and Molly's. I want to take your name for my own and become your wife. I love you Shadrach Jones, and there's no other place I'd rather stand and tell you that, than right here where I want to plant my roots, on the blessed mud under our feet."

Shadrach grinned and held her by the waist. "There is no mud under our feet, anymore."

"Not right here, but I know a mud pit just a short walk away. Past your *fine smelling* chicory fields, if you care for mud colored kisses. But I'll take ash covered today, if you don't mind."

His eyes spoke first with a sparkle even the dusk could not hide. "That would be my pleasure." His mouth dipped closer and would have delivered a kiss had the sound of a horse and buggy not found its way to their yard of dry mud and sweet promises.

"Do you hear something?" Shadrach held his hand up.

Someone jumped out at the end of the lane and swung the gate open before returning to drive in. Dusk and fading light shadowed their visitors, and Finella followed Shadrach for a better look.

"Evening, Shadrach." Goliah Ashe secured the brake and hopped out. "Thought I'd surprise you good people with something I found on the steamer from Melbourne today." He helped his wife from the buggy.

"Some*one*," she whispered.

Agatha rolled her eyes at Finella, but didn't come any closer.

Instead, she stepped aside to make room for Goliah to reach into the buggy, once more. Warmth from Molly's body pressed Finella from behind, but it could not match the gust of cold, when Aunt Sarah stepped from the shadows and set her polished boots on their shell path.

35

"Now?" Shadrach helped Goliah with the buggy. "You couldn't wait until morning?"

Goliah's shoulders slumped. "Morning? As in tomorrow? Do you know what kind of day I've had? First, I sit beside her all the way from Queen's Wharf. I listen politely to her dislike of ship travel, of oceans and even the inconsiderate nature of the wind which brought her here earlier than expected."

He stopped to calm his agitated voice. "Then," he cocked a thumb in the direction of the house and the womenfolk in it, "she sits in my parlor while my good wife pours tea and listens to the same stories I've already heard." He came so close for a moment Shadrach thought he might poke him in the chest.

"You stink, brother. Sorry to say it." He brushed at the tip of his nose. "But here's something worse. Did you know we've set up house all wrong?" He nodded as if he agreed with the revelation, but his wide eyes told Shadrach he was not impressed. "Oh yes, a respectable preacher's hallway should have a *mahogany* hat rack with brass hangers tipped in white china? Did you know that Shad? *White china.*"

Shadrach twisted the reins tighter. The preacher didn't stop for an answer. "And did you know Finella has one such hat rail in her possession, and if tragedy had not robbed her of the position she'd been groomed for, it would now hang in my house? Right where Miss Sarah Mayfield pointed out I did not have such a hat rack?" Goliah swallowed.

"You must be parched." Shadrach didn't know whether to laugh or worry. The pitch in his stomach told him worry would arrive sooner than any laughs might.

The preacher continued. "And here's something you might like to know for when you go laying carpets." He nodded again and leaned back with his arms folded over his chest. "Apparently, Dutch carpets wear out. The one a preacher should have, for parishioners to traipse in and over, should be Venetian." He leaned closer. *"Venetian."* He hissed into Shadrach's ear.

"You're babbling." Shadrach tried to shove all Goliah had whispered aside for the real story. "Did the aunt arrive on your doorstep thinking Finella would be there?"

"Ha." Goliah roared. "You're not listening. I made her acquaintance on the steamer from Melbourne this afternoon, after a meeting with the Diaconate. Seems her ship came in early but she's not afraid of much, Shad. She found her way aboard and asked me if I was on my way to Phillip Island and did I know her niece, Miss Finella Mayfield."

"And she's been with you all afternoon?"

"*All* afternoon. And evening, so far. Started with afternoon tea. Agatha tried to convince her to stay the night, but she insisted we bring her over. I sent one of the young lads over with a note to tell you while we dawdled as much as we could. Didn't he get here?"

Shadrach shook his head. "Never saw him. Unless he came while we were cracking open the brick clamp."

That detail hardly mattered now. What mattered was whatever was happening around his table. He chewed on the inside of his mouth. He'd hardly savored his moment with Finella. He wondered if she waited for him to join her before telling her aunt their news.

"I guess we'd better get inside." He secured the horses and tried to ignore the shift in his gut. But that only made him feel worse. "If the aunt wasn't happy with your carpets and hat rack, imagine what she's saying about my place?"

❦

"Marry him? The farmer? And live here, in this hut? It's out of the question." Aunt Sarah rose and collected her gloves. Closed to further discussion, she'd kept her voice low and in full control. And no matter how Finella tried to explain there was more to this place than what Aunt Sarah couldn't see, her aunt refused to listen.

"No niece of mine will live covered in soot, when I have poured years of work into making you something more. Now, get up."

Finella stood. "Aunt Sarah, please. Won't you reconsider?" Her head thumped and stiffness crept into her shoulders she hadn't felt in months.

"There's nothing to think about. You must come away with me, this night. I won't have you stay here a day longer than you have to." She tapped the table, as if it were to blame. Cold and untouched, tea sloshed over the top of her cup and pooled into the saucer. A single drip stained the Christmas cloth Finella had only just laid on the table. The happy start to their festive decorating. Was that only this morning…?

"I know what this is." Aunt Sarah continued. "I should have thought of it earlier." She turned to Agatha, as if Finella were not even in the room. "The trauma of losing both her father and Mr. Gleeson must have turned her mind. She's a sensible girl. Raised better than this. I cannot imagine why else she would agree to live and work, and *marry* into these conditions."

She slipped on her gloves. "Come along, Finella. Mrs. Ashe offered me a room for the night. I'm sure the invitation extends to you, too, and I don't doubt that includes a bath." She waited, hand held out.

Finella's lungs felt as if that very hand commanded the air to leave the room. She held onto the back of a chair and tried to breathe.

"I am sensible. That's precisely why I live here. Caring for Molly is the most sensible thing I've done." *And loving Shadrach*, but she knew not to waste those words right now.

Her aunt's face flushed crimson. "And did you cast any thought to where you might eventually put me? Did it not occur to your sensible mind that I would soon arrive and need somewhere to stay?" She viewed the two beds, one in which Molly now lay with her back to their visitor.

"I assume the other bed is yours?"

Finella nodded. At least it was properly made and covered with one of her own quilts. No doubt, Aunt Sarah would have recognized it and known there was no other bed for her in this room.

"We didn't expect you to arrive for another few weeks. Your letter said in the New Year, and we've been busy making bricks for an oven." Finella heard the rambling in her words. She took a deep breath and started again.

"I hadn't yet talked to Shadrach about where you might sleep, but there would have been a solution." She rummaged wildly in her head for one now. "Molly could share Shadrach's skillion, while you and I sleep here." Her tepid smile did little to boost her confidence and the quiver in her lips worked against her.

"Regardless, I have no intention of staying. When you wrote to tell me you'd secured work with a local farmer, I assumed a wealthy farmer, with a generous property, other staff, and accommodation suitable for a governess."

"I assure you, Miss Mayfield, your niece has done a sterling job here." Agatha ventured. "My husband and I can vouch for the tender care Finella's shown Molly. The entire community knows it. You have every reason to be proud. And Shadrach Jones is one of the finest men on this island."

Aunt Sarah breathed through her nose. "Pride is a sin, Mrs. Ashe. In the absence of her father, it's my duty to point out, she is living under the same roof with an unmarried man." She turned to Finella. "Did you really think your father would approve of this arrangement?"

Heat and tears welled in Finella's eyes. "I arrived to much less than you thought I would find, Aunt Sarah. And I made the best of something awful."

"Be that as it may, you asked me to take you home. And I promised your mother I would never abandon you." Something gentle tempered her words. "You don't belong here, Finella, and I intend to remedy that, and make sure your mother and father's memory is never sullied with an unsuitable match."

She gathered a basket from the floor and dropped it onto her vacated chair. "Gather whatever of yours is at hand and we'll send for the rest another day. I shall wait outside," she opened the door and recoiled, "in whatever vile smell wafts over this place."

Shadrach couldn't care less about carpets and hat racks. They could rot into sawdust for all he cared. At his sapling door, handkerchief to mouth, Aunt Sarah stood straight as a constable.

"Why's she outside?" he mumbled under his breath.

"Probably doesn't like your drapes," The preacher chuckled softly. "Or perhaps she fancies your fresh *sea breeze*."

Shadrach's chest constricted. He knew Goliah was having fun

with him, and after suffering an afternoon with Finella's aunt, he guessed the man deserved to let off some steam.

"There you are, young man. I do hope it's no trouble to send you back for the horse and buggy. I assume you've only just taken care of the animal, but we are about to leave, if you wouldn't mind, Mr. Ashe." Sarah Mayfield adjusted her sleeve cuff.

"Leave?" Shadrach wasn't sure he'd heard her right. "Is something wrong?"

She peered behind her and pulled the sapling door shut. "My niece and I will be staying with Mr. Ashe and his wife. We'll send for her things in the morning."

"In the…" Shadrach looked from the woman to Goliah. "What?" His pulse quickened.

Aunt Sarah held a handkerchief over her mouth before answering. "I think there's been a mistake. I won't stoop to believe there is anything untoward going on here. I see my niece is truly taken by your sister and her affection is honorable. Only, it's misplaced. Finella is not the kind of girl for farms and…brick stacking." She waved, as if pestering flies assaulted her on all sides.

Shadrach wasn't sure the earth didn't tilt a little, and his vision narrowed onto the woman in the shadows who proposed the opposite of what he'd only just secured.

The aunt's chin lifted by another degree. "Finella's been trained for much more, and when she's ready to hear it, I will tell her of the position I have already found for her. With a young parson in London. He's looking for a suitable bride. I'm sure you'll understand, Mr. Jones. You can find a maid, or whatever Finella is to you, anywhere. They're teeming in Melbourne. I've been told."

Shadrach stared at her. The woman must be mad. It happened to some who sailed over.

"I'm sure it's not your fault, entirely." She looked away. "Let's agree the sudden death of Finella's fiancé has pushed her to hide away in this pocket of bush. In the confusion she seems to think she belongs here, but I assure you, after a decent rest she'll find herself once again."

Find herself? Shadrach's mouth dried to dust and he swallowed what felt like a fist full of ash.

"With respect, Miss Mayfield. I think *you're* confused. Finella does belong here. She's not hiding. From anything."

"Mr. Jones," she spoke as if it were a great imposition just to utter the words. "I am old and tired. I have spent months on a ship which passed over waters where my dear brother is buried. But it's neither weariness nor delusion which prompts me to speak." She sniffed. "It's soot."

"Soot?" Shadrach and Goliah spat the word out in unison.

She delivered a curt nod. "I know my niece better than anyone. She would rather die than live with mud or dirt. She hates it more than I, if that were possible. And now, only five months after I bid her farewell I find her living in a shepherd's hut with no regard to the ash on her face and foul stench of this place." She shook her head. "She needs my care more than I imagined."

"She doesn't need you at all." Shadrach knew his voice rose above what he should use for an elderly guest. But he didn't care. All he cared for was in his *shepherd's hut* and Sarah Mayfield stood between them.

"She needs people to stop making decisions for her and for them to move aside so she can do it on her own." He wanted to bundle her aboard the first rowboat off the island. "Finella knows what she wants. If you only stopped long enough to ask, she'd tell you so herself."

Like a slow sink hole the hut door opened.

"I'm ready." Puffy redness rimmed Finella's eyes, but her face still held the playful fingerprint he'd smudged there earlier. She gripped a small basket like a shield and kept her eyes down.

"Ready for what?" He ignored Agatha Ashe who shook her head at him. "Finella? Look at me?" He grabbed the handle and shared the light load with her. "Where are you going?"

Finella's lip trembled. "Molly's fallen asleep. I don't want to wake her. Tell her I..." A small sob escaped her and she took a flutter of breaths. "Tell her..."

Shadrach touched his fingers to her chin and drew her face to him until their eyes met. Tears stuck to her lashes and she blinked through them.

"Tell her my Aunt Sarah needs me, and I owe her..."

Shadrach waited. His heart smashed against his shirt the same way it did when he thought he'd lost Molly in the bush. Only this time, the girl he loved was about to walk away, right under his nose.

"She'll be resting at the church house with me." Her aunt moved in and took the basket away from them both. "Thank you Mr. Jones."

Her lips pinched tighter, if that were possible, and she dug into the basket. "I expect there's no clean handkerchief in here." She rooted around and drew a napkin out. "Your mother would upend her grave if she knew, but this will have to do." She dabbed at Finella's dirty cheek with one of the Christmas napkins he'd seen Molly admire countless times since she'd washed them.

"You can't take that." Molly crept out. "That's my mum's napkin. You can't take it away."

"Molly, dear." Finella whispered. "Go back to bed, dearest one. You're probably dreaming still."

"But ..." Molly rubbed her eye with a soot covered fist. "The napkin..."

Shadrach wanted to grab his sister's dirty hand from her eye, but

Finella beat him to it. He wanted to lock them in his one room house and tell everyone else to move off before he forced them off his land. More than anything, he wanted time to erase the last hour and take them back to a world where a little soot on one's collar hardly mattered.

Finella cradled Molly's hand. "Remember when we washed the Christmas apron? Remember I said my mother made it when I was a very little girl? She made the napkins too."

Molly shook her head. She wriggled until her hand came free and pointed at Aunt Sarah. "You can't steal from us. The napkin's not yours. And neither is Finella, and we won't let you take her away."

36

Finella couldn't walk away from her girl like this. Not even with Aunt Sarah breathing instructions into her ear. Confused and babbling on the doorstep they'd learned to call home together, the young girl looked to Finella for answers.

So did Shadrach.

Like a captain about to issue orders lest his ship capsize, his heaving chest threatened a bellow of words. Finella didn't know who to turn to first.

Didn't any of them know how hard this would be for her? Did they think she could just bid her aunt farewell, after so many months and losses they'd not yet grieved together?

Finella concentrated on the weakest in their midst. If she could shepherd Molly back to her bed, and spend a day in Agatha's sweet smelling parlor with Aunt Sarah, perhaps she might plead her case and return with her blessing.

To Molly and the farm by the sea, and the man whose blue eyes begged her to never leave it.

She crouched beside her girl. "Molly dear, Aunt Sarah doesn't mean you any harm."

Molly frowned. "She told me, Finella. My mum did. She said her name was Bessie, but when she was a baby they called her Elizabeth. And it says right there on the napkin. E for Elizabeth. I'm M for

Molly, but my mum was E. Like this one. Aunt Sarah can't have it because it's my mum's."

Finella tried to follow the logic. Her head ached and the push and pull at her ankles sent a shake into her limbs she feared would only grow. "The napkin?"

"Perhaps they look something like you remember of your mother's." Aunt Sarah leaned in. "But I promise you; this is the handiwork of Finella's mother, Emma Mayfield. I sat with her while she stitched them. All six of them. Finella was only a baby that Christmas. And I packed them myself into her possessions before she departed."

Molly raised her head. "Six?" She snatched Finella's basket from Aunt Sarah. "One, two… three, four, five." She dropped the basket and collected the napkins to her belly like an owner cheated of her possessions.

Finella stood. There *had* been six, but now there were five. How had that memory stolen its way into this day? She wrapped her arm around Molly's shoulder.

Aunt Sarah looked at Agatha. "The set is incomplete now, but I can vouch they were made by my sister-in-law."

Molly scrunched them into a ball at her chest. "That's a lie. You can't have everything." She spat her words at Aunt Sarah, who reeled and flattened her palm to her chest.

"You can't take my mother's napkin, and you can't take our Finella. Her name is on the brick." She choked on a sob. "Brother's going to marry her and you can't tell us what to do."

Molly pushed through the small crowd of people, stumbled to the safety of Shadrach's skillion and slammed the door behind her.

And no one stopped her.

Finella reached into the skillion first. Heavy with tears, her eyes burned only a little less than her heart. As expected, the girl crouched on the floor in a corner. Scattered around her, Finella recognized the possessions she'd once unearthed in her hunt for a tablecloth. Who knew what she searched for now?

Sucked into the corner of her mouth, the end of her braid didn't stop her from crying.

"Molly, dear." She squatted beside her. "Please don't cry. Aunt Sarah can be a little frightening, but she didn't mean to scare you away."

Molly wiped her nose on her sleeve. "Aunt Sarah lied." Her words caught on another sob. "Look." She thrust the napkins into Finella's lap. "See? Six. I know my numbers. Up to ten."

Six napkins? There hadn't been six since.... Finella's legs crumbled and she could not have held herself up if they'd been girded with iron rods. Her skirt folded over the linens and together with Molly, they drew them out. One by one.

Three in Molly's grip and three in Finella's.

"How, how can this be?" Six, not five napkins, all with the same cherub and trumpet and embroidered E in one corner.

"Which one is yours?" Finella's heart bled a sickening beat.

"This one." Molly sniffed. "Mother hid it in her sewing. She said it was special. It's because it has an E for Elizabeth, isn't it? They called her Bessie, but she was really Elizabeth. She told me."

Finella dropped the others and held Molly's find up to the light of the open door. Elizabeth, Emma. Was it possible another woman with the same initial had worked the same design? It matched the pieces of the incomplete set Finella never imagined would find its missing sixth. Only this one carried a peculiar mark. A stain, not present in the others. A rusty blood-like wipe.

Shadows filled the doorway and Finella lowered the linen. Aunt Sarah and Shadrach crept in, while Goliah and Agatha remained just outside.

Aunt Sarah reached for her hand. "You're greyer than an ash pit. Give me that."

Molly's crying stopped and Shadrach leaned against the doorframe. Time and sound stood still.

Aunt Sarah turned the handiwork over. It trembled in her withered hand, and Finella saw for the first time, how it matched the sadness in the old woman's aged jowls. Perhaps it was the shadows in Shadrach's small skillion, or the memory of happier days, but Aunt Sarah withered right there when the lifeblood drained from her body and out of her hand. She passed the napkin back.

"This is your mother's work," she whispered. "I would stand in a court dock and testify I watched her stitch it." She laced her fingers together and pressed them to her mouth. "But it's been missing since the day a thief stole her basket and left her for dead."

Finella looked around the room, miles from her childhood home in Chingford Green. "But, how would it come to be deep in your mother's belongings?" She trained her eyes on Shadrach. "How?"

He shook his head. "I don't know how."

Molly leaned on Finella's shoulder and stood. "Mum wrapped the spider with it. She let me hold it sometimes when my head hurt. She said the spider would buy Shadrach a home for us."

"A spider? What's the girl talking about?" Aunt Sarah extended her hand for Finella to rise.

"Brother knows." Molly looked to Shadrach. "Remember, the spider with the gems. The one Mum gave you."

Shadrach looked at the floor as if the answers to their quandary were written in the dust.

"It wasn't a spider, Molly. It was a bee, with a ruby body and seed pearl wings."

Aunt Sarah snapped her head around. "Did you say a *bee*? With seed pearl wings and two," she held up her own two fingers like pincers, "garnet eyes. Tiny stones?"

Shadrach looked from Finella to Aunt Sarah. "Yes, a ruby body and red eyes. Didn't look too friendly, no wonder Molly thought it a spider."

"Never mind that." Aunt Sarah straightened. "How in God's good name did you come to have these in your possession when the last time they were seen were on Emma Mayfield, the day she was attacked?"

"My mother gave them to me, when I left for Melbourne. She gave me two things. A pouch of gold dust and the brooch. Made me promise I'd sell only if I came across a place to make a good home for Molly. When these lots came on the market, I bought the land with a pouch of gold."

"And you didn't wonder where she got it all?" The tremble in Finella's voice rose in an audible quiver. She was not sure she wanted to hear the answer, but someone had to ask the questions. "Shadrach? Do you know how your mother came to have my mother's embroidery and brooch?"

Shadrach ran his hands through his hair and sat on the edge of his pallet. His long legs jutted out like the limbs of a trapped colt in a pen not his own.

"She gave it to me the day I left Ballarat. My dad had only been back a few months and I couldn't bear to be in the same house with him. She pressed it all into my hands in one of her own handkerchiefs. Told me it was never hers in the first place, but I always thought she'd found it in someone's pocket. She'd found gold that way too." He looked up at Finella.

"A miner never came back for his laundry order once, and she found a pouch of gold dust in it. The next day, she heard he'd been killed. No one knew his real name and when there was no claim on his washing, his shirts were given away. But, she held onto the pouch. I thought the brooch must've been in there too."

"But Molly says it was always in the linen napkin." She held her hand out for Molly's. "Wasn't it?"

The girl nodded and came closer. "When my head hurt, Mum would let me hold the spider. But only for a minute."

"Do you remember where it came from? It's really important we know. Did your mother ever say?" Finella tightened her grip.

"Not Mum. But Dad did. He said it was a present. From England. I heard him whisper to her one afternoon when he came back from running away. He wanted her to have something fancy to remember our Daniel who died."

"England?" Aunt Sarah exclaimed.

"Your father was in England?" Finella twisted back to Shadrach.

"He was gone four years." He frowned. "He could've been anywhere. I never spoke about it with him. I guess some of the time he could've been in England."

"When was he away? What were the years?" A wild frenzy worked in her head and Finella counted back while she waited for his answer.

"He disappeared when I was fourteen and came back, four years later. Early...1870."

Cold ran through Finella's veins and she let go of the snug hold of Molly's hand to rub her forehead. "My mother was killed the week after Christmas, 1869. The thieves fled and were never seen again. Neither was her brooch, nor the basket she carried that day, lined with this Christmas napkin. Until today."

She hoped some heavenly miracle would stop the shiver in her bones. Dear God, could it be this unfathomable? She collected a slim measure of strength and willed her words into sensible order, unlike her wild thoughts.

"My guess is the brooch and napkin made it back to your home.

As gifts to your poor mother, while we laid flowers on my mother's grave each week and limped through life without her."

"Hang on." Shadrach scrambled to his feet. "There's little about my father I remember that's good, but he could have won the brooch in a card game. Or stolen it from some blind drunk." His voice pleaded with her to look up. To connect and slip in alongside him where she'd been all day.

Finella tripped out of his skillion with Aunt Sarah close behind. Goliah and Agatha parted and made way for her exit, but there was not enough space under God's darkening sky for what she craved. She needed air. Deep gulps, if she were to keep from falling in a broken heap.

She looked to the dusky sky for answers. Had she been living with the family of her mother's attacker all this time? Cared for them, *for him*, with affection she should have reserved for only one man in her life.

The shell path at her feet swam in a swirl of colors.

"Finella. Please…" Shadrach pulled her back. "Listen to me."

She twisted around. "No, you listen to me." She pressed her hand to his chest. "My mother had blood on her fingers and under her nails. I never saw it, because she'd been washed when they let me in her room. But I heard the whispers. She'd fought her attacker. Probably knocked his nose they said, when he ripped at that brooch. And the napkin Molly found still has bloodstains on it. Didn't you tell me your father returned with a broken nose?" She pointed to the skillion where the madness of the afternoon lay strewn in linens at the foot of his bed. "That stain is your father's blood, on my mother's Christmas napkin."

She retched at the thought of that villain's blood on her mother's lace collar. On her beautiful face. On her carefully stitched napkin, now a filthy rag. The gag reached her throat. *God help me, I have to ask.*

Had George followed through with his promise? Had he placed her right where she'd find what she needed all along?

Molly tumbled outside and pressed her shoulder into Shadrach's open arms. The last of the summer evening sun picked up the blue in her eyes, still swollen. Still confused.

"Your father," Finella's words tumbled in uneven breaths, "stole from my mother, while she lay dying in a mud hole. If you think about it carefully, you won't deny it. And he left behind a page of the newspaper from Ballarat where you all lived."

He tried to speak but she ignored him.

They all called to her; Aunt Sarah, Agatha Ashe, but their words drowned in the booming memory of the ship's surgeon and his parting words reaching for her like a gnarled knuckle from the grave.

Evil is carried by the next generation, Miss Finella, as surely as the moon drags the tides. The emancipated convict's blood is just as potent today as when he yanked the chain. Only now, his children carry the brand. Mark my words, the blemish of the convict era hasn't faded and won't anytime soon.

Finella breathed hard. She leaned a hand onto the skillion wall but nothing held up what crumbled inside.

Shadrach shook his head at her in slow disbelieving shakes.

"You can shake your head as much as you like, Shadrach, I don't care. All that's left now is his name." She pounded on his chest as if it were right there for her to reach in and grab. "The least you can do is give it to me in return for everything he stole. So I know how to name the sinner."

She didn't care how bitter her words sounded. How hurtful or numb.

She didn't care about Aunt Sarah's discordant whisper for her to calm down. Even Goliah and Agatha's silent retreat into the shadows didn't stem her boiling anger. All she cared for was the name George had promised they'd find.

"You're right. Our father was a despicable man. He lusted for riches which only made our lives worse. Never better." Shadrach's voice wavered and his eyes flooded with tears.

"Worst of all, he cherished an illusion he'd find us a house where the sun would shine through the windows all the day long and keep us healthy. Fortify our strength. Unlike poor Daniel who died in our reality, my dad retreated to a sun filled fantasy. You're right." He nodded, and his lip trembled. "It has to be him. He hid that newspaper report in his breast pocket and unfolded it whenever the mood took him. Read every word out loud to us as if we'd never heard it before."

"My father did the same," Finella whispered, more to herself that anyone else. Even from outside the skillion, she could see Father's trunks against the wall where they collected dust and awaited someone to break them open. "Father read that newspaper scrap over and over as if it held the answer to our grief. 'Someone from Ballarat,' he'd guess. 'Someone who read the Ballarat Star.' But that's all we knew. But you…" she backed away a step. "You did know. You knew when I told you how my mother died. Didn't you?"

"I didn't want to think it could be him," Shadrach pleaded. "God knows how many others could have read the Ballarat Star and there's a million reasons a scrap of paper might have tumbled from person to person, country to country."

"There may be a million reasons an old newspaper is still lodged between my father's books. But there's only one reason my mother's napkin is here in your skillion." She spat the words and shrugged off Aunt Sarah who tried to draw her away.

"And all those reasons wrap into one. Your father. The nameless man. The man George saw run off with his younger accomplice.

That was your father."

"And you're asking for his name?" Shadrach's voiced remained as low as Finella's had grown in pitch. "What difference does it make, now? If any of this is true, it happened so long ago. So far from where you and I are now. Can't you let the past stay where it is? Can't you forgive?"

"Forgive?" She stepped back before the scream was fully out of her mouth. "Something inside me would have to die for that to happen. And I've seen enough death for one lifetime."

She wiped at her tears. "You don't want me to look back, Shadrach, but my mother asked. Aunt Sarah will tell you. That was her dying wish. And my father stewed over it until he died. How can I not want to know what they were robbed of at the grave?"

"And when you do? What then, Finella? Will you be free? Will you and I return to how we were before Goliah's buggy rolled into our yard?"

She looked away and let fresh sobs take over.

Shadrach wrapped his hands around her cheeks and made her look up. "You already know his name," he whispered like a man defeated. "You've known his name since the day you and I met on that pier. The day I let your brown eyes chip at my heart for the very first time."

Finella peeled his hands away but he wrestled her by the elbows.

"I carry his name, Finella. In full. My father's name was Shadrach Jones."

"No." She dared him to take it back. Anything but that. Not...
Shadrach Jones.

Shadrach Jones, Shadrach, Shadrach, Shadrach Jones. Words swarmed around her like an upended wasp nest. As if a dozen fractured Mollys sang the discordant song over their breakfast table.

It wasn't until her own lungs curdled the air like a funeral dirge, that Aunt Sarah and Agatha dragged her away.

37

Shadrach watched them bundle Finella away from his house, his sister, and anything else he thought might have kept her there.

Goliah tapped Shadrach's back. "It's a sudden blow, Shad. Let's wait and see what morning brings."

Shadrach tore his eyes from Finella's back to Molly, who slipped into the hut and no doubt found her bed. "Morning had better bring you and that buggy with Finella in it. Or so help me Goliah I will come right over myself."

"Easy, now. No use forcing her. You want her to be here because she chooses to. She's got a lot to sort out."

Shadrach ran soot-stained fingers through his hair and pressed at the back of his scalp, as if to keep the madness from taking root in his head. "I asked her to marry me, today. She'd only just said yes. Now, that's all undone in one conversation and her bags'll be packed and out in deep seas before week's end." A fresh stab hit him in the chest. "My father, ruining another handful of lives, from the grave this time."

"Best to let a night's sleep calm us all." Goliah sent him a parting look, half pity half courage, but the pity won out and framed his face with the misery they all fought.

Shadrach watched a cloud of dust rise from their departure. It filled his yard and crammed his mouth. He couldn't tell how long he stood there, watching it float back to the ground through the splinters of the setting sun. None of the crazy thoughts he wrestled made any sense.

Finella had every reason to walk away, but he wanted her back, anyway. He wanted her back...

He wondered about bundling Molly into his wagon and chasing the buggy down, when a smaller puff of dust appeared.

Hope crammed his chest. Was Finella marching back toward him? Instead, Jimmy Callahan rode his horse into the yard.

"Got a note for ya from Mr. Ashe." He jumped off and hunted around in his pocket. "Here ya go."

Shadrach snatched the paper. "Next time, do as you're told and don't take the long way round."

Jimmy's face colored. "How'dya know?" He wiped his mouth with the back of his hand. "Peew...It stinks here."

"Get going." Shadrach didn't care to point out the boy's trouser bottoms dripped with seawater. Who cared now if he'd been fooling with the lads, fishing or poking around the rock pools?

When Jimmy left the way he'd come, Shadrach turned back into his house and sat on the end of Molly's bed. She'd fallen asleep, fully dressed, fingers curled around her brick. He ripped the letter open with a blackened fingernail.

Brace yourself, Shad. Miss Sarah Mayfield's blown in like a gale force wind. Agatha and I will bring her around later this evening.

You'd best polish your boots, lad.
Goliah.

Shadrach scrunched the paper into a tiny ball. He tossed it into the fire without even moving from the bed. The noiseless missile fuelled Shadrach even more.

He paced the room. Looked for something, anything to grab and slam against the slow burning log with a force to equal the rage within.

But there was nothing to burn. At least not in the fire.

"But I want Finella to come back." Molly chewed on her breakfast damper.

Shadrach wouldn't look Molly's disappointment in the face. He leaned against the door and watched the road.

"Brother?"

He sipped his tea. "Finella needs to look after her aunt, now."

"I don't like it in here without Finella." Molly touched her name in the brick. "It's sad."

Shadrach put his mug on the table. Molly was right. The emptiness carved a ditch in his chest. But he didn't need his insides to prove something was wrong.

Unmade beds were only the start. The table still held the cold remnants of tea Finella had brewed the night before. Scalloped paper lined the shelf where the treacle and sugar tins lived, one corner lower than the other, crooked and begging attention. And Finella's apron hung by a single nail in the wall. Its loose strings released of their duty.

But the worse reminder, heavier than the untended room and Molly's wild hair, clung to him like a heady vapor. He couldn't even escape it. For Shadrach Jones had slept in the bed beside Molly's all night. The bed he'd given up for Finella. He'd lain there all night, blinking into the dark, wrapped in sorrow and shame and her sweet smelling quilt.

He inhaled again. An intoxicating draught of rose water, lemons and her. Just her. And it was all he had.

"Which way did they go?" Molly pulled at the rope Shadrach fastened around her waist until the knot rested on her left hip. She wriggled for a comfortable position under the largest quince tree, at the edge of the yard.

"Only one way into the village. They followed Old Lou's track." Shadrach dragged the tin sheet of mortar closer. "Why?"

"I want to know where to look. For when she comes back." She leaned on her elbow and faced the gate. Shadrach breathed in the sweet summer day, but nothing chased the sour taste from his mouth. He hated to keep her tethered to a tree. Even more now that Finella had scoffed at the choice and then used it herself. Everything reminded him of her. He couldn't even lose himself in hard work. His mother always said honest labor was the best distraction, but oven building didn't fit that. Not this oven.

Not when each brick heaped memory upon memory. When bricks split his skin with their rough edge, and sliced his heart in the process.

The sun overhead scorched like a furnace, and so did his longing for Finella.

Molly rested her cheek on her rag doll. "Jimmy Callahan comes by the beach."

"Jimmy and those boys like to scramble over rocks. They're not afraid to wade through Saltwater Creek. Probably use it as a short cut. It's not the way Finella would come."

"Why not?"

He tapped another brick with the trowel and eyed the row for straightness. "The beach might be the quickest road from here to Cowes, but Finella wouldn't want to get her skirt wet. She'd prefer to sit in a wagon and no horse can take you over the beach and rocks the way Jimmy's legs can."

"Can yours?" She kicked off her shoes.

"I haven't tried. I'm too busy being a farmer to wander all over the bush or the beach." He smoothed a line of mortar with his finger. "And you know what a busy farmer likes doing least?"

"What?"

"Being a builder." The trowel weighed almost nothing, but felt like an anvil in his fist. If only he'd married Finella before the aunt had arrived.

"Brother?" Molly squinted. "Will you tell me when she comes back? I don't want to have my eyes closed when she does."

"I will do that for you, Miss Molly." The lane shimmered in the heat with no one either coming or going. "You take that nap, and if anything happens while you rest, I promise to wake you. Quick sticks."

She smiled. "She'll come back. To bake our pies."

38

Finella watched Goliah Ashe pace the floor. His feet cut a circle in his good carpet piece, and if his wife didn't beckon him to sit, he may have left a rut clear to the wooden board beneath.

Lord knew, Finella's heart held a similar rut. A going over of events and words which bled right into her soul. Shadrach's father, the man who robbed her beloved mother. All those years ago. And now she held the jagged pieces of the tale like broken glass.

"Take some more chamomile tea, dear." Aunt Sarah beckoned, and Agatha Ashe lifted the pot. But neither of these women knew what she wanted or needed. Perhaps Finella herself would never know now, either.

Beyond the window, a wink of sky against rustling blue gums and brilliant sun did nothing to take away the gloom. It wrapped around her heart like the skin of a cold stone.

Shadrach Jones. How could he expect her to be near him after such a revelation? How could she in good conscience and decent respect for her mother's memory, engage with him in any way? She shifted in her chair and all eyes fell on her. But she had nothing to say. Nothing they hadn't already discussed a hundred times in the last few days.

A loud rap at the front door drove both Goliah and Agatha to jump to their feet. When they returned, Jon Tripp followed them into the parlor, hat in hand and lathered in a sweat from brow to the end of his long hair.

"Just wanted you to know your things are all at the bunkhouse, Miss Mayfield. Shadrach and I carted it all there this morning."

"Thank you, Mr. Tripp." She hunted for the words needed to acknowledge him. "You've been kind to oversee that for me. It shouldn't be too long and we shall empty your bunkhouse and make our way home."

Weariness and heat hit her with a force she didn't expect. Her spine would not hold up the way she'd been forcing it for too much longer.

"My pleasure, Miss. Although, I have to say, working around Molly wasn't the easiest thing I've ever done. The little chit hung onto every last article of yours and fought me like a terrier. Took all my strength, and Shad's, to get her off your bed for that quilt. In the end, we tied her to a chair at the table and she fell asleep with her head on the tablecloth. Which," he looked around the room at his audience, "we also had to pry away and she was not happy about that either."

Finella cringed. Mr. Tripp could not have wounded her more if he'd entered with a whip and flicked her with it.

"I can only imagine." She whispered, more to herself than the man at the door. When the ever-present tremor of her lips gave way, she excused herself for the bedroom where she could cry herself to sleep, as her dear Molly did, when life bore down on them.

Heartsick with separation, and miserable with loss, Finella never expected the untimely death of George Gleeson would pale into a sweet goodbye, compared with the fresh ripping away of Molly and Shadrach Jones.

January 3 1876

I cannot erase the picture of Shadrach holding Molly back as I screamed pain at them. Stained. I yelled it over and over, until I couldn't see through my tears. Stained, like the napkin. Covered in blood, always destined to carry the mark. The sins of the father. Hadn't I been warned? Why was it such a surprise?

I don't know when I stopped yelling, but I must have. Aunt Sarah took over and Goliah drove us away. How they calmed me down, I'll never know. But I saw myself in the hallway mirror of the little church house. The madness in my eyes. My mattered hair. My shaking, which didn't stop for hours.

I remembered how Shadrach had once before carried me there in haste to see the last flicker of life in George Gleeson. The hush which covered me when all those inside tiptoed around me like an invalid from the darkest asylum.

And here I sit again, in the same room with little to show for my time in this country but heartache of the worst description. There is no fingerprint of God worth recording here. Nothing, from the highest firmament to the dustiest core of this land is worth holding onto. Even the measly flowers I've added here, mock me with withered faces and dead stems.

Agatha Ashe crept into the room. She cradled a small ceramic bowl and clean towel. Finella pushed aside her Everlasting and made room on the edge of the bed.

"You're not napping?" Agatha settled onto the mattress.

"I can't. I keep seeing Molly's frightened face and Shadrach's stony glare. They're like ghosts I can't get rid of. Even with my eyes closed."

"And it's for those very eyes, puffed and sore, I've made you a balm. Sit back and I'll apply some while you rest."

Finella closed her eyes and let Agatha press the cool mixture to the skin above her cheekbones. "It smells sweet."

"My mother's recipe. A grated raw potato and two heaped spoons of applesauce. She had enough practice with me when I was at home. Much crying led to many applications. I think she kept a potato in her pocket most days just for me." Finella heard the smile in Agatha's voice.

"Did you nurse a broken heart?"

Agatha padded her eyes with the towel. "You could say that." She shifted off the bed. "My parents were not in favor of my affections for Goliah. They tried their best to keep their only daughter from marrying the least likely candidate."

"Goliah? Least likely? You make a team I can only envy."

Agatha laughed softly. "We do now. But we fought hard for the privilege."

"I can't imagine why your parents objected. Goliah's a fine gentleman. No one could find fault in him or his generous ways."

"Oh, yes they could. And they did. Loudly and for years."

"But why?" Finella lowered the towel and opened her eyes.

Agatha settled back on the bed. "I've waited until now to tell you, Finella. I knew you wouldn't be able to hear it until you'd calmed down some." She took the towel and folded it in half.

"My dear Goliah is the son of not one, but two convicts. His parents were transported here, separately, served their sentences and found each other after they'd obtained their ticket of leave."

Finella's pulse thundered against her temples. Goliah Ashe? The son of convicts? She twisted in the bed for a better look at Agatha.

"And you still wanted to marry him. Even after you learned that, and your parents disapproved?"

"You've seen him Finella. He's a charmer. And I couldn't help myself. I learned very quickly his parents' sins had nothing to do with the Goliah I knew."

"And that's where we differ." Finella let her head sink back onto the pillow. "Shadrach's father's sin has everything to do with me. He's the one who took my mother away. He stole, he killed. And Shadrach is no better."

"Shadrach? He didn't even know about it until you pieced it all together."

"It doesn't matter if he knew or not, anymore. It matters that he's the son of such a man. Don't you see? It's in his blood. It's what Shadrach's tried to tell me himself, only I wouldn't listen. It's not just me that thinks it. He's the one who thought it first." The balm dribbled and she took the towel from Agatha to wipe her cheekbone.

"And is that what I should think about my own husband?" Agatha tempered her voice with caution. "He's the son of two felons. His father stole a barrow of turnips from market. Harmless enough you might think, but the weight of the law carried him across the sea into jail for his trouble."

"And his mother?" Finella wanted to know more.

"His mother was a young lass when she had a baby on the wrong side of the blanket. She drowned it in a tub after it wouldn't stop howling one night." Finella sucked her breath in at the horror.

"She lived with an uncle who hardly lifted his head from his drinking. The neighbors knew he'd been the one to leave the baby in her belly, and testified she'd been misused by the drunk for years. She was so young, about Molly's age I'd guess. The magistrate must've taken an extra dose of pity on her that day and transported her instead of sending her to the gallows. Quite the miracle if you ask me. But then, God needed her to be a mother to Goliah, so I shouldn't be surprised He spared her."

Finella recoiled at the miserable tale. "How awful."

"That's how these stories go. No one ends up a convict for pretty reasons. Some fall, others are pushed. Australia's offered many a place to find their feet and new start. Goliah's parents for one."

"But not Shadrach's father. He never paid for his crime. He returned with my mother's rubies and passed them onto his wife as a gift."

"And you want Shadrach to pay?"

"He could never make up for what his father did."

Agatha smiled. "Exactly. Because it's not his fault, and he shouldn't be held accountable. And neither should he or you or anyone else make him wear the mantle of sinner because of what his father did."

"But he'll always be that man. The son of the scoundrel who ruined our lives."

"Only if you allow it. Shadrach is his own man. So is Goliah. Neither will give an account to God for anyone else's sins but their own. And you won't have to for any but your own."

"But aren't you afraid, Agatha? What if your children carry the curse?"

The preacher's wife's green eyes sparkled. "Goliah made me learn a scripture from the Psalms when he told me about his parents. One he holds onto as closely as I do. *The mercy of the Lord is from everlasting to everlasting, upon them that fear Him. And His righteousness unto children's children.* I have nothing of the past to fear, and everything of the future to look forward to." She patted her belly and blush turned to grin. "God is a restorer, my friend."

Finella stared at Agatha's hand, rubbing the flat of her stomach.

"You can close your mouth, now." Agatha tapped playfully at Finella's chin with her fingertips. "Yes, we're expecting our first child and I couldn't be more hopeful for its future. If you lined up a hundred and one men born of free settlers, I couldn't pick a better father for my child. I mean that, Finella."

Finella wrapped her arms around Agatha's shoulders. Fresh sobs held back her words, and she hoped the embrace conveyed what her heart wished for her friend. A long and happy life with the man she loved and the babies they would share.

A life Finella could never hope to taste, for in turning away from Shadrach Jones, she'd turned away from the only man who'd stolen her heart and killed her dreams.

39

Shadrach poured another bucket of water around the newly planted mulberry tree. He'd watered it for weeks in the barn where he'd kept it hidden and wrapped in hessian, but Finella's Christmas gift was never presented the way he imagined. Molly appreciated her rabbit blanket, well enough, but no one had taken pleasure in the tree he hoped might shade Finella's mulberry cordial and tea drinking days.

Instead, he planted it alone near the oven he'd made. Also for her.

Not that she'd see that, either. The Christmas Finella had promised and prepared for had come and gone. Delivered by Shadrach to Molly in the hasty opening of the blanket bundle just before bed. He hadn't wanted her to miss out on a Christmas day completely, but had almost nothing in his possession to fill it with. So he'd waited until evening to drag out the present he'd worked on all year. In every other regard, the day looked no different to the one before it and the few that had passed since.

He kicked the empty watering bucket away and looked at the sky. No rain clouds threatened today. All that threatened, he held inside. Like a raging firestorm, crackling and incinerating from within.

A few short steps took him to the door of his house where Molly napped. She'd slept a lot these last few days and complained about a sore head. He wished he could sleep so easily. At least in his dreams he didn't have to wrestle with his own shadow about how he deserved to lose a girl like Finella. How he was never worthy of her in the first place. A man like him. The son of his father. Shadrach Jones.

He peeked into the lonely room. The table held no cloth. The floor didn't wear her rag rug. Extra shelves he'd added to the wall boasted none of her lemonade cups. Even the lace she'd put on the window had been folded up and returned to her.

And he hated the nakedness of this room without her. What he wouldn't give to have her back with all her fancy things, and more. All the fancy he could buy her.

He moved to Molly's bed. His eyes adjusted to the shadows, and he nudged the covers only to feel a loose sheet against his fingers. Where was she now?

He swung around and headed outside again.

"Molly." He cupped his hands around his mouth and called. "Molly. You'd best be hiding well, Miss, because when I find you you'll be in the deepest trouble."

He stormed around the farm looking for, but never finding his sister. Deep silence hung over his fields and no sound of her came from the tracks into the scrub by the beach. If she was paddling in the rock pools, why he'd...

He'd what? Tie her up to her bed every time he needed to fetch a pail of water? Weariness heavier than he'd ever imagined pressed on his shoulders. Finella was right. What kind of home was it when your own brother had to tether you up like an animal to keep you safe? It pained him to think even Finella wouldn't want to take her now.

He reached the sand in no time, looking for signs of Molly. He scoured the beach and found nothing of her in either direction.

Where had she disappeared to now? He trod the track to his fields and orchard. Perhaps she'd tried the road?

A blow hit him in the chest. Surely she wouldn't try to...? No.

He shook the thought away. She knew she'd never make it through the bush to Cowes. Not by foot. Half the time he drove her there she dozed on his shoulder. She wouldn't even know the way... would she?

He hurried to where his shells paths stopped and the red road took over.

⌒

Finella walked the length of the jetty and back again. Her heels tapped little smacks on the boards and waves underfoot swayed and kissed the footings of the pier. She quickened her pace. Anything, to drown the noise of crew loading her belongings onto the steamer to Melbourne, under the watchful orders of Aunt Sarah.

She wasn't the only one searching for something over the water. Holidaymakers from Melbourne strayed from their guesthouses to promenade, lazy and carefree. Finella overtook a trio of older women, intent to plod arm in arm, in time with the slow splash of the water.

She wasn't sure why she needed to pace. Just that she did. Like the tide, she yearned for a new tomorrow to pull her away. Only, there would be no more tomorrows on this island.

The steamer bounced on a wave. As if it strained like a horse at the starting gate. As if the ropes knew they would only hold her there a while longer.

How she hated the notion of another sea journey and yet, it was her only choice. Aunt Sarah never failed to reassure her of the life they would make together in London, even hinted at a possible match for her there.

Finella cared very little for talk of a match. She had nothing to offer anyone, anymore.

She turned her back to the open waves and faced the little cove of Mussel Rocks where Mrs. Lawson lived. Aunt Sarah said goodbyes only brought more grief. She insisted a clean break would bring Finella the quickest healing and help her look forward.

Finella wasn't sure about Aunt Sarah's wisdom, anymore.

The island coastline dipped out of view to the west. To where the sun set each night, and Shadrach's farm called to her.

Shadrach Jones. A name she loved and loathed. She pressed her fingernails into her palms. How had God let her search for freedom only to end in such bondage? She longed for the voice of reason, but reason had a way of twisting her insides and her heart couldn't take another dose of what Agatha preached. Not without it changing her.

She sucked in the sea air as if it were the last breath she'd take. Was there time to pay a call on Mrs. Lawson before they left? She owed the dear lady that much.

The smell of the sea filled her lungs. But her heart refused to be calmed. Why did that napkin have to be mixed in with Mrs. Jones' sewing? Why hadn't a washerwoman, an expert in stain removing not brought that cloth to near new?

Heavy steps took Finella back to the steamer. Everything else in Shadrach's mother's possession was old, but clean. If anyone knew how to rid a napkin of blood, surely Bessie Jones did? So why did she hide the blood stained napkin when she could have starched it and used it herself? Finella's head hurt to think about it as much as her heart did.

"There's no time for dawdling, dear. Time to board." Her aunt fastened the clip on her travelling case. "They're about to loosen the ropes."

They moved past busy seamen and slower passengers until they secured a seat on the upper deck where long benches offered the last view of the island.

Finella closed her eyes. She didn't need to look. Like a scar she'd never outrun, miles of sandy beaches, the dirt road, tea tree scrub twisting up the hill, and village buildings were all scratched deep within her.

Loud voices from the top of the road caught her attention. She peered at the base of a croft of pines on the hill. Jon Tripp poked his head out of the bunkhouse and did the same. A small gathering of villagers pointed westward and their voices carried down to the shore.

"Young Molly Jones disappeared again, did you hear?"

Molly?

"Been gone hours, they say. Shadrach's called for a search party."

Molly!

Finella sprung off the seat and leaned into the steamer's top rail. She strained to hear more, but her ears filled with a whoosh of blood and panic, she could only stare at the growing circle of villagers.

"Sit back, Finella." Aunt Sarah's voice stiffened with instructions. "It's not your concern, now. I'm sure Mr. Jones will find his sister, soon enough."

Finella's stomach heaved. "She is my concern. I'm tired of pretending she's not. I love her and if she's lost, I care very much to know where she is."

A crewman uncoiled a rope from the last bollard.

"They'll find her, dear. Don't make this worse than it need be. Sit here before the sway knocks you off your feet."

Finella looked at her shoes. Mud free and polished only that morning before they farewelled Agatha and Goliah, she stood shod for whatever life brought next. But she didn't want clean shoes. Not anymore.

"It's too late, Aunt Sarah. I've already been knocked off my feet." She pushed into the narrow stairwell and down to the steamer's gangway. But the plank no longer offered passage off the vessel. Someone had lifted it away in preparation for departure, and a blue chasm of water widened between her and all she longed for in this world.

She hitched her skirt and stepped onto the edge of the boat.

"Miss? We're pulling off." Someone called from behind her.

"Finella!" Her aunt called from the top deck.

Someone blasted a horn and cut off all sound. All except an inner voice which sounded very much like Molly calling her name.

Finella launched from the vessel and landed like a newborn foal in a clumsy squat just shy of the pier's edge.

But she didn't stay there long. Long enough to steady her legs and check she hadn't twisted a limb, but the pulse which pushed her off the steamer raged and carried her on. She ran along the pier and up the sandy track, far from the frantic calls of her aunt and the cursing of the steamer master, barking furious orders to throw ropes back to the jetty.

She ran as fast as her clean shoes could carry her and reached the fringe of the villagers in a breathless stop. They talked over one another and hardly noticed she'd joined them.

Mr. Spencer shushed the crowd so they could hear Jimmy Callahan share the news.

"Molly hasn't been seen for hours. Shadrach begged us to check the village and tell anyone along the way to look out for her."

Mrs. Trilloe let the door of the mercantile slam behind her and stepped onto the stoop, shading her eyes with a feather duster. From further up the hill, Goliah Ashe and other men rushed to the base of the pines, where debate began on what they should do next.

Mrs. Lawson arrived, waving her thick arms and elbowing her way in. "I can't imagine she's strayed too far from home. There's no way a girl like that could walk all the way through the bush into the village. And if she knew the way, why isn't she here? How long's she been missing, anyhow?" Everyone listened, asked questions, but no one had answers.

"Where's Shadrach?" Goliah asked the boys.

"At his farm. Dad said he should stay there, in case she turns up. He's turned the place inside out already but I reckon Molly's stuck somewhere. Maybe up a tree..." Simon Callahan added to his brother's story, his eyes wide as the sky, cheeks flaming like the sun.

"If you boys came in along the bush track and didn't see her, and Shadrach hasn't seen her anywhere on his property, where else can she be?" Goliah came close to voicing what Finella didn't want to consider.

Jimmy shrugged. "I guess if she wanted to get into town, the only other way would be to walk all the way from Red Rocks. She'd be mad to try it, but Shadrach said she's likely to do anything in the mood she's in right now."

"Why would she attempt a walk she's never done before?" Finella pushed into the group and looked for answers. "I've walked the beach at Red Rocks with her for months now and she's never once hinted to follow it all the way to the village. She knows she can't manage that on her own."

Jimmy Callahan scraped his shoe in the dust and shrugged. When he looked up, the blush in his cheek matched his brother's. "Shad thinks she wanted to give you something, Miss Mayfield. He tried to tell her you'd left for good, but she wouldn't listen to him. He thinks she's somewhere out there looking for you, to say a proper good-bye."

All eyes fell on Finella. Mrs. Lawson cocked her head and waited, her eyes freshly tuned with accusation.

"I...I didn't..." Finella threaded her fingers together but it did not stop them trembling. Words wouldn't come, and her dry mouth managed no more than the quick breaths she took in.

"Right, Finella, you come with me." Mrs. Lawson pushed through the crowd to stand beside her. "We'll walk back to my house and see if Molly's stumbled her way there. Perhaps Mr. Ashe, you can arrange the rest of this lot to keep looking." She didn't wait for his reply. She snatched Finella by the elbow and pushed her all the way down the track until they were far enough for no one to hear them.

"You're leaving? Without a *proper goodbye?* Is the boy addled in the head from too much sun to suggest such a thing, or are you the one that's lost your mind?"

Finella hurried to keep up. "I wanted to see you, Mrs. Lawson. But, Aunt Sarah said it would be kinder in the long run to leave without goodbyes. She... I... well, so much has happened I hardly know where to start."

"Start with talking. And when you're done talking you'd better take up praying, 'cause I'm not liking the sound of this one bit."

Finella prayed. She prayed along with every soul in the village who had a place in their heart for God and his mercy. She wept until no more tears would come and numbness crept over her like the shadows at Mrs. Lawson's door.

The sun slipped into purple velvet and still no word came of Molly's whereabouts. Night shadows lengthened and the sea lapped not far off, complicit as the sky in the keeping of secrets.

Only the hush of those who came and went filled the summer night, with few words to share and the empty shake of heads.

"Won't you return to the house, Finella dear?" Somehow, Aunt Sarah had managed to follow her back to shore. The poor steamer master probably feared her too much to disobey even one of Sarah Mayfield's commands, but for once, Finella ignored her beckoning.

"Agatha's cut sandwiches for those in the search party. She's eager to have you back."

Finella barely heard her. She leaned against the Lawson's verandah post with her eyes on the sea. She had to stay near the water, where it glimmered through the tea tree gully with splinters of moonlight. She had to stay within earshot of the pier, near the people. The ones who still called and carried lanterns into already searched thickets of bush.

Molly. *Molly*

Against a chorus of crickets and night birds, the cry of the townsfolk pierced the day, fast slipping away.

Where was she?

Finella rubbed her forehead and prayed again. Prayed for God to erase her unkind words from the heart of a sweet girl who never deserved to hear them. And to forgive her for ever uttering them.

"At least, take some barley water Mrs. Lawson's kindly made for us. Please, Finella. I don't like the way you're looking." Aunt Sarah pressed a glass against her fingers.

Finella cradled the drink in both hands. Her trembling spilt the barley water over the rim, and a trickle fell into her sleeve like a teardrop. She closed her eyes to block out the image of Molly, crying in some gully, scared and alone in the dark.

But it made no difference, even with her eyes closed, she could still see her face. Puffy eyes, swollen and weepy, tousled black hair messed up and plastered to her damp forehead in that frenzied search for the sewing box in the skillion.

And Finella had walked away from her. No, had *run* away, without regard for the poor girl's confusion. How could she have been so uncaring?

Her shoulders trembled and she gripped the wet glass. Hadn't she thought all along, that caring for Molly was *God's work?* Had she really let someone else's mistake interfere with that? And what about Shadrach? He'd begged her to listen to him. Pleaded with her until he too stepped back, with tears in his eyes and watched her with the same confusion Molly had.

And she had walked away from them both.

40

Shadrach couldn't sit any longer. He pushed away from the table and paced the inky yard. She had to be somewhere, probably too scared to move from where she crouched.

The road held no signs of people. Mr. and Mrs. Callahan had taken off again to search their property on the other side of Saltwater Creek.

In his heart he knew she wouldn't be there. She avoided Saltwater Creek the way sensible folk avoided snakes. He stopped his pacing and looked in the direction of the sea. But what if she had gone that way anyway, and followed the creek along its inward bend where it snaked into the fields?

But she wouldn't. The bend always frightened her and nothing could drag her near it.

His chest clenched another inch.

Nothing could drag Molly to the fire either, but Finella had managed to get her to cook a batch of glue.

Molly wouldn't let him touch the splinter in her finger, but she'd let Finella remove it altogether.

Until now, nothing could drag Molly past the creek, but if his sister loved Finella the way he did, there was nothing either of them wouldn't do for her. He knew *he'd* wade the dark waters of a river for Finella.

And so he ran. Past his moonlit fields and back through the bush. He brushed past young tea trees and slid down the sandy track to the beach.

He toppled into a dip in the sand, and doubled over. His lungs on fire, his legs more marrow than bone. Waves shattered against the sand and the moon bounced off every crest.

"Molly," he roared against the din of the waves. "Are you there?"

Wet sand shimmered like a mirror under silver nightlights too beautiful to hide a secret so cruel. He stumbled closer to Saltwater Creek. "Do you hear me?" he called into the night.

But his demands went unheard, and the turbulent sea continued to pound.

The further the creek twisted from the shore, the murkier his sight, and he trained his ears on any sound, any whimper he might catch from the scrub.

He waded into the shallows. But neither ear nor eye could prepare him for the tap against his leg and the gentle bob against his shoe.

He dipped his hand in and drew up a mass of wet rags. Nothing that belonged to the sea. It drained into his open palm, and he squeezed it hard.

Only when he shook it out, did it take a shape he knew. Molly's ragdoll. Washed up where it should never be.

"Molly! Molly, do you hear me?" But Molly did not reply.

Something nudged his foot and a tangle of hair wrapped around his leg, dragged by an unwelcome pull.

Ankle deep and getting deeper, the creek swirled in a mass of unthinkable blackness. Shadrach screamed into the night, and sank into the waters where his sister lay.

❧

The scrape of boots on gravel along Mrs. Lawson's garden paths crumbled into Finella's thoughts. Scattered and loose they contemplated the worst and tripped her into places her heart vowed she'd never revisit. Lantern held high, someone trudged their way to the house, muttering to himself.

"Mr. Lawson. About time you showed yourself." Mrs. Lawson wiped wet hands on her apron and met him half way. "What news?"

He lifted the lantern higher and came into view. "They found her."

They'd found her. Finella pressed the glass of barley water to her throat and let its coolness seep through to her skin.

"Oh, thank God." Mrs. Lawson hurried to reach him and the old man came to a stop. "What is it?"

He gave her the lantern and with a shaking hand wiped his mouth, pinched like a clam.

"Harry?"

"They found her, by Saltwater Creek. Shad and the rest. Callahans and some other folks from that way."

The corners of his mouth dipped like a melting candle. "Poor mite was dead before they got to her."

"No!" Finella screamed. "No. They did not. You're wrong. Don't say that!"

She gulped for air and searched their faces. Why was no one else saying anything?

Aunt Sarah slid beside her in a flurry of skirt and hems, and placed a heavy hand on her back. Mrs. Lawson buckled against her husband, and the lantern light quivered.

And from somewhere in the darkness, the smash of glass echoed against the splintering of Finella's soul.

～

The stillness of night only served to magnify the spiral of despair. Even Aunt Sarah paced the little church house kitchen, twisting her handkerchief when it was not pressed to her mouth.

Long after midnight, Goliah and Agatha returned from their vigil beside Shadrach, but the young preacher quickly retreated to his desk. And while Agatha played with her steaming cup of tea alongside Finella's stone cold one, she too excused herself before long.

By four in the morning, Finella was already dressed and back at the kitchen table. No sun poked the day, but a steady sprinkling of early rain blanketed the iron roof. After lighting a lamp, her numb fingers leafed through Agatha's Bible.

Would she find comfort? Was God the only hope left now? Her soul agonized for something to grip before she slipped further into grief.

She opened to Psalm 88 and her eyes fell to the words she'd uttered over and over all night.

Oh Lord. There were no other words her soul could cry, but *Oh Lord.* And here, the Psalmist's words repeated her own.

Oh Lord God of my salvation, I have cried day and night before thee, ...my soul is full of troubles and my life draweth nigh unto the grave.

She closed her eyes against the sting of yet another grave.

I am counted with them that go down to the pit. I am as a man that hath no strength. Free among the dead, like the slain that lie in the grave, whom thou rememberest no more. Thou hast laid me in the lowest pit, in darkness, in the deeps.

Tears stole the page from view and she fought against long buried images. She shook her head, but could not escape the image of her father's body, wrapped in a rust-stained sail. Crude stitches hastily added to keep the edges in place with two small sand bags wedged inside.

Thou hast put away mine acquaintance far from me; thou hast made me an abomination unto them: I am shut up and I cannot come forth.

Finella rubbed her feet together in vain. She breathed a little warmth into her cupped hands. But nothing worked to shake the cold truth of loss.

Lord, I have called daily upon thee. I have stretched my hands unto thee... Shall thy loving kindness be declared in the grave? Or thy faithfulness in destruction? Shall thy wonders be known in the dark?

She'd promised herself she'd never revisit that rainy morning aboard the Aurora. Why now, of all times, did it torment her?

Finella refused to think about the burial canvas, but she could hear the popping of light rain fall and gather in its creases like a sorry stream. No, better to look at the murky horizon and think of the lessons Father had taught her.

She brushed her tears away. She needed fresh words.

But unto thee have I cried, O Lord: and in the morning shall my prayer prevent thee. Lord, why castest thee off my soul? Why hidest thou thy face from me? I am afflicted and ready to die from my youth up. Her shawl did nothing to keep shivers from her bones and Finella let the nightmare in.

The captain took his position and spoke words of the burial service into the rising tempest. The squall's cruel grip snatched away the words the moment they were delivered. Salt spray mingled with tears on her lips, and Mrs. McLachlan held her by the elbow. Finella listened for the hymns. Why were there no hymns? Surely Father would've wanted hymns.

Two men lifted the wide plank and raised it to shoulder height. *But, that's where her father's body lay.* Why were they moving him? No, please, don't tilt the plank any higher. Not any higher, please God, no he'll slip into the...

Black waves lapped the edges of her world and Finella sank into the cold depths of disbelief.

She looked at the page with dead eyes. Only three verses remained.

Thy fierce wrath goeth over me; thy terrors have cut me off. They came round about me daily like water; they compassed me about together. Lover and friend hast though put far from me and mine acquaintance into darkness.

⌒

"Finella." Someone shook her shoulder. "Wake up, dear. You've fallen asleep at the table." Aunt Sarah whispered against her cheek and Finella rose to the copper streaks of dawn at the window. "Have you been here all night?"

Finella rubbed her temples. "Only some of it. I couldn't sleep so I came here to read. I suppose I ended up doing both."

Her aunt lowered herself into the opposite chair. "You look like you've spent more time crying." She drew her chair closer. "But it's time for something else, now."

Finella stared at the old woman who hugged a light morning wrapper around her shoulders. Silver hair hung limp in a thin braid against her collarbone. Many years had passed since her skin had been smooth and now, after a sleepless night, every fold doubled.

"I made a terrible mistake, Finella. I should never have dragged you away from them. Now look what's happened." Her words gave way to tears and she smoothed a wrinkle in the tablecloth. "You must go to Shadrach. Today."

Finella's sore eyes stung with fresh tears of her own. "He'll never want to see me again. This is all my fault and he has every reason to hate me for it."

"Perhaps. But you must go, anyway. I've labored over it all night. Wondered what your mother would've told you to do." She leaned back in her chair, the fight gone from her stiff shoulders.

"I believe your mother would have urged you to seek forgiveness and return it in generous measure. *She* did. As she lay dying. The only words I heard from her on the day she was struck were, 'Do we know his name? Whoever he might be, the Lord have mercy on him.' Who else could she have meant but Shadrach's father?"

"But, all these years I thought Mother wanted to know his name. That if we knew him, we could…"

"Name the sinner?"

"Name the sinner." Finella whispered the a burden she knew she'd never lift. Shadrach Jones. The man she'd wanted to name for six long years. The name she'd searched for. The name she knew she'd hate the minute she heard it. Only now, she knew how much she truly loved it in another man. One worthier. Kinder and more deserving than she'd ever be of finding love.

She couldn't let herself think of poor Shadrach and the night he must have endured. What right did she have to return to him? Now of all times. What would she say?

"Go." Her aunt insisted. "Go. Wrap forgiveness as tightly as you dare around this day. Your mother would want that. And Shadrach can't bury Molly without it. Neither can you."

"But, I can't." Finella sobbed "There's no way I can go to him, now. Not even to obey you, Aunt Sarah. Not even if Mother and Father themselves appeared from heaven and told me to go. There's too much I've already said I can't undo."

"You're right." Aunt Sarah knitted her hands into a tight ball and locked them in her lap. A look of regret Finella had never seen in her, now pulled at the edges of her trembling mouth. "No one can tell you what needs to be done, anymore. This time, you'll have to follow your heart and decide for yourself."

41

Morning winds chased the rain clouds away, and nothing on this beach showed signs of gloom, except the tears between Shadrach and the sea. He wiped his eyes with a sleeve cuff he knew still held the tears of a night's worth of sobbing. Nothing he'd let himself give into, until Goliah and his wife closed the gate behind them, with Mrs. Lawson and the Callahans only a few paces ahead.

Only then, when the whispers of the living had left, did he let his head rest on Molly's damp hair. He'd not wanted anyone to stay the night. What was the point? At least this way, he could howl, kick chairs and fight the fire until sparks spat up the chimney.

But morning brought fresh panic. The need to find air and wind, if only just for a moment. He longed for the crash of the sea to drown the sound of his weeping. He'd lost them both, in a matter of days. Lost the only two he'd promised to care for. The two he'd loved.

His legs folded into a soft sand bank and he sank there, too tired to keep his eyes open, too scared to close them in case he saw the terror of Molly's wet face again.

A sea breeze ruffled his trouser cuffs. They too, told their story. Dried salt left a mark calf high, yet he couldn't remember the cold or the water. Only yelling. Molly. Molly.

Oh Molly. *How did I let this happen to you?*

A whistle of wind sounded behind him. If only it were Molly.

Always at his heels, always tugging the other way.

He heard it again. The swish of a skirt.

Sleep would catch him soon and he'd see her in every corner. Soon he'd think that was her kneeling in the sand with a new sea treasure. Her hem on his shoe.

"Shadrach." A soft voice, thick with tears made him open his eyes. Finella knelt and trembled at his feet. Violent sobs worked her chest and shoulders. "I'm so sorry," she whispered. Her plea so deep, it matched his own. Her sorrow poked at his numbness. *She was here?*

"Finella." He pulled her close and buried his head in her hair. Held her so tight it was a wonder she managed to breathe at all. For a long time he wasn't sure if the crying was his or hers. When he eased the embrace, her cheeks still streamed with tears.

"How did you get here?" He brushed her face with both hands.

"The Lawson's picked me up along the road."

"You were walking here?"

"I had to." She patted her eyes with a well-creased handkerchief. "I had to come, to see…" She hung her head and cried again until shallow breaths and short sniffs were all he could hear.

"Did you go in?" He wanted to know if she'd seen her. A piece of him wanted to know she'd come back to face what he'd had to look at all night. What he knew Mrs. Lawson cried over now. But even more, he needed Finella to share this grief with him, more than he'd needed anything in his life.

"Only for a moment. I couldn't stand to see her like that. So completely gone from us." She looked up at him, red eyes wide with horror. "What happened?"

He pointed to the beach behind her, where the mouth of Saltwater Creek ran in a thin line from the heart of farmlands to the edge of the sea.

"I didn't think she'd follow the creek. It's always scared her, the way it disappears to the left like that. I'd warned her there were snakes along the bank. Never thought she'd brave it."

He rubbed the stubble on his chin and held his hand over his trembling lips until he was sure he could go on. "She must have been confused and thought to follow the creek to town and not the beach. Must have crossed over and tried to scramble up the bank onto dry ground."

He shrugged, not sure of anything except the obvious. "I guess she slipped and hit her head on hard ground because she was bleeding from the ear when I found her. But I was already too late."

Finella touched his hand. "So, she didn't drown?"

"I don't think so. Water's too shallow, even for Molly. She would have pulled herself up, if she could..."

"Is it true what they're saying in the village? Was Molly coming to find me?" Her voice croaked.

What good would it do to tell her anyway? He couldn't speak, until her eyes found him. The beautiful brown he'd come to love, darkened to something stormy now. The pain he saw there almost convinced him to keep the story to himself. She'd suffered enough. Why lay more blame where it didn't belong.

But then he remembered the limp body of his sister. Yes, it was Molly's heart which drove her to tell the truth. Now he could finish what the poor girl had started.

"Let's go back. We can talk better at home." He brushed a tear from her cheek and wrapped his arm around her shoulder. Even with a brilliant sunrise to light the way, the awful truth dawned on him.

I have to tell her the way Molly wanted it said.

She followed him to the edge of the yard. A freshly built oven rose from where Finella never imagined she'd see one on this farm. Not until recent weeks when farm life had taken a sweet turn for all three of them.

But now... now by unspoken agreement they unwound from each other's hold and lingered there where he'd cemented their names in a row on the oven's domed top. Shadrach. And Finella. With Molly's brick fixed between them.

"Oh Shad," there were no words good enough to thank him for what she once thought she needed. How swiftly life had knocked *fancies* from her heart. How complete the loss of Christmas pies she'd promised a blue-eyed girl who only looked for the smallest happiness.

Finella wanted to touch Molly's name, but kept her fingers clenched in fists. God knew she was not worthy to trace the letters they'd drawn together. Not now.

Just beyond them, smoke rose from the chimney in Shadrach's house and she guessed Mrs. Lawson would soon need them inside. A part of her wanted to go in to Molly, but something stronger kept her where she stood.

"Shad?" She ventured. "Tell me."

He leaned against the oven wall, his face as colorless as that morning months ago when he'd woken in delirium. "I remember Mum saying Dad deserved a broken nose for all he'd put them through."

The huskiness in his words stemmed his story, and he took a moment to collect himself. "She said some kind soul had done us all a favor and thrown a punch when we were too scared to sit up, let alone fight back. Your Christmas napkin? Mum kept it as she found it, all blood stained. Said it served as a reminder someone had delivered justice. It wasn't until Molly pulled it out, I remembered how pushed around they'd really been."

Finella listened, too afraid to interrupt Shadrach's awful memory.

"Molly cried and slept for a full day and night after you left. Wouldn't eat a thing. Pleaded with me to get you back. I tried to explain our Father did something bad to your Mother, and this made you sad." His lip trembled, and Finella's heart bruise deepened.

"But she knew you were more than sad. She knew you were angrier than we'd ever seen you, and she pushed me on it. For hours. For days. Why was Finella so angry? Were we really stained? Why did she need Dad's name? Why were we stained?"

Finella sucked her breath in. *Stained.* She had said it. Shouted it across the yard until she'd no voice left. And she could never take it back. Filled with shame, she placed her hands over her face and sobbed.

"I thought I meant those words then, but I don't. I really don't. Please forgive me—"

He gathered her against him while she cried again. Until exhaustion and heartache cloaked them in a heavy quiet.

Shadrach ignored her apology. "I told Molly something George Gleeson taught me years ago. To surrender to what I truly believe in. That no matter what I've done, or where I've come from, I'm whiter than the freshest, brightest laundry my own mother could produce. That's how my faith unfolds. No more stains. Forgiven. Restored."

Finella pushed back. "Did Molly understand?"

"Did she?" He laughed and sobbed all at once. "She not only understood, she wanted to tell you. And show you."

"Me? Show me what?"

He dug into his pocket. "I believe this is yours."

"The ruby brooch?" Neither of them spoke while Finella held it in her palm. Only the sound of Shadrach's breathing filled the air between them. "I thought you'd sold it."

"I sold the pouch of gold dust. I wanted to explain when Molly found the napkin but you were too upset. I figured you needed a few days away from here to take it all in, and then I'd try again. There was just enough gold to buy my land but the brooch I've kept all this time, to sell when I was ready to build a proper house. Timber's not selling for the price of spring potatoes, so I kept it up my sleeve."

"And you showed this to Molly?"

He nodded. "To keep her quiet. She lay on her bed and twisted the gem to catch the light. And then, just like that she jumped up and said we had to return it. Put her good shoes on and insisted I get Old Lou and take her to see you that very minute. When I said no, she had a royal fit and after all her pouting, fell asleep. So I put it in a tin on the top shelf. I talked myself into bringing it to you while I finished my chores. I figured we owed you that much." He rubbed the back of his neck. "I was on my way in to tell Molly to get ready when I noticed... she'd gone."

"With my mother's brooch?" Finella pressed it to her collar in a clenched fist.

"I found it pinned to her shirt when I carried her body home."

"If only I'd not let my temper get in the way of what's true." She wanted to look him in the eye and beg for forgiveness, even though words would never come close to what she owed.

"She didn't just want to return the brooch. I guess she wanted you to see for yourself that she understood grace and forgiveness. Once she wrapped her little mind around it, that girl beamed like torchlight. You should've seen her. Bursting to share it with you like some fine seashell."

Finella needed to hear it, yet flinched with every word. Molly, their own Miss Molly, knew what it was to be forgiven. And didn't withhold it.

"Can you forgive me, Shad? I should have been the one teaching Molly that lesson. Instead..."

She grasped both his hands in her own trembling grip, the brooch trapped between them.

"I'll regret my words all my days. And for my punishment I'll always know I can never ask forgiveness from Molly. Here," she opened her fingers. "If Molly had brought me this, I would have given it back. I... I don't care who your father was anymore. All I care about is who you are. Please take it, if you can forgive me."

He smiled through fresh tears, but the lines remained in his brow. "I forgive you." He cupped her cheek. "But, if anyone's to blame it's me, isn't it? That's my punishment. Knowing how much Molly wanted to see you, I should have bundled her into the wagon. Instead, I let her fuss and sleep and made myself miserable out here digging a hole in the ground." He cocked his head to the left.

Finella brushed her tears away. A mulberry sapling stood in a shallow of water and freshly dug dirt.

"I had it hidden in the barn. I was going to bring it out with Molly's rabbit blanket and your Christmas pies."

Finella gasped. He didn't mean to wound her, she knew that. And if they were to wade through the next few hours, she had to let the hurt not only strike, but as Agatha encouraged, change her.

"You planted a mulberry for me, even after all I yelled at you? How did you not add it to a bonfire after I left?"

"Because I knew where it belonged. I dug a hole so big I could've buried three trees there, not one."

At the word bury, their sorrow deepened. He ran his finger over the word *Molly* on the brick in the centre of the oven arch. "I need you beside me today, Finella. Can you do that?"

Hand on hand, she pressed hers to his and wound her fingers there. She could only see her name and Shadrach's now.

"If you'll let me."

"What about tomorrow. And the next day? Will you stay then too?"

Tears clouded her vision but her heart saw what she needed. What God allowed her to feel again. "Tomorrow, and every other day."

42

"The burial reading tells me I must open to the ancient words of comfort in Psalm 90."

Goliah Ashe ran his finger along the gap between his collar and throat. Too much longer in the blistering sun and Shadrach figured he'd join him in his fidgeting.

Still, he held his chin up even with his good coat scratching his own neck, and busied himself steadying Finella. From the other side, her aunt held a summer parasol over their heads.

He wanted all those gathered at the small bush graveyard, to be sure there was no room for blame or guilt. It's what Molly had chased down. And didn't forgiveness at its purest, come with a high price?

Shadrach was not too sure what Goliah had spoken about in the church. He'd spent all his energy keeping his eyes off the cedar coffin he'd carried in. But here, with bird sounds from the pink gums overhead, he let Goliah's words sink in.

"It's fitting we begin the burial of our dearest Molly Jones by remembering the God she belongs to. For while she's no longer with us, she most certainly is with Him. I want to speak to those who cannot fathom the loss of this dear girl. To you, and me, and those who can barely stand in the glorious sun and contemplate the horror of the last few days."

Finella leaned into Shadrach and while he may have sat at attention, his heart bent at their joint grief. With Aunt Sarah's slender frown the least of his concerns, he wrapped his arm around Finella and squeezed her shoulder.

"Hast thou not known? Hast thou not heard?" Goliah read from his book. "The everlasting God, the Lord, the Creator of the ends of the earth, fainteth not, neither is he weary. There is no searching for his understanding." Goliah's voice grew louder. "He giveth power to the faint, and to them that have no might, he increaseth strength. Even the youths shall faint and be weary, and the young men shall utterly fail. But they that wait upon the Lord shall renew their strength."

Shadrach closed his eyes for the familiar ending.

"They shall mount up with wings as eagles, they shall run and not be weary, and they shall walk and not faint."

Goliah went on. "You might think that's all a preacher needs to say to a gathering of bereaved. That in life's darkest moments, they will find rest and the promise of renewal. While this is true, I am not done.

He looked at the sky before continuing on. "I leave you with this question. Are we to walk away from bitterness with the hope of strength alone? Are we to soldier on for the sake of soldiering on? Perhaps not, dear ones. For God himself, tells us what Molly would want us to think on as we depart. 'Yea, I have loved you with an everlasting love. Therefore, with loving kindness have I drawn thee.'

"Molly shared great love with the people she knew and trusted. Even with her limitations, she tried to express this love as best she could. I think if she were able, she'd tell us *love* is the greatest. That forgiveness allows us an open door to really love and be loved. By one another, and by the Everlasting, Creator of all things."

He closed his book with a sad tip of the cover, and motioned to Shadrach to take a handful of dirt for their final goodbye.

∽

Finella's empty palm trembled. Aunt Sarah offered a handkerchief to wipe her stained fingers, but a smudge of earth remained. Six months ago the stain would've vexed her like a twig in her shoe. Today, she held onto it for as long as she could.

One by one the mourners moved away. To their wagons and jinkas for the ride back to refreshments at the little church house. Finella joined Shadrach in accepting sympathies so raw she could barely stand to hear them. Glad it was over, yet desperate at the thought of leaving Molly where she lay.

And so they stayed. A weak but firm smile from Shadrach assured the straggling Mrs. Lawson they needed one last moment, and even Aunt Sarah let them go with bruised reluctance.

"Can we ever learn to live with our guilt?" Finella asked when the empty graveyard echoed with a magpie's song.

"If we never let it go it means we don't believe God is big enough to take it." They walked away from the grave. "I think we'll mourn her all our life, but not under a cloud of guilt. I don't want to remember her that way. Do you?"

Finella smiled. "No. I want to remember her running across the sand, hair flying everywhere, finger in her mouth because she was too scared to let you touch her splinter."

Shadrach hung his wrist on her shoulder. "Or completely jam-smeared and laying on her bed sorting new shells, the end of her braid in her mouth."

"Me telling her to spit it out." How it crushed her to talk about their Molly like this. Gone forever. But how deeply good to share her, just the two of them.

"When I wouldn't bring her to you, she told me something I'll never forget."

Finella stopped walking. "Tell me."

"She said, 'Finella loves us, Brother. She's cross because it's hot now and not cold like England, and she misses her Mum and Dad. But we have to find her and love her back.' "

Too many to count, the cuts cleft Finella in places she didn't know pain resided, and she lost her battle with tears one more time. "She did?"

"She did." He brushed at her tears with his thumb. "Best way we can honor her is to grow that love for one another and fill our days with it."

She turned to look at the fresh grave. An earthy mound where a sleeping child still held her heart.

"Wait. I need to get something." She ran back to where they'd laid her. Her chest rose and fell a few times before she had enough breath for words.

"I will always love you, my darling Molly. You taught me true forgiveness. Cloaked me in a love I'll never forget. I promise I'll make rosehip cordial every summer and look out for the best shells on the beach. I'll love Shadrach and care for him and always trace my finger along your name between our three bricks. And even without the bricks, I'll never, ever forget you."

She reached for an overhanging eucalypt branch and picked a cluster of gum nuts and fluffy petals. She kissed the tiny pink bouquet, split it in half, and threw one half onto the grave. The other she cradled in her dirt stained hand.

43

Shadrach tossed his empty crates from the steamer deck onto the jetty. Jon Tripp loaded them onto the trolley, along with the trunks of the last wave of January holidaymakers. Another week and they'd say goodbye to summer's visitors.

While his crates may have returned empty, Shadrach's pockets held the reward of late summer crops ripe for market. That and a small tin of fresh raspberries he'd bought at the last minute for Finella.

It was Molly he'd thought of first when he walked past the Eastern Market fruit stalls. Pierced by the sight of berries, he'd stopped to remember the girl who loved red jam. But Finella was the girl he longed to share them with, now.

"Why Shadrach Jones, fancy meeting you here?"

His heart surged, like the steamer pulling away and sending ripples into the deep in all directions. Finella waitied for him. She smiled at Jon Tripp who pushed the trolley, but her eyes found Shadrach and stayed there.

For two weeks, when he'd returned from market, she met him at the pier, a short walk from the guesthouse where she and her Aunt Sarah shared a small room. Her brown eyes still held the veil of their shared grief, and he didn't expect that to ease anytime soon. He knew how it razed his own heart each time he remembered the loss of Molly.

Still, that didn't mean he wouldn't try to add a brightness to Finella's honey flecked eyes. And today, while he had a pail of fruit to begin with, he had a little more tucked away for good measure.

He returned the smile and quickened his step, offering his arm to the beautiful lady who already held his heart. She wrapped her arm in his.

"Did you sell for a good price today?"

"Good enough to bring you back a present."

"You mean the berries? I already saw them." A twinkle played around her eyes and he warmed to see it.

"Not the berries, although they're yours, too. If Jon Tripp doesn't help himself to too many."

"He can have them. I know what I want." She held her chin high and breathed in the sea air. "Nothing too fancy. Nothing as bright as berries or rubies even. I want my Shadrach Jones."

He pulled her to a stop at a wooden bench and let the new arrivals pass them for cool verandahs and the promise of fresh pots of tea. He needed something only Finella could offer.

"Speaking of gems and all things fancy, I want to show you something." He waited for her to sit, and dug into his breast pocket.

"One of the traders at the market imports cargo from America. Anything you care to imagine. American stoves, furnaces, silk bonnets, felt hats. He brings it all. And look…" he sat beside her and pressed a catalogue into her hands. Dog-eared, he'd already marked the page he wanted her to see first. "See these houses? One will be yours, one day. The entire house."

His words spilled almost as fast as his heartbeat, but he carried on, cheered by her growing smile.

"There's floor plans, and see here," he turned the page, "it says everything is included in the kit. The mantels, all timbers, glass panes, shingles, the entire frame and this one..." he turned back to the first page, "has a wash-house."

She poked him in the ribs. "Who needs a wash-house?"

He grinned and sat back against the bench, his arm draped behind her while she poured over the plans. Single storey, double storey, fancy and even fancier, there'd not be enough sunlit hours for her to examine each one today. He knew the glimmer in her eye meant he'd brought more than a daisy for her hair.

"Who would've thought you'd be enamored by house plans so, so..." she stole a look from the corner of her eye, "elaborate?"

He laughed and leaned a little closer. "I'm enamored by you. And if you agree, I'm going to add that bee brooch to my savings and trade them in for the best house a bride's ever had on this island. One to match the brick oven in our yard."

She turned, her smile a little less radiant. Had he figured it all wrong? His heart sank and he pressed his hand to her back. "Unless you really want to keep the brooch to remember your mother."

Finella put the catalogue down. "That brooch is pretty enough for any girl. But I'm not that girl. Not after my Mother and Molly, well... you know." Her words faded, and he reached out for her chin to draw her back.

"So, you don't mind if I work a little harder, sell the brooch and order us one of these? No mud walls, mind you. Only timbers. American hardwoods and the fanlight above the door is etched, see here?"

She didn't even look. Her hand covered his and any of the glass inserts he wanted to show her.

"The brooch is yours to sell. All I need is what's already etched in my heart. Nothing put there by my father, or George Gleeson. Not even by Aunt Sarah. As long as your blue eyes wink back at me, that's all I ask." She wound her fingers through his. "But I do believe a house as pretty as any of these deserves a name. I think we should call it…" She looked across the water where sparkles, lit from the sky, spilled over their waves and rippled along the shallows.

When she looked back at him, her eyes brimmed with the same light. The same hope he'd carried all the way home.

"I think we should call it the Blue Wren House."

Love for her and all she'd brought him flooded his chest. "Kisses come with this house, Miss Mayfield. A lifetime of kisses. It's part of the Blue Wren House package."

She dropped her head onto his shoulder. "Then order us a lifetime supply, Mr. Jones. The fancier, the better."

January 29

Aunt Sarah says I must mark the days. She says they are, each one, touched by God and I must look for his fingerprint at day's end.

But I need not look far. His forgiveness and love have shaped me from the inside, and I will never be the same.

So I press to this book the already dried petals of the sweet pink gum and its leaf of curled green. I mark this day as the one we saw the birth of a field of muttonbird chicks. More than a field, an entire shore of nests.

Shadrach and I explored them at dusk against the urgency of hungry chirps and calls. Tiny creatures of soft grey down, the ends of what will one day become feathers, strong and free.

No one has begrudged us a wedding day and I am to marry Shadrach at the end of March when the last of the summer boats sail away. I shall return to our little island house to make a home beside the only man I have ever desired.

Where the wind stirs soft.

Where the blue wrens spar.

Where the kiss of the tide fills the shallows.

And I am carried home.

The End

Author Note

A writer dreams her story while she's awake.

But the facts still need to be checked. The history-nut in me loves this part and I'm blessed to have people on my team to assist with fact-finding and fact checking.

Many thanks to Raymonde Fauchard who scoured her local history and found a birthplace for Finella, in Chingford Green, England.

All of the food references in *Carry Me Home* come from Australia's first cookbook compilation, The Colonial Cook Book. I've spent hours fascinated by the food choices available in the 1870s and incorporated some of these recipes into the daily lives of Finella and Shadrach.

Local historians believe Shadrach's bricks would have been made from pure clay and that there's a distinction between the words *mud* and *clay*. For the purposes of the brick making chapters, I relied on Victorian Era brick making techniques which set the stage for these scenes. I hope the purists forgive me for using the words mud and clay interchangeably.

Kit homes were available in Australia as far back as the 1830s, thanks to the Hudson Brothers family business. Phillip Island's Glen Isla House is believed to come from an American distributor of prefabricated homes. It is the inspiration for the home Shadrach promises to build Finella at the end of *Carry Me Home*, and the setting of books 2 and 3 in the Blue Wren Shallows series.

Thank you to my co-members at the Phillip Island and District

Historical Society, Secretary Christine Grayden and President John Jansson, who read *Carry Me Home* for historical and local accuracy. I am in awe of your passion for Phillip Island's rich beginnings and ever thankful for all you and the Historical Society members do to preserve its history.

Carry Me Away

COMING SOON

FROM DOROTHY ADAMEK

To learn more about Dotti and her upcoming books, please visit dorothyadamek.com where you can join her mailing list and be the first to hear about the second book in the Blue Wren Shallows series, *Carry Me Away*.